THE DARK SIDE OF THE RAINBOW

Caren Powell

Copyright@2014
Caren Powell
Illustrations by Neil Powell

CAP Publishing
Victoria B.C. Canada

Note for librarians: A cataloguing record for this book is available from Library and Archives Canada at www.collectionscanada.gc.ca

ISBN 978-0-9936607-0-2

Printed in Canada

For Neil

My beloved husband,
friend,
and
illustrator.

AUTHOR'S NOTE

Having lived in South Africa during the apartheid era and the changeover to democracy, I was familiar with the stifling oppression faced by non-white South Africans. I also consulted many newspaper articles, web sites, and books during the writing of this manuscript. Nelson Mandela's *Long Walk to Freedom* was invaluable, as was the *Bible*, and *The Magalisberg* by Vincent Carruthers, amongst others.

This book is based on true life events and the history is accurate. Political characters and events have been portrayed as accurately as possible – although in some instances they have been adapted for the purpose of the story. All of the other characters have been changed to protect their identity. Those who think they recognize themselves, I apologize for the changes I have made to your story as this is a work of fiction. I have borrowed from your stories, given them to other people, and leant you mine.

There is Kazi, whose story is partly true; the white owners of Fairvalley Farm and their black labourers; a young radical, who comes to live on the farm and disrupts everything; a girl brutally raped in the belief that sex with a virgin will cure AIDS; an alcoholic womanizer, who destroys his life and those around him; a black preacher, whose sons are kidnapped in retribution when he refuses to hold subversive meetings, and the terrifying search for them; two boys, one white and one black who become friends in spite of racist attitudes and separatist rules. And Nelson Mandela, who was released after twenty-seven years in jail for sabotage, and encouraged the people not to let up their campaign of mass action to force the government to a free election.

EPIGRAPH

No one is born hating another person
because of the colour of his skin,
or his background, or his religion.

People must learn to hate,
and if they can learn to hate,
they can learn to love,
for love comes more naturally
to the human heart than its opposite.

- Nelson Mandela (1918 – 2013)

Nelson Mandela, an icon of peace, freedom and reconciliation, passed away during the editing of this manuscript. He was an inspiration to millions.

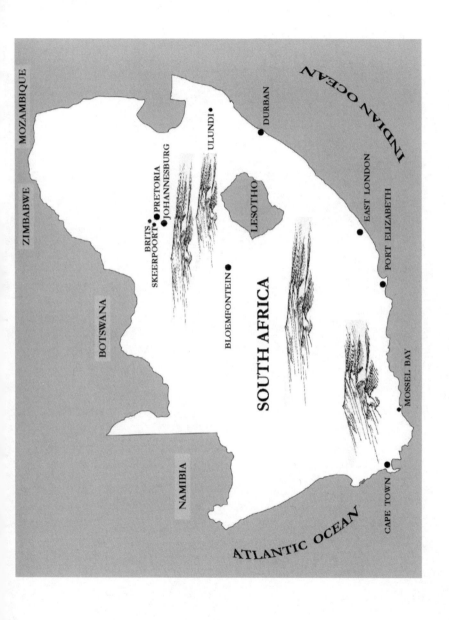

TABLE OF CONTENTS

part one

the farm

ONE

A JACKAL CALLS AT NIGHT

1975 · 1976 · 1977 · 1978 · 1979 · 1980 · 1981 · 1982 · 1983

O n the day the child disappeared, an old man watched a group of girls collect red seeds from under the Coral tree. The children paid him no attention and didn't notice him leave in silence to walk up the mountain, where he lived alone in a ramshackle hut of rusted metal and rotting boards.

As the sun set towards the lower reaches of the valley, it caught the bright colours of a butterfly's wings and the child took a step towards it. The wings fluttered open and closed, languidly flashing yellow, peacock blue, and russet. The child reached out, touched the wing, and the butterfly took off. It lifted into a looping dive and the child laughed and followed, holding up a finger lightly smudged with butterfly dust. He wanted to touch it again, but the butterfly dipped and rose, hovering just out of reach. Stumbling over tufts of grass and pebbles, his small brown hand stretched out, the child laughed each time the butterfly flew away. Higher and higher the butterfly fluttered, well beyond the child's fingertips and he realized he'd lost sight of his mother. He was thirsty and wanted her. His mouth turned down, his chin puckered. He flopped to the ground and pounded his fists. When no one responded to his cries, the little boy pushed himself to his feet and stumbled along, tears eroding tracks through the dust on his cheeks. He reached a fence, dropped to his hands and knees and crawled under the wire strands. His light cotton shirt caught on the barbs and held fast. Kazi, frightened and unable to move, screamed.

The day faded to grey and shadows lengthened. Nearby in his hut on the mountain the old man lay on a straw mattress covered by tattered blankets. He heard the strange cries of the child, but thought they were a jackal howling at the moon.

At the Fairvalley farmhouse Garth Finley stirred in his sleep. The Fox Terriers were barking and he pulled the blanket over his head, then the Rottweiler started up with deep-throated, furious barks. Garth threw back the covers, stretched to his full six feet, ran his fingers through his dark brown hair, kept short because it had a tendency to curl, and rubbed the early morning stubble on his chin. He reached for his khaki pants and shirt.

Caitlin turned over, "What's wrong?" she mumbled sleepily.

"Just the dogs barking, go back to sleep," he said, and hurried outside. Shivering in the pre-dawn breeze he whistled for the dogs. They turned at his call and shepherded a man towards him, the terriers nipping at his heels and the Rottweiler trotting silently alongside, teeth shining in the early light. Garth recognised the man as one of his African farm labourers and called the dogs off.

"*Baas*," the man said. His breath caught in his throat as he bent forward and sucked air into his lungs. "Kazi, he is lost. He wandered off into the mountains while his mother was not looking. We searched all night." He held his hand palm upward at knee height to indicate the size of the child. "We are worried because the boy is still small. He is not even two years old. *Baas*, we must find him before something bad happens. Can we have the day off to look for him?" The man's beard was unshaven, his eyes red from fatigue.

Garth's hazel eyes showed concern as he thought of his own child sleeping in her bed, snuggled against her cherished blanky. "Good heavens, of course you can," he said. "Show me where everyone is and I'll help too."

The man turned and ran in the direction he'd come. Garth picked up his two-way radio and followed until they reached a group gathered near the farm shed.

"Where's the father?" Garth asked. Although only twenty-seven years old, he was used to taking control of his men.

Goodwill stepped forward, his thin shoulders stooped under the weight of his distress. His clothes, unchanged since the search began, were creased and stained with sweat and dirt, and smudges of exhaustion lay heavily under his dark eyes. Of medium height, he looked even smaller and shrivelled with fear.

"*Ek is die pa, Baas,*" Goodwill said in Afrikaans. "I'm the father, Boss," he added translating automatically. A muscle clenched at the corner of his mouth.

Garth was still learning to speak Afrikaans, the language commonly used by the local white Boers – the farmers in South Africa – and their African labourers. Although born in South Africa, Garth spoke only English[1] with a colonial accent, flat and unmelodious.

"How sure are you that he went up the mountain?"

"*Baas*, there are tracks." Goodwill pointed beyond the labourers' houses.

Garth looked at the man who worked for him as a labourer and was also preacher to the black community. He was a lean man, five foot eight, with intelligent eyes etched with fine lines

---

[1] one of South Africa's eleven official languages

from years in the sun and caring for his flock. On his chin was a few days' growth. He doesn't deserve this, Garth thought, and closed his mind to the possibility that they might not find the child who had been born the year he and Caitlin purchased Fairvalley Farm.

Martha, Goodwill's wife and the mother of the missing child, stood next to her husband twisting her hands in an agony of worry and despair. She was a short woman, plump, and usually cheerful by nature. Now her brown skin was ashen, and her eyes were red.

"Martha," Garth continued, "go to the farmhouse and wait there. I have a radio and will let you know the minute we find him. Goodwill, we'll go together. The rest of you divide yourselves into groups. Let's spread out."

A baboon barked up on the mountain and everyone looked up with fear and apprehension etched on their faces. Garth brought their attention back: "Look for tracks, and search under every log, in every hole, and make sure to call the child's name regularly. He might come to you if he hears his name."

By then, sun bathed the land around the search party and, as the men walked in rows, they lifted debris and leaves to be sure nothing was under them, and pushed branches aside to peer under bushes. One man, who saw movement in a hole between two rocks, slid down an embankment and frightened a rabbit from its hiding spot. Two men rushed forward when a flock of birds lifted from a tree – they were sure the child had caused their flight, but there was nothing there.

Time passed. They could not find Kazi, and a deep quiet settled over the search party. Occasionally the child's name echoed across the mountain, but the men only spoke to one another when necessary. The sun rose higher in the sky, the day grew warmer and the men became tired and thirsty.

Martha sat with a group of women under a tree near the farmhouse. They were quiet, lost in their own thoughts. The hours dragged by. Martha dropped her head into her hands and shuddered at the images running through her mind. She imagined a snake slithering up to her son, forked-tongue testing the air – head launching poisonous fangs deep into Kazi's tender flesh. A jackal's howl, a circling vulture, every sound and sight brought new despair.

Near midday, Caitlin Finley made sweetened tea and jam sandwiches for Martha and the women. Shanon, her three-year-old daughter, helped carry the food as she followed her mother outside. Handing out the tea and bread, Caitlin noticed the old man from the mountain walk up the path towards the farmhouse. Under five feet tall, he was dressed in a tattered khaki shirt and pants that hung in folds from his birdlike frame. He had a haze of grey hair and a face like a weathered walnut into which his eyes disappeared when he smiled. He reached the stone wall in the yard, sat down and waited for Caitlin.

"Hello, Juby," she greeted in English when she came to him.

Shanon ran up, an empty plate in one hand and the last piece of bread in the other. "Hello, Juby, I saved this for you," she said, giving the old man the bread.

"Thank you, little *Missus*," the old man accepted the bread.

Caitlin lifted Shanon onto the wall and she sat there licking jam off her fingers.

"Madam," Juby said, looking at the group of women. "Why are those women crying?"

"One of the babies is lost, he's been gone since last night."

He looked at her with milky, cataract-filmed eyes and frowned. "Madam, Juby knows," he said in his slow manner. "I, Juby, heard the baby in the night, the child he is there." He pointed a gnarled finger toward the mountain.

"Are you sure?"

"Yes, madam. It is only now that Juby knows it was a baby and not a jackal."

Caitlin reached for her two-way radio and pressed the call button. "Garth, come in," she said, anticipation in her voice.

The radio crackled and Garth's voice echoed in the air. "Caitlin, go ahead."

"Garth, Juby's here. He says he heard the baby last night. He pointed to the area north-west of his hut."

"Is he sure it was a child and not a jackal?"

"That's what he said."

Garth and Goodwill left the search party in the lower reaches of the mountain and took the shortest route to Juby's hut. They could have stayed on the path that Juby used, the one that bypassed a deep gully, but they had to hurry so they took a short cut. The climb was steep and rocky and when they reached the gully Garth wondered if they had made the right decision. The sides were sheer and covered with loose shale, but he realized there was no choice now. They had to make their way across. He lowered himself over the edge sending shale sliding and small rocks tumbling ahead of him. A rock broke loose under his foot and he slipped and skidded to the bottom of the gully. When he came to a stop, his hip was bruised and his knee and thigh were scraped raw.

He looked at Goodwill to see how he was faring; he had fallen and twisted his ankle, but he seemed oblivious to the pain and to the blistering heat of the sun. Without a word they both got to their feet and pushed on up the other side of the gully, every step an agony surpassing the one before.

At the crest both men turned their eyes towards the point that marked Juby's hut and lengthened their strides. Sun-bleached grass crackled underfoot, dry dust lifted into the air, sucking the moisture from it. Sweat soaked their shirts and their breathing came hard and fast.

When they reached the hut they searched through thick undergrowth, behind a sheltering rock, and under a fallen tree. But there was nothing there other than the distant bark of a baboon.

Goodwill stopped and turned a full circle, calling Kazi's name over and over again in each direction until his voice caught in his throat.

Back at the farmhouse, Caitlin went to Martha and placed a hand on her shoulder. The woman looked up, her heart bleeding sadness into her dark eyes.

"Martha, Juby heard Kazi last night. He's near the old man's hut." Martha curled forward, tears wrenching from her in great choking coughs. "They will have him soon," Caitlin reassured her, groping for words.

A friend pulled Martha against her shoulder and Caitlin stepped away feeling like an intruder to the woman's pain. She walked back to the wall and thought of Juby and the first time she had noticed him watching the children collect seeds. She had been curious and, when he left, she had tracked him up the mountain until he disappeared into his dilapidated old hut. Although he was a squatter living illegally on their land, it hadn't bothered her because he was old and frail and wasn't a threat to her. She had called out a greeting to the old black man.

"*Molo mdala* – hello old grandfather."

Juby had come to the door: "I, Juby, I will go now," he had replied in English. "I will leave the white madam's farm." It had always been a matter of time before he had to move on.

"I'm not here to chase you away," Caitlin had said, "You don't have to go."

Juby's face had showed surprise as her words sank in, and then he had broken into a wide, toothless grin.

"Thank you madam, thank you," he had replied gratefully.

Over time Juby had developed the habit of coming to the farmhouse every day for tea, sugar and provisions. He had never asked for everything he needed at once. He would make the long trek down the mountain and sit on the wall outside the kitchen door until Caitlin noticed him, and then he took only what he needed for that day, so that he could come to the farmhouse again the following day to talk. Caitlin didn't mind, she was his only human contact, and she enjoyed hearing his stories. In the beginning he told her that his beard had just begun to grow when he worked for an English officer during the Boer War. With this information Caitlin had done a rapid calculation and guessed Juby's age at nearly a hundred. Apparently, when the Dutch Boers defeated the English in the early 1900s, Juby's officer had left on a ship leaving him a legacy of a military Sam Brown belt and a pith helmet. And then Juby became a drifter, moving from one place to the next.

In the stillness of the mountain Garth saw defeat in Goodwill's face and tried to sound optimistic. "Maybe he's further over. Caitlin said Juby pointed to the north-west... let's go a little further."

Again, the two men moved in grid formation. The silence broken only by Goodwill's tormented repetition of his son's name: "Kazi." "Kazi." "Kazi."

And then Garth heard a sound, froze and brought his fingers to his lips. "Wait, I think I heard something."

Goodwill stopped and turned in the direction that Garth was looking. They stood without moving, their tension mounting as the minutes stretched on. Only crickets and grasshoppers shrilled and clicked in the stillness.

After some time the men looked at each other and, without speaking, began to walk again. Then the wind changed ever so slightly, and carried with it a barely audible whimper.

Goodwill's eyes opened wide. "Kazi," he shouted.

And this time Kazi heard him and let out an angry scream.

"Caity, we've got him, we've got him," Garth yelled over the radio, barely able to control the tears stinging his eyes as he watched Goodwill untangle his child and lift him into his arms.

With the news, Martha's eyes closed tightly. She wrapped her arms around her chest and cried, rocking back and forth, back and forth, offering her own silent word of thanks.

When Garth and Goodwill reached the farmhouse with the child, Martha ran to them with tears streaming down her face. She took Kazi and sat down on the ground, opening her blouse and baring her breast. Kazi latched on and sucked hungrily, his dirty hand stroking her breast, his eyes locked on hers. Martha crooned, "*Tula Tu Tula Baba Tula*, hush my baby close your eyes," and his eyes closed and flickered, and then he fell into an exhausted sleep.

TWO

WITCH DOCTOR

1975 · 1976 · 1977 · 1978 · 1979 · 1980 · 1981 · 1982 · 1983

Kazi's disappearance had a deeper impact than usual on Caitlin because she herself was pregnant. She watched little Shanon's every move and became anxious if she was out of sight for more than a few seconds. Sensing her mother's mood Shanon stayed close, intuitively doing what was required of her. Caitlin also worried about her future child, perhaps a son that would be more adventurous.

Now, nearly five months later, the press of her bladder woke her. She longed for a few more minutes of sleep, but the baby kept moving, pushing on her, and she had to get up. She threw back the blankets, got out of bed, went into the bathroom and welcomed the feeling of relief as it emptied. She knew she wouldn't go back to sleep, so she walked through to the kitchen and switched on the kettle. While she waited for it to boil she stood at the window and looked out. Her hair hung below her shoulders, a sun-streaked blond, her eyes were a gentle brown flecked with green, and at twenty-three her skin was clear and only lightly sun-tanned.

Her view took in the farm, the valley and the surrounding mountain ridges. To the east the sun was rising at the mouth of the valley, to the north the town of Brits lay beyond a ridge of mountains. Below the house were fields of veld grass where Caitlin wanted paddocks and horses. Beyond the veld stretched the farm lands planted to wheat, and below that a narrow stretch of bush grew alongside the river. Behind and to the south rose the Magliesberg Mountains and fifty kilometres beyond, the city of Johannesburg thrived.

It was now dawn and birdsong filled the branches of the trees. Beneath the window sparrows, finches, and blue waxbills pecked through yesterday's birdseed. Noticing their food was finished Caitlin scooped up a handful of fresh seed, and went outside to spread it on the ground under the protective canopy of a Frangipani tree. It was autumn and a warm wind was blowing as the sun shifted higher in the dawn sky. She remembered the day when she'd learnt she was pregnant again. It had been spring and, noticing a stippling of red blossom on the Coral tree, she had run down to admire the first blush of red blossoms. Now, heavily pregnant, she walked down to the tree and, just as she had then, leant her back against the trunk, drawing strength from it. She looked out at the valley, allowing her thoughts to drift, and watched as a formation of birds flew over, shadowed against the lightening sky. Standing for a moment longer she turned reluctantly, then returned to the house. Shanon would soon be up demanding her cup of milky tea in bed with them, and then the day's chores would begin.

For the rest of the day Caitlin was lethargic. After dinner she rested on the couch feeling her pregnancy and every one of her years. Garth, on the other hand, was filled with restless energy. Something was troubling him. He walked to the window and glanced out as a whisper of wind blew in bringing with it the faint smell of smoke. He frowned and sniffed the air, perhaps a wood fire from the labourers' houses, he thought. To be sure he strode across the room to another window. When he opened it the smell was stronger. He looked south, and noticed a string of fires moving along the crest of the mountain towards Fairvalley Farm. As he looked, the fires caught and combined. Flames leapt into the sky.

"There's a fire on the mountain!" he yelled to Caitlin as he sprinted outside to his diesel Land Cruiser. He turned the key and while he waited for the glow plug to heat up, seconds felt like hours. Finally the indicator glowed orange so he started the engine, and accelerated away towards the shed, tooting the horn as he drove. Several men ran out of the labourers' houses fifty metres away. Some were barefoot, their boots carried along in their hands to be fitted once they were on the way. Others were pulling on their coveralls.

Garth pointed to the flames and yelled, "Load the water barrels and sacks onto the Land Cruiser. Let's go!"

Within minutes, the back of the Land Cruiser was filled with supplies and men, and Garth sped off up an uneven track that led up the mountain. The primitive trail soon disappeared, but Garth kept driving until they reached the base of the fire. A mile long stretch of angry flames, fuelled by tinder-dry trees and logs, ran ahead. Beyond the fire the land was reduced to ashes, burned black.

Birds had flown from their nests and circled overhead, frightened baboons barked over the roar of the flames, and a duiker bounded away.

The men leaped from the back of the Land Cruiser, took the sacks, wet them in the barrels, and strode forward in a line. Garth took his place in the line, no man any different to the other in an emergency, and each man kept the man to his left and to his right in sight. One man called the strike and the sacks came down in unison, they lifted and the strike was called again and the sacks came down. They worked as a team, a rhythm forming, minds closed to discomfort and exhaustion. Their hair singed, their throats burned, and every breath brought a choking, searing agony, but still they pushed on. The heat of the flames dried the sacks and the fire fighters soaked them again and again, returning each time to put out more of the fire.

Back at the farmhouse Caitlin stood outside for a moment watching the fire. The soot-laden wind ruffled her long blond hair and pushed her skirt against her slim legs. She became concerned about the effect of the smoke on her unborn baby, so she went inside and closed the windows. She placed a hand on her stomach and felt the child move, perhaps sensing her distress. She gently stroked it and thought about her previous pregnancy. She could still remember the *sangoma*, the witch doctor, who had offered to tell her the sex of her first child.

The wizened old woman, stooped with age, eyes small and black, had opened a leather pouch on her belt, thrown the bones of a tiny animal on the ground, and turned away without a word about what she had seen. Even though Caitlin didn't believe in tribal medicine and witchcraft, it had upset her. She had wondered if something was wrong with her baby. Why else would the woman have acted in that way? But she'd dismissed the episode. And then months later on the way home from hospital after Shanon's birth, the old witch doctor had been standing on the side of the road, as if she'd been waiting for them. She had stepped into the road and held up her hand, and Garth had stopped the car. She'd clasped her hands and bowed her head and said, "*Baas* Garth, I share your shame that your first born is not a boy, an *amadoda,* to help you when you grow old."

Garth had looked confused, but as they drove away Caitlin had laughed. The witchdoctor had not seen some terrible omen in the fall of the bones, only that their first baby was a girl and not a boy, which in tribal Africa is a sign of strength and virility.

Now, whenever Caitlin crossed paths with the *sangoma*, the old woman pinned her with a dark look as if she wanted to throw the bones again. Caitlin was not interested. It was not that she cared about the sex of her baby. It was more that she was frightened that the witchdoctor would see something wrong.

Caitlin came back to the present, smiled at the thought of her little girl and went into the bedroom to check on her. Shanon had thrown off her covers and was sleeping peacefully. She pulled up the sheet and tucked Shanon's teddy in next to her.

At the sound of the Land Cruiser, she went to the door, looked up towards the mountain and noticed that the fire was out. With a sigh of relief she turned and walked into the storeroom where she picked up a crate of home-brew beer for the men. She went outside and put the crate down.

Garth parked and the men clambered off the back. Noticing the beer, he said, "Caity, you shouldn't have picked up that heavy crate."

She smiled. "I'm fine," she replied, gently putting aside his objection. She handed out the beer, and the men headed home as she and Garth walked down the slope towards the farmhouse.

"I was worried about Juby," Caitlin said.

"The fire never made it across the gorge. He was fine," he assured her.

"Cold Castle?" Caitlin asked, referring to his favourite beer.

Garth nodded as he pulled off his boots, collapsing onto a chair on the veranda.

"Thanks," he said when Caitlin came back with his beer.

She eased down next to him and they sat in silence listening to an owl hooting in the barn. Crickets chirped nearby.

A swarm of flying-ants lifted on silver wings. "That's a sure sign of rain," Caitlin observed.

Garth smiled, "I hope you're right, we need it."

The next morning Johannes, the man who looked after the cattle, arrived at the kitchen door to fetch the milk buckets. It was raining lightly and he was dressed in the standard farm issue of blue coveralls and black gum boots. He was a strong, broad shouldered Ndebele man with a friendly smile and a ready word of advice for anyone willing to listen.

"*Môre Moedertjie*," he greeted Caitlin with the Afrikaans word for mother to acknowledge her advanced pregnancy, and also her status as the mother-figure to the farm workers and their families. Although twenty-three and younger than most of the labourers, they respected her because she was knowledgeable about most common illnesses, provided treatment when she could, sent them to the doctor when she couldn't, arranged the clinic nurse for inoculations and family planning, and provided a listening ear to their concerns.

Caitlin pressed the heels of her hands to her back and leaned into them easing the ache. She smiled and acknowledged the man's greeting: "*Môre,* Johannes."

"*So ja,* I see *Moedertjie* is going to have the baby today," Johannes announced.

Caitlin shook her head and her smile spread. "I wish you were right… but it's not time yet." With effort, she bent, picked up the buckets and handed them to Johannes.

Johannes took them and turned, smiling broadly. "Madam will see. I know when a baby's coming, I have six children." Caitlin shook her head and turned back inside.

But later that day she realized that Johannes was right. The ache in her back came and went at regular intervals. She was in labour. Garth, Caitlin and Shanon left for Johannesburg minutes later. Shanon stood on the seat between her parents, a dimpled hand on her mother's shoulder, her short legs spread bracing against the vehicle's movements. Her auburn hair bounced just above her shoulders, and her hazel eyes, so similar to Garth's, danced with excitement.

Garth wove through the traffic and drove as fast as the Land Cruiser could go while Caitlin lay back against the seat breathing calmly.

Fifty minutes later, he pulled up outside the hospital's emergency entrance. He got out and looked around. Caitlin waited in the Land Cruiser while a contraction passed.

Garth rattled the change in his pockets. "They should be here." Before they left the farm, he had called his parents to fetch Shanon. He looked around. The engine ticked as it cooled.

An ambulance sped in and parked behind them. Medics ran out and ushered a stretcher inside. The hospital doors opened and closed silently. Another contraction pulled Caitlin back onto her seat, but she panted as she had been taught. Shanon's thumb snuck into her mouth, her eyes on her mother. A man stared in at them as he passed.

"There they are," Garth said, relieved. Caitlin turned her head on the seat and saw Garth's mother striding towards them, her tall figure outlined against the sun. Her hair was short, dark and lightly curling like her son's. Her eyes were the same as Garth's, but lined at the corners. Garth's father, the same height and build as Garth, but with straight receding hair, and brown, not hazel eyes, hurried forward to take Shanon's bag. After a few words of encouragement they left with Shanon, her eyes still on her mother as they walked away.

Inside the hospital Caitlin eased into a chair and filled in the admission forms. They were directed to a ward where the smell of antiseptic stung the air and a woman in labour down the hall screamed. Caitlin got changed, climbed onto the bed, and a nurse came into the room and examined her. The next set of contractions began – each contraction building into a pain that Caitlin imagined as a mountain, an uphill climb becoming harder and harder, steeper and steeper, until she reached the peak and could slide with the pain down to a plateau where she could rest before she faced the next mountain.

Twenty minutes later the contractions were five minutes apart and the nurse came back and examined Caitlin again. "Nine centimetres, we're ready to go," she said, taking hold of the foot of the bed and steering it towards the door. Garth followed, but at the entrance to the delivery room the nurse stopped.

"Sorry, Sir," she said to Garth, "you have to wait here. You can only come in when the doctor gets here." Garth looked like he was going to say something. "Rules are rules," she added, brooking no argument. She pushed through the doors and they swung closed before Garth could speak.

Caitlin looked around the sterile confines of the delivery room. Lights blazed down, rows of equipment stared blankly back. She was cold. A contraction pulled through her and she felt nauseous. The door swung open and she turned desperately towards it.

Two masked people in hospital scrubs strode in. One of them walked directly to her and Caitlin recognised Garth's hazel eyes. They crinkled encouragingly and he picked up her hand and squeezed. She smiled feebly, her energy sapped.

The doctor, a stout man, balding with thick glasses, examined her, "Ten centimetres," he announced and then he placed his stethoscope on her stomach and listened. He straightened and hooked the stethoscope around his neck in a slow, deliberate movement. The lights hummed in the silence.

"I don't want you to worry," he said, his attitude suddenly serious, "but we have to move this along."

Caitlin frowned. Now she was worried. A buzzing started in her ears.

"The baby's heart rate has dropped and we don't want it to go into distress."

"What does that mean?" Caitlin asked, fear in her eyes.

"Just that we don't want a protracted labour. I'll see if I can speed things up by pressing down on the uterus during the contractions." He did not mention that the next step would be a caesarean.

Caitlin mustered her strength again as a powerful contraction pulled her forward. Garth squeezed her hand tighter. It passed and she fell back breathing heavily.

The doctor placed his hands on her stomach, "Tell me when the next contraction starts."

"Now," Caitlin told him a few seconds later.

"Okay," the doctor said. "Let's do it. Push," he instructed, and he pressed on her abdomen. "Push," he instructed again. "Don't forget to breathe. Hold on, gently now. Don't push." The doctor's hands disappeared under the sheet draped over Caitlin's knees as he rotated the baby's head and the shoulder came free. "Go ahead now, push." Caitlin bore down and there was no pain as the baby slid from her. She fell back and watched the doctor lift it.

"It's a boy," he announced with obvious relief, and then he turned to the nurse and said, "Suction." His voice suddenly turning cold and emotionless.

The humming in Caitlin's ears got louder and the room closed in around her. She looked at Garth. His face had paled, his eyes glued to their child. Caitlin heard the suction start up. The baby's silence filled the room. She gripped Garth's hand and her legs trembled. Her heart raced while the doctor and nurse worked with strong, confident movements. Still her baby remained silent. Caitlin's legs quivered, her grip on Garth's hand tightened, she prayed silently. The room hushed, dampened, narrowed. After what seemed an eternity, a weak cry emerged from the tiny body, then grew stronger and stronger. At last the doctor turned and smiled. "There we are," he said, placing the baby on Caitlin's chest.

"Scott," she whispered as she touched his cheek. At her touch, he turned his head toward her and opened his mouth.

THREE

TROUBLE AT THE BOTTOM
OF THE BOTTLE

1975 · 1976 · 1977 · **1978** · 1979 · 1980 · 1981 · 1982 · 1983

Summer, three years later, Kazi, now five years old, was expected to help with the chores. An afternoon thundershower had cleared, and the sun was turning orange as it sank towards the horizon. Up at the labourers' houses, Kazi had collected wood, filled the water bucket and escaped before his mother could think up another task for him. He ran, barefoot as usual, after a tire which he hit with a stick, first on one side then the other, keeping it going in a straight line. It zigzagged ahead of him, picked up speed then it hit a stone, leapt away and headed towards the group of men who sat around the cooking fire in the *lapa*.

There were twelve identical *lapas* on Fairvalley Farm, simple structures of a roof and half wall surrounding a fire pit where cooking and visiting took place behind each of the whitewashed houses in the labourers' compound.

Kazi watched in horror as the tire sped out of control. Should he shout a warning, or just hope it would miss them? Before he could decide, it fell over, and spun lazily to a stop. Dust drifted over the men.

Goodwill stopped talking and looked up. "Kazi, go to bed. Did you not hear your mother calling?" His father's voice was firm.

Kazi hung his head. He had been told often enough not to interrupt his father when he was in a meeting; he was, after all, the *maruti*, the preacher. Kazi picked up his tire and walked away, shoulders hunched. He washed his hands and feet at the tap outside the house, went inside, and climbed into bed next to Mandiso and Dumani, his younger brothers. Dumani, the eldest was three and took up most of the space – spread-eagled across the bed. All that Kazi could see of him was the back of his dark head. He was so similar to Goodwill, whereas Mandiso, a year younger, took after his mother. He slept on his back, top-to-tail with Dumani, one chubby hand flung out above his head. Kazi hoped Ntokoso, his baby sister in her crib, wouldn't wake up and demand attention. She did not, so he turned over and fell asleep listening to their sleepy snuffles.

Later that night Kazi woke to voices outside. He tried to ignore them, but Swart Piet, a horrible scowling man all the children avoided, was cursing his wife loudly in a drunken slur. Kazi heard a thump, and a woman call out. Then the sound of scuffling and a stifled scream. He couldn't stand it any longer – he had to see what was happening, so he slipped out of bed and looked out the window. Outside, Swart Piet laughed drunkenly, his back to Kazi, his wife Julia on the ground at his feet. As Kazi watched he swung back and kicked his booted foot into Julia's side. Swart Piet towered above his wife, a rail thin woman in a cotton dress so faded that the pattern was indistinguishable. Swart Piet's face was dark, almost black, and his eyes held a wild unfocused look.

The cement floor chilled Kazi's feet, drawing the cold up his thin legs. He was frightened, but he couldn't turn away.

Swart Piet's boot landed another hard blow and Julia skidded into a pile of firewood. She lay amongst the wood, her eyes on Swart Piet, her hand moving slowly, reaching for a branch. Kazi held his breath; he looked at Swart Piet, terrified the man would see what his wife was up to. But Swart Piet was busy with his own thoughts, cursing his wife and hammering his fist into his hand psyching himself up. Kazi glanced at Julia, she almost had the branch. As Swart Piet stepped forward to hit her again she grabbed the branch, leapt up and struck with the speed of a cobra. The branch hit Swart Piet on the side of his head. He gave a bark of surprise, stumbled forward, reached out to support himself against the wall, and then he staggered away towards his house. Julia stayed where she was, shaking visibly. She had blood on her mouth, and dirt caked the side of her face. After a while, she dropped the branch and went in the opposite direction.

Silence fell and Kazi climbed back into bed soothed by his brother's sweet breath on his face.

The next morning early dew flattened the dust and woodsmoke drifted into the valleys and low spots from eleven of the twelve cooking fires. Kazi dragged sleepily towards the *lapa* and sat down between his brothers. He hadn't slept well after the fight the night before, and he knuckled sleep from his eyes. His mother worked over the fire cooking their breakfast, his father leant against the wall looking out. In the other *lapas,* families ate bowls of *mealie-pap*, thick cornmeal porridge, with milk and a smattering of sugar for those that had any. Kazi noticed that Swart Piet's *lapa* was empty. His fire was not burning.

Goodwill turned from his musings. "Swart Piet was drunk again last night."

"I know, I heard them fighting. It's awful the way that man treats his wife," Martha said. Her full lips turned down, and the flesh under her chin wobbled as she shook her head. A cotton *doek* covered her hair, and she was wearing an old button-down shirt, a dark shapeless skirt pinched in across her thick waist, and sensible work shoes, mud splattered and flattened at the back.

Goodwill turned and his gaze touched affectionately on his own offspring. "God's blessings are often hard to recognise as blessings at the time, but he certainly blessed that woman when she couldn't fall pregnant. Swart Piet would have beaten the children as well as Julia."

Martha lifted the lid off the pot over the fire. "It's also a good thing *Baas* Garth gives us rations and milk as part of our wages. At least Julia has food." She spooned porridge into four bowls for her children, her movements plump and unhurried. "I see she isn't home. She must have stayed with Sophie last night."

They finished eating and Martha filled the bowls again, fastened cloths over them, gave one to Goodwill for his lunch, and kept the others for herself and the children. She fastened Ntokoso onto her back, took Mandiso's hand and sauntered towards the other women where they were getting ready to walk to work in the farmlands. Kazi, as he did every work day, picked up the bowls of food Martha had prepared for them and followed with Dumani.

Julia stood silently on one side of the group of women, her eye swollen and darkly bruised. Her friend Sophie guarded her like a rugby fullback, head forward on hunched shoulders, legs spread. Her broad nose flared angrily, and her low breasts swung as she moved. She was a big woman, strong from years of work in the fields, and her hair was an inch long mess of tight black curls. "Let's see if the drunken pig is awake," she snarled.

Julia walked to her house and the others followed closely behind. She knocked timidly, pushed open the door, and peered in. Kazi peeped past broad hips and skirts. Swart Piet was sleeping on the floor, the air sour from his breath.

"Eh!" Sophie exclaimed. "He is sleeping. I hope he loses his job."

No one else commented. Julia closed the door, and they all left for work.

While his mother worked in the fields, Kazi looked after his younger brothers and sister on a blanket, which was laid out under a tree on the edge of the wheat land. He had to watch Dumani like a hawk, because he tended to disappear if Kazi turned his head for a split second. And Mandiso wanted to be with his mother. "*Umama, Umama,*" he whined constantly, reaching out towards her whenever she came into sight. An inch of flesh showed below his shirt, and his pushed out belly button could be seen through the thin material.

Baby Ntokoso was the only one content to sleep or kick her feet at the leaves moving in the tree above. To keep the children on the blanket, Kazi threw shiny stones, pointed out soaring vultures, and made hand animals that swooped onto their tummies to make them giggle. Sometimes he took them for walks, but it was hard because he had to carry Ntokoso and he wasn't all that big himself. It was boring and Kazi was relieved when it was time to go home. He was also hungry, and he had looked forward to dinner ever since he had noticed his mother collecting morogo leaves for their meal. It would be good to have something with their *mealie-pap* tonight, even though it tasted like spinach.

On their way home, the uphill walk seemed to take so much longer because everyone was tired, and the silent group spread out in a long straggle. At her house, Julia stopped and looked in. This time Kazi made sure that he could see properly. Swart Piet was still there, on the floor, the evening air cooling rapidly.

"Help me lift him onto the bed," Julia said.

"*Eh, eh*," Sophie shook her head. "Why should you care? He beat you. Leave him."

"I'll help you," Martha suggested. She waved two women over and together the four of them heaved Swart Piet onto the bed.

Sophie chuckled, observing their efforts. "In the morning he will have a big *babalas* – a big headache. He won't care that you put him on the bed, he'll beat you again, Julia."

Julia didn't reply. She covered Swart Piet and, too scared to stay, followed Sophie outside.

The next morning, on the way to work, Julia stopped again at the house. She opened the door and this time Kazi was pushed into the room ahead of the women as they crowded in. The warming sun had not entered the house, leaving the room a wretched grey. Nothing had changed. Swart Piet hadn't moved, his breathing was shallow, and the air was stale with the reek of unwashed clothing and stale beer-breath. Julia shook him gently, and he flopped as if boneless. His mouth sagged open.

"Julia, I'm worried," Martha whispered. "Swart Piet does not look right. I think he should've woken up by now, don't you?"

The two women stood watching Swart Piet. He was in what appeared to be a deep sleep.

Martha looked worried. "I think I should fetch Goodwill, see what he thinks."

"Yes, let's fetch him," Julia agreed.

Martha looked at her children, "Kazi, wait here with your brothers," she instructed. She waved the other women away, "Go on without us, we'll catch up with you later."

The women left after one last look at Swart Piet, and Kazi was left alone at the door with Dumani and Mandiso. He kept his eyes on the body on the bed. If Swart Piet woke up he would be very angry if he saw three children in his room, thinking they were stealing his stuff. Kazi gripped his brothers' hands tightly. If Swart Piet did wake up he would have to get the two little ones away before Swart Piet beat them all.

"Get ready to run," Kazi whispered. "If the old man wakes up, he'll kill us for sure."

Mandiso and Dumani's eyes grew wide and, as they stared at Swart Piet, Mandiso trembled slightly. Kazi's eyes hurt from looking so hard and his feet began to feel like they'd put down roots. He wondered how he would lift them in time to run away if Swart Piet did get up.

After a while Dumani tugged his hand. "*Utata, Umama* – Daddy, Mommy," he whispered, and Kazi turned to see his mother and father hurrying towards them with Julia.

Relief swept over him. Swart Piet couldn't get them now, *Utata* would stop him.

Goodwill followed Julia into the room and pulled the blanket away from Swart Piet's face. Kazi stretched his neck to see. He was no longer scared now that his father was there.

"Swart Piet, Swart Piet, wake up," Goodwill urged. "Come on man, wake up." Swart Piet didn't move. "Fetch some water," Goodwill ordered.

Julia ran to her kitchen and came back with a mug of water. Goodwill took it and poured a little on his hands and spread it on Swart Piet's face. It had no effect, Swart Piet didn't move. Goodwill drizzled water into the man's mouth and it trickled out of the corner.

"I don't like the look of this," he said. "I'm going to ask *Baas* Garth to phone for an ambulance."

Goodwill pulled the blanket over Swart Piet's chest and strode out of the house. Kazi raced after him, still worried that Swart Piet might wake at any moment.

At the farmhouse Maria, the maid, opened the door. She was a tall woman with an olive brown complexion, dressed in a maid's coverall and apron.

"Maria, call the *Baas*. Be quick."

"*Baas*," Maria hurried through the kitchen to the dining room door, she knocked. "*Asseblief Baas*, – please Boss, Goodwill has come to see the *Baas*."

"Maria, tell him to come back later," Garth responded irritably. "I'm eating."

From outside Goodwill heard Garth's response. "Maria, tell the *Baas* it's urgent."

Maria repeated what Goodwill said. "Sorry, *Baas*. Goodwill says it's important, *Baas*."

Garth swallowed the last of his breakfast, pushed back his chair with an irritable scrape, and came to the door. "*Ja*, what do you want, Goodwill?"

"Sorry, *Baas*, but we need an ambulance for Swart Piet, he hasn't spoken since Sunday."

"What do you mean he hasn't spoken? Has he lost his voice?"

"No, *Baas*, he isn't moving."

"Hasn't moved since when?"

"Sunday, *Baas*."

"That's odd, was the old bastard drinking?" Garth asked following Goodwill.

"Yes, *Baas*."

"Well, he should've woken up by now. What happened?"

"Julia hit him on the head, *Baas*."

"He was probably beating her up as usual."

"Yes, *Baas*."

When he saw Swart Piet, Garth realized immediately that he was seriously ill. In the five years since they had bought Fairvalley Farm, he and Caitlin had learnt to deal with the drunken Sunday brawls that overflowed from the labourers' houses to the farmhouse and the variety of wounds, cuts, bruises, knobkerrie bashings and stabbings. A well-stocked medicine kit handled most injuries, and a dog-eared medical guide helped with a range of illnesses: boils, fevers, aches and pains. Only labourers with serious injuries or illnesses were sent off to be dealt with in hospital, and this was obviously one of them.

Garth returned to the farmhouse and called the ambulance. It arrived shortly, and two medics ran into Swart Piet's room with Garth and Goodwill. Julia hovered at Swart Piet's bedside.

One of the men pulled back the blanket and felt for Swart Piet's pulse. "This man's a goner, he's not going to last long," he announced callously, and Julia cried out.

The second medic came back with a gurney and between them they loaded Swart Piet onto it, pushed it out to the ambulance and slid it into the back. The doors slammed and, without another word, the two men drove away.

The medic was right – Swart Piet died during the night without regaining consciousness.

On Saturday morning Garth drove to Brits and bought a pine coffin, then he fetched Swart Piet from the mortuary. The labourers dug a grave, bought a goat for the party after the funeral, and Goodwill conducted the service.

After the funeral Garth approached Goodwill. "The police are asking questions about the wound on Swart Piet's head. If they come, Julia should have the right answers."

Goodwill looked at Garth and nodded. It would not be right if a good woman had to pay for her husband's sins.

FOUR

SUN SCORCHED EARTH

1978 · 1979 · **1980** · 1981 · 1982 · 1983 · 1984 · 1985 · 1986

One year rolled into the next – the same droughts, illnesses, births, but thankfully no more deaths. The adults hadn't aged much over the intervening two years but the children had grown. Kazi, reed thin, ran between inventing games and doing his chores, Scott played at the kindergarten in the mornings, and Shanon learnt to read and write at school. However, this year the drought appeared to be worse than ever. The leaves on the trees drooped and the fifth wheat crop in as many years did not look promising.

Garth and Caitlin, dressed lightly to accommodate the heat – Garth in khaki shorts, khaki open-neck shirt, ankle height hiking boots on account of snakes when out on the farm, and Caitlin in a cotton shift and sandals – were discussing the lack of rain on their wheat crop when they heard a vehicle drive up.

"That must be Dries," Garth said as they heard a man whistle for his dog. *"Kom Fox,"* the man called, and Garth went to the door and opened it for his friend.

The Afrikaner had gentle sloping eyes that crinkled at the corners after years in the sun. Black hair curled around his ears. *"Môre boet,"* he said, saying good morning and using the word *boet* as a term of friendship indicating their relationship was as close as that of brothers.

"Môre Dries, come in."

"You look like you're going to your own funeral." Dries observed following Garth inside. *"Môre*, Caitlin. You've also got a long face, what's going on?"

Caitlin sighed. "We're in overdraft again. We've been on Fairvalley for five years and it's been one drought after the other. We occasionally have a good crop, pay off the Co-op loans, buy seed and fertilizer for the next crop, and then we go into debt again and worry about the weather for the rest of the season. Year after year it's the same. I can't take it anymore." She went to the kitchen door. "Maria, *Baas* Dries is here. Bring three cups of coffee please." She turned back to the table as Dries and Garth scraped back chairs and sat down.

"That's farming for you, Caitlin," Dries said, lighting a Dunhill. "Right now there's a drought and you feel like you're on the dark side of the rainbow, but I promise there's light on the other side. Just keep working towards it and you will get there." He took a slow drag on the cigarette and blew the smoke away. "Garth," he said, mulling things over, "why don't you get a government subsidized Landbank loan? The interest rates are lower than independent banks. You could put in irrigation, plant vegetables – a cash crop that would even out the ups and downs."

Garth narrowed his eyes in thought. "You have a good point. I think I'll try that."

After Dries left Garth made an appointment with Landbank and, with the farm as collateral, the loan was approved. After that he, Goodwill, and Jaapie, a black man with a history of finding water, met in the field above the farm lands. Jaapie walked back and forth, a y-shaped stick twitching and sometimes twisting in his hands. He was looking for water using the old way. While he was busy, Garth and Goodwill walked through the field checking the slope towards the lands, looking for a logical place to build a dam. Garth stopped and pointed occasionally, and wherever he pointed Goodwill made a pile of rocks. And whenever the y-shaped stick twisted in Jaapie's hands Goodwill placed another pile.

Dries arrived, looked at what they were doing, and pointed towards a ravine up in the mountain. "Garth, forget the old guy's mumbo-jumbo. If you go by geological reasoning, rainwater collects in underground sills and flows downhill towards the river." His hand swept down the mountain in an imaginary stream. "See where the kloof feeds into that flat area? That's where you'll find water. Tell that old goat to look over there." He pointed his chin at Jaapie.

"Jaapie," Garth called the water diviner, and indicated the place Dries suggested. "*Baas* Dries thinks we'll find water there."

"*Ja, Baas*, perhaps the other *Baas* is right."

Jaapie and Goodwill followed Garth and Dries across the field. Shaka, Garth's Rottweiler, normally at his side, stayed behind in the shade of a thorn tree. His eyes, dark-brown pools that reflected an intelligent, fearless expression, followed his master. Although he was Garth's dog, the family was his pack and he protected them all. Kazi, who hadn't gone to work with his mother, trailed Goodwill. Scott was also there. He stood on the lowest rail of the gate and watched them all. He was bored and wondered if Kazi wanted to play. He looked as if he was about his age, maybe a little older. In fact, although they looked close in age, Scott's fifth birthday was in April, and Kazi was a few months shy of seven.

He jumped off the gate and walked over to Kazi. "Hey, you wanna do something?"

"What?" Kazi asked.

"I dunno, anything," Scott said, scything grass with a stick. Kazi kicked a stone and shrugged. "Okay," he decided, and the two boys walked away together.

Scott was not quite as tall as Kazi and, although sun tanned, was not as dark as Kazi's native brown. Kazi's eyes were a deep mahogany, and Scott's were green, or blue depending on the weather, his mood, or what he was wearing. Scott's hair, a lighter shade of blond than Caitlin's, bleached from hours playing in the sun, lay like thatch on his head. Kazi's black hair curled tightly.

Scott stopped abruptly. "Look!" he said, putting his stick down, snapping off a stalk of grass, and crouching in front of a small indentation in the sand.

"What is it?"

"An antlion sand trap," Scott informed him. Kazi knelt next to Scott, his dark head close to Scott's.

"Watch this," Scott said, twirling the stalk on the surface of the sand. Suddenly sand spewed from the centre of the cone-shaped indentation, and Scott jumped back with a small grub-like insect clinging to the tip of his stalk.

"What is it?" Kazi asked.

"I told you, an antlion," Scott replied. "It waits for an insect to fall into its trap and..." he lowered his voice ominously, "then he grabs it and eats it," he announced dramatically, holding his hands like biting fangs.

The antlion dropped to the ground and scurried away, and Kazi laughed.

The boys stood up, and Scott flung an arm over Kazi's shoulder as they walked off.

Garth drilled a borehole in the spot where both Dries's scientific reasoning and Jaapie's 'mumbo-jumbo' correlated, and found a strong underground aquifer.

The air was hot and dry, the season new, ready for planting. Garth was in a hurry so he rushed through building the dam and preparing the lands. All in record time.

At last it was the first day of planting and Kazi wasn't looking after the little ones. He was working with his mother. And for the first time in his life he was being paid to work because Garth had hired every able hand on the farm, young and old included.

Garth brought the eight-tonne Mercedes farm truck, loaded with cabbage seedlings, to a stop. Scott spotted Kazi, jumped out, and raced over.

"Can't play," Kazi announced feeling very grown up. "I'm working."

"Gee," Scott was impressed, "what are you doing?"

"I have to bring seedlings for my mother. She says I'll get into big trouble if she has to wait for me, but she won't 'cos I want to show her that I'm a good worker. Then I won't have to look after the babies anymore. I can get money for doing real work."

"I want to work too," Scott exclaimed, and Kazi shrugged. He ran to Garth. "Daddy, can I work too? Kazi is, and he's getting paid."

"Sure, but don't get in the way," Garth said.

"Will I get paid?"

"I'll pay you the same as Kazi, but no messing around, you hear? I'll check with Martha at the end of the day."

"Okay, Dad." Scott ran back and copied Kazi; he picked up a tray of seedlings and followed him back to Martha. She smiled and nodded approval when they put the trays down next to her. They continued, back and forth, fetching seedlings, leaving them, taking an empty tray back. But their good behaviour lasted only an hour before they got bored.

Scott raced off down the field. "Race you back, Kazi." He reached the end of the row first, grabbed a tray and turned back.

Kazi overtook him. "Ki ki ki," he giggled, his hard feet speeding over the uneven ground. He dropped the tray next to Martha. "I won," he yelled, spinning around and running back for another tray.

Scott scooped up a handful of mud and threw it at Kazi's retreating back. It missed and sprayed up one of the women's legs. She gave Scott a sharp look and Scott ducked his head. He knew he'd escaped a sharp reprimand only because he was the boss's son.

Martha, bent to her task, hadn't noticed. Ahead of her, Elliphas was preparing the seedbed and she was annoyed. This was the third time she had caught up. She straightened and placed her hands on her hips: "Elliphas, hurry up. The others are far ahead, and we're going to have to work late because of your laziness."

Elliphas ignored her and continued digging, and then he put down his hoe. "I have to go to the toilet," he announced and walked away.

Martha scowled; it was so typical of the man to find an excuse to avoid work.

"Kazi," she yelled, "take Elliphas's hoe and dig the holes, I can't wait for him."

"*Klein Baasie*," she said to Scott, "you must bring the seedlings on your own."

Scott nodded and both boys did as she asked.

There were no toilets on the fields and Elliphas walked along the new dam wall looking for a place that would be hidden from view. He spotted a vertical opening at the end of the dam wall, an outlet for future irrigation lines, and pulled down his pants and squatted. While he waited for his bowels to move he looked into the shaded hole. Something shimmered and he squinted to see if he had imagined it, and then he saw a long gleam of shadow and dark move towards him. It was a snake!

"*Nyoka*, snake!" he screamed leaping to his feet, and took off running without taking the time to pull up his pants. The material ripped apart, fell to his ankles, and he ran across the field towards the women and children with his pants down.

"Snake, snake... big snake!" he yelled, and everyone turned to see what he was shouting about.

"Look at Elliphas!" Kazi laughed grabbing Scott's arm.

Scott turned to look. "Run, man, run!" he giggled.

"Now look at that," Martha commented sourly. "The lazy man can move quickly after all."

"Look at his thingy," Sophie snorted, "it looks like an earthworm!" She cracked up laughing and everyone joined in.

Elliphas came to a stop and looked at them. "What are you laughing about?" he demanded angrily.

Sophie sniggered and pointed at Elliphas's crotch. He looked down, and realizing he was naked, hurriedly pulled the separate legs of his pants up, and drew them together.

Garth strode across the land. "What's going on?" he demanded crossly.

"A snake, a big *nyoka,* this big!" Elliphas stretched his arms to show how big the snake was, and his pants fell down again.

"For heaven's sake man, hold your pants," Garth said. He turned to Scott, "There's rope behind the seat in the truck, find a short piece for Elliphas to tie up his pants." Scott ran to the truck and came back with a length of rope.

"*Dankie Baas* – Thank-you," Elliphas said, tying the rope so that the sides of his pants overlapped. "Big *nyoka,*" he repeated.

Sophie called out, "Elliphas, you didn't see anything, it was your trouser snake." Everyone laughed and Elliphas scowled.

"Elliphas?" Garth questioned.

"For sure *Baas*, there is a big snake in the pipe."

"Why were you on the dam wall when you were supposed to be working?"

"*Baas,* I had to visit the bush to do my business and…"

"What? You filthy bastard," Garth responded angrily, "you went to the toilet where I have to work!"

Elliphas looked remorseful. "Sorry, *Baas.*"

Goodwill came back from the direction of the dam wall. "*Baas,* I pushed a stick into the hole and there's nothing there, no snake."

"*Nnyane* – honest," Elliphas formed his index fingers into the sign of a cross, as if taking an oath. "*Baas,* there is a very big snake in the pipe."

"Okay, Elliphas, I'll give you the benefit of the doubt. Goodwill, go to the house and fetch my shotgun from *Missus* Caitlin. We'll soon find out if there really is a snake."

Garth followed Elliphas to the dam wall, while Scott and Kazi followed like two little shadows. When Goodwill came back with the gun Garth loaded it, aimed, and let off a shot into the hole. He kept the second cartridge in reserve.

Nothing happened for a moment, and then a massive snake slithered out in an angry coil of muscle and scale. It lifted two feet of its length into the air with its hood spread and its mouth open in a gooselike hiss.

Garth pushed Scott and Kazi out of the way. "Get back!" he ordered.

The snake coiled to strike, and Garth fired the second cartridge, blowing away the left side of the hood. As the snake dropped, Elliphas rushed forward with a branch hitting it until it stopped moving. He dropped the branch, and Scott picked it up and turned the grey-brown snake over. Its belly was mottled with blue-black and yellow-brown cross-bars.

"Egyptian Cobra," he said, recognising the snake from his book of reptiles. He knew them all off by heart. "It's a big one."

"It is," Garth agreed, "probably about eight feet long." He turned away from the snake and looked at his labourers, "Okay, back to work." He turned to Elliphas. "And you. I don't want to see you walking even one step away from the job."

"Yes, *Baas*," Elliphas replied.

"And if you so much as look away from your work I'll give you a good hard *klap* across your ear, you hear?" Garth said, holding up a large threatening hand.

"Good," Martha said, giving Elliphas a dark look.

FIVE

WOLF IN SHEEP'S CLOTHING

1978 · 1979 · **1980** · 1981 · 1982 · 1983 · 1984 · 1985 · 1986

A few weeks later, on Sunday, Martha was outside hanging laundry and Goodwill was chopping wood. Kazi had created a car out of old rusted wire, drawn roads in the brushed dirt in front of their house, and was playing when a man approached.

"Hello, Kazi. Nice car, did you make it?"

Kazi looked up and immediately recognized the young man who'd reaped Fairvalley's wheat the year before. He had a flared, broad nose and a handsome well-formed face, his hair a carefully oiled Afro.

"I did," Kazi smiled proudly. "You're Jackson," he recalled. "You let me ride on the combine with you."

Jackson nodded. "Is your father home?"

"Dad," Kazi yelled, "Jackson's here."

Goodwill came around the house. "Kazi," he said crossly, "I've told you before not to shout like that. You must come and fetch me."

He turned to Jackson. "Sorry about that, Jackson. Come, sit," he said, indicating the stools in his *lapa*.

"Thanks," Jackson said, and followed Goodwill.

They sat down, spent a few minutes talking about their families and people they both knew, and when Jackson felt he had spent enough time on polite conversation he cleared his throat.

"Goodwill," he said, "you're probably wondering why I'm here." Goodwill nodded. "I've come to ask your advice."

"I hope I can help."

"You might remember that my wife and I were living in a shed with no water and electricity on my boss's property, and that we have a small baby."

"I do," Goodwill nodded. "We spoke about it when you were working here. You were hoping that your boss would build a house for you. How're things now?"

"Not any better, we're still in the shed," Jackson said forlornly.

"What, you're still in the shed? When we talked about this last year, I suggested you get your heavy-duty driver's licence and find another job if he didn't sort things out for you."

"I did get my licence, but the problem is that no-one will hire me because I have no experience."

"Hmm," Goodwill thought for a moment. "I could ask *Baas* Garth. He'll need a truck driver when the cabbages are ready for market. He's a fair man and might give you a chance. But I should warn you that he's very particular about his vehicles and machinery. And he doesn't have the nickname *Ma-double* for nothing. He has two sides – if he's pleased with you, he's nice, but make him angry and you'll meet the other side, and that won't be pleasant."

"I can deal with that. Will you ask him?"

Goodwill looked at his watch. "They'll be at church now. But *Baas* Garth doesn't like to be hassled on a Sunday anyway. Perhaps it would be better if you came back tomorrow morning. Be here at seven and I'll see what I can do for you."

The next day Jackson arrived ten minutes early and Goodwill walked to the shed with him. They waited until Garth finished speaking to one of the labourers, then Goodwill stepped forward.

"Please, *Baas*. Has the *Baas* time to speak to Jackson?"

Garth glanced at Jackson. "Jackson? Oh yes, I remember you. You're the man who harvested our wheat last year, right?"

"*Ja, Baas*," Jackson nodded.

Goodwill continued. "Jackson has his heavy-duty truck licence now and he's looking for work. He's a good man and I wondered if the *Baas* would need a driver when the cabbages are ready for market."

"I don't need anyone right now, but you're right, I will. How much experience do you have, Jackson?"

"Sorry, *Baas*, I have none."

"Hmm," Garth said thoughtfully. "I remember you worked well last year, and you looked after your machine. I like those qualities." He paused and looked at the eight-tonne truck, then back at Jackson. "Let's go for a drive and see how you do."

"Thank you, *Baas*." Jackson grinned, but his heart had leapt into his throat. He was suddenly so nervous he wondered if he could drive well enough to pass the test.

Fifteen minutes later Jackson drove back to the shed. He parked the truck carefully and Garth jumped down from the passenger seat. Jackson followed more slowly, his expression hopeful.

Garth thought for a moment considering whether to take the risk or not. He pressed his lips together. "I'll take you on," he said, making a decision. "But you'll be on trial for a month," he warned.

"Thank you, *Baas*. I promise I'll look after the *Baas's* truck."

Garth nodded. "You can have the house Swart Piet was in. It's empty and you can move in right away. Goodwill, show him the house," he added as he walked away.

When Garth was out of sight Goodwill patted Jackson on the back. "Well done. Come on, I'll take you up to Swart Piet's house. Then I must get back to work."

They walked up the dirt road to the labourers' houses and stopped outside the house next to Goodwill's.

"This is it," Goodwill opened the door. "The old guy died and his wife moved away." He didn't add that Swart Piet died in the house.

Jackson wasn't really listening. He walked into the house and although the layout was identical to Goodwill's house, he hadn't been further than the small living room.

"Nelly will be thrilled. Look at this, two bedrooms!"

As Goodwill took him out the back door to show him the *lapa,* a young woman walked by, and Jackson turned to watch as she passed. She was beautiful, her face narrow with high cheekbones and a soft honey-brown complexion. Jackson smiled when she looked up, and she glanced away quickly.

"Who's that?" he asked, still watching the girl.

Without looking at him the girl carried on walking towards the last house in the row. The way she held her head, long neck arched elegantly, told Jackson that she was aware of his scrutiny.

"That's Sarina," Goodwill replied. "Her mother works for *Missus* Caitlin. They don't mix with us because they're coloured," he said, referring to a mixed ancestry from the early European settlers and his own native African.

Jackson nodded. "She's very pretty."

When Nelly and Jackson moved in, their few furnishings looked meager in the little house but both were ecstatic with the move. Although they'd never formalized their relationship, which was common in rural black communities, they had been together as man and wife for four years. And they'd lived in the shed for all of that time.

As Jackson lifted the last box off the truck, he looked up and a thrill ran through him. Sarina, the pretty girl, was standing there looking at him.

He smiled. "Hello," he said.

"Hello," she replied softly.

She turned and walked away and Jackson watched her hips swaying as she moved. She must have felt him watching and glanced over her shoulder. He smiled again.

Jackson began work the next day and over the following weeks he serviced and cleaned the John Deere tractors and the Mercedes truck. He drove to the Agricultural Co-operative to fetch fertilizer, pesticides, supplies, and tidied the workshop until, at last, the cabbages were ready to be harvested. On his first trip to the market Garth went with him. He was nervous, aware of Garth's presence watching him, assessing his driving. He concentrated on shoulder checks, his speed, revs, braking gradually at stops, and pulling off at an even speed. At the market he turned in and his heart beat faster at the sight of all the trucks juggling for a position at the loading docks. He took one sweating hand off the steering wheel and rubbed it on his pants, replaced it and did the same with the other, hoping Garth wouldn't notice. His foot twitched nervously on the stiff clutch.

An opening came up, he indicated, pulled into the line between an Isuzu double-axel truck and trailer and a Ford, and moved carefully between the dozens of vehicles. His heart raced and his hands were damp again. He reached the front of the line, turned and reversed towards the ramp, stopped inches from the lip and switched off the engine.

"Well done," Garth applauded. "Come on, we'll go inside while they offload the truck."

Jackson followed Garth into an enormous warehouse filled with people. For Jackson it was overwhelming with the noise of auctioneers shouting, fat Portuguese greengrocers placing bids by raising a hand, farmers arguing prices with worried expressions, and the smell of overripe fruit, onions, cabbages and cauliflower that hung heavily. But Garth moved effortlessly through the crowd. When he spotted a man with a floor manager name-tag he went up to him.

"My new driver," he indicated towards Jackson after greeting the fellow. The white floor manager glanced at Jackson, but, possibly because he was black, dismissed him without saying anything, and turned back to Garth. Garth told the man a joke, which was followed by laughter and a clout on the shoulder, and then Garth and Jackson walked back to the truck.

On the way home Garth said, "You're driving well, Jackson. I think I can safely say that you're no longer on trial."

Jackson grinned. "Thank you, *Baas*."

"And because you've done so well with the maintenance work on the machinery I've decided to put you in charge of the workshop. You'll be getting an increase."

Jackson smile broadened. "Thank you, *Baas*," he repeated.

Garth smiled too. He liked the young man and was pleased that he'd hired him.

A few weeks later Jackson slid out from under the truck, wiped his hands on a rag, and feeling a presence behind him turned around. Sarina was sitting on a pile of tires watching him. She was wearing a floral print dress that showed off her small waist and slim hips. "Oh!" he said in surprise. "I didn't notice you there."

She smiled. "I've been waiting for you. I wondered if you'd like to go for a walk after work."

Jackson knew he was playing with fire, but he couldn't stop himself. "Sure," he accepted grinning. Over the previous weeks he'd found himself looking out for the girl, making excuses to bump into her and speak to her.

He looked at his watch. "It's nearly five o'clock. If you wait a few minutes, I'll clean up and we can go."

He walked into the shed and a warm feeling tingled through his veins. He washed his hands, smoothed his hair and, grinning to himself, walked out.

"Should we go down to the river?" he asked, imagining somewhere private.

"That would be nice," she nodded. He loved the way she spoke, like liquid honey. He felt a slow burn in the pit of his stomach, molten lava radiating outwards. She fell in beside him and he could smell a floral scent.

They traded small talk, and then she asked how long he and Nelly had been together. She asked the question casually, as if the answer wasn't important.

"Too long," he replied, and she smiled. "Do you have a boyfriend?"

"Uh, uh," she shook her head.

"Why not? I would have thought a pretty girl like you would've been snapped up."

Sarina shrugged. "I'm picky I guess," she replied with another coy smile.

"Perhaps that's in my favour," he grinned, and she smiled back.

They were nearly at the river before either of them spoke again. He wanted to speed through the small talk and get straight down to basics. He decided he had nothing to lose. "I've been longing to see you on your own," he said, breaking the silence.

"I know," she replied simply. "I've seen the way you look at me."

"I didn't realize it was so obvious."

"It was," she said, taking his hand.

When they reached the river they found a place on the bank covered in soft kikuyu grass and shaded by trees. Jackson sat down and Sarina sat next to him, her thigh touching his. They chatted and flirted, establishing what they already knew – that they had an irresistible attraction for each other.

Jackson couldn't wait anymore. He was in a frenzy of anticipation. Nellie had been anti since the baby and he was hoping to charm Sarina into having sex with him. Maybe not today, but sometime soon. She had asked to see him, which was promising, but he had to plan his moves carefully. He had to make her feel special. He turned towards her, touched her lips ever so briefly, and ran his hand down her cheek to cup her chin.

"You're very beautiful," he said, admiring her. "I wish you were mine." He looked at her with longing. "But you're too good for me. I could never hope for someone like you."

She raised her eyes to his. "Jackson," she sighed. "I've also wanted you since the first day I saw you."

He couldn't believe his luck. He pulled her face towards his and kissed her softly. His hand moved down her side. She groaned and lay back on the grass. His hand followed her leg, caught the bottom of her skirt and slid it up. He drew aside the elastic of her panties, and she didn't stop him. He kissed her again, his hand lingering.

"Oh, Jackson," she breathed. "I want you."

She lifted the dress over her head and dropped it aside. With trembling hands, he took off his clothes. She slid out of her panties and reached for him, and he lifted himself over her and entered her quickly, his desire almost overwhelming. He wanted to explode, but he held himself back shutting his mind to his urgency. Finally Sarina yelped passionately and he let himself go. He collapsed against her, his breath ragged, and waited until his heartbeat returned to normal. Then he lifted himself onto his elbow and looked down at her. The sun gleamed on the light sheen of sweat on her skin, and he ran his finger over her breast and down her stomach.

She smiled up at him, her eyes shining. "Do you love me, Jackson?" she asked wickedly.

He hesitated. "Of course," he replied, the lie sliding smoothly off his tongue.

After that day next to the river, Jackson couldn't keep his hands off Sarina. Nelly didn't know about their affair, but she knew intuitively that something was wrong.

SIX

BENEATH THE ALGAE DEPTHS

1978 · 1979 · 1980 · **1981** · 1982 · 1983 · 1984 · 1985 · 1986

On the farm the drought continued and the cabbages were followed by carrots and onions. Kazi and Scott became good friends. They dressed alike in shorts and T-shirts, Kazi's worn and handed down, and both boys ran generally barefoot.

On Sunday, the sun just rising, Kazi lifted the lid off his mother's cast-iron pot. It stood over cold embers from the cooking fire and the porridge inside had burnt around the edges. It was left over from last night's dinner and he knew he could take it for bait without getting into trouble. Only the chickens would miss it. He scooped some into a plastic bag, picked up his home-made fishing rod, and ran down the road. From a distance he could see Scott at their meeting place, holding a battered can.

"Lemme see," Kazi asked without saying hello.

"Earthworms," Scott held up the can. "Bet I catch more than you today."

"Never," Kazi grinned. "Fish like *mealie-pap*."

Scott's smile broadened. "We'll see," he replied, turning to go.

Twenty minutes later they reached the river. Brightly-coloured birds slapped the green water in dazzling succession snatching insects, and the occasional fish rippled the smooth surface where algae trapped the sun, leaving the river dark. The sweet, moist smell of undergrowth rose from the bushes behind.

Kazi squashed a ball of meal onto his hook and dropped it into the water. "By the time you get that worm on your hook I'll have caught ten fish," he teased.

Scott threaded a worm onto his hook and cast. "There," he said. "And you haven't caught anything yet."

Kazi didn't reply. His attention was on a man walking along the opposite bank. Although he was quite far away, it was obvious that the man was looking at something in the river.

Scott followed Kazi's gaze. "What's he doing?"

"Following that thing in the water. It looks like a duck."

"He's going in after it."

The man waded into the water and the duck floated away from him towards the middle of the river. He followed lifting his arms above the water as it got deeper, but he kept on walking until the water lapped just below his armpits. He was closing in on the bird when a voice up-river yelled, "Hey! Phineas! What are you doing?"

The boys looked in the direction of the voice, and noticed two men herding cows that browsed ahead of them snatching tufts of grass.

"Who's that?" Scott asked.

"Frans and Johannes."

"Oh yeah, they work for Dad," Scott said, recognising the two men. "Where does that other guy come from?"

"Next door."

"Oh."

The man in the water stopped. "I shot that duck," he called over his shoulder to the two men on the bank. "The bloody thing fell in the water." He held up a slingshot and pointed at the bird twisting and turning on the current.

"Wait!" Johannes yelled. "It gets deep right there." But it was too late. As he spoke Phineas stepped forward, slipped and disappeared under the water.

He came up flapping his arms, and went down again. He came up spitting. "I can't swim," he managed and went under again.

Johannes plunged into the river, swam out strongly and reached Phineas within a few strokes. He dove under, found Phineas and hauled him to the surface. Phineas, frantic with fear, turned in his grip and wrapped his arms tightly around Johannes's neck. Johannes fought to get free, but Phineas was scared and wouldn't let go. There was a brief struggle and the two men sank below the surface. Kazi and Scott could see turbulence, then a stream of bubbles that trickled to a stop, but Johannes and Phineas didn't come back up. Frans leapt into the water, swam out to where they'd last seen the two men and dove under. Again and again he went under, searching for them, but the river deepened right there, eroded by previous summer rain, and there was no sign of them. He swam back to the side and Kazi and Scott ran to meet him.

"You boys stay here. Look..." he gasped, "... for them. I'm going to *Baas* Garth to get help."

Frans ran all the way to the farmhouse and banged on the door. Garth opened it and Frans tried to speak, "B-big one... l-l-little... one d-drowning," he stammered. He was dripping wet and a white froth of spit had formed at the corners of his mouth.

"Who? Who's drowning?" Garth demanded.

Frans tried to speak, he was shaking. "J... J... Johannes."

Garth clutched Frans's arm. "And who?" he asked urgently.

"Ph... Phineas."

"Get in," Garth said, and he ran with Frans and pushed him into the Land Cruiser. "Where?" he demanded. Frans couldn't respond. He pointed directions and Garth drove as fast as he could.

They reached the river and Scott ran to his father. Garth lifted him into the Land Cruiser and closed the door firmly. He could see Kazi at the edge of the river, but there was no sign of Johannes or Phineas. Garth realized it was hopeless. Frans would have taken ten or fifteen minutes to reach the house and the drive back another five. The men had been under for too long. He called Caitlin on the radio. She answered and he gave rapid instructions. "Call the police. Tell them two men have drowned and they should bring divers and equipment." He looked at the two boys and added, "Can you fetch Scott and Kazi? This is not a place for them to be."

"I'll be there now. Who drowned, Garth?' Caitlin asked, her voice sombre.

"Johannes and a man named Phineas. I don't know who he is," he replied briefly.

Caitlin arrived shortly with Johannes's wife Anna, Goodwill and Martha. Kazi refused to leave. He wanted to stay with his parents, and he still hoped that Johannes would somehow be all right. Maybe he'd been swept underwater and had swum to the edge further down the river. He expected him to walk out of the bush at any moment, and then they would all laugh at themselves for being so worried. Johannes would be there tomorrow morning to milk the cows and give him a tin mug of lukewarm milk straight from the pail, and then they would talk for a few minutes like they did every day.

Garth and Goodwill walked down-river searching the bank, and came back looking solemn. There was no sign of the two men. They stood with the others and waited for the police, the river flowing peacefully as if nothing untoward had happened.

When they arrived there were three policemen who, joking amongst themselves, took their time offloading equipment. Two of them eventually tied lines around their waists and walked out into the water. The third policeman remained on the edge holding their lines while they moved slowly, feeling with their feet in the mud. It was a long and tedious job moving back and forth across the river, and they resumed their conversation from when they arrived. To them it was just a job.

Anna, Goodwill, Martha, and Kazi watched silently, while Garth stood to one side, as one of the policemen reached the middle of the river, further down from where Johannes had last been seen, and froze. He held up his hand, pointed down, and his partner waded closer. The policeman on the bank tightened his grip on the rope and the policeman ducked below the water.

As he dove, Anna screamed and held onto Martha, her eyes big in her face.

The policeman surfaced, undid a second rope from around his waist and dove again. His partner went down with him. After a few attempts they came back hauling a weight behind them. When they reached shallow water, Garth and the policeman on the bank waded in to help. Together they pulled on the rope and brought the two drowned men to the surface. They were clutched together and Anna screamed again. This time she didn't stop screaming and Kazi put his hands over his ears to shut out the sound. He ignored the tears that ran down his cheeks. How could this have happened? He had been so confident that Johannes would be fine because he was so strong. He was the strongest man he knew. He should have been able to save Phineas *and* himself.

Kazi watched as the policemen dragged the bodies out of the water. He saw Johannes's face twisted in the agony of drowning, his eyes dark and staring, his mouth open as if gasping for one last breath of air. He turned his face away trying to blank out the sight and buried his head in his mother's skirt.

Two days later Scott found Kazi at home sitting on a bench outside, looking sad. A couple of chickens scratched in the dirt, pecking for food. Next door a dog, ribs showing, lay tethered and panting in the sun. Seven puppies suckled hungrily.

"Come and play, Kazi," Scott said.

"Don't want to," Kazi replied.

"Come on, we can swim in our new pool." Kazi shook his head. "Come on, Kazi, please. Come *on*," Scott needled.

He dragged Kazi to his feet and drew him unwillingly along. They reached the farmhouse and walked around the back. In the garden, water flowed over rocks into a swimming pool that looked cool under the shade of a Karee tree. Kazi held back.

"Kazi, it's a swimming pool, not the river, and you can see the bottom. You won't drown," Scott reassured him.

Kazi stood looking at the water. What Scott said was true, but the memory of Johannes's drowning was still fresh in his mind.

"Kazi, just stand on the top step – c'mon, Kazi." Scott stripped off his own shirt and tossed it aside. "Mom," he yelled over his shoulder, "We're going to swim." He had promised his parents he would let an adult know if he was going to use the pool or go to the river.

Kazi reluctantly removed his shirt and, placing one foot on the first shallow step, brought his other foot reluctantly over the edge. The soft mercury chill of the water cooled his feet, the sun baked down hard on his shoulders, and the water shimmered invitingly. But fear held him back.

Scott leapt into the air. "Kaziii," he yelled, tucking his knees to his chest and landing in a gush that cascaded over Kazi. Kazi laughed and Scott grinned, pleased that Kazi had laughed.

"C'mon, Kazi, get in," Scott urged.

Kazi took another small step and Scott splashed him, the flat of his hand raising a great fan of water. Kazi flinched, and Scott sprayed him again. Now Kazi wanted revenge and relinquished his fear. He dove in and swam after Scott, grabbed him and pushed him under. Scott went deep, kicked off the bottom and came up on the other side with Kazi racing after him.

They were still chasing each other when Garth came outside. He smiled. Johannes's death had hit them hard, Kazi more so than Scott, and it was nice to see them playing again. It had been a terrible thing for children to witness. He and Caitlin had explained to Scott that it was normal to feel fear and grief, and encouraged him not to harbour his feelings. Now it appeared that he in turn had helped Kazi.

He watched for a while, not wanting to interrupt, but he needed their help. He waited a few minutes and, when he could wait no longer, called them. Their noise drowned out his voice, and he had to call again. This time the boys looked up.

"Scott," he said once they were quiet, "could you come here. I want you to do something for me."

"Okay, Dad." Scott swam to the edge and climbed out dripping. Kazi followed and Garth handed them towels.

"I've just come from Brits with Juby. Could you boys take him back to his hut?" He turned and walked into the house with the two boys following, pulling on their shirts.

"Why does he need help, Dad?"

"He isn't well. He's been complaining about pains in his chest. Doctor said it's his heart."

"Is he gonna be okay?"

Garth shrugged. "Hope so."

They walked into the kitchen where Caitlin was putting the final items into a box of groceries. She picked up the box and gave it to Scott.

"Here are his pills," she added, placing the bottle on top. "Make sure he sees where you put them."

"Okay, Mom."

"Kazi, will you carry these blankets?" she asked, passing him two blankets.

"Yes, Mrs. Finley," Kazi said.

"Juby's waiting outside. I want you to walk slowly with him, and when you get there make sure he has enough firewood and water."

The two boys went outside and Scott hurried ahead with the food. Kazi walked slowly with Juby leaning on his shoulder, the blankets under his arm. When Scott got to the small shack, he placed the box in Juby's hut and set off to fetch wood. By the time he returned, Kazi had settled the old man on a stool with a blanket covering his shoulders. Juby was exhausted, his eyes shrunken and darkly smudged, his skin grey.

The two boys set about making a fire, and heating a pot of water while Juby sat in silence, his eyes staring into what seemed a different time altogether. When the water finally boiled, Kazi brewed coffee and added a generous helping of sweetened condensed milk.

"Here," he said to Juby, holding out the mug. Juby took it, but his hand shook so badly that Kazi had to place his own hand over Juby's and guide the mug to his mouth.

Juby took a long sip and smiled. "Thank you," he said softly.

Kazi felt a wave of affection for the old man. He was like a grandfather to him. "I'll come and see you every day," he promised.

Juby nodded tiredly. "Thank you, my boy."

SEVEN

SEPARATION

1978 · 1979 · 1980 · **1981** · 1982 · 1983 · 1984 · 1985 · 1986

Juby improved on the medication, but he was no longer able to make the trek down the mountain. Kazi and Scott, or more often just Kazi, took food to him every day and saw to it that he had firewood and water. The boys also hiked, fished, and played, and the days flew by, bringing the summer holidays to an end and the start of school in January. Scott, turning six later in the year, was starting first grade. Although Kazi had already turned seven the year before, this would also be his first year at school. His mother had kept him at home for as long as possible to look after his siblings.

Kazi's school was a single, whitewashed classroom that stood in the centre of a dusty clearing. A sagging goal post stood at one end of the playground and, at break, children played barefoot under a giant Bluegum tree. The teacher taught several classes at the same time, and the older children were often put in charge of the younger ones, helping them and supervising their lessons. Only the labourers' children went to Kazi's school. Although there were several schools for the labourers' children, (all with one classroom) on various farms in the area, the school with the Bluegum tree was the only one close enough to Fairvalley Farm to reach on foot.

Scott's school had been built by the farmers for their children. It had four, red-brick classrooms, three teachers and a headmaster, and it provided schooling only for white children until they graduated from junior school. Behind their school there was a grass rugby field that doubled as a sports track. A brand new hall, donated by a rich farmer, stood alongside the school.

When Scott heard that he and Kazi couldn't go to the same school, he was furious. He barged into Garth's office, "Dad, why can't Kazi go to the same school as me?"

"Because he's black."

"But why, Dad? What's that got to do with it?"

"Because it's the law. Blacks and whites aren't allowed to go to the same schools," Garth replied with a sigh. Caitlin's father had argued the same point time and time again – the fact was that there was a system of segregated and unequal education in the country. While white schooling was free, compulsory and expanding, black education was sorely neglected. The government had repressed the blacks for centuries by maintaining separate education and reduced spending on black education. In the last year the Nationalist Party had recognised the need to reform apartheid and had increased spending from one-sixteenth to one-seventh of what was spent per white child, but it was still a case of too little. Caitlin did what she could by providing the Fairvalley children with school books and clothes. In summer she bought grey shorts and shirts for the boys, and dresses for the girls. In winter, jerseys and shoes.

Scott's eyebrows lowered further. "But Dad, how come Kazi and I are allowed to play together, but we can't go to school together?" He crossed his arms. "That's a stupid law."

"Scott, it's just what it is. I know it's unfair, but things are changing. One day you and Kazi will go to the same school."

"Well, I hope it changes soon."

On the first day Kazi walked to school with the other labourers' children from Fairvalley. Their farm was the furthest from the school and on the way children from other farms joined their group. The Fairvalley children were all in uniform; the other children were dressed in an assortment of clothing – school uniforms, everyday clothes, and a combination of both. Kazi was proud of his new clothes. But he knew that not all children were as lucky as the children from Fairvalley Farm.

When they reached the school, the children who had been there the previous year searched out old friends, and Kazi was left alone. He looked around feeling nervous. To give himself something to do he walked to the Bluegum tree and looked up into its branches. It was a good climbing tree he thought, and then he walked across to the sagging goal post. He peered into the classroom window and looked at the rows of desks; they were old with holes for ink wells and children had carved their names into the wood. There was nothing else to look at, so Kazi stood and waited. He shoved his hands into his pockets, scuffed his feet and watched puffs of dry dust settle on his brown toes. He wiggled them again and watched the dust settle again. After a while he heard a change in the tone of the other children's chatter and looked up. A black man with a fat belly was unlocking the classroom door. He opened it and whistled. The children seemed to know that it was the signal to come inside so Kazi followed them in.

"Good morning, children," the man said over the noise. He had thick eyebrows, a flat nose in a square face, a strong jaw with a double chin, and his hair had been razor-cut close to the scalp. "Most of you know me. For the new children," he glanced around the classroom, "I'm your teacher, and my name is Knowledge." There was a snicker of laughter from the older children, and the teacher's eyes lost their warmth. He frowned and carried on. "I would like the first grade children to sit in the front row, grade two second row, and so on up. You two," he pointed to two older children who were already seated near the front, "please find your appropriate row. You should know better than to sit there."

Kazi sat down next to a young girl and the other children scuffled around sorting themselves into their grades. Because Kazi was closest, the teacher handed him pencils and a pile of lined paper with the first letters of the alphabet hand-drawn three times each down the side of the page, and asked him to pass them along. "Row one, keep a pencil and paper and pass the rest on. Practice the letters on your page, keep between the lines and make your letters upright and nice and round. Fransina," a girl in the back row stood up, "please get them started. Grade three and four do the sums I've handed out. Grade five, open your arithmetic books on the first page."

Kazi picked up the stub of a pencil. They had all been sharpened many times, and he wished he could've used the pencil Caitlin had given him, but he didn't want to take it out and look like he was better then the other kids. He started the first letter and made a fat circle for the tummy of the A, and then a straight line behind it. But somehow it didn't stick together, so he tried again.

Fransina came up behind him and put her hand over his, she held it and traced over the letter the teacher had drawn. "Do that a few times until you're used to it and then try on your own," she said kindly.

After fifteen minutes his hand was tired, and he realized that his tongue was sticking out the corner of his mouth and pulled it back. It looked like a spider had crawled across his page.

Fransina came back. "Good work," she said and wrote his name in the top left hand corner, and then she took his work and added it to a neat pile on the teacher's desk.

Another girl took her place and handed out photocopied pictures of a barnyard scene, and old margarine tubs filled with an assortment of wax crayons that had seen better days.

"Okay, kids," she said, "get to work."

The sun was shining outside and Kazi wished he could go outside and play. The girl noticed him looking out the window and she wacked him lightly on the back of his head. "Stop day dreaming and get back to work."

Kazi quickly picked up a red crayon (there was no yellow), and coloured the sun scarlet.

After a while a girl called Margaret took over. She made them stand in a circle in front of the class. There were only four of them including her, and she taught them a rhyme about Jack and Jill. They marched on the spot and pretended they were Jack and Jill going up the hill, and when Jack fell, the boys had to copy Jack and roll down the hill. It was fun.

When Kazi got home, he ate quickly and went in search of Scott.

"Yay, you're back. I've been waiting ages," Scott said when he opened the door. "Let's go to the river."

Kazi hesitated, still trying to erase the memories the river held.

"We won't go to the same place," Scott assured him. Kazi watched a tok-tokkie beetle wander about in the sun, occasionally tapping its hard abdomen on the ground to attract a mate. "You don't have to be scared."

Kazi looked up crossly. "I'm not scared, it just makes me sad."

"I promise we'll come back if you don't feel like staying. Please?"

"Okay," Kazi gave in.

"Great," Scott grinned, closing the door behind him. "How was your first day at school?" he asked as they walked down the road.

"It was fun."

"What's your teacher like?"

"I thought he was nice, his name is Knowledge. Do you think that's his real name?"

"Nah, can't be."

"Kids at school call him *Geen Weetenskap* behind his back. You know what that means, don't you?"

"No knowledge," Scott laughed, "that's funny."

Kazi smiled, but didn't quite laugh because they had reached the river and his eyes were on the water.

"I wish we went to the same school," Scott said, skipping a stone across the water. A large bullfrog croaked its annoyance.

Kazi flopped onto the grass. "Did you make any friends?"

"I played with a couple of boys at break, it was okay. There was one strange kid though. His name was Jacobus, and he wore a camouflage jacket to school."

"Why was he strange, because of the jacket?"

"No silly, 'cos he hid in the trees spying on us. Weird." Scott whirled his hand in circles next to his head. "Anyway, our teacher saw him hiding and called him over, and then she saw he had a flick knife so she sent him to the headmaster. Next break he had a chicken's foot for lunch and made the toe move." Scott shuddered. "Then he ate it. It was gross. I can't imagine eating a chicken foot!"

Kazi laughed, "Haven't you eaten chicken feet? They're delicious, but you know what the best is?" Scott shook his head. "When you're finished eating you can use the toenail to pick the meat out of your teeth."

Scott threw a sand clod at Kazi, "Not true, you're teasing."

Kazi jumped to his feet and sprinted away. He ran into the water and fell over. Scott splashed down next to him. For a brief moment they had forgotten about Johannes, and the differences in their lives now that they were at school.

Later, they sat on the river bank drying in the sun, and then they walked home, each with an arm draped over the other's shoulders. In the distance they could see Maria coming down the mountain from Juby's hut. She waved to them indicating that they should hurry.

As soon as they were close enough she shouted, "Something's wrong with Juby. Scott call your mother."

"What? What's wrong?" Scott yelled.

"I don't know, just hurry."

"Kazi, I'll go get Mom. You go to Juby's hut with Maria," Scott said, and sped off towards the farmhouse.

Kazi and Maria reached Juby's hut and went inside. Juby was lying on his side on the floor and Kazi ran forward. He took Juby's hand in his.

"Juby, wake up," he said leaning over the old man. "Come on, wake up." Juby didn't move, his hand slipped out of Kazi's and flopped onto his chest.

Maria said, "Kazi, I think you should leave him. The *Missus* will be here soon."

Kazi started to cry. He took a pillow from the bed and placed it under Juby's head. "Juby, you'll be okay. You'll be okay," he cried, rubbing Juby's cold hand. "Maybe we should give him his medicine," he said.

"No, Kazi, just wait for the *Missus*."

"She said his medicine was important, maybe he forgot to take it." Kazi went to the table. He found Juby's pills, took two out of the bottle, and filled Juby's tin mug with water. "Here, Maria, let's make him sit up."

"Kazi, let him rest. The *Missus* will be here soon."

Kazi gave Juby's shoulder a gentle shake "Juby, Juby, wake up. Come on, take your medicine. Please, Juby. Come on. Please, Juby." Juby didn't move and Kazi started to cry again.

Caitlin arrived and went straight to Juby. Scott stayed at the door, his eyes on Juby.

"Maria, what's wrong?" Caitlin knelt and placed two fingers on Juby's pulse.

"I don't know, *Missus*. This is how I found him."

Caitlin looked up. "I'm sorry," she said quietly, "but he's dead." A tear ran down her cheek and she wiped it away.

"No!" Kazi cried. "No, he's just sleeping." He took Juby's hand again and pulled on it. "Come on, Juby, wake up," he cried. "Wake up."

"Kazi, I'm sorry, but he's gone." Caitlin took a blanket from the bed and covered Juby gently, as if he were cold. "Scott, go and fetch your father and Goodwill."

Maria took Kazi's arm and drew him outside.

"Poor Juby, he was all alone," Kazi cried. "I visited him every day and today I didn't."

Caitlin left Juby and knelt in front of Kazi. She took his hands in hers, "Kazi, Juby was happy on his own. You must remember that he chose to spend his life that way."

"I should've been with him this afternoon," he cried.

"Kazi, it could've happened at any time," Maria said. "He was old."

Kazi continued to cry, it was all too much. First Johannes and now Juby, everyone was dying.

Goodwill hurried up the path and Caitlin turned to him with a sense of relief, "Thank goodness you're here."

Goodwill looked at Kazi. He reached out and brushed at the tears on his cheeks. "Come, Kazi, Juby's in a better place now where there's no illness or suffering." He turned to Maria, "Please take him to his mother, I must pray for Juby now."

Juby was buried in his white uniform, his pith helmet on his chest and his few belongings with him. He had no family or friends, so the funeral was a small and sad affair with the labourers standing silently in a row behind Caitlin, Garth, Shanon and Scott. Kazi stood next to his mother and Goodwill held the service.

EIGHT

CHRISTMAS

1978 · 1979 · 1980 · **1981** · 1982 · 1983 · 1984 · 1985 · 1986

At the end of the year, December was hot and dry. There was no relief in the brief cloudburst, and a dust devil spun lazily in the field nearby, lifting tumbleweeds and dust into the air. Time seemed to have slowed, mainly because Kazi was counting the days to the party on Christmas Eve.

The twenty-fourth of December finally dawned, but the day was endless and the hours dragged on. At last it was time and Kazi got himself, then his sister ready for the party. Ntokoso was nearly three and could be stubborn. She lay on the floor and kicked her feet. Kazi blew on her belly making a loud blurt and she squealed, "Zi-zi," she said, using her pet name for him.

"Stay still so I can put your shoes on." He caught her foot and she giggled as he fitted the shoe. "There, *baba*, now give me the other one." She kicked her feet, laughing up at him. He looked up from his task, "There will be sweets if you let me put them on," he added.

She grinned and gave him her foot. He slipped the second shoe on, lifted her onto his hip, and went into the living room. "Dad, can't we go yet?"

"Just a moment, Kazi," Martha said. "Let me fix your father's tie."

"Please hurry, Mom," Kazi urged.

"Be patient, Kazi. The evening can't start without your father, so don't fret. Where are your brothers?"

"Mandiso, Dumani," she called, "are you boys ready?"

Dumani skidded through the door. "We're ready, *Umama.*"

Martha gave Goodwill's tie a final twist. "Okay, let's go," she announced.

Kazi passed Ntokoso to his mother.

"Race you there," he said to his brothers, and sped out the door.

Dumani, the quicker of the two, was close on his heels. They reached the farm shed, slid to a stop, and walked in laughing happily.

Most of the labourers and their families were there already, and the smell of Lifebuoy soap from clean-scrubbed bodies sweetened the air in the shed. The men were dressed in long pants, their best shirts, and good shoes. The women were also dressed in their best – clean cotton print dresses, with scarves or *doeke* on their heads. Most of the children were barefoot, but their clothes, although handed down, had been carefully washed.

"Let's find a place to sit," Kazi suggested.

"Over there," Mandiso pointed out a place amongst the other children, third row from the front. They sat down on the dirt floor and Kazi waved to Scott, who was helping Caitlin and Shanon sort through a magnificent heap of wrapped parcels at the front of the shed.

Goodwill and Martha arrived and Garth nodded to indicate that Goodwill could start. He walked to the front of the shed opening his *Bible*. Silence fell and he began his story with Joseph and Mary on their way to Bethlehem to register in the Roman census. During his sermon mosquitoes feasted on the abundance of flesh in the shed. Adults smacked at the annoying insects, and children shifted on bony bottoms, stirring up dust. Kazi waited patiently while his father spoke. He knew they would each get a toy after the sermon. He wondered what he would get. Last year he'd been given a football. This year he was hoping for a car like the one Scott had.

At last the sermon ended and, on Martha's signal, the children's voices lifted together in *Stille Nag*, "Silent Night", and as the final notes drifted away to the electric sound of cicadas in a bush outside, Caitlin picked up the first gift.

The children held their breaths – who would be first?

"Zama," Caitlin called, starting at the end of the alphabet for a change.

A skinny eight-year-old girl squealed and jumped up; she scrambled past the other children, stopped in front of Caitlin, and clapping her hands twice, spooned them to receive her gift. One by one the children went up, each one taking their gift in the same respectful manner. Kazi waited his turn, his muscles tensed, ready to leap to his feet when his name was called. He watched the heap anxiously – maybe the green and red parcel would be his. It was about the same size as the car, oh no it wasn't, well maybe the one with gold bells or the one with Christmas trees.

It seemed to take forever before Caitlin looked at him and at last she called his name. He was up and over the rows of children in a flash. He scampered to the front, clapped his hands, spooned them just like Zama had, and Caitlin placed his gift in his hands. It was a square parcel with no bells or trees on the paper. He grinned up at her with a brief 'thank you' before racing back to his place to open his present. He didn't waste time guessing what was in it, he was too excited. He ripped off the wrapping paper and turned the box over. It was a beautiful, green, sports car with a white stripe, and the doors and bonnet opened – exactly what he wanted.

When the children had all received their gifts Caitlin gave each of the women a set of patterned enamel dishes and a scarf, and the men collared shirts for Sunday church and special events.

At last she announced that it was time for the Christmas feast.

Jackson's wife, Nelly, stood by herself. She looked around the shed wondering what she should do. Everyone else had formed into couples and groups, and were laughing and chatting excitedly. She shifted from one foot to the other, looked down at her hands, plucked at a hang-nail, put her finger in her mouth and bit the piece of skin off. She knew no-one and agonised over talking to strangers. What would she say? Jackson was nowhere to be seen. She wished that she had spoken to him earlier and asked him to stay with her. He knew she was shy, why hadn't he thought to stay? She noticed Martha walking towards her and her throat closed up. Martha was looking right at her and smiling. Nelly glanced around hoping that she was smiling at someone else. She tried to make herself inconspicuous and small against the wall so that Martha might walk by without noticing her, but Martha stopped in front of her. Nelly tried to smile.

"Nelly," Martha said. "Are you enjoying the party?"

Nelly tried again to smile. "Oh, it's very nice, it's…" she stopped.

Martha looked at the young woman's crestfallen face. "What is it? I hope you got your present. You weren't left out were you?"

"Oh no, it's not that it's… Well, it's just that I don't know anyone."

Martha took her arm. "You know me," she linked her arm through Nelly's. "Come, let's get some food."

They walked to the table and waited while the children filled their plates.

"How old is your baby?" Martha asked looking at the child strapped to Nelly's back.

"She's two-and-a-half, and yours?"

Martha hefted Ntokoso into a more comfortable position on her back. "Just a few months older than your little one. I also have three sons – Mandiso will be five next month, Dumani is six and Kazi, my eldest, is eight." Martha patted her own stomach and gave Nelly a knowing look. "You're expecting another?"

Nelly nodded, "Oh, it will be quite a while. I'm only five months." She smiled; it felt nice to have someone to talk to.

They moved forward and Nelly took a plate. She filled it, but as she turned to find a place to sit she saw Jackson. He was looking at someone with frank admiration and Nelly followed his gaze. It was Sarina, her eyes large and dark, fixed on Jackson, returning his look. Her dress was low cut, flared at the waist. She was wearing lipstick, and her cheeks had been reddened. A smile hovered at the corners of her mouth. Nelly couldn't move; jealousy burnt like poison in the pit of her stomach.

Martha touched her arm. "Nelly, are you all right?" she asked.

Tears pricked the back of her eyes, she forced them back. "Yes, I'm fine." She turned away and followed Martha to a seat. She held her plate on her lap and picked at the food, pushing it around with the little plastic fork.

When everyone had eaten, Garth, dressed as usual in boots, khaki shorts and shirt, opened two crates of homebrew beer and the men shouted approval. He gave each man two beers and Elliphas took his, downed the first, and danced in a full circle, whooping, and slapping the side of each foot as he lifted it. Everyone clapped as the next man took his place. While the men danced and drank, the children ran between the adults playing with their Christmas presents, and the women gossiped amongst themselves. Jackson took a long swallow and lowered his beer as Sarina walked past. He followed her with his eyes. She looked at him, her eyes flirting, inviting. A thrill swept through him. He left his beer and walked after her. His pulse raced. He lengthened his stride and caught up with her behind the shed. As she turned he pulled her roughly towards him. She lifted her face to his, and kissed him, sucking gently on his lips. He was aroused beyond thought, his desire heightened by the fear of being caught.

Nelly watched them come back separately, minutes apart. Sarina came in first and sat down. Then Jackson walked past Sarina pretending indifference and eased his way back into the group of men. Someone had finished his beer while he was gone, but he didn't care.

On the way home the men could be heard talking loudly. The women walked together, their sleeping babies secured with blankets on their backs, the older children following sleepily. Nelly walked silently next to Jackson. A mixture of emotions threatening to overwhelm her – betrayal, anger, jealousy, fear. She knew her intuition was right, Jackson was having an affair. She was sure of it now.

NINE

DUST DEVIL

1980 · 1981 · 1982 · 1983 · 1984 · 1985 · **1986** · 1987 · 1988

Jackson had been disappointed when Nelly had given birth to another girl, but now that the child was four years old they were trying again. He was still seeing Sarina, although he was careful to cover his tracks. He liked things the way they were, his wife could not be his mistress – she was the mother of his children – and he didn't want his mistress to be his wife.

It was summer again on the farm and a *Piet-my-vrou* flew overhead calling for rain. Dust devils spun through the fields and the sky stretched flat and blue with no hope of relief. It was going to be known as the drought of '86, the worst in decades. There was nothing they could've done to prepare for it. Even the best laid plans were falling apart. Garth couldn't plant a dry-land crop with no rain in the forecast, there just wasn't enough moisture in the soil to germinate the seed. And although the vegetables under irrigation had kept the wolf from the door for the past six years, they couldn't sustain the farm on their own. Not only that, Garth had to face facts. With temperatures soaring it was proving difficult to keep the plants alive. They would get the present crop to harvest, but the risk of the underground aquifer drying up was too great to plant another.

When the men realized that the next crop wasn't going to be planted, Goodwill broached the subject that was foremost on all of their minds.

"Some of the farmers are turning their men away, *Baas* Garth. Our crops look the same as theirs. Are we going to lose our jobs too?"

Garth shook his head. "I won't let any of you go, we'll find something else to do during the drought." He looked at the equipment and sheds as if seeing them for the first time. "But what?" he said, more to himself than to anyone else.

Already deep in thought he walked to the house, sat down at his desk with a sheet of paper, and waited for ideas to flow from his pen. The paper remained blank and the threat of dismissing his men loomed. Caitlin kept him going through the day with cups of strong tea and then later, after dinner, he went back and sat at his desk worrying at the problem.

Three days went by, papers lay crumpled around the bin, one of the numerous cups of tea had grown cold in front of him, and now he rested his chin in his hand and stared at the list he had made.

"Maybe…" His finger stayed where it was on the list. "That's it!" he exclaimed.

From the next room Caitlin heard him and strode in. "What? Did you think of something?"

"I did! A brickyard – we'll make cement bricks and blocks." He followed his thoughts to their conclusion. "The forms and machine won't be expensive. We can use the concrete floor in the shed and we've got the truck for deliveries. It's perfect!"

"But who'll buy the bricks? Don't most people use baked bricks?" Caitlin asked.

"Local builders will buy them. Baked bricks are more common, but cement bricks are used for low cost housing and farm buildings."

He jumped up and went to the shed to tell Jackson and Goodwill. They stopped working and straightened at his approach.

"I've got a plan," he said. "We're going to make bricks, over there," he indicated the expanse of floor in the shed. "Fetch the others and clear everything out of here. I'm going to town to buy what we need."

"Yes, *Baas*," they replied in unison.

Jackson grinned. "Lots of good news today, *Baas*. Nelly had her baby last night."

"Congratulations, Jackson. This must be your third. Is it a boy or girl?" he asked.

Jackson's smile broadened. "A boy," he replied proudly.

"A boy at last, you must be very happy."

"I am, *Baas*."

The first bricks were brittle and cracked. The cement company recommended additives and a different ratio of cement to sand, but they still didn't pass the South African Bureau of Standards test. Trial after trial failed until a representative from the cement company came to the farm to see what they were doing wrong. The man took samples from the small quarry on the farm and immediately identified the problem. The particles were too fine. He suggested they add river sand and a smaller quantity of their own sand from the farm. The bricks would cost more to manufacture but they had no choice, they had to increase the strength or give up.

Garth tried the new mixture and was relieved when the new formula worked. The bricks were strong enough, and production started with the men taking turns mixing the cement and stamping out rows of bricks in long lines across the floor. Once the bricks were dry enough to move the men packed them into stacks to cure for thirty days. The date was written in chalk on each stack to make sure they weren't dispatched too early.

When the first delivery to a local pig farm was finally ready and loaded onto the truck, Jackson climbed into the driver's seat, and turned the ignition. Frans tapped on the window.

"Jackson," he yelled. Jackson rolled down the window. "Can you buy some beer for me on your way home?"

"Sure. How many?" Jackson asked.

"A six pack," Frans said, handing over the money.

Four months passed with only an occasional shower that settled the dust, and the clouds that built up in the afternoons blew away to rain elsewhere. The brick press vibrated with a deafening noise, guaranteeing headaches and aching muscles. But the men laboured in the heat, covered in a fine layer of cement and dust. They had work and food to fill their children's bellies.

One evening at dusk, Jackson parked next to the shed. He ached with exhaustion. No one came to meet him, or to fetch the beer they had asked for, and he was angry. Since that first day when he'd agreed to stop at the liquor store for Frans, he now bought beer for all the men. He walked to the back of the truck, opened the tailgate and looked at the crates of beer. Blood banged in his head, a headache forming. He jiggled the change in his pocket, trying to remember whose it was. He was tired and he didn't feel like carrying the beer to the men's houses. He stood there for a moment longer staring at the crates. And then he walked to the farmhouse, leaving the beer where it was. Garth opened the door at his knock.

"Evening, Jackson, anything wrong?" he asked.

"No, *Baas*. It's just that the men ask me to buy beer every week. It's a lot of work and I get nothing for it."

"So stop doing it," Garth said.

"I can do that. But, well…" he paused eyeing Garth's response. "I was wondering if you would let me open a *shebeen* at my house and sell the beer for profit."

"A bush pub," Garth repeated. "That's not legal."

"I know, *Baas,* but I'll only sell to our men and local people."

"No strangers," Garth confirmed.

"No, *Baas.*"

"And where are you planning to do this?"

"I'll use my *lapa.*"

"Okay Jackson, but if you get into trouble with the police I'll tell them that I don't know anything about it. If there are any fights or noise, I'll shut it down, and remember that I don't want strangers coming to the farm."

"Yes, *Baas,*" Jackson grinned.

Jackson bought an old kerosene fridge from a farmer and word spread that he had cold beer for sale. Customers came from neighbouring farms and from further away. Jackson didn't know all of them and he had already forgotten his promise to Garth. He bought a car from the profits, a small brown Toyota that he parked in a shelter next to his house.

Months later, on a Saturday, Nelly couldn't sleep with the noise from the *shebeen*. She climbed out of bed and went outside. About to step out of the shadows, she noticed Jackson sitting close to Sarina. She stayed and watched. Jackson's head moved closer to Sarina's in response to something she said.

The girl laughed, showing perfect white teeth against olive skin. She lifted her chin and Jackson kissed her.

Nelly broke into a run. "Whore," she screamed, running towards them. Seeing a discarded bottle she picked it up. "Leave my husband alone," she yelled, and hit the girl with the bottle. She saw everything in slow motion. She saw the flesh on Sarina's arm split open, the blood run from the wound, Jackson's hand fall back in its failed attempt to stop her, and the horror on everyone's faces. And then everything sped up again. Sarina grasped her arm and Jackson shouted something at Nelly, then turned towards Sarina. Nelly could feel tears threatening but, she didn't want to cry in front of them, so she turned and ran inside. She heard car doors slam and looked out. Jackson was driving away with Sarina.

Nelly sat down in the darkened living room, but hours dragged by and Jackson didn't come home. She thought about him and the girl alone together. Her remorse turned to anger. How could the bastard go off with that bitch of a husband stealer? She wanted revenge. She left the children sleeping in the house and walked to the brickyard where she picked up two bricks. Then she sat on the side of the road in the dark and waited. After a long time she heard Jackson's car in the distance and stood up, testing the weight of the brick in her hand. The car drew closer, rounded the bend, and she threw the brick.

The windscreen shattered and Jackson braked hard. He leapt out of the car as Sarina slid silently from the passenger side and disappeared. Nelly yelled at Jackson, screaming and calling him names. He walked slowly towards her, his pace measured. He was so angry he wanted to punch something. Nelly recognised Jackson's expression of absolute fury, stopped yelling, turned and ran. Jackson, being taller and faster, caught up. He grabbed Nelly's arm in an iron grip, dragged her home, and threw her onto a chair.

"What the hell were you thinking, you stupid woman? Look what you've done to my car," he yelled.

Nelly was defiant and wouldn't speak. Jackson stormed out. He had to leave before he hit her. "I'm going to bed."

After a while Nelly heard Jackson snoring. She went into the bedroom and eased herself into the same bed, because there was nowhere else to sleep, and turned her back hugging the edge, her body brittle with rage.

Nelly rose early to see to the baby. She was still angry and when Jackson woke up, she started again. He walked away but she followed talking and talking until his head hurt. He had a hangover and just wanted silence. He ignored Nelly and walked faster. She picked up a stone and threw it. It bounced off his shoulder.

He turned. "That's enough! You threw a brick through my windscreen, and now you're throwing stones at me. Do you think you're going to get away with this?"

Something had snapped in him and Nelly could see it. She darted around a tree and ran towards the farmhouse and safety. Jackson had never hit her before, but he certainly looked like he wanted to now. She heard him running after her and she ran faster. They reached the farmhouse and she screamed.

Caitlin heard the scream and came outside. "Stop!" she yelled at the two running figures.

Jackson stopped, and when Nelly saw that he had stopped, she stopped too, keeping a reasonable distance between them.

"What's going on?" Caitlin asked.

Nelly didn't reply. She stood where she was with a sullen look on her face.

"Jackson, what's going on?" Caitlin repeated, looking at Jackson.

Jackson scowled at Nelly. "*Missus*, Nelly threw a brick through my windscreen."

"Why did you do it, Nelly?" Caitlin asked.

"Jackson is sleeping with that whore."

"Who?"

"Sarina, *Missus*."

"Is this true, Jackson?"

Before Jackson could reply Nelly continued, "They drove away in his car and they were gone for a long time."

"Jackson?" Caitlin repeated.

"*Missus*, Nelly hit Sarina with a bottle and I had to take her to hospital for stitches." He lifted his hands and shrugged. "That's all. We just went to the hospital."

"Nelly, why did you hit her?"

Nelly glared at Jackson, "Because Jackson was kissing her."

Caitlin looked at Jackson. "In that case, you should've taken someone with you when you took Sarina to hospital. For heaven's sake, Jackson, what were you thinking?"

Her heart went out to Nelly, but she masked her feelings. African men often took mistresses or a new wife. Their marriages were never formalised and relationships were dissolved when the man simply left the home. She turned now to face Nelly, who was smiling, evidently enjoying the reprimand Jackson was getting. "Nelly, you're also wrong." Nelly's smile faded. "You knew Jackson was the only person who could take the girl to hospital. You shouldn't have hit her in the first place."

Garth drove up and Caitlin told him what was happening.

"Nelly, go home," he said, and Nelly stalked off. "Jackson," Garth said as soon as she was out of hearing, "you're drinking too much." Anger lowered his voice. "You've been late for work a couple of times this month and your breath often smells of alcohol. And now you're fighting with your wife. It's all very well that I allow you to run the *shebeen*, but if it affects your work and your judgement you'll have to close it."

Jackson nodded, "Yes, *Baas*."

"Good. Now go home and sort things out with your wife."

Jackson walked home, on his way he stopped outside Sarina's house.

"Sarina," he called softly.

She opened the door and smiled.

"How's your arm?" he asked.

She held it up. "Not too bad, how're you?"

"I'm okay." He glanced away. "Sarina, I'm sorry but we've got to stop seeing each other."

"No!" Anguish strangled her voice. "Why?"

"Things can't go on like this. I love my children and I have to try and sort things out with Nelly."

Sarina threw her arms around his neck. "Jackson, please don't, don't do this to me. Please leave her. We'd be happy together and we'll have our own children."

"Sarina, I'd lose my job," he replied simply. "*Baas* Garth is already cross with me." He stepped back. "I have to go now. I'm sorry, Sarina."

He turned and walked away. He wondered how he'd manage to see her every day and not be with her. He felt his need for her already.

He walked into his house, Nelly was dressing the baby.

"Nelly," he said. She ignored him. "Nelly," he repeated. "I'm sorry."

She looked up, her eyes hard. "What about Sarina?"

"It's over, Nelly."

"Are you sure?"

"I promise, Nelly, it is over. I was stupid."

"I don't know, Jackson. How can I trust you?"

"Please, Nelly, please give me a chance."

She nodded and turned back to the baby.

TEN

CRASH AND BURN

1980 · 1981 · 1982 · 1983 · 1984 · 1985 · 1986 · **1987** · 1988

S ix years had passed since the boys had started school and they were still best friends. Both had grown over the years. Kazi now looked like a skinny brown grasshopper, all legs and knees, and although Scott had caught up in height, he, on the other hand, looked more like a frisky colt.

Kazi was on his way home from school, his shoes in his schoolbag and the sand soft underfoot. He didn't have much homework and was looking forward to spending the afternoon with Scott.

With his mind on his feet Kazi didn't notice Scott in the shadow of a Saringa tree. He was hiding and keeping as quiet as possible. Even when an insect walked over his nose he didn't move. He stood quietly and waited until Kazi strolled by, and then he leapt out and jumped onto his back.

Kazi fell squawking and flailing his arms, and Scott rolled on top of him pinning him down.

"Let go," Kazi yelled.

"Say you give up."

"I won't." Scott twisted Kazi's arm. "Okay you win, I give up."

Scott climbed off, and Kazi got up and retrieved his bag. "I didn't see you."

Scott laughed. "You weren't supposed to," he said, matching his step to Kazi's.

"I'll get you back." Scott nodded and they walked on in friendly silence.

"What should we do today?" Scott asked after a while.

"Let's see what Jackson's doing in the workshop."

"I think he's putting new pistons in that old John Deere tractor."

When Scott and Kazi reached the workshop Garth and Jackson were there. Garth glanced up.

"Hi, Scott, Kazi," he said as the boys walked in.

"Hi, Dad."

"Hello, Mr. Finley."

"Scott, Jackson tells me that you boys hang around here every afternoon. Is that right?"

Scott looked down at his toes and waited for the usual lecture about getting in the way.

Garth continued, "School breaks up soon, doesn't it?"

"Yes, Dad." Scott looked up and wondered what Garth was going to say.

"Well, I've got an idea that will keep you out of mischief up here."

"Sorry, Dad," Scott thought he was going to be put to work tidying or cleaning, and he definitely didn't want that. "I promise I won't bother Jackson again."

Garth laughed at his reaction. "I'm not going to punish you. Come and take a look at what I've got." Garth turned and took them to the back of the shed where a 1972 Chevrolet Nomad was hidden behind the stacks of bricks. Total body rust and countless accidents had left it looking as if it should have been sent to the scrap yard.

Scott rushed forward. He loved it in spite of its flaws because he knew his dad could restore it.

"I bought it as a learning tool for you. I'm going to cut off the canopy and open it up to look like a jeep. Jackson will work on the engine and get it running. We'll do the mechanical work, but you'll have to help, and then you'll do all the sanding and body prep before we paint it. I want you to learn how a vehicle works."

"Will I be allowed to drive it when it's been fixed?"

"Yes, but only on the farm."

"Yay!" Scott grabbed Kazi's hands and hauled him around in a delirious circle.

"It'll be hard work and there'll be no fooling around," Garth warned.

Scott stopped. "We'll work hard, Dad, promise. You will help, won't you Kazi?" he asked turning to Kazi.

Kazi bobbed his head enthusiastically.

It *was* hard work and each day for the next month the boys went home tired, covered in grease, but happy. Martha grumbled half-heartedly about Kazi's ruined clothes. And Caitlin insisted they leave their shoes outside after she found black footprints tracked across the kitchen and grimy fingerprints on the cookie cupboard. The boys sanded rust until their arms ached, they learnt which tools were which, and worked next to Garth and Jackson like surgeon's assistants. One day Garth announced that all that was left to be done was to replace the battery and fuel.

"Can we do it now?" Scott asked. He was dying to get the Nomad running. It had been stripped and rebuilt and, true to what Garth had predicted, it had a rugged safari look and had been transformed.

"Umm," Garth looked at his watch as if he had something more important to do.

"Please, Dad?" Scott begged.

Garth cuffed him on the shoulder, "Just teasing."

He turned to Jackson. "Fill her up while I install the battery. Let's see if we can get this baby running."

He bent over the engine and connected the battery while Jackson filled the tank.

"Ready?" Garth asked.

"Ready, *Baas.*"

Garth climbed in and turned the ignition. The motor churned, he tried again and the engine caught and vibrated roughly.

"The timing needs adjusting," Garth shouted above the noise of the engine. "Jackson, see if you can get it right."

Jackson loosened the locknut that held the distributor and turned it. The engine shuddered.

"The other way – turn it the other way," Garth yelled.

Jackson hadn't been thinking about what he was doing. His thoughts were on Sarina, he wanted to see her again. He turned the distributor again and the engine settled into a smooth idle.

"Come on, guys, let's see how she goes," Garth said with a swoop of his hand.

They all got in and Garth drove to the intersection on the main road, turned, drove back, and stopped the Nomad in front of the workshop.

"She's running beautifully. Come on, Scott, take her around the shed," Garth said. He was confident Scott could do it, he'd been teaching him to drive since he was ten.

Scott and Garth exchanged places. Scott turned the ignition, added too much accelerator and the motor revved loudly. He dropped the clutch, and the Nomad lurched forward and stalled. Kazi laughed.

"Try again," Garth said. "Just go a little slower on the gas and be gentle on the clutch. It's still new, so you'll find it a bit stiff."

Scott started the Nomad again and drove away reasonably smoothly. This time Kazi clapped.

That night Jackson staggered into their house, holding the door for support. He aimed himself towards the table, mouth slack and eyes bloodshot.

Nelly glared at him. "You're drunk again!"

"Sho what?" Jackson said, lurching to the cupboard. He leant against the counter and stared into the cupboard. He lifted his hand to take something out, but his hand caught the side of a mug and it fell to the ground, splintering loudly.

Nelly stepped out of the way. "Jack-son!" she spat. "I've had enough. I'm sick to death of your drinking and… that woman. I know you're still seeing her."

"Cut it out, Nelly, not in front of the children," Jackson slurred, pointing to them.

"I saw you with her this evening."

Jackson lurched across the room and sat at the table. He forgot about the children and his mouth curved in disdain. "You're imagining things, stupid woman."

Her face twisted. "You're a lying, stinking bastard! I saw you with Sarina again so don't try and deny it."

She strode across the room, swung the baby onto her back. "I don't want to live another minute in this house with you. I hate you!" She grasped her daughter's hand, and stormed out of the house. "Come," she said to her eldest, and the girl followed meekly.

Jackson leapt to his feet, his chair crashing to the floor. He staggered after her.

Kazi was walking back from the outhouse. They could no longer use the toilets in their houses because Garth had decommissioned them when they had blocked up with mealie cobs, newspaper and various undesirable items.

There was a half moon and Kazi kicked a stone ahead of him. He noticed Nelly run past without a glance in his direction, followed by Jackson.

Jackson stopped and looked at him. He swayed on his feet as if they were rocking chair legs. "Where'sh Nelly gone," he asked.

"I don't know, Jackson, what's going on?"

"Stupid bitch took the children."

He stopped talking to Kazi and yelled into the night, "Bring my children back. Bitch!"

He turned back to Kazi and in a quieter tone added, "That bitch is not going to take *my* children. *My* kids," he mumbled stabbing his chest with his finger. He staggered to his car, climbed in and smashed his hand on the dash. "Bitch, fucking bitch! Shorry, Kazi." He rested his head on the steering wheel.

"Jackson, you're drunk. You shouldn't drive."

"Can't walk, too mush to drink," he said with the logic of a drunk. "Mush get my children," he said, fumbling with the keys.

"Jackson, give me the keys. You can't drive."

"Yesh I can."

"Jackson, give them to me."

"No." Kazi realized he couldn't stop Jackson and yelled for his father. Goodwill appeared at the door of their house.

"Dad, Jackson's drunk. You've got to stop him." Jackson managed to get the car started. He revved it, the engine screamed and the car shot forward.

"Wait," Goodwill shouted, and his outstretched hand fell to his side. "He's going too fast."

Kazi and Goodwill watched Jackson's car careen down the dirt track towards the farm road. The Toyota barely missed a drought-stricken pine tree, reached the road, turned onto it, overcorrected, straightened out, and sped on towards the corner. Jackson didn't slow down and entered the corner too fast. The car skidded and whipped around, slewed to the right, left the road, and smacked into a tree stump. It flipped into the air and the lights cut through the sky, spun through the trees. Then they came to a stop, glaring into the distance.

By this time Goodwill and Kazi were already running. When they reached the car, the engine had cut out and it had come to a stop on its roof. Jackson had been thrown clear and was lying face down on the ground. Goodwill turned him over and blood gushed from a wound in his neck.

Kazi stood next to his father, looking down at Jackson's blood pooling darkly on the ground. He wanted to be sick from the seeping odour of petrol, radiator fluid, and dust that blended with the iron smell of blood. He held a hand over his nose and mouth.

Garth ran up, with Scott close behind.

"We heard the noise, what happened?" Garth asked.

"It's Jackson, *Baas*," Goodwill replied. "His throat's cut."

Garth knelt and took in the extent of Jackson's injuries. His first aid training in the army helped him keep a tight lid on his emotions. This type of accident had happened before and would happen again. He just had to do what he had to do.

"Tell Mom to phone the ambulance," he told Scott. "And bring the first aid kit. Hurry!"

Garth continued his inspection of Jackson's wounds. "This is deep, it goes right across his throat." He turned Jackson onto his side, bent his head forward to close the wound, and put pressure on the cut. Blood flowed between his fingers.

Nelly ran towards them, the baby tied with a blanket on her back, her littlest girl clutching her hand, the other following. "What happened?" she asked. "I heard the noise." She knelt next to Jackson. "Jackson, speak to me, Jackson..." Jackson groaned. She was on the verge of hysteria.

Scott came back and placed the first aid box on the ground next to Garth.

"Here, Dad," he said breathing hard. "Mom's phoning the ambulance."

"Thanks," Garth said automatically.

"Nelly," he said, grasping her shoulder with his free hand. "You must help me," he said firmly. "Put your hand here, and keep pressure on the wound while I get something to stop the bleeding."

Nelly lifted her eyes, which were dark and filled with fear. She untied the baby and left the child on the blanket. Her little girl clung silently to her skirt and sucked her thumb, her eyes on her father. The eldest stood silently.

"Nelly," Garth repeated, "put your hand here."

Nelly put her hand where she was told. She retched dryly, and a tear rolled down her cheek.

Garth turned to the first aid box, took out a couple of sterile gauze pads and tore them open.

"Nelly, lift your hand."

A fresh burst of blood pumped out at the release of pressure.

He placed the pads on the wound. "Okay, press firmly," he said to Nelly. Nelly did as she was told and Garth straightened.

Caitlin arrived with Shanon, followed by her cousin Sue-Sue from Johannesburg.

Shanon looked at Jackson. "Is he going to be okay, Mom?"

"I hope so."

"Can I do anything to help?"

"He's going into shock. Bring a blanket, the blue one in the linen cupboard." Shanon turned and went back to the house.

"Oh my God, Garth," Sue-Sue screeched, her lipstick-red mouth a round O. She flapped her hands prissily, false nails matching her lipstick. "Look at all the blood on your hands. How can you deal with this... this blood? Aren't you scared of AIDS? Jesus!"

"Don't..." Caitlin's voice carried the warning. She never blasphemed.

"Oh, oh, I think I'm going to faint," Sue-Sue complained.

"Garth," Caitlin said, ignoring her cousin, "the ambulance is on its way."

Garth looked down at Jackson. "I hope they hurry. There's a lot of blood."

"I told them to," she said. She turned away and lowered her voice so that Jackson wouldn't hear. "When they heard he was black they wanted to send that ridiculous thing they call an ambulance. It's just a *bakkie*, a blooming pick-up truck with a canopy and loose stretchers," she said heatedly. "I told him we were prepared to pay whatever it would cost for the real ambulance with paramedics."

"Good," Garth replied tersely.

"The mosquitoes are biting," Caitlin's cousin grumbled.

"Why don't you go back to the house," Caitlin snapped, and her cousin turned and flounced off.

Twenty minutes later Garth said, "Where the hell is that ambulance? Caitlin, go and phone again. Tell them to hurry."

Caitlin went to the house and when she got back she looked angrier than ever.

"The same person answered. He was so nonchalant I wanted to swear."

At last the ambulance siren could be heard in the distance and everyone willed it on faster. The vehicle slowed as it reached the farm, and at last they saw lights bouncing up the road towards them. It drew to a stop and two paramedics clambered out.

One of them remarked callously, "I heard you were upset. Sorry, man, we had to pick up someone else on the way."

"He's lost a lot of blood," Garth said.

The man looked at Jackson. "Don't worry, these guys are tough."

While he was talking, his assistant, a short dark-haired man, turned Jackson over. Caitlin felt rising nausea hit her. Jackson's eye was gone, a bloody hole in its place.

The paramedic lifted Jackson's chin. "Lucky bugger, just missed his jugular," he said, opening his medical kit and swiftly bandaging Jackson's neck. "He'd be dead if it was."

Caitlin asked, "What about his eye?"

The man poked at the wound. "This?" he asked. He shook his head. "Not the eye," he said. "This is from a cut above the eye. Look," he said lifting a large flap of loose flesh.

"What a relief," Caitlin said.

Garth squeezed Jackson's shoulder. "Did you hear that? You're going to be okay," he said.

Jackson stared up at him, his one eye dark with blood. The paramedics lifted him onto a gurney and slid it into the ambulance. Suddenly, with surprising kindness, the short paramedic asked, "Which of you is his wife?"

Nelly lifted her hand.

"There's space for you if you want to go with him."

Martha pushed her forward. "I'll look after your little ones," she said, and Nelly smiled gratefully and climbed in behind the stretcher.

They took off, dust trailing.

On the day that Jackson was discharged, Garth waited outside Kalafong hospital. It was hot in the sun. He wiped the sweat from his forehead and looked at his watch. Just when he was wondering if he should go inside and look for Jackson, he spotted him.

Jackson was hesitating outside the glass doors. He looked around and, in turn, saw Garth. His hand lifted in a self-conscious movement to hide the scar on his neck and Garth noticed that Jackson's eye drooped.

Jackson walked towards the Land Cruiser and climbed stiffly onto the seat. He greeted Garth without enthusiasm.

"Good to have you back, Jackson," Garth smiled.

"Yes, *Baas*," he responded indifferently.

"Nelly and the kids are excited that you're coming home." Jackson remained silent. "When you get home, take your time and rest. Come back to work when you feel well enough."

Jackson nodded and rubbed at the moisture on his cheek that seeped constantly from his eye.

On the farm Garth drew up outside Jackson's house. The door opened and the children ran out, followed by Nelly.

Jackson's gaze passed over their heads and lingered on his damaged car, which was back in the lean-to. He ignored Nelly, brushed the children aside, and walked inside.

ELEVEN

THE TEARS OF THE INNOCENT

1980 · 1981 · 1982 · 1983 · 1984 · 1985 · 1986 · **1987** · 1988

A month later, Jackson sat outside in the sun. At the sound of footsteps he lifted his head. Realizing it was Sarina he turned his face away, aware of how ugly he must look.

"Sarina," he said. "I don't want to see you any more. It's definitely over now. Leave me alone."

She looked down at him. "I can't, Jackson."

"And why would that be?" he asked, without any real interest in her answer.

"Because I'm pregnant."

His head jerked up. "Are you sure?"

"I wouldn't have said it if I wasn't."

"Sarina, I'm sorry."

"Jackson, what do you mean? Aren't you happy that we are going to have a baby? Now you can leave Nelly and we can have our own family."

"No, Sarina. It's over between us. I can't leave Nelly. I'm sorry, but this doesn't change things. I have to pull my life together."

"But you told me you loved me," she cried.

Jackson shook his head. "Things have changed since my accident."

Sarina spun away. "Fine, if that's what you want. But you're going to support this baby. Just try and get out of it, and I'll see you in court. Bastard," she added, as she stalked off.

Jackson sat on the bench and watched her walk away, her anger evident in every step.

Martha went to see Sarina's baby when it was born. She was pretty with Sarina's light brown skin, but Jackson's round, full features.

"What's her name?" Martha asked as she took the baby from Sarina.

Sarina smiled softly, "Lena," she replied. Lena yawned and a droplet of milk balanced on her lip.

"Are you going to have her christened?" Martha asked lifting her eyes.

"I'd like to. Do you think Goodwill would do it?"

"Of course he would," Martha replied.

"Even though she's illegitimate?" she asked.

"I know he will." Martha nuzzled her nose into the baby's neck and breathed in her baby smell.

Sarina smiled, "I'm relieved you haven't held this against me. It's been hard staying here with Jackson and Nelly living so close by. A lot of people cut me dead, but I've got nowhere else to go. I have to stay with my mother. I have no choice." Lena let out a wail.

"Here, you'd better take her," Martha said. "Don't worry about the others, Sarina, time heals everything."

On the day of Lena's christening, Kazi didn't feel well and, by nightfall, he was coughing badly. Each bout left him gasping for breath and throwing up. Martha sat on the edge of his bed with a bowl for him to be sick into. His lungs ached and he felt weak and hot. She wiped his forehead and he lay back on the pillows.

"Goodwill," she called out.

Goodwill came through from the living room. "Yes, Martha?"

"Please go and ask the *Missus* for some cough mixture."

At the house Caitlin frowned when Goodwill explained Kazi's symptoms. It didn't sound like a normal cough and she decided to see Kazi herself.

Caitlin stepped into Goodwill and Martha's house. Everything was neat and, even though six people lived in the small two bedroom house, everything was in its place. She could hear Kazi coughing and she recognised the tell-tale whoop of whooping cough. She followed Goodwill to the bedroom. Kazi couldn't catch his breath and he breathed in with a deep whoop, and threw up in the bowl.

"I'm sorry," he gasped, embarrassed.

"It's okay," Caitlin said. "Sounds like you've got whooping cough." She walked across the room and bent to feel Kazi's forehead with her wrist. "You've got a fever."

She turned to Martha. "I brought some cough mixture, but it won't help much because it's whooping cough – not an ordinary cough. But I did bring some Disprin, as well, and that will reduce the fever. Give him two every four hours." She turned back to Kazi. "Make sure you drink lots of water.

You've got to be careful you don't get dehydrated." She turned to Goodwill. "How is Jackson? Will he be able to take Kazi to the doctor tomorrow?"

"I'm sure he can, *Missus*."

"Good, tell him I want him to take Kazi."

She turned back to Kazi, "The doctor will probably take a mucus sample to confirm that it is whooping cough and, if it is, he'll give you antibiotics and tell you when you can go back to school. In the meantime keep away from Sarina and her baby. Whooping cough is very contagious, and the baby hasn't been vaccinated yet."

The doctor confirmed it was whooping cough and after two weeks Kazi was well enough to go to school. A number of his friends had also been sick and their tired coughing formed a chorus in the classroom.

A few days later Martha heard that Sarina's baby was sick in spite of all the precautions they had taken. She went to Sarina's house and knocked softly.

"C-come in," Sarina cried.

Martha walked in. The drapes were drawn and the room was dark. Sarina sat on the single bed, tears rolling down her cheeks. Her shirt was undone and her breasts looked painfully engorged. Lena lay in her arms.

"She-she won't drink. Martha, w-what can I do?"

"Let me hold her for you," Martha said. "Express some milk and we'll spoon it into her mouth."

As Martha lifted the baby to her shoulder she noticed that Lena's arms and legs were painfully thin, and her stomach was distended and hard against her. She rubbed her back gently and paced the length of the room while Sarina expressed milk into a cup.

"Has the *Missus* seen her?"

Sarina nodded. "She took us to the doctor herself. I've got medicine, but Lena won't swallow it. The doctor told me to make sure that she got enough liquids, but I can't get her to drink," she sobbed.

"I'll help you, I'm sure she'll be all right," Martha said in a soothing voice.

Sarina finished expressing milk and Martha cradled Lena in her arms so that Sarina could spoon it into her mouth. The first spoonful trickled in and she coughed, spraying the milk back out. She opened her mouth in a fragile wail.

"Try again," Martha instructed.

Sarina did as she was told and Lena gagged.

"Come along, *liefling*," Martha crooned.

The next spoonful stayed down and Sarina smiled with relief. They dribbled milk into Lena's mouth until she fell asleep, and then Martha placed her gently in a nest of pillows on the bed.

"I'm afraid I have to go now," she said. "Try and feed her often with small amounts." She smiled at the young mother. "I'll come and see you tomorrow."

"Okay," she said, her voice uncertain. Sarina put down the cup of milk and wrapped Lena in a swaddling blanket.

"Call me if you need me," Martha said and Sarina nodded.

"Thank you, I will."

Towards midnight Goodwill and Martha woke to hammering on the door. An urgent voice called, "Martha, come quickly."

"Who's that?" Goodwill asked, struggling awake.

"It's Maria. Lena must be worse!" Martha leapt out of bed, pulled a jersey over her nightie, and opened the door.

Maria was turning to go. "Lena is very sick. Please, I don't want to leave Sarina alone while I go and call the *Missus*," she said, her face pinched and drawn.

"Go, hurry, I'll stay with Sarina," Martha said and ran through the labourers' houses to Sarina and Maria's house.

Sarina was on the bed rocking back and forth.

Martha placed a hand on Lena's cheek. "She's hot, burning with fever."

Caitlin and Garth came back with Maria in the Land Cruiser. From what Maria had said, Caitlin realized they had to get Lena to hospital as quickly as possible. She had brought Garth with that in mind.

Caitlin and Maria leapt out of the vehicle as soon as it drew to a halt and ran into the house. Sarina was still on the bed rocking back and forth, Lena silent in her arms.

Caitlin's heart stopped, it was worse than she expected. She took Lena and rapidly removed the blankets she was swaddled in.

"Get me a wet cloth, we have to bring her fever down," she instructed. She lifted Lena's foot and tapped the sole to rouse her. Nothing happened. She stroked her, and still nothing happened. She realized she had to start CPR – the thought terrified her, she had done it in first aid but they had used a doll. She took one more look at the child and pushed her fears aside. If she didn't do it, Lena would die. She tipped Lena's head back as she had been taught, then she took a small breath of air, held it in her mouth, covered Lena's nose and mouth with her own mouth and breathed out gently. She did this five times. Then she put two fingers on the breastbone directly between the baby's nipples, pushed down gently, and then let the chest come back up. She started to count and after three Lena took a breath. Caitlin let out a sigh of relief.

"Okay, let's go," she said, picking Lena up. "Sarina, bring the wet cloth so that we can cool her down on the way."

Garth had the doors to the Land Cruiser open and the engine running. He was ready to go. Sarina climbed in and Caitlin passed Lena up before she climbed in herself. As soon as Caitlin shut the door, Garth accelerated away. By then all the lights were on in the labourer's houses and worried faces looked out as they passed.

Nelly stood next to Jackson in the doorway to their house, a blanket thrown over her shoulders. They both stared as the Land Cruiser passed, their faces filled with concern – Nelly's, as well as Jackson's.

Garth sped down the farm road and onto the deserted road to Brits. It was dark and lonely. Once in a while they passed the shadowy outline of a farmhouse, but not a single soul witnessed their desperate race to the hospital. Caitlin kept her eyes on Lena. If she suffered another episode she would have to administer CPR again. They would have to stop, and she was not qualified to cope with this kind of emergency.

Lena looked as if she was going to drift off to sleep and Caitlin rubbed her gently to keep her awake. She wasn't sure if she should let her sleep under the circumstances. She only knew from her first aid course that children should not be allowed to sleep if they had concussion.

They entered the town and the traffic light ahead was red. Lena was making small choking sounds.

Sarina cradled Lena to her chest.

"Sarina, try holding her on her side. Keep her head lower than her tummy," Caitlin instructed, "she'll breathe easier. Garth, don't stop," she said. Garth had no intention of stopping. He glanced left and right, pushed the accelerator to the floorboard and raced through the intersection.

Sarina did as she was told and Lena drew a shallow breath. Garth checked the next intersection and drove through it too at full speed. Seconds later, they drew up at the hospital and Sarina ran inside with Lena.

The doors slid closed behind her, and Caitlin and Garth drove home. There was nothing more that they could do.

Caitlin sat in silence. She had thought that Sarina understood what the doctor had told her to look out for – high fever, vomiting, breathing problems, all the symptoms that

Lena had. And now the poor little child could die. She put her face in her hands and began to cry. She felt too young, too inexperienced to carry the responsibility of all the people that lived on Fairvalley Farm.

Garth put his hand on hers and she began to cry even harder. "If only I had checked on her again."

"Caity," he said, "you can't be everywhere all the time. You took her to the doctor, and you did what you could."

"It wasn't enough, was it?" she said bitterly.

When Sarina and Lena came home weeks later, Nelly went to see Martha.

The door was open and when she called out Martha came to the door with a child's shirt hanging loosely from one hand, a needle and thread in the other.

"Martha..." Nelly said pausing. Martha waited for her to continue. "Martha," Nelly repeated taking a deep breath, "Jackson said Lena might have brain damage."

Martha nodded. "We're hoping she'll come right in time. She had a seizure in hospital."

"Poor baby," Nelly said, thinking how lucky she was that her own children hadn't been sick as well.

"Martha, I was mad at Jackson and Sarina, but that's over, and I want to put it behind us. Will you come with me to see Sarina?"

"I will, I think that would be a nice gesture."

Martha placed her sewing on the table and they walked to Sarina's house together. Nelly paused outside, then knocked tentatively.

Sarina opened the door.

"You!" she snapped. "Why are you here?" she asked glaring at Nelly. "I suppose you've come to gloat. You're happy now aren't you? You've got everything – healthy children and Jackson. What have I got?" She burst into tears and turned her back.

"Sarina," Nelly stepped forward and touched her shoulder.

Sarina reacted as if she'd been scalded.

"Don't touch me!"

"I'm sorry." Nelly let her hand drop to her side. "I'm sorry this has happened to you. Please believe that I came to put things behind us."

Lena let out an angry squeal from where she lay, and Sarina walked to the bed and picked her up. She turned towards the two women.

"There!" she said, holding Lena towards them. "Now you can see what you've come to see." Lena's head drooped to one side, her mouth sagged and her eyes held a dull stare, one hand twisted inwards.

"Go now," Sarina said, her voice cold and harsh.

"I'm so sorry," Nelly whispered, tears falling as she reached out, begging forgiveness.

Sarina looked away and Nelly turned reluctantly, her shoulders sagging in defeat.

Martha paused on the doorstep. "I'll come back later, Sarina," she said quietly before she followed Nelly.

"That poor baby," Nelly cried when Martha caught up. "That poor woman."

"I know," Martha replied. "Pray for her Nelly, pray for her. That's all you can do."

TWELVE

WHISPER OF CHANGE

1982 · 1983 · 1984 · 1985 · 1986 · 1987 · **1988** · **1989** · 1990

Winter passed and Lena showed no improvement. She did not sit, crawl, or walk. Her brown eyes showed no interest in her surroundings, and her body hung limp within the blanket that held her to Sarina's back.

Kazi, on the other hand, showed no ill effects from the illness. He was old enough not to. Now, months later, he ducked under the fence and ran through a field over patches of thorns without noticing, his feet hard from being barefoot. At his approach a flock of guinea fowl lifted, squawking into the air, and Kazi threw back his head and laughed – foolish birds, he thought. He reached the edge of the field, ducked under a second fence and walked up the road towards home, his satchel on his back. From a distance he could see a tractor parked in front of the lean-to where Jackson's wrecked car stood and, when he got closer, noticed Jackson crouching between the tractor and the car, a cable in his hands.

"Hey, Jackson," Kazi said in greeting.

Jackson straightened, "Hello, Kazi."

"What's up?"

"I'm taking my car to the workshop. I want to get it running again." He looked at Kazi with a calculating look. "Perhaps you could help me."

"Sure, with what?"

"Could you steer the Datsun while I'm towing it?"

"But I can't drive."

"All you have to do is steer in the direction I take, and brake if the cable goes slack. It's easy, I'm sure you could do it."

"Sure, I'll give it a try if you think it's okay," Kazi dropped his satchel and scrambled into the damaged Datsun. Jackson pointed out the brake and the handbrake.

Kazi nodded, "I know where the brakes are."

"Good, let's go then. Just toot if you want to stop, and remember to brake gently."

Jackson climbed onto the tractor and eased forward taking up the slack in the cable. The Datsun gave a little jerk and, as it rolled forward, pulled to one side. Kazi turned the wheel, corrected its direction, and once the car was moving it followed behind the tractor just as Jackson had said it would. It wasn't difficult. Kazi coped easily and felt a growing feeling of excitement behind the wheel. He had always envied Scott and wished he could drive himself. Jackson slowed and Kazi eased his foot down on the brake pedal. The Datsun kept an even distance behind the tractor and when Jackson stopped outside the workshop Kazi brought the car to a standstill. Jackson jumped down and came to the window. "Well done, now pull up the handbrake."

Kazi did as he was told and got out.

Jackson looked at him thoughtfully. "Kazi, if I teach you to drive will you help me some more?"

Kazi's eyes lit up. "You'll teach me to drive? Of course, but what will I have to do?" He was so excited he could've beaten a drum roll on the hood of the Datsun.

"Same kind of stuff you did on Scott's Nomad – sanding, passing tools, cleaning up. That kind of thing."

"It's a deal." Kazi didn't care what Jackson wanted him to do, he would do anything.

"Good, can we start after work tomorrow?"

"Tomorrow," Kazi nodded, picking up his satchel and slinging it over his shoulder. He was still beaming as he jogged up the slope towards home.

Kazi worked with Jackson every evening for a month and then, once the Datsun was running, Jackson carried out his promise. By Christmas Kazi could drive, and during the holidays he and Scott did their usual hiking, swimming, and fishing, but now that they could both drive they wanted to venture further afield. Scott asked Garth if they could leave the farm to drive the back road to a new game farm.

Garth noticed how well they were driving and decided they had enough experience. The road that Scott wanted to drive along was really just a dirt track that wound past two other farms. They would be as safe as if they were on the farm, however there would be one provision: they would only be allowed to drive as far as the game farm. The man was a friend of Garth's and wouldn't mind if they popped in.

Scott was elated. "Can we really?" Garth smiled and nodded.

"You may, but pull over if you see any other vehicles."

"C'mon, Kazi, let's go now," Scott said, restarting the Nomad.

Shanon came out of the house and noticed them opening the back gate. She'd overheard Scott asking to go to the game farm and assumed that was where they were going. She didn't usually join the boys on their escapades, but she'd heard that the farm was used to quarantine game, and wanted to see the animals.

"Are you going to the game farm?" she called out.

"*Ja*, you want to come?"

"Yes, wait for me."

Kazi jumped out and opened the gate, and then he climbed into the back making space for Shanon. She climbed in and Scott drove carefully down the road, pulling over for the occasional vehicle or tractor. When he reached the gate at the game farm, he stopped outside the entrance.

"Is *Baas* Paolo here?" Scott asked the security guard.

"That way," the man pointed to a building within a fenced camp.

Scott parked the Nomad, and they all got out and went through a narrow gate into the camp. It appeared to be unoccupied, but, being the last person through the gate, Shanon made sure that the gate was latched behind them. Walking through the field they frightened a small herd of impala on the other side of the fence, and stopped to watch them scatter, prancing away, tails in the air. None of them noticed a hyena approaching until Kazi heard leaves rustling, turned, and gave a terrified yell. The hyena stood low on its haunches, strong in its forequarters. Its jaw gaped showing vicious teeth, and it held them in a dark stare.

"Run!" Kazi yelled, and the three of them took off, running back the way they'd come, slamming through the gate.

"What's the matter?" the guard called.

"Hyena!" Scott gasped.

"Eh, eh, there is nothing wrong with that animal. Go now. The *Baas* is in the shed." He waved them on.

"No," Shannon shook her head. "We'll wait here for the *Baas*. Call him and tell him."

"*Nee*, you must go now. The animal, he is fine."

Kazi spoke to the man in Tswana[2]. "I've asked him to call his boss," he told the others.

The man disappeared into the gatehouse, came back and reiterated what he'd said earlier, but this time as an instruction from his boss. "The *Baas* says you must go in."

Scott, Shanon, and Kazi stared at the hyena, and it stared back. None of them wanted to go back into the field with the hyena, which looked vicious.

After some time a man appeared in the doorway of the building, and walked across the field.

"Hello?" he said with a lift to the word, forming a question.

"Hi," Shanon replied. "I hope we're not bothering you, Mr. Di Canio. We're from Fairvalley Farm. Dad said he'd spoken to you and it was okay for us to come."

"Oh yeah, Garth's kids," he said, giving Shanon an admiring glance. At sixteen she had long legs and a woman's slim body. "He didn't tell me he had such a beautiful daughter."

Shannon's thick auburn hair fell across her face. She looked away and blushed.

Scott interrupted. "Mr. Di Canio, I'm Scott, this is my sister Shanon, and my friend Kazi," he introduced each of them in turn.

Paolo drew his eyes reluctantly away from Shanon. "Call me Paolo. Come in," he said, opening the gate. He looked exactly how you would expect a game ranger to look – tanned, rugged, khaki bush clothes, ankle length hiking boots, and a revolver in a holster on his hip. He clapped his hands. "Go on,

---

[2] One of the eleven official languages in South Africa, commonly used in the Magaliesburg area

be off with you," he said to the hyena, and the hyena gave a soft grunt-laugh and loped away to look at the impala.

"I was about to feed Mitsi, you can give me a hand. I'm sure you'll enjoy it," Paolo said without explaining who or what Mitsi was, and strode off towards the homestead. When he opened the door they stopped in surprise, and Paolo chuckled. Mitsi was not a kitten or a cute little poodle. She was a baby cheetah.

"You guys can play with her while I fetch her bottle," he said.

Shanon bent down to touch the cheetah. The animal was small enough not to be threatening and emitted a soft purr as Shanon scratched behind its ear. "She's soft!" she exclaimed.

The cheetah rolled onto its back offering its belly, and Kazi ran his hand down the length of her.

"She is," he agreed.

When Paolo came back, he allowed Shanon to feed Mitsi, and then he took them outside to a series of camps where zebra, ostrich, and warthog were kept and they helped feed the animals. Then Paolo took them on a tour and proudly showed them an enclosure he was building for rhinoceros. A massive structure of I-beams concreted into the ground with high-tension, spanned elevator cables, and a steel sliding gate.

"Poor beasts," Shanon said, imagining the enormous creatures in captivity.

Paulo shrugged. "At least they're safe from poachers here. In the bush the bastards hack off their horns leaving them to bleed to death."

Shanon looked at the small enclosure and felt sad. "That's horrible." On one hand there were the poachers killing these massive animals for their horns. On the other were men like Paolo who captured and sold them to zoos or game parks. Both were equally repelling and it showed on her face.

Paolo noticed her expression and put his hand on hers. "If we don't protect the rhinos, like I do, they'll become extinct."

Shanon moved her hand away. "But isn't there another way?" She imagined that his argument was valid but still fuelled by greed.

He shrugged. Of course there was, but his reasoning gave credence to his actions and export game was a lucrative market.

"I hope Mitsi isn't also going to a zoo," Shanon said.

"No, she's mine," Paulo assured her with a smooth smile.

Shanon pretended to look at her watch. Paolo was a lot older than she was and she wasn't enjoying his interest in her. The boys had wondered off so she called them back. "Guys, we promised Dad we'd be home before sunset, we'd better go." She turned to Paolo. "Thanks for showing us around."

"You're welcome. You should come back again. Perhaps on your own," Paolo's gaze was direct, his smile lazy. The boys walked up and Paolo turned his attention away from Shanon. "Come on then, I'll walk you past my guard dog."

He escorted them through the field with the hyena and through the gate, where Scott stopped dead.

"What's that all over my Nomad?"

"Oh dear," Paolo grimaced. "I didn't think to ask where you parked. I just assumed you'd walked here," he shrugged. "You don't look old enough to drive."

Scott didn't reply. "What is it?" he asked again.

"Manure."

"Manure?"

"Yes, manure," Paolo pointed to a small hippo chewing on a clump of ferns. "That's how a pigmy hippo marks its territory."

Scott stared at his Nomad. "But – it's everywhere!" he said with a look of disgust.

Kazi looked at the back seat. "Maybe I should walk."

"No, you drive and I'll walk," Scott said.

Kazi laughed and shook his head. "Your car, your problem."

"Ugh," Scott said, giving the hippo a sour look. "I'm going to have to hose this off when we get home."

Shanon climbed in with a grin. The hippo had missed her seat.

Paolo chuckled. "Come back soon," he said, giving Shanon a significant look.

"We will, thanks," Scott replied, ignoring Paolo's insinuation that it was only Shanon he wanted to see.

They all waved, and the old security guard opened the gate. He'd seen what the hippo had done and was laughing. He said something to Kazi who laughed.

"What?" Scott demanded crossly.

Kazi translated. "He said, 'I bet the *Klein Baasie* parks outside next time.'"

Shanon laughed. "I'm sure he will."

"It's not funny, my jeep's a mess!" Scott moaned.

"We'll help clean it, won't we, Kazi?"

Kazi chuckled, "Maybe."

Still giggling Shanon said, "That was fun, I'm glad I came with you."

The sun was lowering in the west turning the sky a dusky orange, and the Nomad was kicking up a light trail of dust behind them. Scott sobered. "It's going to be hard leaving all of this for boarding school next month."

"At least you can come home every weekend," Shanon said. "I'm only allowed home every second weekend from Girl's High."

"I'm sure it won't be too bad," Kazi said.

"That's okay for you to say, Kazi," Scott said. "You're going to school in Brits and can come home every day."

Although the government had repealed some of the petty apartheid laws and Kazi could now go to the same school as Scott, his parents couldn't afford the fees. Caitlin was prepared to pay for books and clothing for the labourers' children, but she couldn't afford school fees for all of them to attend the newly formed Model C schools, which had a semi-private structure with decreased funding from the state. So Kazi had to remain in the public school system, which was fully funded by the government.

The holidays passed swiftly and on the last day Kazi watched Scott pack his clothes for boarding school as if he were going to prison. They walked outside and Scott placed his bags on the back of the Land Cruiser, then he looked around at the familiar surroundings. He appeared to be committing them to memory.

"I'd better go now," Kazi said, taking Scott's hand and shaking it in the traditional manner, three times, hand over hand. It was the first time that he had shaken Scott's hand, perhaps because he unconsciously realized that they were both leaving their childhood behind.

"I'll see you in a few weeks."

"*Ja,*" Scott turned away and Kazi could see that he didn't want him to witness his anguish at leaving home. He placed his hand on Scott's shoulder. "*Hamba kakuhle* – go carefully," he said, and left.

Scott's leaving dampened his own excitement. During the past few years he'd been teaching the younger children at the farm school and not learning much himself. He was looking forward to high school.

The next morning Kazi jogged to the bus stop. Caitlin had broken her own tradition by giving him two sets of school clothes instead of one, and a pair of shoes. His new shoes pinched and the collar of his white shirt chafed. But he felt confident, in spite of the discomfort, and ready to face new challenges.

An old, dusty bus trundled to a halt, the doors opened and Kazi asked the driver if he was going to Brits. The driver nodded and Kazi climbed on, paid for his ticket and found a seat. On the bus, the same distance Jackson drove in twenty minutes took much longer to travel, and Kazi chewed on a piece of loose nail, worried that he would be late for his first day. At last, the bus drew to a stop outside the school. Kazi climbed down, pausing on the steps and looking at his new school – it was an ugly grey building, long and squat.

While he looked, students pushed past him, shoving him out of the way, uncaring of his newness, his confusion at the size of the school and the milling people.

He moved out of the way and fumbled for an information sheet in his pocket. Making sure he knew where to go, he walked around the quadrangle and found the right classroom. Inside boys and girls his age stood in groups talking loudly. No one seemed to notice him walk to the back of the classroom and sit down at an empty desk. The minute hand on the clock above the blackboard inched forward, and at exactly eight-thirty a portly, middle-aged black man walked into the classroom.

He clapped his hands. "Find a seat please," he yelled above the noise, his double chin wobbling. After a few moments of chaos the children sat facing the teacher.

"Good, now we can start. My name is Mr. Mgani. I am the headmaster, as well as your teacher." He glanced around. "I'd like you to stand when I call your name." He lifted a pair of glasses that hung from a cord around his neck, and as each student was called he wrote on a chart on his desk. "Please stay in the same seat for the rest of the term," he instructed. And then he began, and the lesson passed in a blur of information that Kazi found difficult to follow. When they stopped for a break he was relieved, went outside and sat on a bench in the sun. He scanned through the work. It was lucky he could speak English from hanging out with the Finleys, but he couldn't make sense of the grammar rules and wondered how he would find the answers. His mother and father wouldn't be able to help. He wished Scott was home so that he could ask him. The Finley's wouldn't mind if he asked, but he didn't feel at ease going to them without Scott.

He was still wondering how to deal with the problem when an older boy sat down on the bench next to him.

"This seat taken?" he asked.

"Nope," Kazi said without looking up.

"Looks like you've got a problem with your homework."

Kazi nodded. "Yeah, and it's only the first day!" He held the book up. "Do you know what a thesis statement is?"

"It's a sentence that gives an idea of what the rest of the paragraph is about."

"Oh!" Kazi still looked blank.

"I'll show you." The boy leant over and skimmed the paragraph in Kazi's book. "That sentence," he pointed.

Kazi read the sentence. "Oh, thanks. Now I understand. This is so different to what we learnt at my previous school, I feel stupid," he admitted.

"Farm school was it?" the boy asked with a knowing smile, and Kazi nodded.

"Don't worry, with a bit of hard work you'll catch up."

"Why do we have to take English anyway? Why can't our books be in Afrikaans like in junior school?"

"My father says that Afrikaans is the oppressor's language," the boy replied, obviously using words his father used, "and we must study English if we want to get anywhere in life. He also says that when we take over the government, English is going to be the main language in South Africa. And my father would know." The boy squared his shoulders. "He's head of the African National Congress in Brits," he said proudly.

"The ANC," Kazi whispered, from habit. He looked around to see if anyone had overheard them talking about the banned political party[3].

The bell rang and the boy stood up.

"By the way, my name's Saul."

"Thanks for your help, Saul, mine's Kazi."

The boy grinned, "I'll see you around."

Kazi nodded. "See you," he said, collecting his books.

---

[3] Together with other anti-apartheid groups, the ANC had been banned since the early 1960's, when the ANC represented the main force of opposition against the government.

part two

the struggle

THIRTEEN

SCORCHED HEARTS

1985 · 1986 · 1987 · 1988 · 1989 · **1990** · 1991 · 1992 · 1993

During the course of the boys' first year in high school, President de Klerk came into power and followed President Botha's mission to dismantle apartheid. Early in 1990, with mounting international and local pressure, he lifted the ban on anti-apartheid groups, including the ANC, and promised to release Nelson Mandela, the leader of the banned ANC's armed wing, Umkhonto we Sizwe.

Mandela had been imprisoned when he'd coordinated sabotage campaigns against military and government targets, in an attempt to force the government to abandon apartheid. He had received a life sentence. In the mid 1980's violence had escalated across the country and, to appease the black population, President Botha had offered to release him from prison on condition he reject violence as a political weapon. Mandela had spurned the offer, because the ANC remained banned. In 1989 F. W. de Klerk came into power and he had moved quickly to end the political stalemate by dismantling apartheid.

With mounting international and local pressure, he also lifted the thirty-year ban on leading anti-apartheid groups and Mandela was now going to be released after twenty-seven years in jail.

On the day he was to be freed, the 11th day of February, Scott was home and Kazi walked down the slope to the farmhouse. When he knocked, Scott opened the door.

"Hey, long time no see!" He draped his arm over Kazi's shoulders and drew him towards the living room. "You're just in time to hear Nelson Mandela's speech."

When Scott and Kazi walked into the living room, the Finleys and Caitlin's cousin Sue-Sue, who was visiting again, were watching the event on television. Sue-Sue's hair was a mass of bleached-blond curls, her eyelashes unnaturally long.

On television, a motorcade drew up outside the Grand Parade in Cape Town. Scott and Kazi sat down as Nelson Mandela climbed out of one of the cars. At seventy-one he was greying, but he moved with energy. Everyone leant forward. This was the man whose photograph had been banned from publication for twenty-seven years, whose words had been censured. He had missed the death sentence by the Grace of God, and everyone wanted to know if he had been broken during his incarceration. Beaming, he walked up to the balcony, raised his right fist in the ANC power salute, and called out *"Amandla!"* He was not timid, or cowed by what he'd been through.

The crowd answered, *"Ngawethu!"*

"iAfrika!" Mandela yelled.

"Mayibuye!" the crowd yelled together.

"Kazi, what are they saying?" Caitlin asked.

Kazi translated. "Mandela said 'Power' and the people answered, 'Is ours.' Then Mandela replied, 'Africa' and they answered him, 'Let it come back.'"

Nelson Mandela held up his arms and the crowd settled. He reached into his pocket for his glasses, but they weren't there. His wife Winnie gave him hers, and he began his speech. He thanked the different parties that supported his release, the people and his family. To begin with he was stiff and serious, but as he spoke his voice gained power. All eyes were on him. Then he looked out across the masses and he told the people, "Apartheid has no future in South Africa; the people must not let up their campaign of mass action." He sounded militant, still prepared to die in the struggle against black domination.

Sue-Sue exploded. "They should've executed the bastard when they had the chance. He's a bloody terrorist, and now he's out of jail and back to his old antics urging the blacks to take action."

Garth lifted a finger. "Shhh, we're listening."

Caitlin's cousin pursed her lips, which made her look like she had sucked on a lemon, but she kept quiet.

The crowd on television shouted in unison, some of them raised clenched fists. Nelson Mandela had become a martyr in their eyes; he had been willing to give up his life for their freedom. Mandela let them settle and then he told them that De Klerk had gone further than any other minister, but the sight of freedom looming should encourage them to redouble their efforts. In enthusiastic agreement the crowd began to sing the ANC freedom song, and then Mandela addressed the white people in South Africa.

He said, "No man or woman who has abandoned apartheid will be excluded from our movement towards a non-racial, united and democratic South Africa based on one-person, one-vote."

The speech ended and in the silence crickets could be heard chirring outside the Finley's living room.

"Fuh," Caitlin's cousin broke the silence. "One man one vote... how can black people be expected to know who to vote for? They're uneducated. What the hell do they know about politics? Mandela is a terrorist and the Nats should've thrown the keys away," she said, referring to the Nationalist Party that was in power when Nelson Mandela was imprisoned.

"We had a debate at school yesterday," Shanon's tone was innocent, but her eyes said otherwise. "Nelson Mandela, terrorist or freedom fighter."

"What side were you on?" Sue-Sue asked.

"Freedom fighter," Shanon replied with a sweet smile.

Caitlin's cousin glared, and Kazi privately applauded Shanon – Sue-Sue always acted as if he wasn't in the room, or that he was too stupid to understand.

"He's a bloody terrorist," Sue-Sue repeated, as if she had the winning argument.

Caitlin ignored her cousin. "Do you think Mandela's release will be a step towards peaceful negotiation?"

Garth shook his head, "There's no easy answer. It's going to be a difficult road ahead for black and white people in South Africa. I think the country is going to be split apart, not only through racial conflicts, but also through tribal differences. There's going to be bloodshed before this is over."

Scott looked at Kazi and indicated that he wanted to leave.

The two boys were still close friends in spite of the continuing problems in the country. Garth had predicted change when they first started school nine years ago and there had been some change. But there was still segregation in the most important areas – black people could not vote, and could not own land. Mandela's release was a step in the right direction, but discontent was building, resistance movements were stockpiling arms caches and there were boycotts and strikes. The country was turning into a political hotbed and the world was turning an angry focus on the antiquated rules of apartheid. It was the conversation at every dinner table, around every *lapa* fire and a continuing conversation in the Finley house.

Kazi got up and followed Scott. They had decided to hike up the mountain and Scott picked up a rucksack and slung it onto his back.

They climbed in silence. Tumbleweed roller-coasted down the hill, clouds were building to the west, but overhead the sky was clear. It was hot and Kazi walked ahead, hunting out the easiest route over rocks and through the bush. Scott followed a few paces behind, his feet seeking the same footholds that Kazi had used. When they reached the site where Juby's hut had stood they noticed a pile of stones marking the spot, probably placed there by Caitlin, and they sat down next to each other in the shade of a Kippersol tree. It didn't offer much shade, but it was enough for the two of them.

Kazi pointed. "That's where I was found," he said, referring to the time when he was a toddler and had wandered away from his mother. His parents and Caitlin had told him the story many times over the years, and he knew it by heart.

Scott knew the story, too. He looked at the fence. "I wonder how you walked so far."

"I've often thought about that. I must have been a tough kid. I was only two years old."

"Damn lucky they found you." Scott took two cans of Coke out of his rucksack. "Here," he said, handing one to Kazi.

Kazi wiped his hands over the moisture that clung to the outside and spread it over his face and neck.

Scott took a long swallow of his, then, fishing a stick of *biltong* and a pocket knife out of his rucksack, cut thick slices of the dried meat, and gave some to Kazi.

A baboon barked and a bird whistled three clear notes, *"piet-my-vrou, piet-my-vrou."*

Scott sighed, "I wish I didn't have to go back to school. I just want to stay here."

Nearly two months later, Mr. Mgani walked into the classroom to the usual end of day racket.

"Students!" he yelled, looking over the tops of his glasses while he waited for them to quieten down. "I've heard talk of school boycotts and strikes to force the government to change. I'm personally not in agreement with school boycotts. They can strike and do what they want, but you children are the future brains of this country, and you must attend school so that you can be educated. You," he said, sweeping his hand across the classroom to include them all, "have your lives ahead of you, and without education you'll achieve nothing." He paused. "You *must*," he laid the emphasis on the word, "be educated. You *must* be ready for the time when there's reform in this country. And there *will* be reform! Today we may not be allowed to vote or live where we want, but there's pressure on the government, and things are changing. We have people negotiating for change, and although you are young, you too must all work towards the day when we obtain our freedom and independence, and then you'll be the lawyers, doctors and leaders of our country."

He opened his mouth to continue but the school bell clanged through his next sentence. The scraping back of chairs and noise of books being hastily packed away prevented him from continuing, so he lifted his hands in resignation and packed his papers into his briefcase.

Kazi remembered his father's argument for a peaceful changeover that fell on deaf ears, and also what Garth had said about a difficult road ahead. He was old enough to understand and a curl of apprehension twisted in his stomach.

After school Kazi trudged up the road past the farmhouse towards home. He passed the gardener, Elias, working in the Finley's garden. He was a slight man, grey with age. "Hello, *Mdala*," Kazi said. He always greeted the old man in this way. Although Elias wasn't his grandfather, he called him *mdala* out of respect.

An old man like Elias ought to be at home resting his aching joints after a lifetime of manual work. But Garth employed him and others like him, because the work was their only means of survival in a country where social support was virtually non-existent. Not many people would hire him because of his age, but in exchange for a roof over his head, a monthly ration, and a small wage, he did light work weeding the flower beds and watering the shrubs with a hose. Every day he swept around the house and pool, even if there was nothing there to sweep, and every day he washed the cars whether they needed it or not. It wasn't what he had been told to do; it was what he wanted to do.

When the old man heard Kazi's greeting, he straightened and stretched pressing his hands into the small of his back, easing the ache. He smiled showing yellow tobacco-stained teeth, and the lines around his eyes and mouth deepened. "Hello, Kazi," he said, rolling tobacco into a strip of newspaper. "How are you today?"

"Fine thanks," Kazi replied. "*Mdala*, I see there's a young man staying at your house, who is he?"

"You mean Spyder?" the old man asked, smoke easing from his mouth as he spoke. "He's my second wife's son. He left years ago and she left too, but now he can't find work and has come back," he leant closer and lowered his voice, "Kazi, I have to say that it's not easy having a young man in the house again. There's only place for one bull in a *kraal*."

"I hope he finds work soon, *Mdala*."

"I hope so," Elias nodded and, as Kazi walked on, the old man pinched off the glowing end of his *zol*. Making sure that it was out, he carefully placed the unfinished cigarette in his pocket before going back to work.

At home Kazi dumped his satchel on the floor. He had tons of homework and wanted to get it done, but his mother had asked him to fetch firewood. It was becoming harder and harder to find dry wood for their cooking fire. He had to go further away from the labourers' houses and sometimes even up into the mountain to find it. He didn't want to go up the mountain today because it was hot, so he decided to go to the Black Wattle trees. No one was around, and it would be a good time to sneak off to the secret grove.

Jaapie, the old water diviner, had told Goodwill about the trees. He had smelt the highly-scented flowers and had tracked the smell to the five Black Wattle trees growing amongst a cluster of thorn trees. Goodwill had shown Kazi where they were when he was old enough to take on the chore of collecting firewood. His father had told him not to tell anyone about the Black Wattle trees, and to be careful that no one ever followed him when he went there. It was their secret grove. The reason for secrecy was because the wood from the Black Wattle burnt well with little smoke, and it formed nice, slow-burning coals. Everyone would want the wood, and if the other labourers heard about the trees, they would chop them down, and that would be the end of their supply. Goodwill had shown Kazi how to cut the outward growing branches at a forty-five degree angle, just above a lateral bud that would form new shoots next year. In a few years, those shoots would grow into nice sturdy branches again. Light cutting, he had told Kazi, would stimulate the tree, and if he pruned the tree the right way, it would be a continual source of new wood.

Before setting out Kazi took off his school clothes and hung them on a nail on the wall next to his bed, and then he pulled on an old T-shirt and a pair of shorts.

He decided to take the road down to the irrigation dam and, in case someone was watching, loop around to approach the trees from the direction of the eastern boundary of the farm. The trees grew at the base of the kloof that ran down the mountain from below Juby's house, the same kloof that fed the catchment area for the borehole.

He walked past the dam, reached the boundary and back-tracked across the open field. He looked around as he approached the thorn trees to make sure that no one was following him, and then he slipped through a gap and followed the narrow pathway he and Goodwill had created. As he went he hacked away encroaching scrub that blocked his way, and a few minutes later reached the trees. They had filled out well and he would have a good supply of wood for the winter.

Before he started he studied the trees, selected the branches he wanted to remove, and then he got to work with the saw. It was cool in the grove, and he spent some time working without getting hot. He pruned what he could, chopped the wood into lengths that would be easy to carry and stacked them in a new pile to dry out. Finally done, he tied a bundle of dry branches from one of his older piles, hefted the bundle onto his back and set off home. It was awkward and heavy and he had to stop from time to time to reposition the bundle. When he got home, he was tired and his back was sore, but he took the wood to their *lapa* and stacked it against the wall, then he built a fire ready for his mother to light when she got home from work.

He finished his chores, went inside to do homework until dinner, then went to find his friends.

He heard laughter and found them sitting around an enormous fire in Elias's *lapa*. As he approached he heard someone say, "There's Kazi."

The boy he now knew was Spyder called out, "Kazi, come and join us. I was just asking if you guys knew which girls were good for..." he made a crude movement with his fist against his palm. Without waiting for Kazi to reply he continued. "Fransina has obviously had a few men, and I prefer virgins. Then there's that fat chick Louisa, I liked her. She's got nice big tits, but I'm finished with her now. And what's that skinny girl's name, the one that lives in the house over there?" he asked pointing. "I didn't like her. She's too skinny and got no tits. Maybe she'll develop some when she gets older. I guess she's a bit young, but who cares, no-one's been with her before me." He smiled and pulled off his shirt and became engrossed with the firelight dancing on his muscles as he tensed his arms. He had obviously rubbed his skin with Vaseline or oil because he gleamed in the firelight. For a moment he was oblivious to the others while he admired himself, and then he picked up a bottle of Klipdrift brandy. He twisted the top and threw it down, and then he crushed it under his foot. He took a long swig without flinching. "This is good brandy. Anyone want some?" he asked holding out the bottle.

"Where did you get that?" someone asked. "Jackson doesn't sell it."

"I stole it from that house at the end of the road."

"That's the game farm," Kazi said. "How did you get past the hyena and the cheetah?" Kazi didn't like Spyder and he was sure he had lied about where he got the brandy. He also hated the way Spyder had been talking about the girls – they were all from Fairvalley Farm and the neighbourhood. Fransina wasn't a cheap slut who slept around. She had helped him with his letters on his first day at school, she was a nice girl. He had asked about the brandy because he wanted to say something to stop Spyder from saying these things, to show his friends that Spyder was a liar and a bragger.

"I don't know about a hyena, I didn't see one, but that fucking cheetah gave me a fright, so I slit its throat. I wasn't expecting a fucking cheetah in the house," Spyder said.

Kazi was suddenly terribly angry. He felt like someone had their hands around his neck and was squeezing, squeezing so hard that he couldn't breathe. He felt the blood drain from his face and pain build in his chest. He remembered the cheetah's name, how soft she had felt, and how they had played with her. She wouldn't have hurt anyone.

Spyder didn't notice his anger and continued as if nothing was wrong. "Did I tell you guys about the time that I beat our Shangaan foreman when I was working on the mine in Johannesburg?" He paused. "Makwe, put some wood on the fire," he said, as if Makwe was his minion, his underling at his beck and call.

Makwe didn't seem to mind. In fact he jumped up looking thrilled that Spyder had asked him. He fetched a couple of branches from a heap outside the *lapa* and threw them onto the fire.

A flame caught and as it flared Kazi noticed a seed pod, a curled grey-green Black Wattle seed pod, hanging off one of the twigs and he recognised the branch as one of those he had collected that afternoon. There was only one place on the farm where you could find Black Wattle, and no one else knew where that was.

"Where did you find this wood?" Kazi asked. If Spyder had been looking he would have noticed that Kazi's eyes were filled with loathing.

Spyder barely glanced at Kazi. "Up there behind the houses," he said, and continued the story about the fight with the Shangaan. It was obvious that he had no idea where the wood came from, and it was obvious that he had taken Kazi's wood.

For the first time in his life Kazi was so angry that his anger threatened to overwhelm him.

"You stole it from our *lapa,* didn't you," he said.

Spyder stopped talking and took a long deliberate swig of brandy. "Really?" he said his voice so low that Kazi was only sure that he had spoken from the movement of his lips. "Prove it, little boy," Spyder said, and a red flame flickered in his black eyes.

Kazi looked at the burning wood and a crushing rage overpowered him. The death of the cheetah, the demeaning way Spyder had spoken about the girls, the theft of brandy, and now the theft of his own wood was almost too overwhelming for him to contain. The crackling of the branches that fed the fire sounded like gunshots. He gritted his teeth, fighting for control. His entire body shook with the effort. He had to leave; he had to go before he did something rash.

At six thirty the next morning Maria knocked on Caitlin and Garth's bedroom door, "*Kok-kok* – knock-knock," she called as she always did when she couldn't knock. "Tea, *Missus.*"

"Come in, Maria," Caitlin said. Garth was in the bathroom getting dressed and Maria placed the tea tray on the bedside table.

"*Missus*, Elias said to tell you that his son Spyder is helping him today."

"Why does Elias need help? Is he sick?"

"No, *Missus,* Elias is fine. It's just that his son doesn't have work, and he wanted to come with Elias today."

"I guess it's okay. Thanks for the tea," Caitlin said, dismissing Maria.

Garth came out of the bathroom and drank his tea.

"I'm going to check on the level in the dam," he said. "Can we have breakfast early? I have to go to Brits."

"No problem. I'll jump in the shower and have it ready when you get back."

Garth pulled on his boots and whistled for his dog. Shaka had died several years before and Gotcha had taken his place. Caitlin heard them leaving as she climbed into the shower. She washed her hair, got out and, towelling herself, went to her dressing table. Then as she lifted the blow-dryer she caught the fleeting impression of a face in the mirror, a shadow that slipped away. "Spyder," she thought and got up angrily. She looked out of the window, but saw nothing. Perhaps she was just feeling jumpy, but she had noticed how Spyder looked at everything, absorbing the details. She felt bad that she'd jumped to conclusions, that she was suspicious. But she was sure the man had been staring in at her, was spying on her. There was that feeling that someone had been there, that fleeting glimpse that could've been a person, a branch moving in the wind, or the shadow of a bird. She gave herself a shake and decided not to tell Garth. What she could tell him anyway? That she had seen a vague shape in the mirror that was possibly her imagination?

Garth was walking back towards the house when he noticed a black man standing at his bedroom window.

"Hey!" he yelled and took off at a run towards the farmhouse. Gotcha sped ahead.

"Wat die fok maak jy? Jou bliksem!" Garth yelled. "What the fuck are you doing? You bastard!"

The man disappeared, the Doberman-Rottweiler on his heels, Garth racing after them. When he caught up, Gotcha had the man on the ground. It was Spyder.

"Down," Garth instructed. The dog dropped to his haunches, eyes focused on the man. The slightest movement would trigger another attack.

"What are you doing at my house?" Garth demanded. "Why were you looking through the window?" Adrenaline raced through his system raising his awareness. He could see the boy was up to no good.

He glared at Spyder who stared unflinchingly back, his eyes contemptuous. Garth felt blood rush to his face. His nails dug into the palms of his clenched fists; he wanted to hit the boy.

"*Nee Baas*," Spyder's tone was insolent. "I was just sweeping."

"If you were sweeping, why don't you have a broom?"

Garth knew instinctively that Spyder was lying. The labourers didn't call him *ma-double* for nothing. He knew when something wasn't right. He could sense it and often followed a hunch.

Spyder didn't reply. He continued to stare and Garth lost his temper.

"*Fokken kaffer, ek sal jou fokken bliksem*," he shook his fist in front of Spyder's face, and Spyder took a step back. Gotcha bared his teeth and gave a warning growl.

"If I ever see you near my house again, I'll beat the shit out of you, you little *tsotsi*," Garth yelled. "Now get out of here, and don't ever come near my house again." He stormed inside without wiping his feet, and left a trail of mud down the passage.

He marched into the bedroom and yelled, "That *kaffir* was looking in the window! What the hell is he doing here?"

Caitlin looked at him. He only used the word *kaffir* when he was very angry. She decided that she definitely couldn't tell him that she thought Spyder had been looking at her. If she told him she knew he would go after Spyder, and things were bad enough as they were. So she only told him that Spyder was working with Elias and Garth stormed back outside.

"Elias!" he bellowed.

Elias dropped the hose and came running, "*Ja Baas?*"

"I don't ever want to see that son of yours near my house again, you hear?"

"*Ja Baas*," Elias nodded and looked down, deep lines had formed between his eyes and down the sides of his mouth. If he lost his job he wouldn't have a roof over his head. "*Ja Baas*," he repeated.

Kazi avoided Spyder after the argument in Elias's *lapa* but, one afternoon as he walked along the pathway behind the labourers' houses, Makwe called him. Makwe's father had recently come to work on the farm, and he and Kazi had struck up a friendship. Kazi enjoyed his company and he walked over.

He was already past the point of no return when he realized that Spyder was sitting amongst the group of boys. Spyder had torn the sleeves off his shirt to show off his arms and was flexing his muscles as usual. As Kazi watched, Spyder's hand reached up above his head. He spread his arms, and then he leant forward, his fists moving, obviously describing his fight with the Shangaan foreman. Kazi sighed, *he's repeating that same stupid story*, he thought. He sat down and crossed his arms over his knees, pulling them towards his chest. Spyder barely looked up and, ignoring Kazi, finished the story with the powerfully strong Shangaan beaten and begging for mercy. Kazi imagined his own version of the fight and it gave him some pleasure to visualize the Shangaan punching Spyder full in the face. Spyder's nose had been broken sometime in the past, so maybe there was some truth in Kazi's version.

Makwe broke into Kazi's daydream and whispered, "Have you heard that Spyder's forming a gang? Are you going to join? I am," he said enthusiastically. Kazi shook his head – he wanted nothing to do with Spyder. "Spyder says we should drop out of school, and he'll teach us everything we need to know to join the fight for freedom. We're going to join the armed struggle," Makwe said proudly.

"Makwe, don't be stupid. You mustn't drop out of school."

"I'm not being stupid. He says he'll teach us karate, fighting, and about guns. I heard he's been to a training camp in Mozambique." In those days, Samora Machel, the Marxist President of Mozambique, hosted South African guerrillas of the ANC and allowed them to use Mozambique as a staging post for training and also for terror attacks in South Africa. "It was Russian or Cuban, I can't remember."

"I don't believe you," Kazi said.

"Well, we asked and he didn't say no, so it must be true."

Over the next weeks Kazi watched his friends, one by one, drop out of school and join Spyder's gang. They stole to support themselves and, one day, Kazi had to walk away when he saw a group of them go into a house where an old woman was alone. He had heard her mumbled protests and the sadistic laughter as the boys took what they wanted from the house. The old woman had followed them out into the sun with tears on her cheeks. Spyder's gang did what they wanted and took what they wanted. They stole from the labourers, the farmers, friends, and family. It didn't matter to them.

One day Spyder waited for Kazi to return from school.

"I want to speak to you," he growled, stepping in front of him.

Kazi looked over his shoulder, hoping that someone would come up the road. Spyder had been furious when he had refused to join his gang, and Kazi usually tried to steer clear of him.

"Tell me where the Finleys keep their guns. You're the white boy's friend and I know you go into their house."

"I don't know," Kazi said. Spyder grabbed the front of his shirt and lifted him easily off the ground. He leant in close, his breath on Kazi's face, "Of course you do, now tell me, you little piece of dog shit. Tell me!" he demanded.

"I-I don't know," Kazi stammered.

"You do, and you'd better hurry up and tell me."

"I promise Spyder. I've never seen where the guns are kept. I don't think they have any."

"I don't believe you." Spyder gave Kazi a hard shake and let go.

Kazi's teeth jarred as he hit the ground. He felt his school pants rip across the knee and a burning pain sear his hands.

Spyder laughed. "You're a fool if you think you can get away with this," he said and sauntered off.

When Kazi got home he didn't tell Goodwill. He had been raised to fight his own battles, and he would fight this one too. Spyder was just a bully.

The next day he caught the school bus as usual. It stopped and started and Kazi's mind wandered as he stared out of the window. Everything had changed since Spyder had arrived. Even the friends on the farm he had played with all his life shunned him now. He decided to talk to Scott on the weekend; he had to warn the Finleys about Spyder. Ten kilometres from the farm, Kazi was still deep in thought when he saw Spyder and his gang jogging on the side of the road. As the bus drew closer, Spyder lifted his hand and the group stopped, running on the spot, knees high, eyes forward, arms pumping. Spyder gave another signal, and they shifted into a sequence of karate kicks and punches. Spyder's eyes narrowed as the bus drew alongside; he stared at Kazi's face frozen in the window and drew his hand across his neck.

A shiver ran down Kazi's spine. The message was clearly for him.

That night there was the smell of wood smoke and a chill in the air. Kazi finished his homework and went outside to relieve himself before going to bed. He walked a short distance into the bush and, instead of going to the outhouse, stood behind a tree, opened his zipper and waited while his bladder emptied onto the dry leaves on the ground. The sound of it muffled a noise. He closed his pants and shivered slightly, rubbing his arms. He looked around and listened. Perhaps it was just a night animal, he thought. Then he heard it again, this time more clearly. It was a groan deeper in the bushes, someone in pain. He frowned and walked towards the sound. The bush thinned and he saw the outline of a man in the light of the full moon. He could see that it was Spyder. A girl lay at his feet, her skirt twisted at her waist. Spyder's pants were open and it dawned on Kazi that the moans could be those of pleasure. But, as he turned to go, he saw Spyder lean over and wrench the girl's knees apart, and heard the girl cry out.

Kazi realized that this was what had been happening – those girls that Spyder had been bragging about hadn't willingly had sex with him, they'd been raped!

Kazi yelled. He had to stop Spyder, and he ran forward.

The girl lashed out with her foot and caught Spyder on his thigh. He retaliated, pushing her legs down, pinning her to the ground with the weight of his body. He seized both her hands with one of his own, holding them above her head. He spat into the other and, using the saliva to moisten himself, thrust into her.

"Noooo," Kazi yelled at the same time that the girl screamed. He was already sprinting through the bushes pushing aside branches, as thorns caught his arms and legs and ripped his clothes.

"No!" he yelled again, "leave her alone!"

Spyder still didn't appear to have heard him and he yelled again, "Stop it, you bastard!"

Seconds passed that felt like minutes. Kazi was running faster than he ever imagined he could, but it felt as if he was in a nightmare where he couldn't reach his destination.

Spyder heard him and looked up, his teeth flashing in the dark. He held the girl and thrust again, his eyes on Kazi running towards him. He looked as if he was taking pleasure in having Kazi witness what he was doing. He ground his hips into the girl and she screamed a loud piercing cry.

Spyder smashed his fist into her face. "Shut up!"

Kazi leapt over a log. He was frantic – he couldn't get there fast enough. It was a nightmare.

Spyder held the girl effortlessly and thrust again, his eyes locked on Kazi. The girl screamed again and the sound was filled with pain. Spyder had a horrible grin on his face, obviously enjoying himself. His hips moved fast and hard. The girl let out another scream that pitched higher and higher, a sound of utter agony, and then it cut off to a silence more dreadful than the stiletto point of her scream.

A hot rage welled up in Kazi that made him want to kill. He raced the last few yards across the clearing and threw himself at Spyder, knocking him off the girl. He kicked him in the groin and pounded him with his fists.

"Stop it, stop it!" he yelled.

Spyder swung back and punched Kazi hard, once just below the heart, and once in the face. A terrible pain rose in Kazi's chest, and his legs wouldn't work. He slid to the ground, choking on the metallic taste of blood in his mouth. He looked across at the girl on the ground and realized that it was his sister, his ten-year-old sister.

"Ntokoso," he groaned, and she turned towards his voice looking at him with a look so filled with pain, a look filled with such horror, that Kazi knew what he had just witnessed would be with them both forever. He crawled to her and wrapped his arms around her, a black coal of hatred settling in his heart, a hatred he would nurture.

Spyder stepped back, blood darkening his thighs. He pulled on his pants and looked down at Kazi and smiled.

"The witchdoctor said a virgin could protect me from AIDS. I have what I came for, I am finished here." And he turned and walked away without looking back.

Kazi lay very still, held Ntokoso, and let the hate come in. He knew it would never leave him, and he did not want it to.

Ntokoso began to cry like a child. She fought for breath, snorting through her nostrils. Eventually her breathing slowed, but she continued to whimper. Kazi's hands clenched, he thought of the sound of Spyder's bone and cartilage breaking beneath his fists, of Spyder begging for mercy.

He realized he was no match for Spyder now, but the day would come when he would be strong enough to take revenge.

FOURTEEN

THE LEOPARD STALKS HIS PREY

1985 · 1986 · 1987 · 1988 · 1989 · **1990** · 1991 · 1992 · 1993

The next morning Garth drove through the village, through Skeerpoort, passed a deserted and crumbling building that used to be the café where, as children, Scott and Shanon had spent their pocket money, passed Scott and Shanon's junior school, and then the Afrikaans Dutch Reform church, where they went to church.

He could still remember the first time he and Caitlin had visited the church before they became members, how the congregation had turned virtually as one to stare and titter, "*Hier kom die engelse* – here come the English."

The Afrikaners spoke of Garth and Caitlin as 'the English', (even though they were third generation South Africans and had no close connection to Britain), because Garth and Caitlin spoke English at home.

Twelve years had passed since then, and now they regularly attended the church without the turning of heads or the tittering of gossip. They had been accepted, spoke fluent Afrikaans, and had made close and long lasting friendships with Afrikaners. Close enough to tease each other about being an *Engelsman* or a Dutchman – an Afrikaner – with the easy equanimity of good friends.

Garth turned onto the Hartbeeshoek road, pulled up at the general store, and parked in the dusty forecourt where chickens pecked for insects, and a mangy crossbreed dog panted in the heat.

On the bare cement porch in front of the shop, scruffy children argued over a handful of sweets, and a group of tired looking men leant against the railing smoking hand-rolled cigarettes. The acrid smell of their smoke blended with the aroma of curry and spice that drifted out of the open door.

A woman on a stool near the door was watching dust motes and, as Garth approached, gave him a vacant smile, then turned back to the spin of light and dust. In the dim interior, bolts of material, blankets, and pillows were stacked against the windows shutting out the light. Racks held hardware items and cookware, while another section was packed to capacity with fishing and camping gear. Floral dresses and shirts hung from the ceiling.

The shopkeeper stood at a counter near the door, and behind him were more shelves packed with cigarettes and food, and a large fridge.

"Mr. Garth, Mr. Garth!" Ahmed shouted from behind the counter, his protruding belly jiggling the folds of his Muslim robe. "How are you today?"

"Good thanks, Ahmed, how're you? I see your sister is well." Garth indicated the woman staring at dust motes in the doorway.

"I'm fine, Mr. Garth," Ahmed leant closer and whispered, "Don't tell anyone," he said in strongly-accented English, "but she watches everyone who comes into the store and lets me know if someone's stealing. She looks, well…" he looped his finger in circles next to his head. "But she's only deaf and dumb, she's not stupid. She just acts that way so that she can see without being seen. She sits at the door and gives me the nod when she sees a thief at work. Then I nab him likkedy-split. The blacks haven't worked out how I catch them," he chuckled and waved at his sister. She smiled back and returned to her daydream. "Miss Caitlin phoned with the list of rations and said that you must also bring milk, eggs, bread, and some of that special yogurt she likes. She said you had the wages cheque and gave me the breakdown."

"Thanks, Ahmed," Garth said. "You've saved me a trip to the bank. Oh, I nearly forgot, could you include twelve packets of chicken pieces for the men? They've worked well this month."

"No problem, Mr. Garth. One moment and I'll have everything ready." He yelled at a staff member to bring Garth's order and a youngster came from a room at the back carrying boxes of groceries.

"Put them on the back of Mr. Garth's Land Cruiser, hurry, hurry. And be adding twelve packs of chicken pieces. Make sure they're fresh, the ones from underneath, special for Mr. Garth," he instructed.

He turned and led Garth through a door into a small office, unlocked the safe, removed bundles of currency in five, ten, and twenty rand notes and, consulting a scrap of paper, gave Garth the money Caitlin had requested.

When Garth pulled up at the labourers' houses with the rations, Goodwill came outside and Garth beckoned.

"Goodwill, help me drop off the rations, will you?"

"Yes, *Baas.*" Goodwill climbed onto the back of the Land Cruiser, and Garth pulled away. At each house Goodwill off-loaded a fifty-kilogram bag of meal and a package of groceries that included tea, coffee, sugar, candles, matches, tobacco, curry, salt, soap, soap powder, and the chicken.

When they returned to Goodwill's house, Goodwill climbed off and walked around to the driver's side.

"*Baas* Garth, may I speak?" he asked.

Garth nodded for him to continue.

"*Baas*, it's Ntokoso."

"What is it, Goodwill?"

Goodwill lowered his eyes. "It's… well," he stopped and looked away struggling to say out loud what he had on his mind. He took a deep breath. "A man has forced himself on her, *Baas*."

"You mean a man raped Ntokoso? Who? Do you know who it is?" Garth demanded.

"*Baas*, we cannot say."

"Why not?"

"He is a dangerous man, *Baas*."

"Where does he live? Does he live on this farm, in the neighbourhood?"

Goodwill didn't reply, he closed his mouth and looked away.

"Come down to the house after I've paid the wages, and we'll talk about this further. Does Ntokoso need to see a doctor?"

"No *Baas*, Martha has tended to her. She knows what to do. Ntokoso is all right, but Martha asked me to ask the *Missus* for Disprin. Ntokoso has a lot of pain and is crying all the time."

"You should report this to the police. Go and speak to Martha and Ntokoso about it. We have to stop the bastard before he does it again."

"*Baas*, the police do not care if a black girl is raped, they will do nothing."

Garth looked at Goodwill. What he was saying held some truth; it wouldn't help to call the police. The man would be picked up and held for a few hours before being released, and then he would return to take revenge.

"I'll give you the pills when you come down for your wages."

"Thank you, *Baas*," Goodwill said. He lifted his bag of meal and rations and carried them into the house, and then he followed Garth.

Caitlin was in the shed with the wages book when Garth drew up. The labourers were standing in groups outside waiting to be paid.

Garth parked the Land Cruiser and went to her. "Kazi's sister Ntokoso has been raped," he said, in a low voice no one else could hear.

Caitlin's eyes filled with grief. She closed them, as if to erase the image of a child raped by a man from her mind.

"Is... is she all right?"

"Apparently she is and they don't want a doctor. I've tried to persuade Goodwill to lay a charge." He shrugged hopelessly. "I don't think they will. They're scared of the man, but I'm going to speak to Goodwill later and see if I can convince him."

"Can I do anything?"

"Martha asked if she could have some Disprin for Ntokoso."

"I'll go and get some, and I'll take them to Martha myself. I want to speak to her. I think Ntokoso is too young to have started her periods. She's only ten or eleven, but I'd better make sure. It would be dreadful if she fell pregnant." Her mind had already gone into damage control. "And she could be bleeding from vaginal tears. If she is, she must see a doctor." She was all business now, her grief and horror set aside.

"Here's the wages book, I'm going to see Ntokoso."

She turned and ran down to the farmhouse. In the kitchen she turned on the kettle then she went to the linen cupboard, where she selected a hot water bottle with a soft pink cover. In the bathroom she took out a box of Disprin and a bottle of Bach Rescue Remedy, a naturopathic remedy for trauma and shock. She returned to the kitchen and filled the hot water bottle with boiling water from the kettle and made a flask of hot cocoa. Then she went to Shanon's bedroom and selected a doll with a pretty face and a pink dress from a box in the closet. She knew that Shanon wouldn't mind if she took one of her dolls for Ntokoso. Shanon would have given it to Ntokoso herself if she'd known what had happened. Now that she had everything she needed, Caitlin placed the items in a basket, and walked up to Martha and Goodwill's house. She knocked tentatively on the door and a few seconds later Martha opened the door.

"Can I speak to you privately?" Caitlin asked. Martha nodded and the two women walked a short distance away so that their conversation couldn't be overheard. "Martha, I heard what happened last night. I don't want to intrude, but I have to ask if Ntokoso is bleeding? If there's a lot of blood it might indicate that she has tears inside and should see a doctor. She might need stitches and antibiotics."

"Nee, *Missus*," Martha shook her head, "she's not bleeding anymore, just a little bit at first."

"Okay, one last question. I know Ntokoso is young but some girls start their monthly bleeding early. Has she started her periods yet?"

Martha shook her head. "Nee, *Missus*, dit ook nie – No, *Missus*, not that either."

Caitlin sighed with relief, "Thank goodness, now may I see her? I promise I won't upset her by asking questions."

Martha nodded, "Dis reg, *Missus*," she said and Caitlin followed her into the house. Kazi was sitting next to Ntokoso on her bed holding her hand. His eyes were swollen from weeping, and he had a nasty bruise on the side of his face. It looked like he had tried to intervene and help Ntokoso during the rape.

Caitlin noticed but kept her focus on Ntokoso. She took the hot water bottle and placed it gently on Ntokoso's stomach, "When it gets cold ask Kazi to fill it with hot water again. It'll bring you relief."

She turned to Martha and gave her the box of Disprin. "Give her two every four hours. And here's a bottle of special medicine for the shock; she should have four drops on her tongue four times a day. Give Kazi some, I think he needs it too."

She put the cocoa on the table and then took the doll out of the basket. "Ntokoso, I know you don't want to tell us what happened but I brought this doll for you. When you're alone with her, I want you to tell her everything."

Ntokoso looked at Caitlin, her eyes large and frightened. She nodded and wrapped her arms around the doll.

Garth paid the wages and the men formed into small groups. It was common practice for them to combine the salaries of three or four men. Each man kept enough money for necessities and gave the balance of his wages to the person whose turn it was, in a three or four month rotation depending on how many men were in the group – they called it *gooi oor*.

Elias was excited because it was his turn to take all the wages. He counted the money as each man passed it to him, and placed it in his inner pocket.

"Come on, Elias, let's go and drink beer," Elliphas suggested.

"No, no," Elias laughed. "Not today. I'm going to Ahmed's to buy a radio with my money."

"Just one beer, Elias," Elliphas urged.

"No," Elias shook his head. "If I drink one, then it will be two and then I'll get drunk, and when I wake up, all the money will be gone. I'm going home." He went home and took the bundle of cash out of his pocket and looked at it; he needed to work out how much money to take to Ahmed's shop.

He left the money on the table, walked outside and brought his bag of meal into the house, then he went out again for his box of rations. He placed it on the table and rummaged through the box for his tobacco, which he placed in his pocket.

When he looked up, Spyder was leaning against the door frame watching him.

"So, old man, today is your chance for *gooi oor*." The young man stepped forward, towering over Elias. "Give the money to me."

"Please, no," Elias begged, his voice thin and pleading. "Please, Spyder, not this month. I want to buy a radio. Please."

"Why do you think I care? Give the money to me, you stupid old man."

"No," Elias whispered.

"What? What did you say? Are you refusing?" Spyder scowled. "Just so you know – I'm not asking, I'm telling you. Now, for the last time, give me the money."

Elias stepped in front of the table where the money was lying in plain sight; he hoped that Spyder hadn't seen it.

"I suppose I'll have to show you how to give it to me," Spyder growled walking into the room. He grabbed the front of Elias's shirt and lifted the old man off his feet. He pushed him against the wall and backhanded him across the face with his free hand. Elias's head cracked against the wall. His bladder released, and water seeped down his leg.

Spyder let go. "You're a useless old man," he sneered in disgust, and Elias slid to the floor.

Elias looked up at Spyder. "I'll-I'll give you the money, Spyder."

"Too late," Spyder said. He stepped forward and kicked Elias. The air whooshed out of the old man's lungs and he curled into a ball and coughed. Spyder kicked him again. "That'll teach you a lesson," he said.

Elias lay against the wall unable to move. The next kick caught him low on his back. Spyder turned to the table and picked up the money.

"Next time," he sneered, "you'll remember to give it to me faster."

Elias stayed on the floor. The cold from the concrete floor seeped into his body and his teeth chattered. He wasn't aware of how long he lay there, but gradually the shaking stopped and he tried to hear if Spyder had left. He couldn't hear anything and pulled himself gingerly to his feet. He crept to the door and looked outside. Spyder had left and Elias decided to go to the farmhouse. Each step was agony and he had to walk carefully, one foot carefully placed in front of the other. When he reached the house, he knocked at the back door, his body hunched in pain.

Caitlin opened the door. "Elias!" she exclaimed.

Elias staggered and Caitlin caught his arm. "Maria, bring a chair. Garth, come quickly!" she yelled.

Maria brought a kitchen chair and Elias sagged into it.

Garth hurried out, "Elias, what the hell happened?"

"It's Spyder, *Baas*," Elias's voice cracked. "He stole my pay."

"Bloody Spyder, all I hear lately is Spyder's name. I've heard enough! I'm going to call the police and have the bastard thrown into jail."

He strode off and when he came back he yelled, "Maria, fetch Goodwill, I want him to speak to the police too."

When Goodwill arrived, Caitlin was cleaning the wound on the back of Elias's head, and Elias was dabbing at the dried blood beneath his nose with a wet tissue. Goodwill reached out and gently touched Elias's face.

"Mdala, what happened?" he asked.

"Spyder," Garth replied angrily. "Spyder did this to Elias. The bastard beat up his own stepfather."

Goodwill looked down at Elias and shook his head. "I'm sorry, Mdala."

Garth turned to him, his lips a hard, angry line. "Goodwill, it was Spyder who raped Ntokoso, wasn't it?" he demanded.

Goodwill nodded. "Yes, *Baas*," he replied, his voice barely a whisper.

"Well, the police are on their way. Are you going to lay a charge now that this has happened as well?"

"*Baas*, I don't know."

"Goodwill, we've got to stop this man. I'm going to sort this out, once and for all."

Goodwill nodded. He walked to the low wall behind the kitchen and sat down, silent in his own thoughts.

After what seemed to be a long time, the yellow police van drove into the driveway, and Garth went to greet the two policemen. They spoke briefly, looked in Elias and Goodwill's direction. Garth pointed towards the labourers' houses, and the two men got back into the police van and drove off in the direction of Elias's house, dust trailing. They heard the vehicle stop, a brief silence, and then a man's shout. Raised voices could be heard, a door slammed and a few minutes later the dust plume headed back. The police van skidded to a halt and both policemen clambered out. One of them walked to the back of the van and yanked on the door. He reached in and carelessly dragged Spyder out. Spyder staggered and nearly fell, his hands cuffed behind his back, and a bruise forming under his eye.

"You the father?" the policeman asked Elias.

"Stepfather," Garth corrected.

"*Ja Baas*," Elias replied in a small voice, not looking at Spyder.

Spyder took a step towards his stepfather and spat, and then his eyes raked across Goodwill and he grinned. Goodwill's face twisted and it was obvious from the look on his face that he wanted justice now.

An angry dam of anger and hatred burst within Garth, and he slammed his fist into the centre of Spyder's face, following the punch with another. Spyder fell to his knees, his hands still locked behind his back.

After the third punch one of the policemen stepped forward and hauled Spyder to his feet. "I think that's enough, *Meneer*."

"*Ja*," the second policeman said with an admiring glance at Garth. "We should take this piece of filth away. Pity he fell down the steps and got those bruises. *Meneer*, you'd better bring those two to the police station," he jerked his head towards Goodwill and Elias, "so that they can lay charges. Don't bother to hurry. This one will be locked up, the longer the better."

Spyder turned his black gaze on Garth. "You can't stop me, I'll be back."

For a moment Garth had regretted hitting Spyder while his hands had been manacled behind his back, when he couldn't retaliate, but now Spyder had wiped out any feeling of regret. Garth stepped forward, his face inches from Spyder's, his hands clenching and unclenching at his sides. "If you ever put a foot on my farm again I'll shoot you, you bastard!"

"Steady there, *Meneer*, I think we can handle this." The policeman grabbed Spyder from behind and, lifting him easily by his collar and belt, threw him into the van. Spyder crashed onto the floor, slid to the back, and his head cracked loudly against the side. "That'll keep him quiet for a while," the policeman grinned.

When Spyder was released, he returned to the farm under the cover of darkness and no one told Garth. They were too scared.

FIFTEEN

INTRUSION

1985 · 1986 · 1987 · 1988 · 1989 · **1990** · 1991 · 1992 · 1993

At school Scott wasn't aware of what had happened on the farm. That night he was in a deep sleep and, when he woke up, wondered what had disturbed him. His eleven roommates were asleep and there was silence in the dormitory. Perhaps a bad dream, he thought. And then he heard the rhythmic sound of somebody masturbating. He pulled the pillow over his head and turned to face the other way. But just as he dosed off again he heard someone yell, pulled the pillow from his head, and looked up as a dark figure ran past. Footsteps receded rapidly down the passage.

He turned on his flashlight and looked around. To his left Michael slept soundly and, to his right, Russell was sitting bolt upright in bed.

"Someone was in the room," Russell said.

"I know, I saw someone run out," Scott replied. They both looked at the door. "It was a man, but he's gone now." Scott shone his flashlight further around the room and the beam picked out the pale outline of the boy in the bed next to Russell. He was on his stomach, his pants down, his bottom propped up and exposed. Both boys gasped.

"Damon!" Scott exclaimed.

Damon woke up at the sound of his name. "What's going on?" he scrambled to cover himself. "Why are my pants off? Is this some kind of a joke?" His words came out in short frenetic bursts.

"There was a man in the room," Russell said.

Damon's face turned a livid red. "How do you know?"

"I woke up and saw him standing next to your bed. I think he was jacking off."

By now all the boys in the dormitory were awake and talking excitedly.

In School House hostel, the juniors were separated into four large dormitories, with seven beds along one wall and five along the other, opposite a glass panelled, lockless double-door. The older boys were housed in Buxton House, except for four prefects who supervised the juniors. The prefects each had their own bedroom adjoining the separate dormitories. A cubby-hole with a sliding wooden door opened into the dormitory so that the prefect could keep an eye on the boys. This door now opened with an audible, angry crack.

"Why are you little scumbags making such a noise? Do you boys want to do twenty sit-ups and twenty push-ups, or run around the rugby field ten times, or both?" their prefect, Chris, roared with all the fear he could provoke. "Are you going to shut up and go to sleep, or do I have to come in there myself and make you regret it?"

The noise continued and Chris came through the door and switched on the light. His stare could have withered a thorn tree.

"Chris, there was…"

"Call me 'your highness', or you'll be my skivvy for a week!" Chris yelled. Prefects demanded that the boys called them by a respectful prefix, or they would be punished. When Chris was in good mood his punishment for a normal infraction was to fetch something for him from the tuck shop or to deliver a message. But when he was as in a bad mood, as he was tonight, he would invoke any one of a string of imaginative tortures: sit-ups and push-ups, laps around the rugby field, cut the grass with scissors. Sometimes the punishments were cruel and demoralising, but the worst of the punishments was to be his skivvy.

A skivvy had to wake up before the rising bell to make the prefect's coffee, polish his shoes, run errands before and after school, and generally be at his beck and call. It could last a week or even a month before someone else took your position, or if you did the job well he would retain you for longer. But if you did it badly he would double the punishment.

"Your Highness, Chris," Scott began again. "Russell saw a man standing over Damon jerking off."

"Nonsense!"

"I promise its true, Your Highness," Russell said.

"Was it a boy from one of the other dorms? I'll kill the little bastard if I catch him."

"No, Your Highness it was a tall person, a man."

"Who else saw him?"

"I did, Your Highness," Scott replied. "When Russell yelled, he ran past me and down the passage."

"I didn't see anyone when I came through. Are you sure?"

"I am, Your Highness."

"Did you see who it was?"

"No, Sir, it was too dark."

"Who else saw anything?" The other boys shook their heads. "Skivvy, where's my skivvy?" Chris yelled.

One of the boys stepped forward. "Come closer, man," Chris yelled in an even fiercer voice than earlier and the boy came to stand directly in front of Chris. "Go and tell the other prefects to search the hostel, and fetch the housemaster," he ordered.

"Yes Sir, Your Highness." Chris's skivvy darted out of the room before Chris could add a punishment for dawdling.

"You boys had better have something worthwhile to say to Mr. Connor, or my balls will be on the line for waking him in the middle of the night. And then I'll make you suffer. All of you."

The other boys stepped away from Scott and Russell. Even Damon stepped away. They weren't prepared to take on someone else's fight and be punished for it, no way; Scott and Russell were on their own.

The skivvy returned with Housemaster Connor.

"What's going on here?" he demanded. He had thrown a track suit on over his pyjamas and he looked very annoyed.

Chris spoke up, "Sir, Russell here says there was a man in the dorm."

"Russell, what do you have to say, boy?"

"Sir, I woke up and there was a man standing over Damon," Russell said. "Scott saw him too."

"Scott, what did you see?" The master turned the full force of his gaze on Scott.

"I saw a tall man," Scott said, standing upright in front of Mr. Connor. "But not clearly, Sir, he was running out of the room and it was dark."

"And the man was masturbating, is that right?" The master looked from one to the other. Russell nodded. "Did he touch you?" Mr. Connor asked.

"No Sir, he was over there," Russell indicated towards the bed next to him.

"Did the man touch you?" he asked Damon. Damon shook his head, but didn't look up.

At that moment the prefects come in armed with cricket bats.

"Did you find anything?" Connor asked.

"No, Sir."

"Sir, the boys in Buxton house said they chased someone a few weeks ago."

"Why wasn't it reported?"

"It wasn't confirmed, Sir."

"I'm going to phone the police. Boys, don't touch anything until they get here," he said, stalking out.

Scott realized that his heart was racing. He looked at Damon who was pale and shaken. "Come and sit over here," he said. Damon went across and sat on the chair next to Scott's locker. "Are you okay?"

"I guess so. He didn't touch me. Honestly."

"There's stuff on your bed," one of the other boys observed.

Damon shuddered and turned away, unable to look at his bed. His eyes filled and he glanced down so that no-one would notice.

The police arrived shortly and interviewed Scott, Russell and Damon. They asked a lot of questions and made notes, and then they removed the duvets and bed covers from all twelve beds in the dorm for forensic testing and evidence. After they left, Damon stripped the rest of the linen off his bed and threw the bundle of blankets and sheets under the bed. He turned and looked at Scott. "Would you mind if I sat in your chair again?"

"Sure," Scott said. "I can't sleep anyway."

"Nor can I," Russell said.

The lights were turned off and one by one the others dropped off to sleep. They were not allowed to talk after lights out, and it was taboo to be out of bed, but tonight was an exception. Scott, Russell and Damon had formed a protective triangle and were prepared to flout the rules. It began to rain, and they sat in the dark listening to the steady drum of the rain and the occasional boom of thunder. From time to time, lightening lit Damon's pale face. One of the boys murmured in his sleep and another tossed and turned, visited by his own nightmares.

"Would you like something to eat?" Scott whispered.

Damon shook his head. "No thanks." He was silent for a while and then he said, "I feel so dirty. I would have liked to shower and scrub myself clean."

"Nothing got on you," Russell said.

"I know, but I still feel dirty."

"At least he didn't do anything to you," Scott said, hoping that it was true, and Damon shuddered so hard that Scott could feel it from where he sat. Scott imagined how he would have felt waking up without his pants and a paedophile in the room. He wondered if more had happened that Damon didn't want to talk about.

"Do you think the others believe that he didn't touch me?" Damon asked. "That maybe I encouraged it?"

"I'm sure they believe you, and if anyone says anything different I'll set them straight."

"Thanks, Scott. I wonder if we can have a light on at night. I don't think I could sleep in the dark again."

"They'll have to do something."

Damon talked on in loops, going over every detail, sniffing occasionally and shuddering. Scott pulled out his tuck box, made a hole in the top of a can of condensed milk, drizzled some of the thick, sweet contents onto a couple of Marie biscuits, and passed them to his friends. This time Damon ate.

Finally the sun cracked the horizon and the three boys fell asleep; Russell and Scott in their beds, and Damon on the chair with Scott's pillow behind his head and Russell's blanket tucked to his chin. They slept until the early rising bell, and then Damon took his towel and went down the passage to the showers. When he returned he had scrubbed himself from head to toe, his skin was pink and he had a determined look on his face.

At school that morning all twelve boys from their dormitory were called to the headmaster's office. After retelling the story they were told their parents were coming to fetch them. The other nine boys were excited they could go home a day early, but Damon, Russell and Scott were subdued.

When Caitlin received the phone-call from the school secretary, she called Garth on the two-way radio.

"There's been an incident at the boarding school, we have to fetch Scott."

"Is he okay, what happened?"

"He's okay. Apparently a man was in their dorm, but Scott wasn't involved. It was another boy."

"I'm on my way."

Before he'd finished speaking Caitlin heard the aggressive roar of the Land Cruiser as Garth pumped the accelerator and shifted through the gears.

By the time Garth got to the farmhouse his relief that Scott was okay had turned to anger. He strode into the bedroom where Caitlin was throwing on a sweater.

"A child molester in the hostel – I'll castrate the fucking boff with my bare hands," he said angrily. "I can't believe it, a paedophile in my son's dorm. How did the bastard get into the school? Did you know that it happened to me? My housemaster wanted to check if I had swelling in the glands in my groin when I had twisted my ankle running cross-country. I was too young to know what he was up to, but knew something was wrong. I managed to extricate myself and it came out later that he had molested other boys." Emotions

165

flickered across Garth's face, from revulsion, to anger, to concern for Scott.

Caitlin was silent in the face of Gath's tirade. She was so upset she could weep. Were they telling the truth? Were they hiding something? Was Scott really okay? Even if he was, how was this going to affect him? A strange man in the dormitory! She wanted to bring Scott home, to keep him there, but she knew she couldn't. She had to harden her heart and keep her feelings to herself. But if the school didn't address the situation, then there would be no question, they would have to move Scott to another school.

"Did they tell you how it happened?" Garth demanded following Caitlin out the door. "I'm going to take Scott out of the school. This is not on, it's not acceptable. "

"Which car do you want to take?" Caitlin asked. Garth had recently bought a silver BMW 535i.

"The BMW," Garth snapped. "It's faster." They climbed in and Garth drove hard and fast, pushing the BMW into the corners, ignoring the speed limits and driving angrily, as if defying a cop to stop him.

"I wish both the kids could've stayed at home." Caitlin was miserable. "What can we do? We can't send him to Brits; the schools just aren't good enough."

"I told you we should've sent him to Kings."

"No! We've had this conversation before. We're not sending Scott to Kings College. I know you and your father went there, but I'm not sending Scott to a boarding school eight hundred kilometres away. I wouldn't be able to get there if he was sick or if there was something wrong, and we'd only see him during school holidays. It's bad enough that he's a weekly boarder, so let's not go there again," she snapped angrily.

Garth clamped his mouth shut and they drove in simmering silence for a while. They reached the school in less than forty minutes, and Garth went to speak to the headmaster. Caitlin went straight to the hostel.

Scott and Damon were sitting outside and Caitlin ran up the stairs. Scott got up and walked towards her. She hugged him. "Are you okay?"

"I'm okay, Mom."

Caitlin drew back. "You sure?" she asked, trying to read his eyes.

"I promise, Mom, I'm fine."

"I've been so worried. Come on, let's get your bag and get out of here."

"Could we wait for Damon's parents? I don't want to leave him on his own."

"Of course. Is he the boy this happened to?" Scott nodded and Caitlin walked over. "Are you okay?" she asked.

"I'm okay, Mrs. Finley," Damon said without meeting her eyes.

"Come and sit in our car until your parents get here."

"Thanks, Mrs. Finley," Damon picked up his duffel bag and followed Scott and Caitlin.

A few minutes later Garth came striding up and got into the car. "You okay, Scott?" he asked gruffly.

"I'm okay, Dad. This is Damon," he introduced Damon and explained that they were waiting for his parents.

"The headmaster says they're doing everything they can to prevent this from happening again. They're installing security gates in the passageways, and there are going to be security guards on patrol."

Damon's parents sped in and leapt from their car. Damon got out of the BMW.

"Oh, my God, Damon!" his mother cried drawing him into a tight embrace. "Are you all right?"

Damon's father looked at Garth and Caitlin, a muscle bunched at the corner of his mouth. "Thanks for looking after Damon until we got here," he said gruffly.

Caitlin smiled sympathetically. "Let us know if there's anything we can do to help."

Damon's father nodded and turned to his son.

Garth started up the BMW and drove slowly out of the school grounds.

"What if it's someone inside the school?" Scott asked, watching Damon walk away. "The security doors won't help squat."

"They're going to lock the dormitory doors, and the keys will be kept in cases behind breakable glass in case of an emergency."

"Do you want to move to another school?" Caitlin asked.

"I want to stay at home."

"You know we can't do that, we live too far from town," Caitlin replied sadly.

"I could stay with Grandpa and Granny, they live in Johannesburg."

"They travel too much."

"So what option do I have? I don't want to move to another boarding school."

They were silent on the drive home, each with their own fears, their own thoughts and regrets.

Shanon came home from school that evening and the next morning, with the sun streaming onto the veranda, she sat with Scott drinking tea in the warm winter sun.

"He didn't touch you, did he?" she asked, going straight to the point.

"No," Scott replied firmly.

"Good. In that case, I know you feel bad and what happened was dreadful, but you're okay and that's what you must focus on."

"I know, Sis, but it's easier said than done. I hate boarding school as it is," Scott said. "I hate the prefects. I hate the bells. First bell, second bell, everything is regulated by bells. I hate the food; I don't know what they do to it but it's revolting slop. And I can't stand hearing Beethoven's *Fur Elis* being practiced all day long. Over, and over, and over again. I even hate the smell of the floor polish in the corridors! I hate everything, it just sucks. How do you cope? You never complain, you never say anything."

"That's because I know there's no choice," Shanon replied pragmatically. "It's easier if you just get on with it, than let it get you down."

Kazi came around the house and sat down.

"Hey, Kazi," Scott greeted him.

"Hey," Kazi replied, taking his place next to them on the step.

"Want some tea?"

"No thanks, but I'll have a rusk," Kazi replied, taking a biscuit.

"Did you hear about Scott's incident at school?" Shanon asked. Kazi shook his head. "Tell him, Scott."

"A man broke into our dorm, a paedophile."

Kazi looked at Scott. "What's a paedophile?"

"A grown up who does bad things to children," Shanon explained. "Like touching them on their private places."

"Oh." Kazi didn't say anything more, he was thinking of his little sister being raped. Then he looked at Scott, "But you're all boys?"

"It can be boys or girls," Shanon said.

"So what happened?"

"He pulled one of the boy's pants down while he was sleeping and jerked off on his blanket. Or maybe the man touched him, I don't know, he didn't want to talk about it."

"Did he touch you, Scott?"

"No, the police thought he'd jerked off on my bed too, so they took my eiderdown." He pulled a wry face. "I guess I won't get it back, not that I'd want it after that. Ugh."

"What, that old blue thing?" Shanon laughed, she was trying to turn the conversation in a more light-hearted direction to make Scott feel better. "That's no loss, Scott. That thing was ancient, I think it belonged to Granny."

Kazi remained silent. This was nothing compared with what he had been through, but he didn't want to talk. Not yet, he still felt too raw.

"Are you okay, Kazi?" Shanon asked. It was unlike Kazi to be so quiet. And for the first time she noticed the fading bruise on his face. "What happened to you?"

"Nothing, just walked into a branch," Kazi replied.

Shanon traded a look with Scott and Scott said, "Come on, Kazi, let's go and look at the horses." He knew whatever was troubling Kazi would come out after a while.

Kazi nodded and the two boys got up and walked down to the paddock. Caitlin had bought two ponies for herself and Shanon, and Garth had built an enclosed camp and a stable. They were Nooitgedachts, a South African breed of Basotho-type ponies crossed with Arab horses.

The two boys walked past the Corral tree, bare at this time of year, and across the dry winter grass to the paddock and stood at the fence. Ruben, Caitlin's horse, cantered across the field and came to a halt in front of them. Shaking his big head, he blew air out of his nostrils and nuzzled their hands for food. Cleo, Shanon's horse, trotted up to see what was going on, and Kazi leant forward and blew softly into her nose. She huffed in response, her nostrils spread wide. It looked as if they were having a private conversation.

"What're you doing?" Scott asked.

"I'm talking to her. Try it."

"No thanks, she'll bite my nose off."

Kazi stepped back. "That guy at school didn't do anything to you, did he?" Scott shook his head and Kazi replied, "That's good."

"Kazi, what happened here this week?"

"You know Spyder, Elias's son?" Kazi opened up. "Well," he sucked in a breath and let the words flow. "He raped my sister, beat the crap out of me, then he stole his father's money and beat him up too. Your dad was furious so he called the police, and before they put Spyder away he beat him up, in front of the police. Then he threatened to shoot him if he came back to the farm. My dad told me."

"*Jislaaik*, Kazi, and here I've been jabbering on about some stupid guy that came into our hostel and wanked!"

"That's okay, you didn't know."

Ruben nudged Kazi and he reached out and stroked the horse's neck. "Why don't you ride?"

Scott realized that Kazi wanted to change the subject. "I guess I just prefer wheels."

SIXTEEN

STRANGERS ON THE DOORSTEP

1985 · 1986 · 1987 · 1988 · 1989 · 1990 · **1991** · 1992 · 1993

O n the surface everything was quiet on the farm. Scott went back to boarding school – the security doors were locked at night and so were the dorm room doors, but they offered little security as the seniors had duplicate keys and came and went at will, sometimes leaving them unlocked. Spyder was out of jail, but came and went at night like an invisible shadow. Elias was too scared to tell Garth, so Kazi stayed close to Ntokoso.

It was as if everyone on the farm had taken a collective breath while they dealt with their separate ghosts. And then the strange car arrived and disrupted everything. The black BMW drew up outside Goodwill's house and the shoes were the first thing Goodwill noticed about the two men when they stepped out of the car – they were shiny and black. Also their suit pants were carefully ironed.

Goodwill drew away from the window. "I wonder what they want," he said.

Martha peered over his shoulder. A tall, well-built African was striding towards the house, a second followed closely behind. The moon was full again and the night was alive with pale energy.

"They don't look like they're from around here," Goodwill commented.

"Maybe they're lost." Martha gave him an encouraging nudge. "Go and find out, before I do."

"Okay, okay, I'll go." Goodwill opened the door before the men knocked and light streamed out onto the two of them. "Can I help you?" Goodwill asked.

"You must be Goodwill," the tall man stated.

"Yes?"

"I am Vusi," he indicated the stocky man behind him, "and this is Amos."

Goodwill shook their outstretched hands but didn't move to invite them in.

"Um... could we speak to you for a minute, Goodwill... privately?" Vusi looked pointedly at Martha.

Goodwill stepped out of the house. "We'll go to my *lapa*. The fire will have burnt down by now, but it will hold some warmth."

He led the way and pulled three wooden stools closer to the fire. Vusi took out a handkerchief and wiped the stool before he sat, but Amos just plunked himself down and took out a packet of cigarettes. He tapped the packet so that two cigarettes slid forward and held them out towards Goodwill. He seemed to be a nice guy so Goodwill took a cigarette. Amos placed the other between his own lips, lit a match, and held it out. Goodwill leant towards the flame. The cigarette caught and he let the smoke flow slowly over his tongue, savouring the smoothness of it compared to the cheap tobacco he was used to.

"I won't waste your time, Goodwill," Vusi said. "We've come to see you because you're the *Maruti.*"

"I am the preacher," Goodwill admitted, "but why are you looking for me?"

"We need your help."

"*My* help?" Goodwill queried, glancing from one man to the other.

"Yes, Goodwill, we're looking for people who can organise meetings for our council."

"What council would that be? What kind of meetings?" Goodwill asked.

"You'll get all the information you need later. I can't tell you anything further except that we're part of a large organisation mobilising the people. Our plan is to force this government into negotiations for a free leadership."

"How?" Goodwill asked.

"Through our meetings. We'll arrange school and work boycotts, and massive strikes that will cripple the country and force the government to the bargaining table."

"What do I have to do with this?"

"You, Goodwill, will arrange meetings for us," Vusi said. "You see, you already hold church meetings, so the police and secret services won't suspect anything."

Amos leant in towards Goodwill. "We have lots of ministers like you who are organising meetings all over the country. They're persuading the people to take action. You see, it'll only be through militant action that we will gain our freedom from this racist regime. We have to stockpile arms and ammunition and, when we are ready, we will strike where it hurts most." He smacked his fist into the palm of his hand.

"I don't think I can," Goodwill said, shaking his head.

"What do you mean you can't do it? What are you worried about? You're an influential man, the people respect you and you have a clean record with the police."

"No, it's not that," he looked up at them, his face sincere. "I'm a man of God and I cannot condone violence."

"Goodwill you don't have to do anything, just arrange the meetings," Vusi coaxed. "We need people like you to get the message to the people. You don't have to do any of the fighting yourself."

"When we're free from white rule, the new government will give every black man a house and a car. You'll be one of the first," Amos promised.

"No," Goodwill shook his head. "I'm sorry, but I can't put my people in danger. I won't use my church for your meetings."

Vusi scowled. "Goodwill, you're saying a very stupid thing. Our council doesn't like to be refused. We'll forget what you said tonight, and we'll come back tomorrow." He hunched forward, his face inches from Goodwill. "Think carefully of your answer." He stood. "Come," he said to Amos and strode towards the BMW.

As he rose to follow Amos whispered, "Goodwill, don't refuse."

"What do you mean?" Goodwill asked.

"They'll come for you and your family. People are often found victims of an unexplained death. One man," he whispered glancing towards Vusi, "had a heart attack and fell into a fishpond and drowned. Ask yourself what the chances are of collapsing with just your head in the fishpond and not on dry land – one in a hundred perhaps? You understand?" he asked looking very serious. "The man didn't die of natural causes. Do you understand what I'm saying?"

The car started with an aggressive growl. The window opened and Vusi yelled, "Amos, hurry up."

Amos's eyes met Goodwill's. He gave a barely discernible shake of his head, and then he turned and hurried after Vusi.

As they drove away Martha walked out to the *lapa*. "What did they want?"

After Goodwill had recounted what had happened, he dropped his head into his hands. "I don't know what to do." His fingers rubbed his scalp as if he were drawing the pain of his decision out of his head.

"Goodwill, let's pray for guidance." She took his hand and they sat in silence, each praying their own separate prayers.

After a while Goodwill lifted his head. "I think it would be a good idea if we left. I can't do what they want, and if what Amos says is true, then we have to get the children and ourselves to safety."

"Where will we go?" Martha asked.

"To my brother in the Magoebaskloof Mountains. It's far from all of this, and no one will know we're there. Martha, go and wake the children. Pack only what we can carry."

He followed her to the house, went into their bedroom and slid his hand along the top of the wall where it met the sloped roof, until he felt the envelope he had hidden there. He brought it down and drew out the bank notes that were inside. They were pitifully few, but he placed them in his pocket anyway and turned to pack. He could hear Martha in the children's bedroom and their sleepy protests. After a while she came back and began to get her things together, her apprehension evident.

In the other bedroom Kazi stared at the small bag his mother had given him for his belongings. He thought about Scott and wondered what he would think of their leaving during the night like this, without saying goodbye. He picked up a schoolbook that was lying on the table. What should he take? He threw the book angrily onto the bed. "Why do we have to go?"

Dumani looked up from his own packing. "What are you worrying about Kazi? It'll be fun."

"And we get to miss school," Mandiso grinned.

Kazi glared at him. "We'll fail if we don't go to school. But I guess you're stupid anyway, so it won't make any difference to you."

"I'm not stupid, you're stupid!"

"You're stupid!"

"Hush children, don't fight," Martha called out from the other room. "Hurry up and pack!"

Kazi scowled at Mandiso and placed the schoolbook in his bag. He chose another book and sorted through his clothes, adding the essentials. He took one last look around the bedroom and, closing his bag, followed Dumani, Mandiso and Ntokoso into the living room where they waited in silence.

Goodwill walked in. He looked at them each in turn and then said, "let's go," and led them out.

Martha followed but at the front door she stopped, turned and walked back into the living room where she ran her hand along the back of the couch as if she longed to stay.

"Come," Goodwill said quietly.

She nodded, squeezed her eyes shut once, and then she switched off the lights and walked out. Kazi closed the door behind her and paused with his hand on the door handle wondering how long it would be before they returned. His gaze swept over the other houses. The lights were out, the inhabitants asleep. He wished he could have left a note with some kind of explanation.

"Let's go," Goodwill said in a low urgent whisper and set off down the road, his stride determined.

Martha and the children followed in silence. When they reached the main road they walked on in single file with the occasional truck or car whizzing past. As each vehicle drove by Goodwill lifted his thumb asking for a ride without enthusiasm

177

or much hope, and they watched as their lights disappeared quickly in the dark.

After a while Kazi took Ntokoso's bag from her and she smiled gratefully. She looked so thin and frail, and Kazi worried that she wouldn't hold out for long. He felt tired himself and longed for a rest. As time passed he kept his eyes on the ground, concentrating on placing one foot in front of the other, not on the ache in his muscles or the weight of the bags on his shoulders. He looked up as a large ancient truck lumbered past and juddered heavily to a stop.

"Hey, *baba* – friend," the driver called out. "Want a ride?"

"Thank you," Goodwill yelled back, and they hurried forward. Goodwill opened the passenger door.

The driver looked down at him. "I'm going as far as the Pretoria market. Kids can go on the back with the vegetables," he said with a jerk of his head towards the rear of the truck. "You and your wife can sit up front."

Goodwill smiled with appreciation. "Thanks," he said, climbing into the cab after Martha.

Kazi lifted Ntokoso onto the back and passed their bags to her. Dumani and Mandiso followed, and he climbed up behind them. Ntokoso moved over and he slid into the cramped space next to her, facing Dumani and Mandiso. They all had to bend their knees and it was uncomfortable. The smell of onions was overpowering, but when the truck took off, they were grateful they had them as a buffer against the wind. After forty minutes Kazi's knees began to ache and he longed to stretch his legs. He wondered how much further they would have to go, and peered through the railing. He noticed that they were entering the outskirts of the city and after a few minutes the truck drew to a stop.

Goodwill came around to the back. "This is as far as he can take us," he said, and they clambered down. Goodwill pointed, "The station is only a couple of blocks in that direction," he said, and they hefted their bags and began to walk again.

"Dad, how far is Magoebaskloof?" Ntokoso asked.

"The train goes as far as Pietersberg, about three hundred kilometres from Pretoria. It'll probably take us most of the day to get there, and after that we'll take a taxi to Magoebaskloof."

The train was divided into four sections: first class, second, third and cargo. The first and second class sections were reserved for whites only. Goodwill guided his family onto the train and they found seats in the third class section. The seats were benches facing each other, hard and uncomfortable, but Kazi settled into the corner and fell asleep soon after the train pulled away from the station. He woke sometime later with his head against the window and his shoulder stiff and sore where Ntokoso lay against it. He didn't want to wake her so he stayed still and stared out at the passing countryside, not really seeing anything. His mouth was dry and his stomach growled hungrily. Goodwill snored softly, his head back against the seat, his mouth open. Dumani and Mandiso were also asleep beside Martha.

It was mid-afternoon when the train pulled into Pietersberg and the others woke in blurry confusion. "Don't leave anything behind," Martha said, her voice still thick from sleep, as they collected their belongings and clambered off the train.

Kazi took Ntokoso's hand and followed behind Dumani. People jostled against them, and Kazi tightened his hold on Ntokoso's hand.

"C'mon, Ntokoso," he urged.

A big man pressed in between him and Dumani, and Kazi tried to get around the man, but more people came between them. He tried to keep his father's head in sight, but it moved further and further away until he couldn't see him anymore. He began to feel frightened and pushed his way through the throng of people, pulling Ntokoso after him, and then he started to run, shoving people out of his way. At last the crowd thinned and he stopped and looked around, his heart beating hard. He had lost them.

His eyes swept the crowd. "Where are they?" he asked.

"I don't know," Ntokoso replied in a small voice.

"I suppose we'll just have to wait here and hope they find us," Kazi said. They stood in silence, Ntokoso's hand damp within his own, as seconds dragged into minutes.

Ntokoso pulled his arm. "There! There's *Utata*, there he is," she exclaimed, pointing.

"Well done."

Goodwill was looking around, searching the crowd. Kazi waved and he spotted them. He smiled with relief. "There you are! Thank goodness," he said as Kazi and Ntokoso walked up. "Come, the others are over there."

When they got to Martha she threw her arms around them, holding them close. "I was so worried."

Goodwill said, "Stay here while I find a taxi. We can't waste any more time. We've got to get there before dark."

He approached a line of white mini-vans, and spoke to one of the drivers who pointed to a mini-van further down the line. Goodwill went up to the nearly full taxi, spoke briefly with the driver, and waved hurriedly for the rest of the family to join him. When they got there, Goodwill had already paid, and the man indicated that they should get in. There was an opening at the back and Kazi climbed through and squashed himself in next to a very fat woman whose armpits smelt strongly. There were four people in a row, five rows, and nowhere for his bag, so he placed it on his lap. It was hot in the mini-van and the woman's thigh sweated against his. He moved his leg away and hers slid into the gap, leaving him with less space. He shifted his bag into a more comfortable position and, after a long wait to fill the one remaining seat, the mini-van lurched into the flow of traffic, pressing Kazi against the woman. The stench of her armpits enveloped him, and he turned his face away. He caught Ntokoso's eye and wrinkled his nose, she smiled and his spirits lifted.

A few minutes later, the mini-van veered off the road to the blare of horns and the squeal of brakes. The driver in the car behind lifted a stiff middle finger as he sped by, but the taxi driver didn't appear to notice the commotion he had caused by pulling off the road without warning. He skidded to a stop, enveloping two men on the side of the road in dust. The men opened the passenger door and forced themselves into the already full cab, and the taxi driver took off again at an alarming rate, ignoring the other traffic, as if his was the only vehicle on the road. It had become obvious that the vans were operated on a fixed route, but there appeared to be no set stops. Passengers simply indicated to the driver when they wanted a ride or wanted to get out. Dumani turned and looked at Kazi, grimaced and rolled his eyes, and Kazi made a face in return.

As the taxi wound its way up the mountain, they passed the occasional waterfall that streamed over smooth, dark rock edged with lush foliage, and the air became moist and cool. Looking out of the window, Kazi noticed that the trees that grew to the edge of the road were plantations of pine, wattle or saligna. They passed the occasional sign and traffic became sparse as the taxi continued to stop and go, dropping off passengers and picking up others with complete disregard for other vehicles. And then it swung off the road. This time the driver pointed at Goodwill and indicated that they should get out. Goodwill opened the door and climbed out with Martha, Dumani, Mandiso and Ntokoso, but the fat lady had to get out before Kazi could get past. After he got out, she clambered back in and the taxi took off, leaving them all alone on the dusty roadside.

"Well, this is it," Goodwill said, looking around and familiarising himself. "Thank goodness we made it here before dark. I'm not sure I'd have spotted the sign for the farm." He pointed to a plank nailed to a tree and covered in vines. It was hard to make out the word Pinewell etched onto it. "Come on, it's just a short walk down that dirt road."

Goodwill's brother, Samuel, and his wife Edwina worked on the fifty hectare farm, which was planted with pine trees. The owner, a businessman, lived in Johannesburg, but when he was on the farm he stayed in a modern brick house that stood on a hill, where it took advantage of the view. Further down, two mud huts stood amongst tall pine trees, and a tendril of smoke rose invitingly from a fire outside. The walls of the huts were made from woven wattle sticks plastered with clay, and ethnic patterns in earth colours camouflaged the uneven walls. Course thatch covered the round roofs, and a wall circled the huts. A crude lean-to linked the huts, and the smoke came from a fire in the lean-to. Suspended above the coals was a three-legged black pot, and a smaller pot which stood next to the fire. Behind the walled *kraal,* a few thin goats, a cow, and two mules stood in a fenced enclosure, their tails flicking listlessly at flies.

When they drew closer, Goodwill shouted a greeting to a woman who peered out and a man who came from behind the huts. The man was lean, the same height as Goodwill, with the same dark intelligent eyes. He was dressed in very old corduroy pants and a patched jacket. The woman followed her husband more timidly. Her thinness was accentuated by a long wrap-around skirt, and she was wearing a threadbare jersey. Her careworn face showed the effects of years of worry and hard work.

"Goodwill!" the man shouted, striding towards them, his hands outstretched. "I don't believe my eyes! Is it really you?"

"Samuel," Goodwill hugged his brother, then his sister-in-law.

Martha stepped forward and hugged them both, and then she reintroduced each of her children, who had grown considerably since the families had last seen each other.

Samuel and Edwina didn't have any children – it had been a great disappointment for them.

"For what reason do we deserve this honour?" Samuel asked beaming.

"We'll talk later. In the meantime, how is our father and…"

Kazi half listened to the conversation as he looked around. After a few minutes he strolled away along a faint path towards a creek and walked along the bank. A light mist rose from the river, and the air smelt of pine needles and rich, fertile soil. He stopped at an old, gnarled apple tree, covered in moss. Ferns hung rootless from its branches, and he reached up and picked a small apple. It looked sour but he was hungry so he bit into it and grimaced. The apple was terrible, but he ate it anyway, and then he turned and walked back.

The murmur of conversation and the enticing smell of food reached him as he crested the hill. While he'd been away, the others had carried tree stumps to the fire, and now they sat on them close to the warmth of the fire.

"Kazi, I am relieved you're back." Edwina said as he approached. "I was worried. You mustn't wander off like that, you might get lost in the forest."

Samuel glanced up. "Edwina, he's a big boy, I'm sure he can look after himself."

Edwina ignored Samuel. "Come and sit down, Kazi, we are ready to eat."

The mountain air was cool and damp, so Kazi walked up and hunkered down next to the fire and warmed his hands. "Thank you, Aunt, I am hungry," he said. The sour apple had hardly helped stem his hunger, and he was suddenly ravenous. "I'm sorry I worried you."

Edwina nodded and turned to Mandiso. "Mandiso, don't play with that stick in the coals – you'll make sparks and set the forest on fire."

"There's no wind tonight, let the boy be," Samuel said, but Mandiso put the stick down.

Edwina opened the three-legged pot and spooned *mealie-pap* into enamel bowls. "I'm sorry I'm not more prepared for your visit." She added a spoonful of *morogo* leaves from the other pot and passed the bowls to Ntokoso, who handed out the food. "Tomorrow we'll have to slaughter a goat," she said, with an anxious glance toward Samuel.

"Yes, we will," Samuel agreed. "And tomorrow I'll go to the store."

Goodwill looked up. "Samuel, I'll pay for the food. We appreciate your hospitality but we don't expect you to feed us all."

Edwina looked relieved and Samuel smiled and nodded. "We'll work it out in the morning. Let's eat now."

"Thank you for sharing your meal with us, we are grateful," Goodwill replied, and then he blessed the food, and they ate.

Like everyone else, Kazi squeezed some of the firm porridge between his fingers and dipped it into the *morogo* before eating it. He took his time chewing and swallowing, hoping to cheat his stomach into thinking it was full because there wasn't much in his bowl, and he'd noticed that the pot was now empty. There would be no seconds. A mongrel slunk in amongst them and Kazi rubbed behind its ears, "Sorry little guy, I've got none left."

Once the dog realized that Kazi had no food it moved on and rubbed up against Ntokoso. She wiped her bowl with her fingers and held them out for the dog. He licked them and lay down at her feet hoping for more.

After dinner the women collected the plates and, as Kazi stepped away from the fire, he heard his father talking about the two men in the black BMW. He stopped and listened.

Goodwill continued, "…they want me to arrange political meetings for them."

"Why you?" Samuel asked.

"Because I'm a minister, they said I could organise large meetings without raising suspicion."

"So what did you say?"

Goodwill looked up from rolling a cigarette. "I told them I wouldn't use my church for secret meetings and put my people in danger."

"Is that when they threatened you?"

Goodwill nodded. "Yes. The man called Vusi told me that I couldn't say no, and then after he left the other one, Amos, said that I should be careful because they, whoever they are, would come after my family and force me into holding the meetings."

"So you don't know who they are?" Samuel asked.

"No, they only told me their first names. I'm scared, Samuel," Goodwill said. "These people are powerful. Amos implied that they have murdered people who... " Goodwill looked up and noticed Kazi. "Go and help your mother, Kazi."

"Yes, Father," Kazi said and walked away. So now he knew why they had left so quickly.

In one of the huts he found his mother, his brothers, and his sister stuffing hay into grain sacks to be used as mattresses.

"Where have you been, Kazi?" his mother said. Without waiting for a reply she continued, "Take this sack and fill it, but don't fill it too much or there won't be enough for everyone. You'll need two sacks because you're tall. You can lay them out end to end."

Kazi took the sack, pushed hay into it and then he closed it roughly with twine. He threw it down and started on the next one. Ntokoso and his brothers were struggling to make themselves comfortable under thin blankets.

"It prickles," Ntokoso complained.

"I know, just try and sleep," Martha commiserated.

When he finished filling the second sack, Kazi lay down on his make-shift bed. He thought about home and wondered if they would ever go back. He lay for a long time thinking of what his father had said, and trying not to move. He could feel Dumani's unnatural stillness next to him and knew that he couldn't sleep either. But finally exhaustion took over and he fell asleep.

SEVENTEEN

SHADOWS LURKING

1985 · 1986 · 1987 · 1988 · 1989 · 1990 · **1991** · 1992 · 1993

The next morning they got up scratching from fleas that had hatched overnight from the warmth of their bodies.

"I'm itchy," Ntokoso whined. "That stupid dog must've had fleas."

"Spit on your finger and rub it on the bite, it helps," Dumani said.

"Mom and Dad have gone already," Mandiso observed, spitting on his finger and applying it to his bites. "I wonder why they didn't wake us up."

"What would we do anyway? There's no school or anything to get up for," Dumani replied.

"I suppose," Mandiso's expression lifted.

"Let's go and see what Dad and Uncle Samuel are doing," Kazi suggested.

Outside Martha and Edwina were nowhere to be seen, but the smell of cooking *mealie-pap* came from the pot over the fire, and the men's voices could be heard from somewhere behind the huts. The boys walked in that direction where they found Goodwill and Samuel in the animal enclosure. Samuel was milking the cow. Goodwill was leaning against a post chewing on a stalk. He spotted the boys.

"Hello, sleepy heads," he called out, and they grinned sheepishly.

"Samuel," Goodwill shifted the stalk with his teeth. "I'd like the boys to help with the chores. Perhaps they could look for firewood."

Samuel laughed. "Wood is one thing we don't have to look for, we live in a forest," he said, chuckling. "I already have lots."

Goodwill grimaced at his stupidity. "Old habits die hard; we're always looking for wood. What I meant to say was, is there something we can all do to help?"

Samuel finished milking the cow and stood up. "Perhaps the boys could take the animals out to graze after breakfast." He held out the milk pail. "Could you give this to Edwina while I finish off here? Mandiso can stay and help me."

Goodwill took the bucket, and Kazi and Dumani walked with him to the cooking area. Edwina was busy with a broom.

"Morning, Edwina," Goodwill said.

"Morning, Goodwill, I hope there's enough milk for our porridge." She seemed to worry about everything, and their presence seemed to have added more tension to her already anxious nature. She propped her broom up against the wall.

"You can put the bucket over there," Edwina said, leading Goodwill into the lean-to. She lifted the lid on the pot over the fire and gave the porridge a stir with a long ladle, then she cupped her free hand to her mouth. "Come and eat," she called.

Martha and Ntokoso came out of their hut where they had been spreading Bluegum branches to ward off the fleas, and Martha went to help Edwina serve the porridge. Ntokoso followed and stood silently next to her mother, ready to help when asked.

Samuel and Mandiso came out of the animal enclosure. Samuel latched the gate with a loop of wire and they strolled across to join the others. Samuel had his arm slung over his nephew's shoulder and they were laughing at something.

Samuel, taking his bowl and sitting down, said, "Goodwill, we'll slaughter the goat this morning when the boys take the other animals out to graze. Martha and Ntokoso can help Edwina pick *morogo* and fetch water from the river. I think we'll go to the shop tomorrow."

After breakfast the morning passed quickly and by lunchtime, the skinned goat hung from a post with flies crawling over the freshly slaughtered meat. Another pot of *mealie-pap* and a pot of *morogo* cooked over the fire, and they ate it for lunch. Afterwards, Edwina washed out the pots and put a hunk of goat meat into the smaller pot to cook all afternoon. There were no more chores to be done, so Samuel suggested that Goodwill take the children to an outcrop of soapstone, a soft metamorphic rock they could use for carving.

The soapstone was a short hike from the huts and, when they got there, the children clambered around on the hill looking for loose rocks. There was nothing large enough, so Goodwill used the crowbar Samuel had given him to loosen some pieces, and soon had a nice pile to choose from. The children took what they wanted and, when they got home, asked Edwina if she could spare a couple of old knives. She scratched around in a pile of discarded items and soon unearthed four, rusted, blunt-nosed knives that would do the job without cutting their fingers.

Dumani turned his stone over. "What do you think I should carve, Kazi?"

Kazi reached for the stone and turned it this way and that. "Maybe a horse, this part could be the legs and," he pointed to a rounded lump on top, "this could be its head."

"Good idea, thanks," Dumani agreed taking his stone back and setting into it with his knife.

"And you, Ntokoso?" Kazi asked. "What are you going to make?"

"An ashtray," she replied, showing him a hollowed out piece of soapstone.

"Great. You could give it to Dad, he'd be pleased." He walked over to see what Mandiso was doing.

Mandiso grinned up at him. "It's a secret, Kazi. You'll see when I'm finished."

Kazi smiled at him and walked away. He didn't feel like carving. He felt deeply unhappy. He wondered if Scott knew they had left. Maybe he wouldn't find out until he came home from boarding school for the weekend. Mr. Mgani, his teacher, probably had him marked off as sick. He hadn't been gone long enough for the school to wonder where he was yet. Tomorrow, he decided, he would read his schoolbook and see how far he could get on his own. Maybe he would set up classes for the other three so that they wouldn't fall behind. He pulled himself short and laughed at himself for thinking he could persuade Dumani and Mandiso to do school work.

That night, broth pooled around the mound of *mealie-pap* in Kazi's bowl, pieces of goat meat sat on top, and globes of fat glistened in the broth. He ate all of the porridge first, dunking it in the broth and only when it was finished did he eat the meat. It was tough but good. By the end of the meal his stomach was full, and he felt tired and more content than he had in days. He thanked his aunt for the meal and walked off on his own, as he often did now. He needed to be alone. He walked towards the owner's house, which stood empty and dark, and lay on his back on the lawn. The moon hung in the west and stars spread above, and he felt better when he realized that the people at home on Fairvalley Farm could see the same stars. He lay on the damp grass gazing at the sky until he heard Dumani calling. He wished he could be alone but he answered, "Over here."

Dumani and Mandiso came and lay on the grass next to him. "Show us the stars, Kazi," Mandiso asked.

Kazi pointed, "That's the evening star – there, that very bright one," he said, repeating what he had learnt from Scott.

Mandiso grinned into the darkness until he found the star.

Kazi continued, "And those are the Seven Sisters over there. If you count them you'll see that there are seven stars," he assured them. "Later on we'll see Orion's belt, three bright stars in a row."

They lay looking up at the bright points of light in the dark sky and talked. They spoke about any number of things, but none of them broached the subject that was foremost on their minds: when they would go home.

They stayed until Martha called, and only then did they go reluctantly to their torturous beds.

The next morning the three younger children took the animals out to graze and Samuel hitched the two mules to an old cart. Goodwill, Kazi and Samuel clambered on and as they rode away Edwina called after them, "Do you have your jackets? Samuel you didn't forget your wallet, did you?" Samuel waved to show that he had heard her and that all was well.

The mules seemed to know the way to the store, so they trundled along the forest track without much direction from Samuel. The air was filled with the scent of pine, and Kazi sat on the back soothed by the sound of the wheels muffled by fallen pine needles and the cart's movement in time with the mules plodding.

After a while Samuel pulled on the reins and the cart stopped. He pointed into the forest. "See those trees?" he asked, and Kazi and Goodwill looked in the direction he pointed. Dozens of mature trees had been felled and left to rot where they lay. Vines and ferns grew over and against them, claiming them as their own. It looked like they had been there for years.

Samuel continued, "A woodcutter removed the safety guard on his chainsaw so that he could cut faster. There was a light rain, he slipped, and the saw cut his head off. Yep, right off," he nodded. "Now the others refuse to come back, they say there's voodoo here."

Goodwill shook his head. "If the cutters believe in voodoo, the farmer should call in the *sangoma* to get rid of the curse. Then they would come back."

"Hah," Samuel barked a derisive laugh. "The white farmer doesn't believe in what he calls mambo jumbo, he would rather see his trees rot." He clicked his tongue and the mules moved on. "The shop is not far now," he said.

They rounded a bend and the store lay ahead. It was a small whitewashed building. The inside was cool and gloomy, and the only light came from a grimy window and the open wooden door. The shopkeeper greeted them in the same patronising tone that most white people seemed to reserve for black people, and Goodwill and Samuel went up to the counter. Kazi noticed a pay phone in the corner and realized that it was Saturday and Scott would be at home. He walked over and dialled the Finley's number. Scott answered and he was relieved it wasn't someone else in the family. He dropped a couple of coins into the slot.

"Scott," he said when the telephone connected.

"Kazi, where are you? Your dad didn't say anything about going away, nor did you. What's up, where are you?"

"Scott we had to go. I'm sorry I didn't leave a note, I couldn't."

"Why? What's going on?"

"I'm not sure."

"What do you mean?"

The phone beeped for more coins and Kazi felt in his pocket for more. He didn't have enough, so he put the phone down. He was relieved that he had at least spoken to Scott. The conversation had been frustrating, but at least Scott would know that he hadn't just left without thinking of him. He went back to the counter. Goodwill was paying for the groceries from his envelope and, when he was finished, Kazi reached into his own pocket and brought out the few cents he hadn't been able to use in the pay phone. He asked for chewing gum and handed the money to the woman. She tossed the coins into her till, turned to a jar of gum on the shelf behind her, and took out a few pieces. As an afterthought she reluctantly added another and Kazi placed the gum carefully in his pocket to share with his sister and brothers when he got back.

On the return trip the mules trotted eagerly now that they were headed home and the whip lay unused next to Samuel. The two men rolled cigarettes and smoked, and Kazi took out one of the pieces of gum and leant back against the bag of meal. This time, instead of the smell of pine leaves, tobacco smoke wafted over and the men's voices lulled him away from his thoughts.

They arrived home and the mules stopped automatically in front of their enclosure. Everyone clambered off the cart, and Kazi offloaded their purchases while Goodwill and Samuel unhitched the mules.

"Goodwill," Martha shouted running towards them. "Have you seen Dumani and Mandiso?"

"What do you mean, have we seen them? You know we went to the store. They took the animals out to graze, aren't they back yet?"

"No they're not. Ntokoso said two men came and asked for Goodwill. And then the boys went with them to find you. Ntokoso came back by herself."

"Ntokoso," Goodwill shouted.

Ntokoso ran out of the hut. "Yes, *Upapa*."

"Who were the men that Dumani and Mandiso went with?"

"I-I don't know. They asked if we were your children and then they wanted Mandiso to show them which way you went. Dumani didn't want Mandiso to go on his own, so he went too."

"Oh God," Martha cried. "Goodwill, I thought they had gone to find you and would come back with you. Who are these people? I thought we were safe here."

"Come on!" Samuel said. "We mustn't waste any time. Kazi come with me, we'll run down the road and see if they are there."

"We just came that way," Goodwill reminded him. He walked towards the fire and sat down on one of the stumps. "They've taken them," he closed his eyes for a moment. "How could they have found us?" He dropped his face into his hands. After a while he seemed to pull himself together. "We must wait here," he decided. "They will come back, and I'll do as they say, and then we'll get the boys back."

Edwina took Martha's hand and drew her to a seat, guided her down onto it and stoked coals under the kettle.

Samuel sat down next to Goodwill. He rolled two cigarettes, lit them, and handed one to Goodwill. The two men smoked in silence and watched Edwina pour tea leaves into the steaming kettle. She added milk, a generous amount of sugar for the shock, and then divided the brew between six mugs. She handed Martha a cup, but her hand shook and the tea slopped over the side. Edwina knelt, her hands over Martha's. "Take a sip, it will calm you. We must have faith."

Martha looked at her. Her eyes dark, tears brimming at the surface.

Kazi hadn't moved and still stood next to the cart, the bag of meal at his feet where he'd left it. Ntokoso came and took his hand. She looked up at him, her eyes round and frightened.

"It wasn't my fault, was it, Kazi?"

"No, little sister, how would you have known?"

She turned her head into his chest and he held her tightly. "Come," he said, loosening her hands. "Let's…" he looked up and stopped speaking. There was a man barely visible in the shadows. He stood by himself under a tree. "Dad," Kazi yelled. "There's someone here."

Goodwill leapt to his feet when he saw the man. "Where are my children?" he shouted. "Who are you?"

The man replied, "Goodwill, I'm just a messenger, I don't have your children. I've been told to tell you to go home and follow the instructions that will be brought to you by the man named Vusi."

Martha dropped her mug and was on her feet. She ran towards the man, a tigress ready to protect her young, and Goodwill caught her arm. "Where are my boys?" she screamed, her voice reedy and thin with fear.

The man turned his gaze on her. "Your boys are safe. They've been taken to our camp and will be kept as long as necessary. Go back home and do the work you've been told to do, and your boys will be returned to you when you're finished."

"Wait!" Goodwill shouted as the man turned to go. "Wait!" he shouted again, but the man was gone.

Samuel strode forward. "We'll follow him."

Goodwill stared after the man. He shook his head, "No," he whispered. "We'll have to do what they say. We'll leave in the morning." He turned and walked into the hut and from outside they heard his grief break.

Dusk was falling by the time Kazi finished packing and he walked outside looking for solace amongst the trees. He noticed the soapstone carvings left where the boys had been working, and stopped to look at them. He picked up Dumani's carving of the horse and turned it over in his hand. His feeling of loss welled into a physical pain in his chest, and his throat ached from unshed tears. I *am* going to find them, he promised himself.

The following morning they woke to a light rain, and Dumani and Mandiso's absence was a hollow scream in their heads. It began to rain harder, cold hard drops as Samuel loaded their things onto the cart and took them as far as the main road. Goodwill's shoulders were sloped with grief and Martha, even now, was barely under control, her eyes red and bruised. Ntokoso stood straight and stiff, only her grip on Kazi's hand gave away her feelings.

EIGHTEEN

TOW THE LINE

1985 · 1986 · 1987 · 1988 · 1989 · 1990 · **1991** · 1992 · 1993

When they reached Fairvalley Farm they were drained, both physically and emotionally, and their house stood in darkness, the way they had left it. Goodwill put down his bag and went straight to the farmhouse. Garth's dog came to meet him, his hackles up, and Goodwill held out his hand. Gotcha sniffed cautiously, recognised him and allowed him to continue to the front door where Goodwill rang the doorbell. He heard someone approach and Garth opened the door. His eyes registered surprise. Goodwill had aged in a matter of days – he was thinner and his cheekbones stood out above hollowed cheeks.

"Where have you been?" he asked.

"To see my brother, *Baas*," his eyes slid away from Garth's. "He was sick. I had to go to him."

"But why didn't you tell me, or at least Jackson?"

"I had to leave in a hurry, *Baas*," Goodwill replied.

Garth looked perplexed. "I don't understand; you've worked for me for fourteen years and you've never done something like this before. I would've given you time off if you'd asked."

"Sorry, *Baas*."

"You do understand that you can't just leave without explanation?"

"Sorry, *Baas*," Goodwill repeated. He rubbed his hands, constantly moving them, one over the other.

Garth noticed the nervous movement and the dark smudges under Goodwill's eyes. "What is it, Goodwill?" he asked. "What's going on?"

Goodwill looked at him. "Nothing, *Baas*." And then he dropped his eyes, but Garth had already seen the pain that lay there. When he realized that Goodwill wasn't going to say anything further, he nodded.

"Okay, we'll leave it at that. Go home and get back to work tomorrow then."

A week later Garth found Jackson alone in the workshop. "Jackson," he said, "What's going on with Goodwill? Since he came back he's been acting strangely. Sometimes he doesn't seem to be listening when I speak to him."

"I know, *Baas*. Maybe it's because he left two of his children with his brother. He told me they were sick and had to stay there, but I think there's something odd about his story, and Nelly says Martha cries all the time." He shook his head. "Neither of them will talk about it."

"Perhaps I should tell him to go and fetch the children, they must be better by now. I suppose he doesn't want to ask for more time off after what happened. Come with me and we'll speak to him."

Together they walked to the brickyard where Goodwill was working. He looked up at their approach.

"Goodwill," Garth said. "You've not been yourself since you came back. Take a few days off, go and fetch your children."

Goodwill thought for a moment and a muscle bunched in the corner of his mouth. "Thank you, *Baas,* but I think it would be best for them to stay there for now." He turned away politely, signifying the end of the discussion.

Garth looked at Jackson and shrugged. "Right, if that's what you want. Let me know if you change your mind."

Goodwill straightened and turned again to face Garth. "*Baas...*" He stopped and took a deep breath. "I'd like to arrange a church meeting this Friday night if that's all right with the *Baas.*"

Garth smiled. "Of course it's all right," he said with a feeling of relief. Perhaps he'd been wrong to worry about Goodwill.

Every Friday after that, Goodwill held a meeting. On the fourth Friday, towards midnight, the sound of drums and chanting woke Caitlin. She realized that Garth was already awake and could sense his tension.

"You're awake," she said.

"I am." Garth slid his arm around her waist and pulled her closer. "I can't sleep with that noise. It's the same kind of chanting and drums as when my dad used to go out at night to the riots when he was a police reservist in Rhodesia."

"Do you think these meetings might be political?"

"I'm not sure," Garth replied, "but there are a lot of strange things happening."

Caitlin sighed. "I agree. Goodwill's church meetings used to be only for the locals. Now people come in cars."

"I don't think these are ordinary church meetings," Garth said. "And there's one particular car I've noticed every time, a black BMW with two sleazy looking guys. I've a feeling they have something to do with this."

"But Goodwill's been with us at Fairvalley since we moved here. He's always been trustworthy. Surely he can't be involved in something bad."

"I don't know," Garth rolled onto his back and folded his hands under his head. "I'm not sure if I understand any of this." There was silence while they listened to the toi-toi of drums and distant chanting. "And I don't think Goodwill's children are really with their uncle. I wonder…"

"Why don't you ask him?" Caitlin suggested.

"I can't. Ever since he came back he's been distant and… I don't know how to describe it."

"Something's wrong, maybe you should put a stop to the meetings."

"I can't do that, Caitlin, not without proof."

"Well, I'm scared. Old man Smit and his wife were attacked last week, and someone broke into Johan's house. Let's at least put up a security fence."

"That's a good idea." Garth said. "We should both get revolvers too, just in case." He turned over and spooned his body around hers.

"Did you hear about the Schuttes?" she asked, referring to farmers that lived nearby. "Five blacks broke into the house while they were asleep. They beat him up with his own gun, and she said they would have shot him if they'd worked out how to release the safety catch. Garth, they tied her to the coffee table with ties and belts and threatened to rape her. Thank goodness they didn't, and luckily their children didn't wake up."

"I heard about it. Please let's not talk about this now, let's go to sleep."

"Did I tell you about Makwe?"

"No, you didn't," Garth sighed. It would have been better to talk about these things during the day.

"Makwe told me he couldn't read the blackboard, said he needed glasses. I asked if he had a letter from his teacher, but he couldn't produce one. Anyway I said I'd send him for an eye test, but he was insistent that I go with him. I don't know why, but I felt uneasy, and the more insistent he became the more uneasy I became. I couldn't understand why he wanted me to go with him." Garth sensed her shaking her head in disbelief. "I know I shouldn't be afraid of Makwe, he's just a teenager. But there was just something in the way that he looked at me, something in his attitude that I didn't trust. Maybe it's because I saw him with Spyder's gang that I'm suspicious. Garth, is this how things are going to be now? I don't feel I can trust the blacks anymore. I used to think that if I was good to them, they would be good to me, but I don't think there's any loyalty anymore."

"Let's talk about this tomorrow." He turned her over and spooned his body around hers again. "I love you."

"I love you too," she replied and after a while she felt his breathing settle. He began to snore softly, but she couldn't relax and her heart quickened to the beat of the drums as she lay there unable to sleep.

Kazi and Ntokoso lay in their beds at home listening to the same chanting and drums that kept Garth and Caitlin awake. When Kazi had asked his father why the people hadn't brought his brothers back, Goodwill had turned away, seeming angry with him for asking the question. The drums were a reminder of his missing brothers. He wondered where they were and his thoughts of them tormented him.

Later in the night he woke up with a start, and realized that he must have fallen asleep because he could now hear his parents in the room next door, and the drums and the chanting had stopped. After a few minutes there was silence in the house, but Kazi couldn't go back to sleep. His mind churned with terrible images of his brothers, cold and hungry, held in a dark strange place with guards, possibly even beaten and tortured. They had to be found soon. He wondered who would help – perhaps Jackson or Garth Finley. Mr. Mgani's name came to mind. That's who he'd speak to, he thought, Mr. Mgani could be trusted. Kazi turned over, smiled to himself and resolved to go back to sleep. On Monday, when he went to school, he would go and see Mr. Mgani and begin his search. His father's hands may be tied, but his weren't.

On Saturday Scott stayed at school to watch rugby, and Garth picked him up late. The first thing Garth did when Scott climbed into the car was to show him the brochures for the weapons he was buying.

"A CZ 83!" Scott nodded appreciatively, admiring the image of the gun on the front cover of the first brochure.

"It's a semi-automatic 38 special," Garth replied with a boyish grin.

"Hmm," Scott said, turning to the specs. "Nice," he said, when he reached the last page.

"And I bought this one for Mom," Garth said, pointing to the second brochure.

Scott picked it up. "A Glock 17," he said skimming the details. "Sounds like a nice light weight pistol for her. Don't the military use them?" He carried on reading without waiting for Garth to respond. "When will you get them?"

"When our licences are approved. Now check this out," he said proudly handing over yet another brochure.

"A 12 gauge pump action shotgun," Scott's eyes were shining with excitement. "Sounds like you're going to start the third world war," he laughed. "Can I try it?"

"I don't think so, but you can try out the 38 and the Glock. We'll set up some targets on that flat area above the house."

"That would be awesome, Dad!"

They drove in silence while Scott studied the brochures.

"I wonder," Garth was thinking aloud, "if I can get hold of some hollow point bullets."

"What are those?"

"They're bullets that expand on entering instead of going through. At point blank range they're pretty much lethal. In a life and death situation, I want to know that the first bullet is going to do the trick."

They drew up outside the house and Caitlin trotted up on Ruben.

"Mom, have you seen what Dad's buying?" Scott waved the brochures, and the horse spooked sideways.

Caitlin laughed; she loved it when the horses were frisky. "Whoa," she said, drawing gently on the reins. The horse calmed and she dismounted to hug Scott.

"You smell of horse," Scott wrinkled his nose, hugging her anyway.

Caitlin looked at the brochures. "What have you chosen?" she asked Garth.

"I bought a 38 special for myself, a Glock for you, and a pump action shotgun."

"Do we need so many guns?"

"I think so. When we get them Scott and I are going to set up targets up there," he said as he pointed to the area he was referring to. "It's a safe place for us to practice. It's also visible. I want all the blacks to know that we've got guns, and that we know how to use them."

It was a short weekend for Scott after getting home late on Saturday, and he had to be back at boarding school by 7pm on Sunday. Caitlin went with them for the drive.

On the way Garth asked Scott, "Have you seen Kazi lately?"

"No," Scott replied in a clipped tone. He was in a bad mood because he was going back to school.

"Why not? You used to hang out all the time," Caitlin observed.

"I know, but the weekends are short and Kazi's busy. I haven't seen him for weeks. Why?"

"Just wondering if he'd told you anything."

"About what?"

"Where they went when they disappeared off like they did, and why they didn't say anything about going away. And also, why they haven't gone back to fetch his brothers. It's all very strange."

"We're worried that Goodwill might have been drawn into something politically motivated," Caitlin offered.

"Why do you think that?"

"It's the church meetings; something's changed since he came back."

"Kazi hasn't told me anything yet."

"If you get the opportunity try and find out."

"Okay. Next time I'm home."

They drew up outside the school and as soon as Scott disappeared inside Garth and Caitlin left for home. They didn't have to take Shanon back to school, because she had started university in Stellenbosch, so they turned onto Grosvenor Road instead of heading towards Pretoria.

"I'm looking forward to getting back home," Garth said.

"Me too, it's a long drive. But it won't be long before Scott goes to university, then we won't have to do it at all."

"I can't wait." Garth glanced at the rear view mirror, "Get off my tail, arsehole," he said to a white Mercedes tailgating on his bumper. The Mercedes slid out to pass on a blind rise and Garth protested, "Watch out, idiot," he signalled his irritation with a finger, accelerated, and the Mercedes fell back. "Jerk," he added.

The Mercedes sped up and, as it drew up alongside, two of the passengers held up guns and pointed them in their direction.

"Car-jackers," Caitlin gasped. "Turn left – go, go, go!" She leant forward, her seatbelt tight across her chest, her hand gripping Garth's thigh where it had been lying relaxed seconds before.

Garth turned and accelerated, racing through the gears, and the Mercedes leant over hard as the driver executed a last minute turn. For a moment it looked like it was going to roll, and the engine screamed. Caitlin held her breath, hoping they would crash, but the car levelled out, the tires screeched and it was after them again. It pulled up alongside clipping the BMW's wing mirror. Garth kept his foot down on the accelerator. The Mercedes edged closer pushing them to the side of the road. The BMW's rim caught the sidewalk and their car bounced. One of the men lifted a hand and indicated that Garth pull over. Garth searched for a way out but the Mercedes drew ahead, slowed and pulled up at an angle in front of them, cutting off all hope of escape.

Garth swore viciously. "Phone the police," he said.

The Mercedes doors opened, and four black men climbed out and walked towards Garth and Caitlin. They all had guns.

Caitlin keyed 1011 into the car phone, the emergency number for the police. "Come on," she urged the ringing phone, "come on."

The men split into pairs and came towards them, two on each side of the car. The phone continued to ring.

"I wish I had a gun now, I'd blow these fuckers' heads off," Garth growled.

One of the men rapped on the window with the barrel of his gun. "Get out," he snarled, pointing the gun at Garth. Another man aimed a gun at Caitlin. She put down the phone and raised her hands in submission. Garth opened the door and climbed out, his movements slow and deliberate.

The man pushed him, "Get down!" he ordered.

Garth did as he was told and the man put his booted foot on the side of his face, shoving his head onto pavement. "So," he said, "what have you to say now that I'm in charge?"

Garth remained silent, trying to hear what was happening to Caitlin. The boot pressed harder and stones dug into his cheek. He heard a man on the other side of the car say "... get her pants off." Caitlin screamed and he heard a loud smack. He tried to move.

The man above laughed and ground his foot down even harder. "Move and I'll shoot," he snapped.

"Get the woman out of the car. We don't have time for that," a fourth voice urged. "Hurry up, take her watch and jewellery."

Garth heard a thump and Caitlin screamed again. "No!" he yelled. "Take what you want, just don't hurt her."

The man above him laughed a derisive, grating hack. He leant down and pulled Garth's watch from his wrist, reached into Garth's pocket and took his wallet too. "Where are the car keys?" he hissed. Garth opened his hand and the keys slid out.

The man lifted his foot off Garth's head, picked up the keys and kicked him, hard. "In the new South Africa I take what I want." He laughed again and turned away. "Come on, let's go," he called out, climbing into the BMW.

The other three scrambled into the Mercedes and they sped away in the two vehicles.

Caitlin got gingerly to her feet and went to Garth. She crouched next to him, "You okay?" she asked.

"I-I'm... just... winded." He took a few shallow breaths. "Hold on," he said gasping as he sat up. He reached out and touched the bruise forming on her cheek. "Are you okay?"

She nodded and swallowed thickly. She was deathly pale.

Garth grimaced and stood. "Feels like a broken rib," he took a shallow breath holding his arms around his chest. "Let's get out of here," he staggered forward, taking a few more tentative steps, "before the immobilizer kicks in and the car stops. They'll come back and shoot us for the code."

The immobilizer was an anti-theft device that Garth had installed in the car. If the security code wasn't entered within ten minutes the engine would cut out. The reason for the delay was that potential car-jackers could drive away from the scene of the theft, and not force the security code out of the owner. The car could hopefully be retrieved once it had been abandoned.

"Maybe we can get help over there," Caitlin said, pointing to a row of roofs above a series of formidable walls and security gates. They walked towards them, and Caitlin pushed the intercom button on the first gate. There was no response. She moved on to the next gate and a voice asked her identity but, realizing they didn't know who she was, ignored her. She went on to another gate, but it was the same at each; no one would let them in. Eventually a woman offered to phone the police, but left them standing outside.

A vehicle approached from the direction the robbers had gone, and Garth grabbed Caitlin's arm.

"They're coming back!"

"It can't be them, maybe it's someone else. Maybe it's the police."

"No, it's them. I recognise the sound of their engine."

"What are we going to do? They'll kill us this time."

"Into the donga, come on." Garth pulled Caitlin into the ditch. It had been eroded by storm water from the summer season and was about four feet deep. He winced as he landed. The bottom was now dry and khaki-bush grew up the sides and on the verge. Garth and Caitlin crouched low as lights cut around the corner. Something rustled through the dead leaves at their feet and Garth held his breath. A snake or the robbers

– which could be worse? Lights flashed over the grass and weeds above their heads and the vehicle drove past. Garth sneaked a look; it was the robbers' Mercedes. The leaves rustled, and the Mercedes slowed and turned. It drove towards where they were hidden and twin beams of light cast along the edge of the road. Garth's nerves strained tighter. One of the robbers yelled something in Xhosa and let off a shot into the air. The sound cracked and the bullet thumped into a wall behind the ditch. Garth pulled Caitlin towards him and her body trembled against his. The Mercedes cruised by for a second time, and then it revved loudly and sped off with an angry squeal of tires. Caitlin moved slightly and Garth's grip tightened on her arm. "Stay," he whispered in her ear. He lifted his head above the rim of the ditch and looked around. There was nothing, but the night was charged with uncertainty and menace. He waited another five minutes until he was sure that the robbers weren't going to return, and only then did he turn and help Caitlin out of the ditch.

The police hadn't arrived and probably wouldn't, so they began to walk. They reached a café and, although they had no money, the Greek owner let them use his phone. Garth called his father, who arrived after a few minutes. They didn't search for the car in case the robbers had it staked out, or were stripping it as they often did, and went straight to the Bryanston police station. A policeman asked for his identity documents to fill in the statement and Garth lost his cool.

"I just told you, everything's been stolen! My wallet, my ID, *everything!*"

"Well then," the black policeman sneered, "Come back tomorrow when you do have something to identify yourself with."

"Listen, if you send someone out now, you'll find my car before they strip it. I had an immobilizer, the car will be ten minutes down the road," Garth insisted, leaning forward with his fists gripping the counter. "You'll also get the identity documents you want – they're in the car."

"Listen here, you don't pay my salary, so don't tell me how to do my job." The policeman picked up a pen. "First we fill out a statement, and then *I* decide what I'm going to do." He shook his head. "I don't know why you're making such a fuss anyway. You're obviously a rich man. I can see that because you drive a BMW, and you've got a fancy watch. You can buy a new car with your insurance money. The man who stole your car probably needs the money more than you do."

On Monday Kazi dressed quickly and caught the bus to Brits. He sprinted to the headmaster's office and tapped on the door. Mr. Mgani looked up from marking papers.

"Kazi," he said with some surprise. "Come in!"

Kazi walked in, and when the headmaster indicated that he sit down, he did.

"What can I do to help you, my boy?" Mgani asked. "I hope you aren't worried about being absent last month, you've caught up already."

Kazi cleared his throat. It suddenly seemed so difficult. He felt foolish that he hadn't thought this through more carefully. Would this man believe his story? It seemed so far-fetched.

"Go ahead, Kazi," Mr. Mgani smiled encouragingly.

"Well…" Kazi took a deep breath. "To tell you the truth, Sir, I don't know where to start."

"You're one of my better students. I can't imagine what it could be that would trouble you so much." Mr. Mgani leant back in his chair, folded his hands in his lap and waited.

Kazi looked at him and plucked up the courage to start. When he finished his story Mr. Mgani was leaning forward, his eyes intent on Kazi's face.

"I hope you believe me, Sir," Kazi's voice cracked. Telling the story had brought his emotions dangerously close to the surface, and he struggled to contain himself.

Mr. Mgani looked down at his hands. He tapped his thumbs together and was silent for a moment, and then he looked up. "Kazi, I do believe you, I've heard the same story from other people. You're not alone." He paused. "I understand your eagerness to help your father and your brothers, but you have to remember that you're a child." He held up his hands. "No, no, don't take me wrong. Let me re-phrase that – you're a young man, but not old enough to tackle these people who are obviously dangerous. Remember they've already taken your brothers. There are countless extremist groups that are fighting alongside mainstream political groups who could be involved here. There are too many to name but the main ones are the ANC, with their military wing Umkhonto We Sizwe, and the Zulu Inkatha Freedom Party, who are trying to infiltrate the Transvaal area and undermine the African National Congress position. Then there's Apla, a part of the PAC, and the Azapo liberation army, to name just a few. Many groups have already started affirmative action to force the government to hand the country over to black rule. Because I'm the headmaster of the school I'm careful not to show an affiliation with any one group, but I have friends, Kazi. Perhaps I can get someone to go to one of your father's meetings. They might be able to get some information for us." He stood. "Kazi, we're both late for class. We'll talk again but, in the meantime, I want you to do nothing further."

"Thank you, Sir, I promise I won't."

"Good. Now go," Mr. Mgani said. He watched Kazi leave. He hadn't told Kazi that boys were often taken from their families and placed in rogue military camps where they became child soldiers, never to be seen again.

NINETEEN

THE GIRL WITH THE CARAMEL EYES

1985 · 1986 · 1987 · 1988 · 1989 · 1990 · **1991** · 1992 · 1993

Three nights after the car-jacking Caitlin moaned in her sleep, "No, no…"

Garth touched her shoulder. "Wake up," he said softly. Caitlin's eyes shot open. "It's the car-jacking, isn't it?"

Caitlin stifled a sob. "Those men were coming for us in my dream, and I couldn't run. I was paralysed, and then I tried to scream but I couldn't. It … "

"Turn over, let me hold you," Garth said. "It was just a dream."

"I know, but I keep reliving it; those men threatening to shoot you, and their hands groping at my jeans, trying to pull them off…" she shuddered.

"Shush now, try to sleep."

"I can't."

"You need a change. Perhaps we could go to Mossel Bay and get that same house on the beach that we had last time."

"That would be nice. School breaks up for the December holidays in a few weeks, we could go then."

When they told the children about their idea, Scott immediately asked if Kazi could go too.

"Where would he sleep? You and Shanon were going to share a room," Caitlin asked.

"We'll sleep in the den," he said, referring to the rumpus room where the guys threw down mattresses if there were a lot of people staying in the house. "I'd love to show him the sea," he added.

"What do you think, Garth?"

"It's a small town, having a black kid with us may raise a couple of eyebrows, but it's okay with me. I don't mind."

"I don't either," Caitlin shrugged, and Scott ran up to Kazi's house to tell him.

When they asked Goodwill, he was relieved. Kazi had been restless since they came back from Magoebaskloof; he tossed and turned at night and had been asking probing questions. He had looked after his brothers and sister since he was five, and now it was obvious that he still felt responsible for them. Goodwill was worried Kazi would do something stupid in an attempt to find his brothers, and he had enough on his mind worrying about Mandiso and Dumani, the meetings, and Ntokoso since the rape. It would be a relief to have Kazi in a safe place for a while. He was holding the meetings and doing as he was told; hopefully Dumani and Mandiso would be home by the time that Kazi got back from the seaside with the Finleys.

At 5 am on the morning they were to leave, Kazi ran down to the farmhouse with his towel over one shoulder, and a bag, containing a swimsuit Scott had given him and a couple of pairs of shorts and T-shirts, slung over the other. He was wearing a baseball cap, the only pair of shoes that he was taking and was grinning from ear to ear. Scott and Shanon were carrying suitcases out of the house and Garth was packing the car. Caitlin added the finishing touches to their lunch and, after a few minutes, locked the house.

They left taking a southern route that bypassed Johannesburg with its tremendous yellow-gold hills that towered several hundred feet in the air, dusty reminders of gold mining operations. After three hours they pulled in at an Ultra City station for petrol and to use the bathrooms, then drove on until lunch-time when they stopped to eat their lunch on the banks of the silt laden, slow-moving Orange River. Once across the river they entered the semi desert plains of the Karoo, where windmills turned on a slow hot wind and herds of black-headed sheep grazed on spiney shrubs. After a couple of hours the road rose towards the Swartberg Mountains, and then dropped into a gorge and followed a route alongside a pebbled river between steep granite cliffs.

Outside Oudtshoorn, ostriches grazed in camps on sun-browned grass, the males dancing and beating their wings for the females. Then the car began the climb up the Outeniqua Mountains through Robinson's pass and, just before the peak, Caitlin suggested a competition to see who could spot the sea first. Kazi leant forward, his eyes ablaze with excitement, and when they topped the rise, Shanon nudged him hoping that he would see it first. But he didn't recognise the slight difference between sea and sky where they joined on the horizon, and even when they pointed it out, he couldn't see it until they descended onto the coastal plain where he could make out the coastline and the full extent of the sea. When he did see it at last, he sat motionless absorbing it all. He had seen the sea on television, but this was the first time in real life, and it was much more than he had expected.

Down on the plain the road curved west to follow the coast alongside cliffs and long sandy beaches, and Caitlin opened her window to the fresh smell of salt, seaweed, and heather. She breathed in deeply and sighed, and her face lost the pinched look she'd had since the car-jacking.

The holiday house was a thatched bungalow that stood amongst others on a cliff overlooking Danabaai. Down on the beach, sandpipers followed the tide, probing the sand for food, and seagulls and gannets soured above the waves.

"Mom, can we unpack later?" Shanon asked.

"Sure, just put your bags inside," Caitlin replied, and before she'd finished her sentence, Shanon, Scott and Kazi were racing down the stairs to the beach like young children.

They ran along the water's edge with the waves lapping around their ankles, receding, and coming back higher, chasing them up the beach. When they reached a rocky outcrop, Kazi noticed a girl looking into a tidal pool. She seemed absorbed and he wondered what she was looking at. His curiosity got the better of him and he clambered over the rocks to see.

"What are you looking at?" he asked.

"Sea anemone and starfish," she said, glancing up. She was Kazi's age, and had a naturally honeyed complexion. Her hair was tightly woven into rows of short black braids, and she had caramel-brown eyes. She wiggled her fingers in the water and a crab scuttled away kicking up a little cloud of sand and shells. "And crab, of course," she laughed prettily.

A wave broke on the rocks and the wind blew a fine spray over them. The girl giggled. "There's an octopus," she said, touching Kazi's arm to get his attention.

The sensation of her touch swept through him. He'd never seen an octopus, but he found it difficult to tear his eyes away from the girl. He'd noticed the details of her tiny ears and the delicate flare of her nose, the colour of her skin, the caramel of her eyes, the small dimple in her cheek when she smiled. And, as she bent towards the pool, his heart was sent racing as her T-shirt stretched over her slim back. She glanced up and caught him staring. Heat rose in his cheeks. He glanced quickly into the tidal pool and saw the octopus. Normally it would have amazed him, but now he just wanted to look at the girl.

"Can you see it?" she asked. He nodded and tried to find his voice.

"I can," he said. It was all he could think of saying at that moment.

"Some people eat them. Ugh!" She shuddered delicately.

Kazi looked at the octopus. "Sounds gross. Have you tried?"

"No way, have you?"

He shook his head. "I'm from the Transvaal. The only fish we eat are what we catch in the river."

"Where about?" she asked, referring to where he lived.

"Skeerpoort," he replied. She didn't know where that was, so he sat down on a flat rock next her and explained as best he could. "Do you live in Mossel Bay?" he asked.

"No, I'm just staying with my grandmother for the holidays. I live in Cape Town."

"Where does your granny live?" Kazi asked.

"D'Almeida Township. And you? Where are you staying?"

"In one of those holiday houses," he pointed to the strip of houses above the cliff. "With the Finleys, my father's boss. I'm friends with their son."

"Lucky you!"

Speaking of Scott and Shanon he realized he hadn't seen them for a while, and looked around. They weren't in sight and he was relieved. He leant towards the pool and touched a sea anemone. Its tentacles curled on the tip of his fingers and it withdrew into a closed disc.

"Didn't it sting you?" the girl asked.

Kazi shook his head. "It tickled. You should try."

The girl reached out tentatively and touched the anemone. "You're right. It does!" Her laughter rang pleasantly.

A voice called and the girl looked up. "There's my friend, I have to go."

Kazi's face dropped. "I hope I'm going to see you again." He knew he was being forward, but he really did want to see her again.

"I'd like to see you too. Will you be on the beach tomorrow?"

Kazi's face lifted, he nodded, and as she turned to go he realized that he didn't know her name and asked.

"Thandi," she replied. "Yours?"

"Kazi," he smiled. "I'll see you tomorrow, Thandi," he said, testing her name.

Thandi gave a little wave, dropped down off the rocks and ran up the beach, her feet flying over the sand, the sun flashing on her bare legs. Kazi watched until she was gone and then turned to look for Scott and Shanon. They were further up the beach, Shanon collecting shells and Scott wading in the surf.

"Who was that?" Scott asked when Kazi caught up.

"Just a girl," Kazi replied.

Scott grinned at his friend. "Just a girl, huh," he teased. "Are you going to see her again?"

"Tomorrow," Kazi replied with a shy grin.

The following day Kazi ran down to the beach after breakfast. A mild breeze carried the fragrance of heather, and it was such a clear day that he could see all the way to a smudge of cliffs in the distance and a far-off point of land. But Thandi was nowhere in sight.

Scott followed at a more sedate pace with his towel over his shoulder. "I don't see your girl," he said, looking up and down the beach. "Do you want to swim while you're waiting?"

Kazi hid his disappointment, and looked sceptically at the crashing waves. "Is it safe?"

"You'll be fine, come on." Scott pealed off his T-shirt and hurled it behind him as he waded into the surf.

Kazi left his T-shirt with Scott's and went in slowly, feeling his way with the undertow pulling at his feet as the tide receded. When the waves flowed back in it did so suddenly, reaching waist level. The water was cold and he sucked in his breath.

Scott laughed. "It's better if you get it over and done with quickly. Don't pussy foot around, just dive in." With that he plunged in, slicing through the waves.

Kazi followed suit. After the initial shock his body got used to the temperature, it wasn't as cold as he expected, and it was surprisingly buoyant. He swam after Scott, ploughing through the water without looking, and a wave broke unexpectedly over his head tumbling him head-over-heels, returning him to the beach. He came up spluttering, tried again running hard into the surf and diving when he could, but the waves tossed him back again. This time he lay in the shallows coughing and shaking water from his ears while he took stock of things. After a while he looked up and noticed two pairs of legs. To his embarrassment he realized that Thandi and Shanon had been watching him, laughing.

"Hello, Thandi," he said self-consciously. Standing up and adjusting his shorts he hoped she wouldn't notice the bulge of sand in the crotch.

"Hi," she replied, grinning from ear to ear with the cutest smile, and the nicest teeth Kazi thought he'd ever seen.

"How come you're together?" he enquired, glancing from Thandi to Shanon, and wishing he hadn't been caught looking like a beached whale in front of Thandi.

Shanon glanced at Thandi. "I noticed Thandi walking along the beach. From your description I knew who she was the minute I saw her."

"I was looking for you," Thandi said, and Kazi felt better. "You looked like you were having a tough time out there."

Kazi nodded ruefully, "I've swallowed gallons of water."

Thandi grinned mischievously. "You've also got tons of sand in your shorts."

Kazi blushed, and Shanon laughed. "Didn't Scott show you how to dive under the waves?"

"More or less, but I couldn't get it right."

"C'mon, I'll help you," Thandi said, heading out into the waves. She had on a pretty little one-piece swimsuit that hugged her body and showed off her curves. Kazi would've followed her anywhere. "Just before that wave crests, dive under, and kick as hard as you can," she instructed. A wave came towards them, it began to break and she yelled, "Dive!"

Kazi did as she said and dove and kicked and came up on the other side of the wave. Thandi laughed, "See, it's easy."

Kazi grinned triumphantly. "It was. Thanks."

They spent the morning swimming, walking along the beach, and collecting shells, but at lunch time Thandi had to leave.

"Hey," she laughed, "don't look so glum. There's a beach party on Second Beach tonight, why don't you come."

"Where's Second Beach?" Kazi asked.

"At the bottom of Heide Road. Shanon and Scott can come too if they like," she said.

"Great, what time?"

Thandi shrugged. "After dinner, around seven I guess."

"See you later," Kazi said, happy in the knowledge that he was going to see her again that day.

In the afternoon Kazi went with the Finleys to the harbour and walked along the pier between the fishing boats. Caitlin bought a fresh kabeljou from an old Hottentot fisherman with a weathered face and a gap-toothed smile and, when they got home, she wrapped it in wet newspaper and Garth roasted it over coals in an open fire. They ate it dripping in lemon butter with small baked potatoes, and a crisp Greek salad. It may have been the finest food that Kazi had ever eaten, but he hardly noticed. His mind was on the beach party and seeing Thandi again.

After dinner he was a bundle of nerves, choosing and re-choosing a T-shirt. Eventually Scott leant him one of his so that they could leave, and they ran down the stairs taking them two at a time.

Shanon ambled down and they had to wait for her, Kazi shifting from one foot to the other.

"C'mon, Shanon, please hurry up," he begged.

Shanon laughed. "What's the hurry Kazi?"

"*Ag*, c'mon, Shanon, stop teasing."

"Okay, okay, I'm coming." She skipped down the last of the steps, and they walked to Second Beach. From a distance they could see shadow figures around a fire on the beach.

"Do you think she's there?" Kazi asked.

"She'll be there," Shanon replied.

They reached the people around the fire and Kazi stared into the crowd. "How am I going to find her?"

"Walk around, maybe she'll see you if you don't find her first," Scott suggested.

"I guess you're right. I'll see you later," Kazi said and walked off in search of Thandi. There seemed to be at least seventy-five or eighty young people, black, white and coloured, and ten minutes later he still hadn't found her. He meandered back, but Scott and Shanon had blended into the crowd. He wished he'd asked them to stay with him until he'd found Thandi. He glanced around feeling stupid, and then, just as he turned away, he saw her outlined against the flames. He stopped and watched her talking and was suddenly nervous. She threw back her head and laughed at something, then she must have sensed his presence, and she turned and looked at him. She smiled shyly and he walked towards her. He'd been waiting for this moment, and now he was unsure of what he was going to say. Again he wished he'd asked Scott or Shanon to stay with him.

"Hi," his voice came out gruffly, but he was relieved that it hadn't gone high instead.

"Hey, Kazi," she replied, grinning.

His heart pounded and his tongue felt thick. Silence hung between them for a moment, then they both started talking at once and she laughed.

"C'mon, let's sit down," she said.

He followed her, and they sat on a log someone had dragged onto the beach. He watched her wriggle her feet into the sand. Her toes were painted pearl pink, and he couldn't think of what to say. After an awkward silence she asked him about his family, and once he started talking there seemed to be so much to say and so much to ask. She in turn told him about her kitten, and her parents, about her childhood, where she lived in Cape Town, that she was also going into her final year at school, and that she was hoping to study psychology next year.

By the time Shanon came to tell Kazi that it was time to go, he felt as if the evening had only just begun, yet hours had passed already.

"I'll see you on the beach tomorrow," Thandi suggested.

"See you tomorrow," Kazi said with a broad smile.

The next day, it rained. They had finished breakfast and Kazi stared down at the deserted beach.

"She'll be there tomorrow," Scott said, guessing who Kazi was thinking about. "Tomorrow will be a nice day."

Kazi turned away, wishing he had asked Thandi for her address.

"Let's sit outside," Scott suggested, so they went out and sat on the covered porch.

"Kazi, what's going on at home?" Scott asked.

Kazi's face shifted. "What do you mean, Scott?"

"I know there's something wrong, something that you haven't told me. You've been avoiding me for the last couple of weeks."

Kazi looked out at the rain and the white peaks on the wind-ruffled sea. He narrowed his eyes and remained silent.

The rain eased and a couple of seagulls screamed on the railing above the cliff while others swooped away on the wind.

"It's your brothers, isn't it? Where are they, Kazi?"

Kazi shook his head. "I don't know," he said quietly.

Scott frowned. "What do you mean you don't know?"

"I don't," Kazi replied, "and I can't tell you any more."

"Does it have something to do with the meetings at your father's house?" Scott asked. Kazi closed his mouth. Scott noticed the movement. "My dad thinks they're political meetings, and that your dad might be in some kind of trouble."

Fear coursed through Kazi at the realisation that the Finleys had guessed so much. "Scott, I-I can't tell you. If your father gets involved, then things could get really bad."

"What do you mean?"

"Scott, please," he looked directly at Scott, "please, don't ask any more."

"Why? We've always spoken about everything."

"Things have changed, everything's changed." Scott's face fell. Kazi said, "You don't understand, do you?" He lifted his hands and dropped them back into his lap. "You don't understand what black people in this country are going through."

"What the hell do you mean by that, Kazi?" Scott demanded crossly.

"For instance – do you worry about going into a restaurant and being chased out because you're black? Do you get upset by the tone of voice that a person uses when they speak to you, or that they think you're stupid just because you have black skin? Do you worry that someone might get upset that you're swimming on their beach," he said, pointing down at the beach. "And," he turned and glared at Scott, "what about school boycotts?"

"I hadn't thought about it," Scott replied, simmering down.

"My point exactly. School boycotts are something that you only read about in the newspaper. They don't affect you. To me, school boycotts mean that I won't graduate this year, and that in turn means that I won't go to university."

"Kazi, I'm sorry, I had no idea. I'm such an idiot."

Kazi stood up and walked to the edge of the porch. It was raining harder again, and raindrops fell in a steady stream off the roof. He watched the squalls moving over the sea for a few minutes before turning back. "Sorry, Scott. I'm sorry I blew off like that."

"No, I'm the one who should be sorry. Look, if there's anything I can do to help just let me know."

"Thanks. I know you're a good friend, and I'm sorry I can't tell you everything right now."

Scott remained silent for a few minutes. He decided to leave Kazi's family problems alone, as it was obvious he wasn't going to talk about it. "What can you do if there are school boycotts?"

"There's no 'if' about it, it's when, and we won't be able to go to school, so that's that."

"Aren't there teachers who would give lessons during the boycott?"

"I don't know. But where would we go? We can't use the school."

"Maybe we should speak to my parents, they might have some ideas."

"Maybe," Kazi shrugged.

The next day Kazi scoured the beach for Thandi, but she wasn't there. He gave up and went to a restaurant at the point with the Finleys. The waitress scowled at him because he was black but didn't say anything, and he ignored her surly attitude. After lunch he stood at the end of the pier and stared at the waves foaming and breaking against the rocks. His emotions were in turmoil. He couldn't understand his feelings for Thandi, the way she had taken over his every thought, the way he longed to see her again.

It was late by the time they got home, and Kazi and Scott went immediately to look for Thandi. They walked towards Second Beach and noticed another bonfire burning invitingly. As they walked towards it Kazi's heart beat faster in anticipation.

"I hope she's there," he said.

They heard a shout and Scott grinned. "I think that's your girl. I'll leave you to it. I'm going to look around for the guys I met last time. See you later."

Thandi was running towards him and Kazi left Scott to look for his friends.

"Hi," she gasped breathlessly.

"Hi," he grinned, "you haven't been around."

She gave a rueful smile. "My grandmother wasn't well. C'mon, let's walk." She took his hand and smiled up at him.

They walked and talked, each subject running into the other. After a while they stopped to watch phosphorescence swirling on the tide. He felt her shoulder touch his and her warmth next to him and turned towards her. When she looked up at him, he longed to kiss her and leant forward and kissed her for the first time. She put her arms up around his shoulders and looked into his face, and as he pulled her closer he felt her breasts against his chest. It felt wonderful so he kissed her again, deeper this time and his hands moved down her back. She returned his kiss, holding him close.

After a while she leant away from him until just their hips touched and looked into his eyes. "I think I'm falling in love with you, Kazi," she whispered.

He touched her face. "I fell in love with you the first moment I saw you." He leant forward again and kissed the soft part of her neck and followed the line of her chin with his lips until he reached her mouth. Her lips parted and they stood together like that until they heard people. They broke apart and walked to a sand dune where they climbed to the highest point to sit at the top. Once there they spoke for hours without interruption. When they ran out of things they wanted to say, they watched the surf, comfortable in their own silence. After some thought, she turned to him with a slight frown.

"Kazi," she appeared so serious that Kazi's heart froze in fear of what she might say. "I know that we've only known each other for a short time and perhaps I shouldn't ask." She hesitated before she seemed to decide to go on with what she wanted to say. She took his hands in hers and looked right at him. "We've talked and talked, but you haven't told me what's wrong. There's something on your heart. I know because I've seen the pain in your eyes, even when you're laughing, even when you said that you loved me."

He felt something inside him break. It wasn't what he had expected her to say, but now he found that he couldn't stop himself. He spoke haltingly at first and then the words flowed from him as if he was cleansing his soul. He found that he trusted her as he'd never trusted before. While he spoke she sat still, afraid that any movement would stop this floodgate of emotion. When he had finished, she put her arms around him and held him. She lifted her face to him and whispered, "Kazi, thank you for telling me. I hope your problems are halved now that there are two of us."

He leant towards her and kissed her and felt the world recede.

During the remainder of the holiday, Kazi and Thandi became inseparable and often started to talk only to find that their thoughts were already woven together. Their words followed the same course, and their minds seemed to know each other's thoughts. On the last evening, they took a blanket to the beach and lay together on the sand, hating the thought of being separated.

"Thandi," Kazi said.

"Yes?"

"I love you," he said simply.

She lifted herself onto her elbow and looked down at him. "I love you too."

"I wish I didn't have to go back home."

"I wish you didn't either. Why can't you finish school in Cape Town? You could stay with us."

"I have to find my brothers."

"Why, Kazi, why you?"

"Because I must, I've always looked out for them."

"Your father will get them back."

"By then it will be too late, I must get them back now. Promise me that you will wait for me?"

"Oh, Kazi, I will! I will wait for you," she whispered, lowering herself until their lips met.

At her kiss he felt his body quake as he breathed the smell and taste of her. He wanted to drink her down into his lungs so that he would never have to part from her again.

TWENTY

RESOLUTION

1985 · 1986 · 1987 · 1988 · 1989 · 1990 · **1991** · **1992** · 1993

When they got back to the farm after their holiday, the Finleys parked outside the farmhouse, and Kazi walked up to his parent's house with his bag slung over his shoulder.

His mother saw him right away and jumped to her feet. "Kazi!" she called.

Goodwill and Ntokoso heard her and came outside as well. "Kazi," they both shouted and Ntokoso threw herself into his arms. They had never been apart before. "I missed you!" she cried.

"I missed you too, little sister," he replied dropping to his haunches. "And I brought you a present," he said, taking an ostrich egg out of his bag and placing it in Ntokoso's hands. "If we make a small hole in each end we can remove the egg without damaging the shell, and then you can keep the shell forever and Mom can cook the egg."

"Wow, it's beautiful! I've never seen such a big egg before."

"It is big," Goodwill agreed, taking the egg from Ntokoso and admiring it. "And it's heavy," he remarked, weighing it in his hand.

"It's the equivalent of twenty-four chicken eggs," Kazi replied.

"That's a lot of egg!" Martha exclaimed. "I'll give some to Jackson and Nelly, and maybe Sarina and Lena as well."

"How is Lena, Mom?" Kazi asked.

"Poor child, she'll never be normal."

"I haven't seen her for a long time. Can she walk yet?"

"She manages to walk from one thing to another, but she has to hold on. It's as if the whole one side of her body is slower than the other."

"How old is she?"

"Around four, I think."

A thought struck Kazi and his face fell. "She had whooping cough, didn't she? Was it my fault, Mom?"

Martha was sorry she'd mentioned Lena. "No, Kazi, a lot of children were sick. It wasn't you," she said sadly, knowing how the weight of guilt would lie on Kazi's shoulders if she suspected that he had made Lena sick. He was such a sensitive boy; he would carry the world's problems if you let him. "Thank you for the egg," she said, changing the subject.

"I'm glad you like it." Kazi got up. "I'm going to put my things inside. I'll be back in a few minutes." He walked into the house and put his bag in his bedroom. As he did so, he caught sight of Dumani's carved soapstone horse. He picked it up and sat down on his bed, stroking the horse as he often did, and felt the familiar ache in his chest. Time had not helped, and he felt his brothers' loss as sharply now as he did when they were first kidnapped. Every day that he was free and they were not made him feel worse – he had been free to swim in the sea, to meet a beautiful girl, and to have fun. Suddenly his emotions overwhelmed him and he began to sob. He held the horse and cried deep, racking sobs. He had to find them.

After a while, he stopped crying and realized that he had to pull himself together. He couldn't go outside with his eyes red and swollen. His parents would notice and they would be upset. He stood up, opened his bag and took out his T-shirts and shorts and placed them on the shelves he'd made from a couple of planks he'd stacked on top of bricks from the brickyard. He turned back to the bag and at the very bottom were the shells he and Thandi had picked up on the beach for his mother and Ntokoso. He opened the packet and the fresh smell of the sea on the shells caused all the memories of the holiday to come flooding back: the breeze, the smell of heather, the sound of Thandi's laughter. He picked up a shell, a cowrie, and remembered Thandi's excitement when she had found the little shell that looked like porcelain. How Thandi held the shell in the palm of her hand with her slender fingers. And the light colour of the skin in the middle of her palm. And how he had kissed her. He missed her so much already. He wondered when he would see her again. He wanted to be with her and to share his life with her. He sat on the bed feeling sorry for himself, and then it dawned on him that he could do it. If he worked really hard and got distinctions in all his subjects, he could get a university grant and go to university anywhere he chose. He would move to Cape Town and go to a university in the same town where Thandi lived. But first he had to find his brothers.

He decided he would stop at nothing now. He picked up all the shells. He had to stop feeling sorry for himself, he had to be strong. He would do what he had to do. He squared his shoulders, turned and walked outside to the *lapa* with a smile on his face so that his parents and Ntokoso wouldn't suspect his thoughts. They looked up at him expectantly and he gave them the shells and, while they admired them, told them about

Mossel Bay and Thandi. By the time that he went to bed it was too late to write to her, but in the morning he knew he would.

The next day Garth went to the post office and, as he drew up, noticed Dries fetching his mail.

"Dries," he said as he approached.

"Garth, how was your holiday?" Dries asked in Afrikaans.

"Great *boet*," Garth replied in the same language. He was completely bilingual now.

"Things are getting ugly," Dries said once Garth had finished telling him about their holiday. "The cops busted an arms cache in Broederstroom, and the place is rife with bloody terrorists. You guys must watch out, there are rumours that the quarry next door to your farm might be another one."

"What do you mean? An arms cache?" Garth asked.

"Who knows if it's true or not." Dries shrugged. "There's no work going on in that quarry and I've heard that people have noticed strange vehicles driving in and out of the place. Nobody seems to know who lives there."

"That's disturbing," Garth looked concerned.

"*Ja*, as I said, you and Caitlin better keep an eye on the place." He took out his mail and locked his mailbox. "How's Caitlin since the car-jacking?" he asked.

"Better thanks," Garth replied. "In fact I'm hoping our gun licences are in the mail. I think a gun will give her more confidence."

"You should also put up a security fence with all this going on. I have."

"*Ja*, you're right. Caitlin's mentioned it too. Who did you use?"

"Dawie Hendricks, I'll tell him to call you if you like."

"Thanks," Garth said, opening his own mailbox. He riffled through his mail. "Here they are," he said, slitting open the envelopes and holding up the gun licenses. "Consider us armed and dangerous," he grinned. "If you speak to Hendricks ask him to come over on Monday. I'd like a quote for a fence and burglar proofing too. What did you get?"

"A six foot, heavy-duty, barbed-wire fence with razor-wire on top. I also got him to install security bars on my windows and an automatic gate; you don't want to get out of your car to open gates in the middle of the night. I've got battery back-up as well."

"I'll probably do the same," Garth agreed.

Garth said goodbye, went home to pick up his and Caitlin's identity books and drove to Pretoria to fetch the firearms. While he was at the gun shop he also bought a safe, which he anchored to the brick wall in their bedroom with Rawl bolts. The safe would have to be opened to reach the bolts, making it and the guns impossible to steal.

He had been taught how to use guns when he was in the military and Garth decided to teach his family how to shoot. The next day he and Scott set up targets. For the first part of the lesson they sat around the dining room table while Garth demonstrated how to load the magazines for both guns, how to chamber and eject a chambered bullet, and how to remove the magazines.

They were just finishing off when they heard a car pull up. "I guess that's your cousin, Caity." As they stood to greet their guests he added, "One last thing before you go – always make sure that your gun is pointed in a safe direction when you aren't pointing it at the target. And another rule to remember is that you should never leave your finger on the trigger. It's a natural reflex to squeeze if you get a fright, and you could end up blowing a hole in your foot, or shoot someone by mistake. Well, that's it for now." Garth pulled a face and walked to the door. "I guess we should go and meet the fray."

Caitlin gave an apologetic smile. "Try and be nice, Garth, I know it's difficult, but I'm the only family Sue-Sue has."

"I'll try," Garth said with another grimace, and then he put on his best imitation of a welcoming face as they went to greet Sue-Sue, her new husband, and their three-month-old baby. Sue-Sue's hair was jelled into flame-red spikes. She was wearing large earrings, a knuckleduster ring, and her eyes were heavily mascaraed.

She flounced into the house with barely a greeting for anyone. "Bloody little brat cried the whole way. I'm going to have a nap." She drilled her husband with a commanding look. "Bring the suitcases, David," she said as she walked off, leaving her baby screaming blue murder on the back seat. Scott rolled his eyes, Shanon giggled and Caitlin gave them a mock-stern look.

Sue-Sue's husband was tall with sand-coloured hair, a good contrast to Sue-Sue's red. Before scurrying after his wife, clutching items of luggage, he greeted them hurriedly with an apologetic smile that reached his sloping Labrador eyes. Garth hefted a couple of bags, gave Caitlin a look as if to say, "told you so," and followed Sue-Sue and David inside. Caitlin went to the baby and lifted him out of the carrycot.

"Poor baby, what's wrong? Looks like your mommy's deserted us," she said, retrieving the nappy bag and walking inside, all the while soothing the baby with silly words. She put him on the couch in the living room. "Let's see why you're crying. Nappy first and then we'll see if mommy packed a bottle for you. You're probably hungry." She changed him, fed him, and settled him down to sleep, and Sue-Sue emerged, mysteriously overcoming her exhaustion.

After lunch they left the baby sleeping. Maria would call them if he woke, and they took the guns and went up to the place where the targets had been set up. Garth loaded the Glock and went over the details again for the benefit of Sue-Sue and David. Then he walked up to the line he had drawn in the sand and faced the beer cans they were using as targets.

"Now, you'll be shooting two-handed so your hips should be at a 45-degree angle," he demonstrated. "Place your left leg forward and the right leg back," he said. "You'll be balanced in all directions, and it'll be easier to aim the gun at the target. Remember to hold the gun firmly, keep the sights straight in line and hold the trigger in the crease of your finger," he said, aiming. "The front sight must be centred in the notch of the rear sight, must be level with the top of the rear sight, and there should be an equal amount of light on either side. Keep looking at the sight lined up on the target." He held the gun steady, pulled the trigger and the first beer can went spinning away with the other two following in quick succession. He stepped back. "Okay, Caity. You first." He set the safety catch and gave the gun to Caitlin, keeping the muzzle angled down. "Hold it down while I set up another row of cans," he reminded her.

He came back. Caitlin set herself up, released the safety catch, pulled back the slide and chambered a round, stepped back with her right foot and angled her body at 45 degrees as Garth had showed her, and raised the gun.

"*Ag*, no man, Caitlin," Sue-Sue whined, "You're not going to shoot that awful thing are you?"

"Yes, she is," Garth said. "Now stay behind the shooting line." He turned back to Caitlin. "Remember a nice hard grip, sight, and then roll the trigger smoothly. Be ready for the recoil."

Caitlin looked down the barrel of the gun.

"You want a smooth, even, uninterrupted pull," Garth said.

David added, "You can say to yourself, sque-e-eze the trigger, and squeeze it like a tube of toothpaste." He seemed to be a nice guy, logical too. Garth wondered why he had married Sue-Sue of all people, but now that he thought about it he realized that it must have had something to do with the baby arriving well before their first anniversary. There couldn't possibly be another reason.

Caitlin lined up the sights, her hand wavered and she saw the target move; she steadied, breathed in and held her breath as she pulled the trigger, squeezing it slowly as Garth had told her. She hit the first beer can.

"Beginner's luck! Let's see if you can do it again," Garth dared her, and Caitlin shot off another two shots sending another two cans flying.

"Ha-ha," she said with a triumphant grin, feeling pleased with herself. She'd been nervous at first, wondering if she could cope with a gun, with the thoughts of destruction and anger that it carried with it, but the gun made her feel strong. It made her feel in control. Since the car-jacking she had been frightened, scared by every noise, of being alone in the house or in the car. She looked at every black man on the street worrying about being attacked again. Now she had no doubt that she would use this weapon if she had to. She noticed Garth looking at her and realized that he understood. She had the knowledge now that she could defend herself, and that was what she needed. She was a woman, but she was not weak and would not allow herself to be a target.

"Let me try," Sue-Sue whined, forgetting her earlier objections.

"Okay," Garth said, hoping that if he let her shoot now, she would be quiet and the rest of them could practice in peace.

Caitlin clicked the safety catch into position, reloaded and passed the gun to her cousin keeping the muzzle down.

Sue-Sue took the Glock. "Show me how it works," she said, turning to face her husband and raking the gun in a circle.

"Watch out!" Garth yelled as everyone ducked for safety.

"What's the matter with you?" she asked sulkily, "you know the safety catch is on."

"Sue-Sue, the first rule about guns is that you don't point them at anybody, ever! Not ever, not even when the gun isn't loaded, and definitely not when the safety catch is on. It could misfire. Never, okay? That's the rule."

Caitlin's cousin stuck out her tongue and this time pointed the gun at the beer cans.

"Don't forget to release the safety catch," David said.

"I know, I'm not stupid," she snapped. She lowered the gun and looked at it searching for the safety catch. "This little doo-flabby?"

"Yes, that little doo-flabby," her husband replied patiently, and Garth gave a little smile that he quickly hid.

David reached over and slid the safety catch into the off position. "There you go, Sue-Sue," he said, and she aimed again and blasted off two wild shots.

"Try again," her husband said, adjusting her stance. "Now hold the gun firmly so that you counteract the recoil."

She shot off another three bullets that hit the ground meters away from the beer cans.

"What are you doing? You're not even close," David said.

"It's the stupid gun's fault, it jumps up as I pull the trigger and puts me off," Sue-Sue complained.

"Here, let me help you," David said and walked up behind her. She was standing squared to the target, and he adjusted her stance again. Then he showed her how to hold the gun and line up the sights. He stepped away and said, "Okay now, hold the gun firmly as you pull the trigger, and remember to squeeze the trigger nice and slow. Ready?" Sue-Sue nodded and pulled the trigger.

David chuckled, "No wonder you can't hit the target silly, you're closing your eyes when you pull the trigger," he said.

"Don't laugh," Sue-Sue said crossly. "So what if I shut my eyes. I've aimed already and I can't stand the noise."

"You can't shut your eyes, sweetie. You have to keep them open all the time."

"But I can't," she whined.

"Yes you can, now keep your eyes on the target," David said. "Try again." Sue-Sue shot three more rounds and missed the target.

"That's it," Garth said with a frustrated sigh. "Now it's Shanon's turn."

"Just one more," Sue-Sue clutched the gun possessively.

"Okay, one," Garth was getting angry.

"Keep your eyes open this time," her husband encouraged.

She missed again and handed the gun to Garth. "It's not fair," she pouted.

"Sweetie, you should check on the baby anyway, he's probably awake by now."

Sue-Sue put her hands indignantly on her hips and strutted angrily towards the house muttering something about the baby spoiling her fun. Garth turned to Shanon and went through the procedure with her. She took the Glock and clicked off the safety, chambered a round, and then she followed Garth's instructions to the letter and struck the first beer can with her second shot and then she blew the other two off the bales with a laugh.

"Well done!" Garth said, taking the Glock. He loaded the magazine again and slid it into place. "Scott, let's see if you can beat the girls."

"Okay, Dad, but you don't have to show me, I know what to do." He did everything exactly as Garth had told him and hit the beer cans in quick succession with a big grin plastered on his face, and immediately asked if he could try the 38 special.

"It's David's turn now, and then we'll try out the CZ," Garth said, and Scott passed the Glock to David.

David had been in the military (military training was compulsory), and shot the Glock with easy familiarity. When he'd shot a couple of rounds, Garth loaded the CZ and they all had a turn with it.

While they practiced, the labourers from Fairvalley Farm and from neighbouring farms stopped occasionally to watch. Garth wished the two men in the black BMW would drive by, but he was confident they would find out about the guns and that they could all shoot accurately. They would hopefully take it as a warning.

Garth hoped that they wouldn't have to use the weapons but, if the time came, he was satisfied that they would be ready.

School began, and a few days into the school term the headmaster sent a message to Kazi instructing him to come to his office. When Kazi knocked on the open door, Mr. Mgani was on the phone. He indicated with a sweep of his hand that Kazi could come in and sit down. Kazi sat on the hard chair opposite the headmaster and waited until he had finished.

When Mr. Mgani put down the telephone, he looked at Kazi over his reading glasses. "I assume you had a pleasant holiday?"

"Thank you, Sir, I did," Kazi replied.

"Well, let's get straight to the point. Have you heard anything further regarding your brothers and the threats to your family?"

"No, Sir. I'm not allowed to attend the meetings, and my father won't talk about it. Since my brothers were taken away, he obeys these people. He's frightened something will happen to my sister and me."

"Well, Kazi, I've found someone who will go to the next meeting. When is it?"

"It's on Friday at seven o'clock, Sir."

"Good. I'd prefer that you don't know who the person is, so I'm not going to tell you. And I'm also going to ask that you keep away from the meeting like you usually do. He will report back to me."

Mr. Mgani picked up his pen to continue working. Realizing that the conversation was over, Kazi got to his feet and left, thanking the headmaster.

On Friday, Kazi watched people arrive. He wondered who the headmaster's man might be, but no one looked at him particularly differently or greeted him any more or less. He realized that he would have to wait for Monday when the headmaster would tell him what had happened, so he went home.

He arrived an hour early for school on Monday, and was waiting outside the headmaster's office when Mr. Mgani arrived and unlocked his door. Kazi followed him into the office and without sitting down Mr. Mgani began immediately.

"Kazi, my informant tells me that the people running the meetings are violent and will stop at nothing. When I agreed to help you, I didn't realize the extent of things, and now I strongly advise that you get on with your schoolwork and leave this be. I'll continue making inquiries but I'm sorry, I don't hold out much hope."

"But, Sir, I must know who it is! I must find my brothers!"

Mr. Mgani lifted his hand to stop him. "Kazi, look at things realistically. You're just a young boy; there's not much that you can do."

"Sir, I have to find them."

"Now listen carefully, you can't fight this, and if you do, you will get into trouble. Your parents don't want to lose another son."

Kazi dropped his eyes and vowed to himself that he would continue, regardless of what Mr. Mgani said. But this was a major blow to his plans.

"Do I make myself clear, boy!"

"Yes, Sir." Kazi lifted his head and added, "Thank you, Sir."

"Good. Now get to class before you're late."

"Yes, Sir, thank you, Sir," Kazi repeated.

Kazi sat through the morning's classes thinking about his brothers, unable to concentrate. At last the bell rang for break. He went outside and sat down on a bench under a Jacaranda tree. He had been so sure that Mr. Mgani would help him. There had to be another way to find his brothers. He stretched out his legs and rested his head against the back of the bench. A brown finch hopped from one branch to another above him, and a *bloukop* lizard gazed down. After a while the lizard looked away and bobbed its blue head up and down. Kazi realized from its defensive manner that someone was approaching. The lizard stopped bobbing, and the bird flew away. Kazi wished he could've been that bird, and hoped the person would leave.

"Hi, Kazi." It was Saul. "I haven't seen you in a while."

Kazi didn't feel like talking, but he sat up anyway. He had spoken to Saul occasionally since that first day when he had helped him with his English homework.

Saul took one look at Kazi's face and asked, "What's wrong this time?"

He'd caught Kazi at a vulnerable moment and, to Kazi's surprise, it all tumbled out. He hadn't meant to tell Saul of all people, someone he hardly knew and someone he certainly didn't know well enough to trust.

Saul didn't say anything for a while then he said, "Maybe I can help. My father's a member of the ANC, and there's a meeting in a barn outside town this Saturday." He tore a page out of a notebook and drew a rough map, which he handed to Kazi. "You'll soon realize that the ANC have nothing to do with your brothers' disappearance, but maybe you'll learn something."

On Saturday Kazi told his parents he had soccer practice and instead he went to the address on the piece of paper Saul had given him. When he arrived, he saw that men had been placed as lookouts in case of a police raid. He went inside and found people already listening to a man who was speaking emphatically.

"We must unite and bring the government to the bargaining table," the man brought his fist down with a loud bang. "We rejoice in Nelson Mandela's release from jail two years ago, but we can only stop when we have a democratic and free society. Only through action will freedom be won." There was silence throughout the barn. "We claim South Africa for all, we demand equal rights! We will not stop until we have one man, one vote."

The crowd stood up, fists raised in the ANC salute. A man shouted, "We want freedom in our lifetime, long live the struggle." And the people began to sing *Nkosi Sikelel' iAfrika* – God Bless Africa.

When the meeting was over, Kazi turned to leave, wondering why Saul had thought it important for him to come; he hadn't learnt anything in particular. At that moment Saul came towards him.

"Hey there, Kazi," he called, "wait up." Saul reached him and said, "My father owns a shop and delivers supplies to the

Umkhonto we Sizwe military camp. Do you want to come with us next time – to see what it's about?"

"Umkhonto we Sizwe," Kazi repeated. "That's the ANC military wing."

"Yes," Saul replied. "Do you want to come?"

This might be the opportunity he needed to explore one of the camps where his brothers might be held. Kazi kept this thought to himself and answered, "I'd like that, thanks."

"We'll be going at the end of the month if you want to tag along, but you'll have to keep in the background, and don't say anything to my father about your brothers."

"I won't," he promised.

"You'll see that there are no prisoners at the camp and no children. No one is kept against their will," Saul said and scribbled an address on a piece of paper detailing where his father's shop was, and where they were to meet.

Kazi took the instructions and, at the same time, decided not to tell Goodwill about the impending visit to the ANC military camp.

TWENTY-ONE

BLOWN TO SMITHEREENS

1985 · 1986 · 1987 · 1988 · 1989 · 1990 · 1991 · **1992** · 1993

A few weeks later, on the evening of the explosion, everyone on Fairvalley farm was startled. The people up in the labourers' houses stayed where they were. They knew where it came from, and they knew what had caused it. They didn't want to get involved. But in the farmhouse Garth leapt to his feet, his heart hammering in his chest.

"What the hell was that?" he exclaimed, reaching for the pistol he now carried at all times. He ran outside and stood listening in the direction the sound came from; it was not close, but close enough. Caitlin turned on the security lights, and followed him onto the veranda.

It was as if everything was holding its breath. The frogs had stopped croaking, the crickets were silent, and the night birds had fled.

"I wish we had the security fence now," Garth said.

"I agree. What do you think that was?" Caitlin asked.

"I don't know, it sounded like a hand grenade or some kind of small explosive."

They stood in silence for a while and listened, but nothing moved. After a while Gotcha slunk out of his kennel, tail between his legs, and pushed his head under Garth's hand. He stroked him absentmindedly.

"It came from the direction of the quarry," Garth said. "Maybe its true there's an arms cache down there. Something bad must have happened."

"I heard about the arms cache in Broederstroom, but surely you don't think there's one next door?"

"Anything's possible – there's no white supervision at that quarry. They could hide anything they wanted. Dries warned me about this."

"I'm going to phone the police," Caitlin turned to go inside.

"Turn off the security lights on your way in. I can't see anything even with them on, and if there is someone out there I don't want them to see me."

Caitlin flicked the switch off and Garth stood alone listening in the dark, but there was nothing to hear. Everything was calm and slowly, one by one, the frogs began to sing again. After a while Caitlin came back.

"There's only one policeman in the duty office. He says it's been a busy night and everyone else is out. He's going to call for back-up, but they won't be here anytime soon."

"I'm going to call Dries. If it is an arms cache, I want to see what's going on down there before they hide everything." He turned and went inside, and Caitlin followed closing and locking the door behind them.

"Damn," he said after dialling Dries's number, "there's no answer. Well, I'm going to have a look anyway." He put the phone down and went into the bedroom to the gun safe. He took out the CZ's holster, some extra ammunition, and fastened the gun to his leg.

Caitlin followed him into the bedroom. "Garth, you can't go on your own."

"Caitlin, we've got to know what's going on, it's next door."

"Then I'll come with you."

"No, you won't!"

"Honey, you can't go on your own. What if you need help?"

"I'll be fine. I'll only go as far as the fence."

"I'm coming with you."

"Caity, I don't want you to come."

"Well then, I don't want you to go. Wait for the police." Garth took the pump action shotgun out of the safe and loaded it. She looked at him. "I'm serious, Garth."

"All right, you can come."

"And you promise we'll only go to the fence, no further. And if I feel uneasy, I want you to leave without any argument."

"Agreed," Garth said, taking her Glock out of the safe and passing it to her. It was loaded, so she checked the safety catch before fastening it in a holster to her hip.

Garth handed her a flashlight and hooked his nineteen inch Maglite through his own belt. It gave good light and doubled up as a baton.

Caitlin called Gotcha. "I'll put him inside so that he doesn't follow us."

"Good idea, last thing we need is him barking and attracting attention."

They went outside, Caitlin closed the door, and Gotcha gave her a disappointed look through the window.

There was a partial moon so they could see without turning on the flashlights. They left going east through the field next to the house and, after a few minutes, passed by Kazi's grove of thorn trees and Black Wattle. Then they scrambled through a small donga and clambered up the other side, entering thick bush and negotiating their way through it until they found the boundary fence, and turned left towards the quarry. They could hear voices, and as they drew close, Garth put out a cautionary hand indicating down, and Caitlin crouched. The warm air pressed against her – her pulse raced. Garth moved forward and Caitlin followed a few feet behind, keeping low until they reached the edge of the bush where they hid in the shadows.

Dust still hung in the air and something lay on the ground next to a hollow depression. It looked like the remains of a person. The metallic smell of blood, burnt flesh, and cordite drifted over. Caitlin felt bile rise in her throat. She put a hand up and covered her nose and mouth. Three men were yelling and another was staring at the thing on the ground. Boxes stood open nearby.

"It is an arms cache," Garth whispered. "Looks like a grenade went off by accident. They were probably making a booby trap and that guy must've caught the full blast."

Caitlin interrupted his observations. "We've seen enough. Let's go." She wanted to be sick. She had to get away.

"Wait." Garth moved forward to see more clearly.

"Garth, come back." Her voice was low and urgent. "They might see you."

Garth held up a hand.

Caitlin grabbed his arm and put her mouth to his ear. "Garth, you promised," she said in a hoarse whisper. "Let's get out of here before they see us." She gave one last tug on his arm and crept away. Garth turned reluctantly and followed.

When they got back to the house he called the police again and told them what he had seen. There was still no one available to come out.

He cursed under his breath and dialled Dries's number again. This time he answered. "Dries, it's me, Garth." Without waiting for Dries to respond he continued. "There's been an explosion in the quarry and one of the bastards has blown himself to pieces."

"*Wonderlik!* The only good terrorist is a dead terrorist."

"The police can't come out and the buggers will be gone before they get here. Let's get some of the guys together and catch them." He was talking fast, adrenaline still pumping through his veins.

"*Is jy vokken mal in jou kop* Finley – have you lost your mind? They've probably got AK47's and more, from what you say. That place will be a nest of vipers."

"Come on, Dries, we've all got guns."

"Garth, our guns aren't worth shit against AK47's."

Garth took a breath and realized that Dries had a point. "*Ja boet,* you're right. I'm just angry that the buggers are going to get away and continue to be a threat to us all. We can't rely on the police anymore."

"There are a lot of farmers who feel the same way." Garth could hear Dries taking a long, slow drag on one of his eternal cigarettes. "Some of them have formed their own *Burgerlike Beskerming* groups – their own civil defence force. Maybe we should do the same. We're all armed, and we're all in the same predicament. We'll just have to watch each other's backs and forget about the police."

"Good idea, let's do it tomorrow. I'll call Theunis and Wouter and we'll meet for coffee at my place to discuss it. Maybe Caitlin will make some *pannekoek,*" he said, referring to crepes with cinnamon sugar.

"I'll call my neighbours and get as many people together as I can," Dries said.

"*Ja,* I'll do the same," Garth said.

Dries arrived for coffee the next morning and when Garth opened the door he held out a box. "I have a present for you," he said to Garth.

"What is it, *boet?*"

"The hollow point bullets you wanted," he said. "Make sure the first bullet in your magazine is one of them. They're not as accurate, but they're excellent for close range. If someone's broken into your house or up close and personal you want to make sure you get him good. You can load the rest of your magazine with normal bullets."

Garth took the box and opened it. Inside were six bullets. He took one out and held it up to the light. The sun gleamed on the copper casing. "So this hollowed out shape in the tip is what it's all about," Garth said.

"Yes, that bullet will mushroom out when it hits the target and expand to one and a half times its width. If you hit the guy on his arm he's not going to use it ever again, in his chest and he's *moer-toe*, he'll meet his maker and that's not God. He'll go to the devil where he belongs."

A group of men, including Theunis and Wouter, arrived and they went inside. They had just sat down to coffee and were about to tuck into the *pannekoek* when two policemen arrived. Caitlin took them through the house to where the men were sitting on the veranda.

They introduced themselves and Sergeant Botha said, "There's nothing left at the quarry, Mr. Finley." He looked mature, like he had at least fifteen or twenty years on the police force.

The men made angry sounds, coffee cups thunked on the table, lighters clicked as cigarettes were lit.

"Just bits of flesh in the trees and a big hole," Botha's side-kick Sergeant Venter said, hoping to placate them.

"Fuck it! I told you to come out right away, now they're gone," Garth exploded. "There were boxes and boxes of arms and ammunition."

"Could you tell us what you saw?" Sergeant Botha asked. "Venter – write everything down."

Venter did what he was told; he flipped out a notebook and began to write as Garth described the scene at the quarry.

When Garth finished, Botha nodded. "Thanks, Mr. Finley. Our best guess is that it was a grenade, but our explosive technician is on his way from Pretoria to confirm."

"I thought it could've been an antipersonnel grenade," Garth agreed.

"*Ja,* but if it was, there would've been more people dead or injured. They have an effective kill range of five meters and a casualty radius of approximately fifteen meters. From what you say there was only one body and no injuries."

"I figured that the guy was making a booby trap when it went off, and he shielded the blast with his body."

"You could be right. Well, our explosives guy will be able to tell us more when he gets here."

"Listen, I don't really care what blew up or how many of the bastards could've been injured. What I care about is that they got away. They're still in business."

"We're understaffed, Mr. Finley. Things have changed from the old days when we dealt with the odd fight in a farm compound or went around arresting blacks who didn't have passes. Now the bastards have guns more powerful than ours. It's not easy."

"Well, I just want to tell you that we're taking matters into our own hands. If you guys can't respond in time to an emergency, then we have to rely on our own defences. We're going to form our own civil defence group; we've all got weapons and radios."

"Why don't you join your local commando unit?" Sergeant Venter asked. "You've all done your military training so you'd be supplied with R1 rifles, and if your wives pass the shooting courses they'd be issued with Uzis. Our commando units are voluntary, part-time and they fall under the South African Army and the South African Police Service."

"I don't want to be called up for camps," Theunis said.

"You won't have military commitments outside your area. Each community is divided up into small sections called cells and you'll be responsible only for the safety and security of your own cell in your community. One of you could be a cell leader."

"I don't know," Dries said. "Being part of the commandoes would entail manning road-blocks, and doing foot and vehicle patrols, wouldn't it? And we would have to go for training even though we've been in the military. I have friends who are in the commandoes and they're always out when they should be at home protecting their own families."

"You're quite correct, but there are benefits," Sergeant Venter replied.

"What do you think?" Garth turned to his friends.

"Nope, not me thanks. I'm for our own civil defence group," Dries folded his arms across his chest.

"Me too, we'll watch each other's backs," Theunis agreed, his mouth a grim line.

The other men nodded and Sergeant Botha stood. "Either way is fine with us, we appreciate your help," he added, ignoring the antagonism.

At the end of the month, Kazi told his parents he was going to another soccer practice.

Goodwill felt relieved. Kazi was doing well, getting good marks, playing soccer instead of hanging out with gangs like a lot of the other boys, and appeared to have accepted things as they were. He seemed to have settled down since coming back from Mossel Bay. Most of this was true, but what Goodwill didn't know was that Kazi wasn't playing soccer. He was going to an Umkhonto we Sizwe camp.

Kazi arrived on time at the shop and helped Saul and his father load provisions onto the back of a three-tonne Isuzu truck. When they were finally ready to leave, Saul climbed in first and sat between his father and Kazi, and Saul's father took off in a westerly direction and then turned north. It was hot in the cab, and Kazi immediately opened the window to let the breeze flow through. He felt a surge of excitement. He was finally doing something to find his brothers.

Saul's father wasn't very talkative, so Kazi and Saul talked about school and Kazi told Saul about his holiday and the seaside. Over an hour later Saul's father turned onto a dirt road. Dust streamed in leaving the taste of dirt in their mouths and Kazi closed the window. With the windows closed heat built up even more in the cab. Kazi's legs sweated against the vinyl seat. Dust continued to seep in through the old rubber seals on the windows and doors making it difficult to breathe. It was uncomfortable, and the boys were silent, each coping with his own discomfort. Twenty minutes later they veered off onto a rough track and Saul's father slowed down to negotiate the road.

"Bloody road gets worse every year," he grumbled.

They came to a stop at a set of closed farm gates and two armed guards spoke to Saul's father.

Turning to look at Kazi one of the men asked, "Who is this?"

"He's come to help. Now hurry and open up," Saul's father replied.

The man looked at Kazi again and, shrugging his shoulders, opened the gates. They drove slowly up to a derelict farmhouse, a shed and a couple of old shacks. Saul's father parked the truck and he and Saul walked away to make arrangements to offload the provisions. Kazi looked around with interest.

The buildings were almost impossible to see amongst the bush, vines, and weeds that were reclaiming the abandoned farm. It appeared to be a perfect hideout. He had been told to stay at the vehicle, but it was hot and he became bored. He couldn't see anybody, but he could hear voices and followed them to a group of young men doing exercises. He slipped in behind some shrubs and watched. He couldn't make out their features, so he pushed his way though to where the shrubs thinned out, and peered through the leaves. He still couldn't see well enough. Everyone in the clearing was absorbed in what they were doing, so Kazi decided that no one would notice him. He stepped out of his hiding place and sneaked forward willing his brothers to be there. He could already imagine taking them home with him, his parent's joy, and his brothers' gratitude. How happy he would be. He stopped in the shadow of a large tree and looked through the group, studying each person. None were young enough to be either of his brothers. He turned to leave as an iron fist clamped over his shoulder.

"Vat are you doing?" growled a foreign voice in Kazi's ear. The man was obviously from Russia.

Kazi froze, realizing that he should've done what he was told and not strayed from the truck.

"I'm here with Mister... um..." he couldn't remember Saul's father's name. "I'm here with the truck." He pointed.

"Well then, what where you doing over here? Are you spying?"

"Nothing S-Sir," Kazi stuttered. He was becoming worried.

"You're lying," the man grabbed his arm and shook him roughly. He was dressed in camouflage military clothing.

"I'm not."

"You *vil* address me as comrade!" The man turned Kazi and pushed him towards the house. Kazi staggered forward, beginning to feel really scared.

"Comrade, Sir, please I mean no harm, I…" he looked frantically around for Saul and his father.

"Quiet." The Russian mercenary pushed him again.

They reached the house and the man shoved Kazi through the open door and forced him onto a chair. Kazi's thoughts raced through his head, not sure what to do.

Long tense minutes passed before a tall black man, obviously in charge, entered. Without a word he walked directly up to Kazi and struck him a violent blow across the side of his face. The chair toppled and Kazi staggered back trying to maintain his balance. In the semi-darkness of the room his knees began to shake, pain radiated through his face from his cheek, and he could feel his lip swelling and his eye closing. He lifted his hand to wipe his nose and it came away bloodied. He thought about his brothers and wondered how his parents would cope if he disappeared as well. His thoughts turned to Thandi and his love for her, and he felt a deep aching sadness at the thought that he might not be able to say goodbye.

"Pick it up," the man yelled, pointing to the chair.

Kazi bent to do as he was told and the man kicked him hard. Kazi collapsed onto the floor. He tried to drag himself up, but the man pushed him down holding him on the ground with his boot.

"Tell me the truth! Who are you? How did you get here?" he demanded.

Kazi's face was pressed against the floor and dust rose in little puffs as he tried to breathe. He couldn't answer.

"Who are you?"

"Kazi Matebane," he managed.

"Louder."

"Kazi Matebane," he repeated.

"Why were you spying on our troops?" the man growled.

"I wasn't."

"What were you doing?"

"I... "

"You *were* spying, weren't you?" the man yelled. He towered over Kazi, about to strike him again.

Kazi sensed another person entering the room and he became aware of voices. Then someone was helping him up. He staggered, but the hand held him firmly and Kazi heard Saul's father ask, "Comrade, what's going on here?"

At that moment Kazi realized he had never felt so relieved in his entire life.

The Russian pointed at Kazi. "Comrade, I caught him spying."

Saul's father scowled at Kazi. "Comrade, this is a misunderstanding, he came with me. He's just a curious young boy, not a spy."

The man glared at Kazi, who quaked inwardly. He could feel sweat running down the backs of his legs.

"I'm sure you will understand that a young boy gets bored when left for long. It is my fault. I should not have left him." Saul's father pressed his fingers painfully into Kazi's shoulder. There was anger in the grip of his fingers.

"If he is with you, then take him away and don't let me see him back here again, or you for that matter. Comrade Lyov, escort them to the gate." The man spun on his heel and strode angrily out of the house.

"Come with me," Comrade Lyov commanded. He marched them back to their truck and drove with them to the gate.

When they were alone again Saul's father turned on Kazi. "You stupid boy, I told you to stay at the truck. Remember in future to keep your eyes and ears to yourself. Now I'm going to have to pull in every favour owing to me to get that contract back." He turned to Saul, "Don't ever invite one of your friends again. You hear?"

Saul nodded and stared out of the windshield as they drove in an uncomfortable silence back to town. Kazi felt the throb of pain in his back, and his face ached. He opened and closed his jaw trying to get the blood flowing to his lips and face. He wished he had something cold to hold against the swelling and the bruises he could feel forming, so he opened the window and let the breeze blow on his skin. He thought about the day and realized that he had messed up his first attempt to find his brothers. He wondered now if he would ever find them, or if they were even alive.

When he got home, he went first to the tap outside and washed away the blood and dirt. Then he went in through the back door and changed his shirt before his parents saw him. When he walked into the living room they were listening to the news on the radio and the announcer was saying, "... The Bureau of State Security have uncovered a plan by the ANC to sabotage power supplies, railways and government buildings, and the government has declared a state of emergency to contain any forms of subversion. Thirty-four people have died in unrest between black factions in Kwa-Zulu Natal. Two men died in a gruesome faction fight outside the Diepkloof mine hostel. The men cannot be identified as they were burned to death in a neck-lacing. Petrol-soaked tires forced over their heads and set alight. And now for the weather..." The announcer's voice hadn't changed at all between murder and the weather.

Goodwill turned off the radio. "Where will this stop? Black people are killing white people, white people are killing black people, and black people are killing black people." He turned for the first time towards Kazi and noticed the bruises on his face. "What happened to you?"

Martha looked at Kazi too. "Gracious, what happened?" She jumped up and crossed the room to where Kazi was standing. "You look terrible," she said, looking at the bruising, her fingers feeling for broken bones.

"It's nothing, Mom, I was tackled at soccer. I didn't mean to get you worried, I just came to say goodnight." He turned to leave the room.

"But Kazi, you haven't eaten," Martha said. "You must eat."

"Don't worry, Mom, I'm not hungry. Goodnight."

"Goodnight," they both said and Kazi walked out, concentrating on not wincing.

He was exhausted and although his body ached from the beating, once in bed he soon fell into a deep sleep.

TWENTY-TWO

A BIRD IN A GILDED CAGE

1985 · 1986 · 1987 · 1988 · 1989 · 1990 · 1991 · **1992** · 1993

Maria called from the new security gate. "Kok, kok," she said. Caitlin opened the gate from the remote next to the bed and, ten minutes later, Maria came in with a tea tray, put it on the bedside table, and left. Caitlin took her cup of tea to the window and looked out. The sky was turning a gunmetal grey as night turned to day. The birds had migrated north and the trees were silent. A light frost lay on the ground and a trail, left by Gotcha's night vigil, ran around the inside perimeter of the fence.

"I feel so trapped," she said, looking through the burglar bars at the fence and the Coral tree on the other side. In the distance she could see the valley, a light mist rising from the river. One of the horses whinnied from the paddock. A patchwork duvet lay in a tangle on the bed behind her. The blue drapes had been pulled aside to let in the morning light. A bedside lamp glowed. "I used to love walking down to that tree with the feel of the wind in my hair and the smell of the *veld* in the early morning. I never expected the fence to be like this."

Garth came and wrapped his arms around her from behind. "I know it's horrible, but we had no choice. Come on, let's get back into bed and enjoy our tea. I have to get going soon."

Caitlin stared at the fence. "Our lives will never be the same again."

Garth sighed and went back to bed on his own. "We could sell the farm and move to the Cape if you want. Both kids will be in Stellenbosch next year. We'd be closer to them, and there's not as much crime there."

"The reverse of the Great Trek," Caitlin replied cynically. The Great Trek was the migration of the early settlers into the interior of South Africa. Now she felt they would be going in the opposite direction. "And where would we go after that, into the sea?" she asked bitterly. A cool river breeze came in through the window. She closed it, turned back into the room, put down her cup and went into the bathroom to shower.

Garth finished his tea and got up. He was upset that Caitlin was unhappy. He had bought guns, put up the fence, and installed burglar bars to keep them safe, but he couldn't stop the rising tide of crime and violence. He walked out to the shed with his head down, a host of thoughts going through his mind.

Caitlin climbed into the shower and allowed the water to run hot over her head and down her back, and then, once dressed, dragged herself into the office and, setting her depression aside, did accounts and cost projections for the rest of the day. By mid-afternoon her desk was clear, the weather had improved, and she was about to go for a ride when the phone rang. It was Scott. Her heart plummeted. It was unusual for him to phone during the week; something was obviously wrong.

"It's okay, Mom," he assured her. "I just wanted to let you know that I was sick. Matron said it's probably just flu and gave me some Panado."

"Do you want us to come and see you tomorrow? We're going to fetch Shanon from the airport. We could pop in at around two before we pick her up."

"That would be great. Thanks, Mom."

The next day, when Garth and Caitlin arrived at the school, the matron was standing at the door dressed in beige woollen stockings, sensible shoes, a brown dress, and her hair was pulled back in a bun. The day had cleared, it was 17 degrees Celsius, and Scott lay in the warming sun under a leafless Jacaranda, his head resting on his bag. Matron was watching over him, making sure he was safe. She had sent him outside because he had a rash of chicken pox spots, and she didn't want the virus to spread throughout the hostel. As Garth and Caitlin drove in, she lifted her hand in acknowledgement and turned back inside. Scott looked up, got to his feet, and ambled over to the car. They looked surprised to see his bag, and he climbed in with a wry smile and lifted his shirt in explanation.

"Not chicken pox!" Caitlin exclaimed.

"That's what Matron said."

"I haven't had it, nor has Shanon," Caitlin complained as she picked up the car phone and dialled the doctor's phone number. "That means anti-viral injections for both of us."

After that the day went reasonably smoothly. Shanon's flight was on time. At the medical office they were the last patients, and the doctor was waiting. The drive home was uneventful. As they drove through the new gate Shanon looked at the fence and sank back into her seat without saying a word.

Jackson was waiting to see Garth before he left for the day, and Garth went up to the workshop with him. Caitlin took

Ruben's bridle and ran down to the paddock, captured the horse, and rode off bareback. From the workshop Garth watched her riding through the lands towards the river. He knew she hadn't taken her Glock and he worried for her safety. He feared that Spyder, or a man like him, could be hiding, waiting to settle the score. He decided to speak to her about keeping her gun on her, even when she was riding.

Scott and Shanon went inside with Gotcha sniffing at their heels.

"How's university?" Scott asked, following Shanon. On the way home the focus had been on the explosion in the quarry. Now Scott wanted to know about Stellenbosch and what Shanon had been doing. He walked into the kitchen and stared into the snack cupboard. "Want some popcorn?" he asked.

"Sure," Shanon took a university magazine out of her bag. "Here," she dropped the magazine on the counter as the smell of popcorn filled the room.

The microwave pinged and Scott took it out. He added salt and put the bowl down next to the magazine. "What's this?" He picked it up.

"Our '*varsity* mag. I wanted to show you what you have to look forward to during initiation week next year."

"Great," Scott took a handful of popcorn and turned the pages. He stopped at a dog-eared page. "Who's this?" he asked, and Shanon blushed. "Aha!" Scott exclaimed. "You like him, don't you?"

"Maybe," she said with a wistful smile.

Scott studied the photograph and scratched at a spot on his face. "What's his name?"

"Chad," she replied, taking another handful of popcorn, "and don't scratch, you'll get scars. Go and get some of that cream the doctor told you to use."

Scott took the last mouthful of popcorn, "You just want the rest of the popcorn."

"You're right." She stared into the empty bowl and gave him a playful cuff on his shoulder. He spun away laughing, and went to fetch the cream.

Alone for the first time since getting home Shanon walked to the window and looked at the same view Caitlin had looked at the previous morning. She stood, her hand flat against the cool glass, and stared at the fence. Everything was changing. The farm had always been her safe haven that she visited in her mind when things weren't going well, and now even that was slipping away.

After dinner Scott went to bed and Shanon to her room to finish an assignment.

At ten-thirty Garth and Caitlin said goodnight to Shanon, who was still working, and Garth locked the house carefully. He was still in the habit of locking all the inter-leading doors in the house, even though they now had the fence and burglar bars.

It was well into the night when Garth and Caitlin woke to the sound of gunfire.

"Not the quarry again," Garth grumbled. A fresh volley of gunshots sounded, and he turned over and switched on the bedside light. "I can't believe they've come back. I'm going to make sure the police come out and arrest them this time."

"Garth, those shots aren't coming from the quarry, they're closer." Caitlin's words trailed off as more shots were fired.

"You're right," he said, sitting up, "that's close. Radio for help on the civil defence channel; see if you can get hold of Dries and Theunis. Tell them to bring as many men as they can." He was already pulling on khaki shorts and a shirt. He opened the safe and removed Caitlin's Glock while she was speaking on the radio to Dries, Theunis, and two other men who had responded to her call. His CZ revolver was within reach on his bedside table, and he picked it up.

Satisfied that help was on its way Caitlin cradled the radio. "We've got to get to Shanon and Scott," she said, pulling on a tracksuit.

Garth nodded, "They'll be safe in their rooms – no one can get through the burglar bars."

Caitlin's hands were shaking when she took her gun from him.

"I've checked it, and chambered the first round for you." He didn't want her wasting time chambering a round if she had to shoot in a hurry. The two seconds that it would take could cost her life. "And the safety is on. Don't forget that your first shot is a hollow point bullet so just point and shoot if you have to, don't worry about accuracy," Garth said. Another series of gunshots went off and Caitlin looked worried.

"I think they've cut the fence. Garth – they're outside the house!"

"Odd that Gotcha isn't barking." He didn't add that he was worried that the dog was dead.

Garth unlocked the bedroom door, and moved forward, keeping close to the ground below the windowsills. "Stay low, leave the lights off."

"Okay," Caitlin said as she copied Garth, creeping through the dark house. Another door loomed and Caitlin stayed down, inches from Garth's feet. He stretched up and turned the key. The door swung open and Garth eased forward. The windows in the living room were low and their elbows chafed on the carpet as they crawled through the room.

The shooter let another hail of gunshot loose. The sound was coming from the east side of the house where the kitchen and Scott and Shanon's rooms were located. There was no sign of them.

"Shanon, Scott," Caitlin called out. More gunfire drowned out her words.

A door rattled and it sounded like the kitchen door. Sweat beaded Garth's forehead. "Who is it?" he yelled. "*Identifiseer jouself!* Identify ..."

More banging wiped out the rest of his sentence.

"Garth," Caitlin whispered, she gripped her Glock with trembling hands, "Who do you think it is?"

"Maybe someone needs help. It could be someone we know. *Identifiseer jouself,*" he yelled again.

"We'd better..."

Again loud, demanding hammering interrupted what Caitlin was saying, and this time someone yelled, "Open the door!"

"B-but, that's Scott!" Garth swallowed thickly. "Why's he outside?"

"Scott!" Caitlin screamed.

"Mom," Scott shouted. "Let me out," he yelled. "I'm locked in my room."

"Oh," Garth got to his feet and pulled Caitlin up.

"What's going on?" she asked perplexed.

"I must have locked him in by mistake when I said goodnight."

"But what was all that shooting?"

"I don't know."

Garth unlocked the door and Scott, fever-flushed, pyjamas bagged at the knee, stood in the doorway. On his palm lay a strip of red fireworks.

"Sorry, did I give you a fright?" he asked, observing their panic stricken expressions. "I had to get your attention somehow because I needed the bathroom, and realized that the door was locked. I tried to get out through the window, but I couldn't fit through the burglar bars."

Garth was gruff with embarrassment. "Sorry, son."

"That's okay, Dad," Scott grinned. "You couldn't hear me, so I thought I'd light some crackers and throw them out the window to get your attention," he said.

"You certainly got our attention; you nearly scared the wits out of us!"

"I think you've been watching too much *MacGyver*," Caitlin laughed with relief, referring to the television series that evolved around the clever solutions the secret agent implemented to solve seemingly unsolvable problems. His main asset was his inventive use of common items.

Garth laughed too. "Well, I'm relieved it wasn't a bloody terrorist... Oh no," he exclaimed. "We've got to stop Dries and Theunis."

"Too late, here they come," Caitlin said, cocking her head towards the sound of approaching vehicles.

She walked over to the control panel and opened the gate before the intercom buzzed.

Shanon came out of her bedroom. "What's going on?" she asked sleepily.

"Didn't you hear all the noise?"

"I fell asleep with my headphones on and didn't hear anything until now," Shanon replied. "What's going on?"

"Dad locked my door by mistake, and I needed to pee."

"Why didn't you just pee out the window?" she asked. "You're a guy, you've got the equipment. Did you have to wake the whole house?"

Scott looked shamefaced, "I thought of that, but then I got worried about being locked in my room. What if there'd been a fire?"

They heard the crunch of gravel and vehicles.

"Who's that?" Shanon asked.

"Scott lit fire crackers to get our attention. We thought they were gunshots and radioed for help."

Shanon shook her head.

"Scott," Caitlin said, "you'd better take your chicken pox germs back to bed before the cavalry arrives."

"I'm going too," Shanon said. "I don't want them to see me in my pyjamas."

Garth and Caitlin opened the front door as Theunis leapt out of the leading *bakkie*, a revolver in his hand. Dries climbed out of the second, and Wouter and Jan, the two other men who'd responded to their call for help, followed out of a third vehicle. Wouter was a wiry man who moved like a ferret. His face was narrow with a pointed chin and small eyes. Jan lumbered behind. He had a moustache and thinning brown hair. They were all armed.

"What going on, I thought you needed help?" Dries asked, noticing them standing calmly at the door.

"It's a long story," Garth said, introducing Caitlin to Wouter and Jan. "You'd better come in."

Wouter looked at Caitlin, her Glock in its holster on her hip. "So what have you go there, little woman? A pee shooter?"

"A Glock 17," she replied in spite of the implied insult.

"Do you know how to use it?" he asked condescendingly.

"You'd better know it," Garth boasted, "she's bloody accurate." Caitlin held back a smirk.

"Really," Wouter said doubtfully. "Can I have a look at it?" he asked Caitlin.

She removed the Glock from its holster, ejected the bullet from the chamber and removed the magazine before handing the weapon to Wouter.

Wouter lifted his eyebrows at her deft handling of the gun. "Wouldn't mind one myself," he said, admiring the gun and testing the weight in his hand, "Nice and light."

He handed the gun back.

Caitlin turned to the others. "Would you guys like some coffee?"

"Or maybe something stronger," Garth grinned.

"*Ja,* something stronger," Wouter nodded and the others agreed.

Garth led them inside to his pub, a converted den with a counter and six bar stools, dark shelves filled with bar paraphernalia, and a stereo. He poured drinks without the help of a tot-measure, added ice, and a small amount of mix.

Dries lit a cigarette and took a long drag, smoke easing from his nostrils. He squinted against the smoke. "Okay, Garth, tell us what happened. You said there were gunshots."

Garth took a deep breath. "That's what we thought," he said, and relayed the entire story from the beginning. He paused dramatically at the point where he and Caitlin crept across the floor, and stopped.

"Come *on,* Garth, tell us what happened," Dries urged.

Caitlin couldn't hold out any longer and burst into peals of laughter. "It was Scott," she giggled, "locked in his room."

"What do you mean Scott? What about the gunshots?" Dries asked.

"Fireworks," Garth said. "He was throwing fireworks out the window to get our attention."

"Fireworks? You mean there were no gunshots?" Dries's laugh began deep and erupted in a loud hoot. He pulled a hanky from his pocket and dabbed at his eyes. "Fireworks," he said again with a shake of his head.

Theunis chuckled and held up his glass. "You know, Garth, you're a *dom Engelsman*! Cheers!" he said, taking the insult out of his comment with a smile.

"What can I say?" Garth laughed. "Tonight I was an idiot, and I admit I am an Englishman." Theunis was joking, but he really did feel foolish. It must have been the explosion at the quarry that made them so jumpy. Garth lifted his glass and clinked it against Theunis's glass. "Cheers," he repeated.

After they'd finished complaining about the crime, the ineffective police force, and comparing their weapons, the conversation turned to politics. Caitlin went to fetch peanuts. When she got back Jan was making a point, stabbing an angry finger.

"I'm telling you I'm sick and tired of the way things are going," he was saying. "The country's going to the dogs."

"*Ja,* you're right," Theunis took out a pack of Camel, offered them around and lit one himself.

"The blacks are getting away with murder. They're even allowed to use our public toilets now," Jan looked as if he had a bad smell under his nose. "How can my wife be expected to use a toilet a black *meid* has used?"

"*Sis,*" Wouter shuddered and swallowed a slug of brandy. His Adam's apple lifted and fell.

"They'll be allowed to buy houses in white areas soon," Theunis's head wagged incredulously.

"Imagine blacks living next door." Wouter pointed outside.

Jan shook his head. "Uh, uh!" His beady eyes narrowed.

"What's the difference?" Caitlin opened the window to let the fog of smoke out, "We've already got labourers living next door. They're black."

Jan's lips thinned into a slit. "That's different, they work for us. They don't *own* the land."

"FW's given them a pinkie," Wouter continued, holding up his little finger, "And now they're not going to be satisfied until they've got everything, and chased the white people out of South Africa."

"It's all because of bloody sanctions," Jan continued. "*Vokken* Yanks, *wat die vok weet hulle* – what the hell do the Americans know about South Africa? Do they realize that the blacks were ignorant savages when white people arrived in this country? And now they want us to give them the vote!"

"We can't. They don't know anything about politics," Theunis pronounced. "They'll just put a cross next to a black face, just because they're black. Without knowing anything about them, or what they stand for."

"What do you think will happen if the blacks are allowed to vote?" Smoke streamed from Wouter's nose. He took a long swig of his brandy and coke. "There are thirty million *kaffirs* and only five million of us."

"They'll take over and redistribute businesses and land. We'll become like Zimbabwe, you've seen what happened there," Jan said, and Dries nodded. He'd been largely silent during the whole debate.

A muscle bunched in Wouter's cheek. "We'll form our own *volkstad* before that happens. A place for whites only, where we can live without them."

"I think there should be an education requirement to vote," Dries said.

"But Dries, how can you say that?" Caitlin said. "Half a century of apartheid has left most black South Africans poor and under-educated." Caitlin's father was head of the institute for black education. She knew what she was talking about.

"Nonsense," Wouter disagreed, "they're not under-educated, they're genetically stupid. They can't be educated, and they should have their own schools so they don't drag our children down. I agree with Dries, only educated people should be allowed to vote."

"Did you go to university, Wouter?" Caitlin asked, baiting Wouter. "College?" Wouter shook his head. "Matric?" she asked, referring to South Africa's graduation year. Wouter didn't reply.

"So what do you think it should be?" Caitlin asked. "Standard eight, matric, college, university? If you make the level above standard eight, you'll be taking away a lot of white votes."

"*Ja,* standard eight would be good," Wouter replied without admitting his own education level. It was probably standard eight.

"What do you think about people like Goodwill and Jackson?" Caitlin asked. "They're both smart guys, but they were taken out of school at a young age to help support their families. They didn't have the resources to carry on with their education."

Wouter made a movement as if to wipe her comment away. "Blacks shouldn't be allowed to vote. And that's that!"

Garth poured another round of drinks; it was the same old argument that would go around in circles. He would have enjoyed the discussion with Dries, and possibly Theunis, but not with these other two blokes who appeared to be right wing fundamentalists. He was surprised that Caitlin was taking them on.

Caitlin said, "Look, I think it's going to be hard to argue that South Africa's a white man's country when whites account for less than ten percent of the population. We're going to have to allow them equal rights, whatever we think." She knew she was pushing the envelope.

"*Twak jong,*" Wouter put his palms flat on the table and leant forward. He glared at Caitlin. "Nonsense man, we all know that apartheid's not new, it's in the *Bible.*" He thumped the table. "It's true," he insisted. "Bring the *Bible, vroutjie,* and I'll prove it." Caitlin looked as if she was going to tell him to get it himself, but fetched the *Bible* anyway, and handed it to him with a skeptical look. She wanted to see what he was going to prove.

"*Dankie,*" he thanked her. "Deuteronomy, Chapter 32, Verse 8," he mumbled as he paged through the book. "You'll see, it says everyone must live separately. We're not supposed to live with *kaffirs.*" He found the place. "Here, I'll read it. 'When the Most High gave each nation its heritage, when he divided all mankind, he laid down boundaries for people.'"

Wouter's steel-blue eyes flashed, he skimmed a few pages. "And what's more the *kaffirs* are supposed to work for us. Joshua, Chapter 9, Verse 27. '... from that day he assigned them to cut wood and draw water for the community.' It's all here," he tapped his finger on the open *Bible* proving his point.

Caitlin looked at Garth. She was at the limit of her endurance, there was no logic to the conversation.

"Why don't you fetch some coffee, Caity," Garth suggested, trying to put some distance between her and Wouter.

"*Ja, vroutjie,* your place is in the kitchen, not with the men," Wouter smirked. Caitlin felt the breath suck out of her lungs, the blood rush out of her face. She went quiet.

Dries jumped to his feet. "I'll give you a hand," he said moving her to the door.

As they walked out they heard Wouter expanding his tirade. "Garth, *jy moet jou vrou in toom hou, man* – you need to keep your wife in check, man." Caitlin tried to turn back, enough was enough, but Dries put a strong hand on her arm and propelled her on towards the kitchen.

"Don't worry about him, he's a fool."

"Ignorant bastard," Caitlin's eyes contracted. "He has no right to speak the way he does."

"Caitlin, ignore him."

Caitlin opened the cupboard, took out mugs and slammed the door. It bounced back open and she slammed it again. "I can't stand the man."

"You have to understand that he truly believes that the Afrikaner volk have been planted in this country by the Hand of God, destined to survive as a separate volk with its own calling."

"How can he twist religion for his own benefit like that?" Caitlin asked, filling the kettle. "It's unbelievable!"

They heard Garth say something to Wouter, then a few minutes later a vehicle drove off, and Garth came into the kitchen with Theunis.

"They've left," Garth said.

"Why didn't you support me, Garth?" Caitlin turned on him angrily.

"I'm sorry, Caity," Garth said, "but it's no use arguing with someone like that. You're not going to change his mind. And anyway, I don't know what the answer is."

Caitlin rounded on him, "What do you mean you don't know what the answer is? Everyone should be allowed to vote, that's all there is to it."

"Caitlin, you can't just throw it out there like that. Things have to move slowly. Perhaps an interim government or something."

"*Ja*, Caitlin," Theunis said. "If the blacks get the vote tomorrow, South Africa *will* have a black government, and it'll be a complete bugger-up. They won't know how to run the country. They've got no experience."

Dries stubbed out his cigarette; he could see that everyone was getting hot under the collar. It was time to leave. "Caitlin, I don't think I'll wait for coffee, it's late."

"*Ja*, me too," Theunis agreed. "I'll have to sleep in the dog kennel if I don't get home soon."

"Are you sure? How about a *loop dop*, one last drink for the road," Garth suggested hoping his friends would stay. He knew he was going to get an earful when they left.

"*Ag*, I'd love to, Garth, but I have to get up early tomorrow."

"*Ja*, me too," Theunis said, following suit.

"Okay," Garth said with a long face. He got to his feet, "Thanks for coming," he said.

"Anytime, Garth, we had a good laugh. I can't wait to tell Annarie." Dries knew that Garth and Caitlin would sort things out once they left, he wasn't worried about them. "Bye, Caitlin. Thanks for the drinks, Garth."

"*Ja,* thanks for the drinks, Garth. Bye, Caitlin, *lekker slaap* – sleep well," Theunis said.

TWENTY-THREE

BOYCOTTS

1985 · 1986 · 1987 · 1988 · 1989 · 1990 · 1991 · **1992** · 1993

Kazi was worried, he wanted what everyone else wanted – the freedom to vote – but he felt as if he was being dragged into a vortex into which everything was being drawn. Strikes and demonstrations were happening more and more often, and boycotts of schools for blacks were a certainty. He remembered his conversation with Scott, and decided to find out if the Finleys could help.

Scott was at home for the weekend and he found him at the farmhouse. Together they went in search of Garth and Caitlin, they were in the office.

Scott poked his head around the corner. "Can we come in? Kazi wants to speak to you."

Garth looked up from what he was doing and nodded. "Sure," he said, putting down his pen as the two boys came in. "What's on your mind, Kazi?"

"Mr. Finley, I'm worried that there are going to be school boycotts," Kazi said, "and I don't know how I'll finish school this year."

Caitlin turned from filing documents. "Do you really think there'll be boycotts?"

"It looks like it, Mrs. Finley," Kazi replied. "Last week there were people outside our school with 'Liberation before Education' banners, and the talk is about when it's going to happen, not if."

Caitlin nodded, "Well, then we'll have to start planning for it."

Garth thought for a moment. "If you want to continue your schooling during the boycotts, you'll have to find teachers willing to ignore the boycott, and I guess you'll have to find a safe venue for your classes." He thought a moment. "I think I know a place, an old crop sprayer's hanger about ten kilometres from Brits. It would be big enough to house a number of students if that's what you need. It's old, but it does have running water, a toilet, and electricity. But teachers," he shook his head, "I can't help you with that."

"I'm sure our headmaster will help, he'll find teachers," Kazi said with confidence.

"Good, that would be a start," Garth said. "I'll phone Johan and see if we can use the hanger. He doesn't fly anymore, so I'm sure it'll be available. Kazi, will you speak to your headmaster about teachers? And Caitlin, could you find out what we can borrow in the way of desks and books?"

"I'll get hold of my dad," Caitlin said. "He organises corporate sponsorship for the Freedom School." The Freedom School was a school for black children disadvantaged by government policies and the subsequent secondary education standards. "I'm sure we'll be able to borrow books and desks from the headmistress. She's a friend of Dad's, and she'll understand our problem. Kazi, could you ask your headmaster for a list of things he'll need, and I'll make sure I get them for you."

"Thank you, Mrs. Finley. I'll get the list as soon as I can."

"Excellent," Garth said. "So that's the venue sorted out, and the books and desks. The rest is over to you, Kazi. I'm sure we can get this school rolling when we need to."

"Thank you, Mr. Finley, thanks Mrs. Finley," he said.

He and Scott went off together, relief evident in the slope of his shoulders.

Two weeks later during school assembly, Mr. Mgani told the students he had been accosted by activists while marking papers in his office. He had a light graze, which showed across his temple, his hands clenched anxiously at his sides, and his face held a grim expression.

"Students," he said. "I've been told to tell you all that the people who did this to me, 'comrades' as they called themselves, will be back. This was just a warning," he lifted his hand to the graze on his face. "The ANC are calling for school boycotts and, if we disobey, they will burn the school down."

One of the students called out, "Liberation first, education later." Someone else yelled, "No! Education above all else." And an argument broke out amongst the students.

Mr. Mgani clapped his hands to silence the students' angry outbreak. "I know we're being intimidated, and I know you're all angry, but I fear that if we refuse there will be personal reprisals, not just the burning down of the school. I don't know what we're going to do. Many of you are heading into the final months of school and should be writing your graduation exams in November. As your headmaster, I'm committed to your education, but there's not much I can do. We're going to have to obey the boycotts, which are set to begin on June 16th if negotiations don't improve, but we'll continue with classes as usual until that date." He stepped away and left the classroom without another word.

Kazi followed the headmaster to his office. He knocked tentatively.

"Sir," he said, when Mr. Mgani looked up, "Could I speak to you privately?"

"Certainly, Kazi," Mr. Mgani said and Kazi entered the office.

Mr. Mgani closed the door. "Sit," he said, and Kazi sat down on the chair allocated for students and visitors. Mr. Mgani walked around his desk and sat down opposite Kazi.

"Sir," Kazi said. "I think I know a place where we can continue with our lessons, that is if you know of any teachers willing to teach us during the boycott."

"Kazi, do you realize what the repercussions will be if we disobey the boycott?"

"Sir, no one would find out. This place is completely hidden. It's an old, unused aeroplane hanger, and we would only let the matric students we trust come to our school."

Matriculation, usually shortened to 'matric' was a term commonly used to refer to the final year of school and the qualification received on graduating from high school. Although strictly speaking, it referred to the minimum university entrance requirements.

"Kazi, this is an outrageous idea." He tapped his chin thoughtfully and was silent for a few minutes, then he jumped up suddenly.

"You know, I actually think you have a good idea." He walked to the window and back again. "I think we can do this," he said and started planning aloud. "There will be teachers sympathetic to our cause who will help us. We'll screen the students, and take in only those we trust." He looked at Kazi. "We must be very careful who we speak to. Not a word of this must leak out."

Kazi grinned. "Yes, Sir," he said.

Mr. Mgani frowned, "But there's still the problem of desks and books. Where will we get supplies from?"

"Sir, the Finleys, the people who own the farm where I live, have offered to help us. Mr. Finley is the person who is going to arrange the hanger, and Mrs. Finley has someone who will lend us books and desks."

"Can we trust them?"

"Yes, Sir, their son Scott has been my friend since I was six."

"Okay," he nodded. "So how will we get the desks to the hanger if Mrs. Finley manages to borrow them?" Mr. Mgani asked seeing gaps in the plan.

"I'll ask Mr. Finley if we can use the farm truck."

"Who'll drive the truck?" Mr. Mgani asked, thinking through every step.

"Jackson. He's the driver on the farm."

"And what about him, can we trust him?"

"I'm one hundred percent sure we can."

"It looks like you've given this a lot of thought, Kazi."

"Yes, Sir. One last thing, Mrs. Finley asked me to get a list of things we'll need."

Mr. Mgani nodded. "I'll give it to you tomorrow."

They talked for a few more minutes going over details, then Kazi caught the bus home and went directly to the farmhouse to tell Garth and Caitlin to put their plan into action.

On June 16th, the ANC did call for mass strikes and school boycotts. Students across the country burnt their books and schools were vandalised, and violence escalated as different groups came under attack, those for the People's Education against those for the People's Power. Emergency clinics were swamped with casualties, and police vans patrolled the streets throughout the day and night.

The hanger that Garth found for the clandestine school was beyond a field of wheat on a bumpy dirt road, and quite hidden from sight. A crop spraying company had used it for their aeroplanes, but it had stood neglected for years. A sun-bleached windsock hung forlornly from a pole, and weeds grew on the runway. When they opened the doors of the hanger, dust filtered through the air, and the weak winter sunshine did little to warm the shed. But it was a safe place, and that was all that mattered to the students. They swept the floors and, when Jackson arrived with the farm truck loaded with the assortment of desks and tables Caitlin had borrowed, they brought them inside and arranged them in groups so that the students could be divided into classes and subjects. Jackson also left five boxes of books and supplies on the teachers' tables at the front of the hanger and, by lunchtime, the school was as ready as it would ever be.

On the first morning the students made their way to the school with security foremost on their minds. Jackson drove some of them in the farm truck, the others were brought by relatives and friends who they stayed with near to the school. The first lessons were soon underway and went reasonably smoothly, except for the cold that crept up from the bare concrete floor in the early morning. Everyone was nervous of infiltrators and, although the atmosphere was charged with tension, the mood was positive and the students and teachers proved to be a dedicated team.

By early October their numbers had swollen considerably, and the days went by in a daze. Green buds opened on the skeletal branches of the trees and the wind blew warmth into the shed, bringing with it the promise of rain.

Outside their little haven things were getting worse. The ANC suspended all dealings with the government and held the largest political strike in the history of the country with over one hundred thousand people marching on the parliament buildings in Pretoria, the capital. Mr. Mgani reported that the school in Brits had been broken into and ransacked, and a mob of thugs hung about on street corners looking out for anyone attempting to go to school.

The police were becoming jumpy and nervous and in September, on the way to the hanger with a group of students, Jackson was stopped at a police roadblock.

A policeman stepped up to the driver's window. "Where are you going, *kaffir*?" he asked. "Why aren't these children at school, hey?"

Another policeman, enthusiastic for trouble, joined his partner. "*Ja*, its people like you," he shook his finger in front of Jackson's face, "that are the cause of the problems in the country. Bloody strikes and boycotts! You should be at work," he said. "And these children should be at school, not causing trouble."

Jackson had remained silent up until now. "*Meneer*," he said in the nicest tone that he could muster. "I'm taking these children to town for my boss, Mr. Finley. I have a letter," he said, handing a note to the policeman. Luckily Garth, foreseeing this kind of situation, had given him the letter.

The policeman glanced at it and sniffed contemptuously. "Garth Finley, that bloody *kafferboetie* – kaffir lover," he said just loud enough for Jackson to hear, and with an abrupt wave he said, "*Ry maar* – go," and turned angrily away towards the next car in the roadblock.

The danger of exposure came from all different directions. On the way home, Jackson dropped Kazi off in Brits to buy more notebooks and writing paper for the school. Caitlin had sent an envelope of cash with Jackson, and Kazi bought what they needed. Because he didn't want to be seen outside a shop that sold school supplies, he walked two blocks north and waited for Jackson to pick him up.

While he was waiting, Spyder sauntered up and stood next to him. When Kazi realized who it was he wished a hole could open up and swallow him. He would prefer anything other than a confrontation with Spyder just when Jackson was about to drive up the road towards him.

Spyder took a cigarette out of his pocket and lit it with a deep drag. He slit his eyes against the smoke and blew into Kazi's face. It took everything Kazi had to ignore Spyder. He stared ahead, his hands clenching and unclenching within his pockets.

"So where do you go every day, Kazi?" Spyder sneered. "There's no school, so I wonder what you're up to."

Over Spyder's shoulder Kazi could see Jackson pulling away from the traffic light. He knew the truck would be loaded with students that Spyder would recognise, and thought quickly. He casually picked up his bags, as if he had been resting for a moment and not waiting for someone, then he turned in the opposite direction to that which Jackson was coming from, and walked away. To his relief Spyder followed, taunting him and plucking at his bags to see what he was carrying.

"What's this? Books? I wonder what you would want books for. There's no school. No teachers, no school for little Mister Smarty Pants," his lip curled. "You're going to fail, ha-ha," he laughed. "Or maybe you're hiding something – why else would you be buying so many books?"

Kazi looked back to see where Jackson was, and noticed that the truck had turned down a side street. Jackson must have summed up the situation and would wait for him there.

"I'll find out sooner or later," Spyder laughed horribly and sauntered off, leaving Kazi clutching his bags and staring at his enemy's receding form.

At that moment his anger outweighed his feeling of relief, but by the time he reached the truck and climbed in, he realized how close they had been to being caught and felt only relief.

"That was close," he said to Jackson.

"*Yebo*," Jackson agreed and pulled away.

"You played it cool, thanks."

"We must watch that man. He's evil and will be watching you now."

Kazi nodded and they drove on in silence for a while.

For Kazi the following months passed in a haze of learning, and tension was building up as the date for finals drew closer. But, at the last moment, the Department of Education would not allow the students to write exams in an unlicensed venue and without a registered invigilator. Mr. Mgani met with various heads of departments and inspectors, but he encountered a cold indifference. Time was running out, the date for the exams was approaching rapidly, and no one seemed to be sympathetic to their problems.

And then, with just a week to go, Mr. Mgani finally managed to get an appointment with Mr. Sebong, a grey-haired man, and head of the education department. He listened to what Mr. Mgani had to say and, without a word, took out a series of forms and registered the headmaster as an invigilator so that he could supervise the writing of the exams. Then he listed the venue as private.

They were going to write their finals in the hanger! Leaving the offices, Mr. Mgani walked down the steps, grinning triumphantly and waving the papers clutched in his hand at Kazi and Jackson who were waiting in the parking lot.

The exams went without a hitch and on the last day, Kazi looked for Mr. Mgani. When he found the headmaster, he took his hand and shook it.

"Sir," he said, gripping his hand. "Thank you for all you've done for me and for the other students," he choked up. "We couldn't have done it without you. We know it was dangerous and we'll always be grateful to you and to the teachers who helped us."

Mr. Mgani smiled proudly. "We had a great group of students to work with. They were dedicated and the type of people our new South Africa will rely on." He reached into his pocket. "Kazi," he hesitated, "you've carried out your promise to me and finished school. I know you're going to search for your brothers now. Here's a name," and he handed a piece of paper to Kazi. "It's all I could find for you. I hope he can help."

Kazi looked at the piece of paper in his hand; it was like gold to him. "Thank you, Sir."

"Goodbye, Kazi, and good luck. Remember to contact me if you need anything."

Overjoyed at finally being free from school, Kazi walked across the old landing strip and, finding himself in a field, began to run. With his legs pumping beneath him, he ran and ran, feeling the freshness of the air flow over him. He ran until his chest felt as if it would burst, then he dropped onto the grass under a giant Wattle tree and lay gazing up at the blue sky through the leaves. White clouds drifted gently by, and he looked at them, thinking of Thandi's favourite game; identifying the shapes of the different clouds. His heart began to still its frantic beating as he lay there, spread-eagle in the dappled shade, feeling at ease and relaxed for the first time in months.

TWENTY-FOUR

THE LION'S DEN

1985 · 1986 · 1987 · 1988 · 1989 · 1990 · 1991 · 1992 · **1993**

Six weeks had passed since school ended and Kazi felt restless and discontented. While he waited at the shed for Scott, he watched a hawk hunting for prey as it turned into the wind, its piercing eyes searching the ground for movement, and wondered what it would be like to fly. He was thinking about his brothers and Thandi, longing to see her.

He had graduated with several distinctions, and received a scholarship that Caitlin had applied for through her father. He wanted to go to UCT, the University of Cape Town, but he couldn't leave yet. He had to fulfil his oath to find his brothers, and he also had to earn some money. His scholarship would cover living expenses and university fees, but he would need money to pay for the train to Cape Town, clothing, pocket money for odds and ends, and to take Thandi out. He could ask Garth for a job, but he was already indebted to the Finleys for all they had done for him, and he didn't want to push the boundaries of his friendship with Scott. The other problem was that he didn't want to be tied down to a nine-to-five job while he was looking for his brothers. He had to be free to leave if he received a lead.

He noticed the dust plume before the Nomad came into sight, and within moments Scott was there. Kazi climbed in and Scott pulled away. He had also finished his exams and was on holiday until he started his engineering degree in Stellenbosch.

As they sped off in the direction of Ahmed's shop, Scott glanced at his friend and, sensing his mood, kept quiet. He knew that Kazi would tell him what was on his mind when he was ready. He turned on the radio and the two drove in silence, enjoying the wind and music. When they reached the shop they greeted Ahmed's mute sister at the door, and went inside where it was, as usual, a hubbub of different cultures and languages mixed into a pleasant chaos. It wasn't long before they had found what they wanted and lined up to pay for their purchases. Ahmed was in his usual position behind the counter.

"Scott," a heavy hand landed on Scott's shoulder. "Remember me, Jacobus from junior school?"

Scott turned reluctantly, remembering the scrawny schoolboy Jacobus dressed in army fatigues, a dagger on his belt. Jacobus was now in typical farmer's khakis and had grown into a heavy-set young man. His nose was flattened from a break at some time, his square jaw jutted forward, and his head appeared to flow straight into thick-set shoulders. His arms hung away from his sides in an aggressive stance. Like a baboon, Scott thought.

Scott smiled reluctantly, "Of course, Jacobus. How are you?"

Jacobus nodded. "Good," he said. His glance raked over Kazi. "I see you still hang around with that *kaffir*," he said as if Kazi couldn't hear.

Kazi felt his temper rising and wanted to leave, but Scott held up his hand as if to say wait.

"You English," Jacobus smirked, "do you think the *kaffirs* are going to treat you any differently than us Afrikaners when the time comes? Don't you see that your skin is white, man? 'One settler one bullet,'" he said, quoting black radicals. "I'm sorry to inform you," the R's rolled within his guttural accent, "but that's you, as well as me, my friend," he said, pointing between his own chest and Scott's, and glaring pointedly at Kazi.

"Kazi is …" Scott started. He wanted to say 'my friend', but Jacobus interrupted and continued as if Scott hadn't spoken.

"President De Klerk thinks he can just hand over our country. Well, we're not going to take it lying down. We'll stand up and fight to the last man to protect what's ours."

"Really?" Scott asked without interest.

"*Ja*, man," Jacobus grinned eagerly. He obviously thought Scott was interested. "We're making guns in our workshops, do you want to see?" He glanced at Kazi, "You can bring your *kaffertjie* if you want."

Scott looked at Kazi and Kazi shrugged his indifference. He didn't want to give Jacobus the benefit of knowing that he had got to him.

"Sure," Scott said, intrigued now, "why not."

"Let's go then," Jacobus suggested.

Scott paid for his purchases and Ahmed gave him a pitying look with a roll of his eyes towards Jacobus.

"Please be giving my good wishes to your parents," he said in his accented English.

"Thanks, Ahmed, I will," Scott said and turned to leave. He and Kazi walked outside in silence, climbed into the Nomad and followed Jacobus's diesel *bakkie* out the parking lot.

"I'm sorry he spoke to you like that," Scott said, remembering their conversation in Mossel Bay.

"Don't worry, I'm used to it," Kazi replied with an unreadable expression.

"What's all this about? Do you know?"

Kazi stared at the back of Jacobus's head in the vehicle in front of them. "I heard that he's part of the Afrikaner *Weerstandsbeweging.*"

"I've heard about them, but I don't know much. I've obviously been away at school too long."

"The Afrikaner Resistance Movement is a group of white supremacists who believe that black people are inferior. They're talking about forming their own separate homeland."

"I can see a person like Jacobus belonging to a group like that." Scott indicated, turned the corner and, with a nod, said, "My dad says that racism was taught to people like Jacobus in the cradle. They'll never change. There will always be people who believe in supremacism, like the Nazis and the Klu Klux Klan."

Jacobus turned down a rutted farm road. Scott followed and they came to a halt outside the open doors of a workshop where a group of black labourers could be seen inside.

Scott followed Jacobus inside. Freshly milled guns were lined up on the workbench. Scott picked one up – he could feel the heat in the barrel that had been recently bored and rifled.

"Aren't you worried about sabotage?" he asked, sighting down the barrel. "You're using the same black guys you're threatening to shoot to make your guns."

"How would they do that?" Jacobus looked confused.

Scott resisted a smile. "They might bend the barrels," he said, crooking his finger into a U shape to point back at his own chest.

Jacobus looked at Scott, then gave an uncertain bark of laughter. He slapped Scott enthusiastically on the shoulder. "You're just making a joke, ha, ha. You know *ou* Scott, for an *Engelsman* you're not so bad, man," he said, and Scott realized that Jacobus had missed his poor attempt at sarcasm.

He decided to leave things as they were, replaced the gun, and held out his hand. "I'd better get going," he said.

"You'll see, you English guys will come running to us *Boers* when the shit hits the fan with the *kaffirs*," Jacobus said, shaking Scott's hand.

"*Ja*, maybe," Scott replied dubiously. "Thanks for showing me what you're doing."

"Anytime," Jacobus said, turning to go back into his workshop. He was already yelling insults at his labourers, and cuffed one across the back of his head.

Kazi and Scott climbed into the Nomad and as they drove away Scott started to laugh. Tears streamed down his cheeks and Kazi eyed him quizzically. In explanation Scott formed his hand into a gun, crooked his index finger into the u of a bent barrel and Kazi threw back his head and laughed too. It was a relief to laugh and release the anger and resentment he felt towards Jacobus.

Eventually they stopped laughing and Kazi cleared his throat. "Scott," he said, "can I ask a favour?"

"Sure, what's on your mind?"

"Please say no if you don't want to."

"Okay."

Kazi shifted on the seat. "I have to go to Bloemfontein and wondered if I could borrow the Nomad."

Scott glanced at him, "Sure, but why Bloemfontein?"

"I want to look for my brothers."

"But why Bloemfontein?" Scott repeated. "Your brothers could be anywhere. They could be in Mozambique for all you know."

"I don't know, but I have to start somewhere, and I've been given the name of a man in Bloemfontein who might help me."

"Of course you can take the Nomad." Scott glanced again at Kazi. "You'll be careful, won't you?"

"I will, I promise I'll take care of it."

"No, I meant *you* must be careful."

"I will be, I promise."

They stopped outside the farmhouse and Scott took Kazi inside to phone Thandi. He wanted to find out if she could meet him in Bloemfontein.

She was excited when she heard his voice. "How did your exams go? How did you get around the boycotts? We didn't have any in the Cape, I was lucky," the words tumbled out in a rush. She took a breath.

"Thandi," Kazi took advantage of the break in her conversation, "I'm going to Bloemfontein, I know its a thousand kilometres from Cape Town, but is there any chance that you could ..."

"That I could meet you? Yes, oh yes!" she interrupted eagerly, "I have an aunt who lives in Bloem, we can stay at her house. And I can hitch a ride with one of my cousins. He drives a transport truck between Bloem and Cape Town."

They spoke for a few more minutes, then Thandi gave Kazi directions and they arranged to meet in two days' time.

After the call the two boys drove to the workshop and asked Jackson to service the Nomad before the trip.

As Kazi prepared to leave, Goodwill drew his son aside. Over the years since Mandiso and Dumani's disappearance, the lines on his face had etched into a look of permanent worry, and his eyes showed a deep inner sadness. If he knew of Kazi's quest to find his brothers, he never spoke of it. Now he placed his hand on Kazi's shoulder.

"Please be careful." His brown eyes glistened with moisture. "May God travel at your side, my boy," he said, as he turned away to hide his tears.

Kazi hugged his mother and Ntokoso, and then he leapt into the idling Nomad and accelerated off. As the Nomad moved away he gave a final wave goodbye. In the rear view mirror he saw his mother turn, take his father's arm, and draw him into the *lapa* towards the fire. Ntokoso remained where she stood and carried on waving until he was out of sight. Kazi had noticed that she looked thinner than usual, and her shoulders stooped inwards with a listlessness that was unusual for her. It dawned on him now that she must have been sick for a while. Her coughing had woken him at night for months, and he had noticed that she often got up to change her sodden sheets, obviously damp with sweat from a fever. He decided that when he got back he would persuade her to see a doctor. There was definitely something wrong.

He turned onto the main road, and put his concern for Ntokoso aside as he followed the familiar route that Garth had taken when they went to Mossel Bay. The traffic eased as he travelled through Johannesburg's outer limits and, giving little attention to the passing scenery, he became absorbed in his thoughts until he realized that he was hungry. Nearly three hours had passed already, so he looked around for a picnic spot. He noticed a rest stop on the side of the road with a couple of wooden benches and tables under a tree. He pulled up, chose a table, and opened the parcel of food his mother had given him; a jar of sweetened tea, thick slices of white bread spread lightly with jam and, if that wasn't a treat in itself, she had also included two hard boiled eggs. It was a special meal that she must have saved up for, and he smiled fondly. After eating, Kazi set off again and decided to make a concerted effort to set aside the worrying details of finding his brothers.

He began to imagine his reunion with Thandi, and his longing for her formed a pleasant ache in his chest. It had been a long time since he had seen her, but the memory of her laughing and running on the beach was still clear and sharp in his mind.

He drove at an easy pace, and when the radio cut out it was peaceful, mile after empty mile, with only the sound of the wind. He stopped for fuel just before Bloemfontein and, by mid-day, took the off-ramp and drove into the native township. The street seemed to need repair and the surface had several potholes. The houses were more or less identical, small and drab, and in front of most of them grass and weeds grew tall. Only black and coloured children, some of them in old and ragged clothing, played in front of the houses. But regardless of how they were dressed, they played happily together and, when they saw him approaching, made way for him to pass, then came together again to continue with their game.

He found the house, parked the Nomad in the street, and walked up the dirt pathway. Thandi had told him that her aunt would be away and he looked on the window sill for the pot of geraniums, wilted and yellowing but still recognisable, where he'd been told the key would be. He found the key and opened the door.

The house inside was small, but clean, and set out on a plastic tablecloth on the kitchen table were the makings for coffee, and a note instructing him to help himself. He put the kettle on to boil, made his coffee, then he sat down to wait for Thandi. A cockerel crowed in a nearby back yard, and the soft clucks of hens and children's laughter could be heard from inside. He looked at the clock and wondered how long Thandi would be. When he finished his coffee he looked at the clock again. He walked to the window and looked left, then right, picturing the truck that would bring her, persuading it to come. But the street remained disappointingly empty, so he went back to his seat and looked at the clock. Time seemed to have frozen since he last looked. He picked up a magazine and flipped aimlessly through the pages, not really seeing anything. At last he heard a truck and jumped up. A door slammed and, as footsteps approached, he rushed to the door and threw it open. It was Thandi and she ran into his arms.

"At last you're here," he said, grinning.

She smiled happily. "Yes, at last. I've missed you so much," she said, embracing him.

She turned to wave at the truck driver, and Kazi drew her into the house to the kitchen table where they talked for the rest of the afternoon, each hardly finishing a subject before starting another. They spoke about the year that had passed since they had been together on holiday in Mossel Bay – school, the boycotts, exams, and Kazi's search for his brothers. Thandi asked about Scott and Shanon, and the months apart seemed to melt into moments, and hours passed unnoticed.

After all was said he pulled her into his arms, held her tight and breathed in the smell of her, the soft familiar scent of her skin. "Thandi, I wish I never had to leave you again. I want to be with you forever."

Thandi pulled back and looked up at him. "I want to be with you too," she sighed.

He kissed her again, this time deeply and long. He wanted to touch her body, to feel her, to know every inch of her. He slid his hand under her shirt, and groaned. His heart pounded. He couldn't catch his breath.

She responded, pushing against him, running her hands down the muscles of his arms and shoulders. They had filled out from the manual labour he'd been doing. She cupped the back of his head and deepened their kiss, her mouth soft and welcoming.

"Thandi," he said pulling back. "Thandi, I can't do this. If we carry on I won't be able to hold back."

"It's okay, I don't want to stop," she breathed, kissing him again, holding his face in his hands and looking into his eyes.

He leant away from her and looked back into her eyes. "Are you sure?"

"Yes," she whispered softly. "I've dreamt of being with you."

He kissed her softly running his finger across her bottom lip. He kissed her again where his finger had lingered.

"Oh Thandi, if you want me to stop you have to tell me now."

"I don't want you to stop," she repeated moaning at his touch. "But I don't want to fall pregnant. Have you... have you got anything?" she asked shyly.

"I do, don't worry," he whispered, feeling relieved that he'd followed Jackson's advice and stopped to buy condoms on the way into town.

His hands shook as he eagerly unbuttoned her shirt and slipped it from her shoulders. He ran his hands down her arms. Her breasts were small and firm and he reached for them, cupping them in his hands. She gasped with pleasure and he felt his body harden in response. His heart beat furiously. He kissed her again, and then he pulled back and slowly removed the rest of her clothes. He was struggling to keep his breathing steady. His gaze travelled down her slender body, "You're so beautiful."

"Oh, Kazi." She felt shy in front of his scrutiny. "Let's go to the bedroom," she breathed.

Kazi could barely restrain himself. He ran his hands down her sides and hips, lifted her easily and carried her to the bedroom, placing her gently on the bed. He reached into his bag and removed a condom, then fumbled with his own clothes, pulling them off and throwing them down onto the floor. Then he climbed onto the bed next to her. He tore open the foil, his palms sweating. Fitting it wasn't as easy as he thought and by the time he had it on he was in an agony of anticipation. He lay down and took her into his arms.

"Thandi," he whispered, kissing her.

He traced down the outside of her arms with his fingertips, stroked the undersides of her breasts. He couldn't believe this was happening. He slid his hand down and felt the moistness of her, couldn't wait any longer, and lifted himself over her, knowing instinctively what to do.

"Are you sure, Thandi? Absolutely sure?"

"Yes, yes." She gripped his back, pulling him towards her.

He entered her, and when she gasped it took all the control he had to stop. "Are you okay?"

"Yes, don't stop," she was breathing fast, out of control herself.

She relaxed and, as he slid into the whole depth of her, the feeling was so intense that he came right away. He tried to keep going but to his disappointment he felt his erection dwindling.

"I'm sorry," he said, rolling off her but keeping her in his embrace. "Give me a few minutes," he said, kissing her face, her neck and her breasts, desperately wanting to satisfy her.

"It's okay," she whispered, and she kissed him and ran her hands down his chest.

"You're so beautiful, Thandi. I love you."

"I love you too, Kazi."

He kissed her again and, as she took him in her hands, felt himself harden again. This time he withheld himself, savouring the moment, then slowly and gently entered her. He moved slowly, matching his rhythm to hers and her breathing increased.

She took a sharp breath, her eyes widened, and she threw back her head and began to moan, panting rapidly.

Kazi concentrated on holding back, on her happiness, and, at last she cried out, and only then did he allow himself to let go for a second time.

Afterwards Thandi smiled contentedly. "I feel like I'm floating in heaven. I wish this night could last forever."

"I know," he agreed and, hugging her to him, fell into a deep sleep.

At dawn Thandi woke to find the bed next to her empty and cold. Kazi had told her that he was going to meet a man, someone Mr. Mgani knew, and had carefully slipped from the bed so as not to wake her. She snuggled under the blankets and smiled at the memory of last night. Hugging Kazi's pillow she fell asleep again, breathing his lingering scent.

Kazi had left after kissing her softly without waking her. He had stood for a long time looking at her, absorbing her features, watching as dreams turned up the corners of her mouth in little smiles. He had wanted nothing more than to climb back into bed with her. He felt torn between his commitment to his brothers and his longing for her but he left, knowing that if he found his brothers, he could be with her for the rest of his life.

The man was waiting when Kazi drew up. The early morning light caught a scar on the side of his face, but as he turned towards Kazi, his expression was open and friendly. He looked fit and lean, and was dressed in jeans, an open neck shirt, and runners. A ball cap on his head.

"Kazi?" the man asked.

"Yes," Kazi replied. "Isaak?" he enquired.

The man nodded and stepped forward to shake Kazi's hand. "Leave your vehicle here, we'll take the bus."

Kazi locked the Nomad and pocketing the keys asked, "Where are we going?"

"I'll tell you on the bus. Hurry – we don't want to miss it."

Kazi fell in beside him and they jogged to the bus stop. Arriving just as a dusty bus was about to pull away, they climbed on and sat down.

"Thanks for helping me," Kazi said.

"It's a pleasure, Kazi. Your headmaster is a friend of mine. He's told me a lot about you."

"So you know all about my brothers and their abduction?" Kazi asked.

"I do. It's a sad but common story."

"Do you think I'll find them?"

"We'll try, Kazi, we'll try."

Kazi nodded. "Where are we going?" he asked again.

"Brandfort, it's a few miles north. The people I want you to meet are one of the youth group factions started by Winnie Mandela, Nelson Mandela's wife. She had a strong influence on radical youth in Soweto during the time that coincides with your brothers' disappearance."

"My brothers weren't radicals," Kazi said defensively.

"I know, I know. I'm just trying to give you some background about this group. It's just a starting point."

"Isaak, I don't understand. My brothers were kidnapped. Are you saying they may have freely joined up with one of these groups?"

Isaak nodded. "Kazi, those boys were young and impressionable when they left. They've been gone for a number of years. You must accept that they could possibly be on their own by now, and may have changed from the innocent young farm boys that you remember."

Kazi shook his head in disbelief. "So why Brandfort?"

"The government sent Winnie into internal exile in Brandfort to reduce her political power, but she continued when she got there and formed another group. Then when she was released from exile, this particular group remained in Brandfort."

Kazi looked out at the countryside. He was worried that this whole trip was going to be a waste of time. After a while the bus drove into a black township on the outskirts of the town, which was as bleak and desolate as Kazi felt.

"Come on, Kazi." Isaak stood up. "Don't jump to conclusions too quickly. We have a number of routes to follow while you're here."

The bus drew to a stop, and they swung down onto the dusty pavement. They walked for about fifteen minutes and, after a couple of turns in the shanty town, Isaak led Kazi up to a tin-roof shack. He knocked on the door and they entered to find a group of youths sitting around a table.

Isaak introduced Kazi to the first youth. "This is my brother's son Daniel. Daniel, this is Kazi." Daniel looked up sullenly and mumbled a brief greeting. His cap was on backwards, his shirt open to his navel, gold chains layered around his neck. He had fat lips, hooded eyes and a flattened nose. He must have been nineteen or twenty.

"Kazi is looking for someone. He'll be going to the ANC meeting with me this afternoon. After that I want you to take him to the compound."

Daniel's only acknowledgement of the conversation was to take a lazy draw on his cigarette and blow the smoke towards the ceiling. It curled and twisted, rising to join the haze already hanging against the ceiling. Kazi felt out of place and annoyed by the attitude of the militant and sulky youths, but he realized that he should hide his feelings. He didn't hold out much hope of them helping him, but it would be better to stay on the right side of them.

Isaak sat down and pointed to a stool, indicating that Kazi should also sit down. He turned to Daniel and spoke quietly and persuasively, and while Isaak spoke to Daniel, Kazi sat down and watched the other youths so similar in age to his brothers. He thought about Mandiso and Dumani, mourning them and nursing his hatred for their captors.

After a long silence Daniel looked at him through eyes slit against the smoke. "Who are you looking for?" he growled.

"My brothers," Kazi responded. "They've been missing since 1989."

"How old are they now?"

"Mandiso would be sixteen and Dumani seventeen."

Daniel stubbed out his cigarette. "Okay," he said grinding it into the ashtray. "Tonight, nine-thirty, be here." He stood and marched abruptly from the room while the others followed in a more desultory fashion.

"Good," Isaak smiled with relief. "Now let's get to that meeting in Bloemfontein. You can come back tonight."

At the venue for the ANC meeting, a stage had been built at the end of a sports field and thousands of impatient feet churned dust into the air. There were more men than women, no children, and only a few white people. A hot sun beat down and someone started to sing in a lone pure voice that filled the air.

"Nkosi sikelel' iAfrika Maluphakanyisw' uphondo Iwayo, Yizwa imithandazo yetho, Nkosi silelea, thina lusapho Iwayo."

People stopped talking and gradually other voices joined until the song hung vibrant and full above the field, the lone voice rising above the others in a haunting melody. It lifted, holding Kazi in the song, until at last it softened to an almost mute note and then it faded into nothing as it let him go.

Nelson Mandela walked onto the stage. He looked older than his seventy-five years. Sun damage marked his cheeks, his hair was more white than black, and deep grooves ran alongside his mouth and lined his eyes. Since his release from prison in 1990 the government had tried to push for a two-phase transitional government with a rotating presidency, and

Mandela had been fighting for a single stage majority rule. In the last months the main parties had been aiming for a settlement with increased determination, and he was now going to tell them the outcome. He lifted his hand and the crowd fell instantly silent. Then he gazed out over the field of heads, smiled, and told them that the government had finally agreed to a five-year government of national unity, after which a single majority rule government would take over. "Elections could be held as early as the end of 1993!" he shouted triumphantly, his fist raised, and the people roared with approval.

Then, as he did when he had been freed from jail, he called out.

"*Amandla*! – Power!"

And the crowd enthusiastically responded with, "*Ngawethu*! – Is ours!"

"*iAfrika*!" Nelson shouted back.

"*Mayibuye*! – Let it come back!" The crowd yelled together.

Nelson Mandela left the stage and Kazi remembered his search for his brothers and turned reluctantly away.

"Isaak, I'm going to look around," he said. "I'll meet you at the entrance."

Isaak nodded and Kazi hurried off, hoping that Isaak was right. Maybe his brothers were free and perhaps they were there too. Rather here than with that group of radicals. After seeing Nelson Mandela he was filled with hope. He reached the gate and people streamed past talking. He tried to find something to stand on, but there was nothing, so he climbed a short way up the fence and looked down on the mass of people. After a while his enthusiasm waned and he realized how stupid he was to believe that his brothers could be at this meeting, or that he would find them in the crowd, but in spite of his reservations he stayed where he was and watched until Isaak touched his leg to gain his attention.

"Come, we must go."

He jumped down as the last people filtered past and Isaak continued, "I've made contact with an old friend who has a suggestion. It appears that you've concentrated your search on ANC camps and meeting places, but there's a possibility that the IFP, the Inkatha Freedom Party, attempted to infiltrate your area, took your brothers and forced your father into helping them. They have a large centre in Ulundi, Kwa-Zulu Natal," he paused. "I suggest that we go there if you don't have any luck with Daniel tonight."

Kazi nodded. "Isaak, you're right. It could be anyone who took my brothers. I just wish my father could tell me more." He shook his head in frustration. "I'm ready to try anything but I'm in a borrowed car. I can't take it to Kwa-Zulu Natal."

"We'll take the train."

Kazi looked at him. "Thanks," he said simply. "I appreciate your help."

"You're a good boy, Kazi," he said, joining a line of people at the bus stop. The bus drew up and Isaak said, "Here's the bus that'll take you back to the township. I have to go somewhere so I'll see you tomorrow. Do you know where to get off?" he asked.

Kazi nodded and climbed onto the bus, and Isaak turned and walked away with someone else. Kazi checked with the driver that he was on the right bus and sat down, wondering if he was on a wild goose chase, a futile search for his brothers. But he had taken an oath and he intended to follow every lead he could.

Thandi leapt up when Kazi walked in and she threw her arms around him. "Oh, Kazi," she breathed. Light makeup accented her eyes and rouged her lips. She smelt like jasmine. "You're back at last. You must be hungry."

"I am," he replied as he eased himself gratefully into a chair, and while she cooked he told her about his day. She laughed when he described Daniel, but when he told her of his plans to go to the compound that evening and then to Ulundi the next day, her eyes filled with tears.

"Kazi, please," she begged. "Please stop this crazy search. Your father wouldn't want you to go."

"Thandi," he replied. "I must do this for my own peace of mind. Isaak will be with me, and we'll be careful."

She turned away and busied herself with the food, and silence hung between them. Kazi looked at her back and sighed. How he wished that things could've been different. He would have done anything in his power not to hurt her.

After a few minutes Thandi turned to face him. "Kazi, if this is something you have to do, I won't stand in your way. Then when it's over we'll live our lives without regret."

He stood up and went to her and took her in his arms. "Did I tell you that you're the most wonderful girl in the world?" he said tenderly.

"Not yet," she said smiling. She pushed him gently away. "Sit down now, you must eat if you have to go soon." She piled food onto a plate and placed it in front of Kazi.

"Aren't you eating?" he asked.

"I ate earlier," she said. "Go on, eat while it's still hot."

He picked up a fork and tasted the food. "This is good," he said appreciatively.

He ate hungrily and when he was finished he pushed the plate away, took her hand, and gently stroked her fingers and the soft inside of her wrist. Then he pulled her up and onto his lap. She laid her head on his chest and was soothed by the steady beat of his heart, the regular rise and fall of his breath, and closed her eyes. After a while a distant clock chimed the hour. It was time to go. He lifted her chin with his finger and gently kissed her. Then he stood up and placed her like a small doll on her chair.

"I'll be back later."

She touched her fingers to her lips and placed them on his. "*Hamba kakuhle*, go well."

He nodded. "I will, Thandi, I will."

He walked out, closed the door softly, and stood for a moment, leaning his forehead on the rough wood, wishing he could stay. Then he turned and walked down the steps and climbed into the Nomad. Thandi waved from the window and he waved back.

The Nomad started roughly, blowing a cloud of smoke from the exhaust. Jackson had told him to look out for blue smoke as the first sign of an engine problem. He turned now and checked the colour, which was grey not blue, and he realized that it was just running rich. He adjusted the choke and pulled away, noticing that the smoke dwindled away as the engine warmed.

He drove to Brandfort and, after a few wrong turns, found Daniel's tin-roof shack. He parked on the street and, leaving the Nomad idling, walked the few paces to the door. It opened as he lifted his hand to knock.

Daniel strode out followed by two of his surly friends. "Let's go," he said.

Kazi's irritation at their attitude returned but he put it aside, and turned and walked back to the Nomad with them. They all climbed in. Daniel had a cigarette dangling from his lip.

"The car's not mine, no smoking. Please," Kazi added as an afterthought.

Daniel flicked his cigarette out of the window, pointed, indicating the direction, and Kazi pulled away from the curb. After a few minutes, Daniel snarled, "Kazi, I'll help you because my uncle wants me to, but that doesn't mean that I like you or that I trust you."

Kazi nodded in silent confirmation, the feeling was mutual. He suspected that Isaak was right about Daniel being one of the ANC mavericks who followed people like Winnie Madikizela-Mandela, Holomisa, and Peter Mokaba. These were township militants who felt they were betrayed by all sides and were disillusioned and resentful.

Without another word Daniel pointed when Kazi was to turn left or right and, when they reached a dilapidated building, he held up his hand. "Park here," he said.

Kazi pulled up and a boy stepped out of the shadows with an AK-47 slung over his shoulder. Kazi looked at him in surprise, but Daniel seemed unaffected. He identified himself, and the boy returned to the shadows. Daniel and his two friends strode towards the building and Kazi followed closely. They opened a corroded metal door and entered what appeared to be a deserted factory. Daniel didn't turn on any lights, possibly because there didn't appear to be electricity, and the only light was from the open doorway and windows where the moon filtered in. In the shadows Kazi could see machinery, most likely too large to remove, and work benches that ran the length of what was essentially one large room. Papers and leaves had collected in the corners and the place smelt of old oil, metal, and rust.

Daniel crossed the room to a flight of stairs and they climbed to a second level of what must have been offices – a series of rooms off a hallway. Daniel entered the first room, spoke to various people, and moved on to a second and then a third room without introducing Kazi. There were no women, and the young men, all between the ages of sixteen and twenty-five, except for one or two young boys, played cards, smoked or just sat in brooding silence. There was a pent-up energy, an undertone of aggressive defiance. In each room Kazi glanced briefly from one person to the next, his eye searching for his brothers' familiar faces.

In the last room a commanding young man sat with a group of others around a paraffin lantern that illuminated papers spread on the table. Kazi gazed around the room. There was one window, a single cot in the corner, several beer cans served as ashtrays. Even in the low light he could see that the room hadn't been painted in a long time. The carpet had been pulled up to reveal raw concrete, and there were no drapes or blinds. The people in the room looked up when they entered and the young man turned the papers over, hiding their contents. He appeared to be older than the others. "Hello Daniel, you've brought a friend," he observed, looking at Kazi. His eyes were hard and questioning. He looked like the kind of man who enjoyed trouble, and the type you didn't want trouble with.

"Jabu, this is Kazi. He's looking for his brothers."

"And you think they're here?" Daniel lifted his shoulders and let them drop. "What do they look like? How old?" Jabu asked in a clipped tone.

"Their names are Dumani and Mandiso, they're sixteen and seventeen, and they both look like me," Kazi said, speaking for the first time since entering the building.

Jabu looked hard at Kazi. He shook his head. "No, I haven't seen them. But I'll put out the word," he said. "What's their surname?"

"Matebane," Kazi replied.

Jabu turned away. "I'll contact Daniel if I hear anything."

"Thanks, Jabu," Daniel said. "Come," he said to Kazi.

Kazi followed Daniel down the stairs. He felt disappointed, although he hadn't expected the meeting to come to anything.

"You'd better not tell anyone that you've been here," Daniel snarled. "Most of these boys have a reason to be here, and they don't want to be found."

Kazi nodded. "I won't."

Daniel walked as far as the Nomad. "Now go, and remember what I told you."

"You don't want a ride back?"

"No." Daniel walked away and Kazi didn't waste any time watching him leave. He climbed into the Nomad and drove out of the grim little town.

The trip back to Bloemfontein went quickly. The streets were dark and deserted except for a lone marauding cat scratching hungrily through garbage, and tethered dogs barking their frustration. Only one or two windows were lit, perhaps a mother tending her child, or a person who couldn't sleep. A thin moon hung low on the horizon as Kazi drew up outside Thandi's house. She had left a light on at the front door and he entered quietly, slipped off his clothes, and eased into bed next to her.

She turned sleepily. "I love you," she whispered.

"I love you too," he said, spooning his body around hers and quickly falling into a deep and exhausted sleep.

In the early hours of morning the sun burned across the bed waking Kazi. He reached for Thandi, and in those first moments of dawn they made love tenderly, knowing that they had to finally say goodbye.

TWENTY-FIVE

UNDER THE RADAR

1986 · 1987 · 1988 · 1989 · 1990 · 1991 · 1992 · **1993** · 1994

B ack at the Finley farmhouse the Karee tree threw a canopy of shade over Garth and Caitlin. Shanon floated on an inflatable chair in the pool, a book in her hands. Scott lay on a towel drying in the sun. On the other side of the fence a troupe of Vervet monkeys chattered in a tree, waiting to raid the vegetable garden. In the past it would have been a peaceful scene, but the fence was a stark reminder that all was not peaceful, and Garth and Caitlin's conversation was equally unsettling. They were discussing whether to stay in South Africa and accept the way the country was going, or not.

"Why don't you think things will improve after the elections?" Caitlin was asking.

Garth shrugged. "The problem I foresee is that the ANC have promised every black person a house if they win the elections. They'll definitely get all the squatter's votes, so they'll win the elections. The Zulus will be unhappy, so will the

Afrikaners." He looked at Caitlin. "Then once they get in, the ANC won't be able to fulfil their promise because they won't have the budget. There are millions of squatters."

Maria called from the house and the monkeys scattered at the sound of her voice. Garth's head lifted.

"What is it, Maria?" he demanded.

"*Ekskuus Baas,*" she apologised. "Goodwill is here. He wants to know if the *Klein Baas* has heard from Kazi."

Scott looked up, "Sorry, Maria, I haven't. But I wasn't expecting him to call."

She thanked Scott and turned to Caitlin. "I'm finished the ironing, *Missus,* is there anything else?"

"No thanks, Maria. I'll see you tomorrow. Just let yourself out."

Maria nodded, "*Ja, Missus, dankie, Missus.*"

Garth continued speaking after the brief interruption. "It'll be like Zimbabwe. The squatters will be happy until they realize they aren't going to get their houses. Then they're going to take what they want with violence. They'll take our houses." Garth swatted irritably at a fly. "Our farm will be gone, and we'll have nothing. We should sell up before that happens. Maybe we should move overseas."

Caitlin slumped into her chair. "I don't know if I could leave, but I'm also not sure if I can live like this either." Her eyes swept over the fence and came to rest on Garth's gun on the table next to him.

"Caitlin, be realistic. Look at what happened in Zimbabwe, Angola, and the Congo. The people who stayed can't leave now because their currency is worthless." He stood up and poured a drink from the tray. "Want one?" he asked. Caitlin shook her head.

She gazed thoughtfully out at the river and valley. She recognised the truth in what Garth was saying, but she wondered if they would adapt to another culture if they moved. They would have to leave their friends, their family, her grandparents. And then she thought about all the things Garth had said and realized that she didn't want to fight the same battles the white Zimbabweans were fighting.

"I guess you're right. But where would we go?" she asked.

"Australia, New Zealand, Canada," Garth's shoulders lifted in another shrug. "At this stage I just want to get some money out of the country so that we've got a safety net if we have to leave. The truth is that we don't know what the future holds, but we should prepare for the worst."

"How? We can't legally transfer money out of the country without Reserve Bank approval."

"I've heard Dries and the guys talking about someone they know who moves money on the black market. His name is German, something like Berndt," he thought for a moment. "I think its Berndt Fischer."

Caitlin put her doubts aside for the moment and concentrated on the facts. "Is it safe? I've heard about people being ripped off."

"If the funds are transferred before we made the payment, we can't be ripped off, but the commission is higher. The other route is that we pay first."

"How much is the commission?"

"Fourteen percent."

Caitlin's eyebrows lifted. "Wow!"

"I know it's high, but at least there's no risk."

Caitlin thought for a moment. "Okay," she agreed reluctantly. "Look into it. But I also prefer the first route, the transfer first and payment on receipt, not the other way around." She held up her glass. "I think I'll have that drink now." Garth got up and refreshed their drinks. She took hers and continued. "We could sell our annuities, but how do we go about transferring the money?"

"As far as I know the first step is to open an offshore bank account."

"How?" Caitlin asked.

"I'll ask my dad, he's been involved in international business for a long time. I know he's got friends in Barbados, which is a tax free haven that doesn't share information with foreign countries. Perhaps they can help us."

"So once we've got that set up, how do we transfer money into the offshore account?"

"Dries knows a bank manager who's leaving South Africa and is willing to bend the rules. We'll open an account with him. It'll be a numbered, untraceable account so that deposits and cash withdrawals can be done without any questions asked.

"We'll sell our annuities and deposit the money into the numbered account. Once that's been done we trigger the transfer. When it's been confirmed that the money has arrived in our offshore account we pay Fischer. In cash," he added.

Shanon climbed out of the pool and Garth and Caitlin stopped speaking. They didn't want to involve the children in the discussion just yet.

On Monday Garth placed several calls, one to Dries to get Berndt Fischer's number, and then he spoke to Berndt Fischer himself. After that he spoke to his father who introduced him to David Brown, a portfolio manager in Barbados. Then he faxed their details to David Brown with instructions to open an offshore account, called his broker and placed a sell order on their investments, and last of all he made an appointment with the bank manager Bernd Fischer had referred him to.

Two days later Garth fetched the cheque from his investment broker and drove to Vereeniging. When he entered the town he followed the directions he had been given, found the bank without difficulty, parked, and went inside. It was a small bank in a single story strip mall. A customer was leaving and he held the door open before entering. Inside there were two tellers behind a counter and a reception desk. At the reception desk, he asked for the bank manager and the woman behind the desk told him to take a seat. She pointed to a chair and Garth sat down feeling nervous. He looked around and wondered if he was doing the right thing. He would go to jail if he was caught, but he hadn't done anything wrong yet, he could still leave. He decided he should and was about to when a man approached, dressed in a dark suit, white shirt, solid colour tie – banker's attire. He had a nice open face and gave Garth an appraising look, obviously assessing him too.

"Garth Finley?" he asked.

"Yes," Garth replied, standing up.

"Peter Collins," the man said, holding out his hand. They traded a firm handshake.

"Thanks for meeting me," Garth said, hoping he was doing the right thing.

"You come with good references, Garth. You don't mind if I call you Garth, do you?"

"Not at all."

"In that case, call me Peter."

"Thank you."

The bank manager turned and led Garth into his office. He closed the door and went behind his desk showing Garth to a chair facing the windows and a view of the parking lot. Both men sat down.

"I understand from Berndt that you're emmigrating. Where are you moving to?"

"We haven't decided yet. We thought we might take an LSD trip, you know – Look. See. Decide," Garth replied with a smile.

Peter chuckled; he'd heard the joke before. "My wife and I have decided on Australia. We should have lunch together, share some ideas."

He removed a form from his desk drawer. "Let's cut to the chase. For this I don't require any identification. As you know it's an untraceable, numbered account so that it can't be linked to you. Here's a copy for you," he said, scribbling an indecipherable signature on the bottom of the page and passing it to Garth.

Garth realized that if he had any last minute concerns he should pull out now. He looked at the form and hesitated, and then he withdrew the cheque from the sale of the annuities from his briefcase and placed it on the table.

"Is this what you want to deposit into the account?" Collins asked.

"It is," Garth nodded.

Collins picked up the cheque and looked at it. "Two hundred thousand Rands," he said, attaching it to the form with a paper clip.

Two hundred thousand Rand was worth roughly eighty-three thousand US dollars at the time, depending on the exchange rate. The exchange rate varied daily. And the amount would be further reduced when the commission for the black market transfer was deducted. In the end Garth and Caitlin could expect to receive approximately seventy-one thousand dollars in their offshore account, if everything went according to plan. It was a good start, but Garth knew that he and Caitlin would have to sell the farm and all their assets to build up a sizeable nest egg. Starting over again in a new country wouldn't be easy.

Peter stood up. Garth followed suit and held out his hand. He remembered that he had another detail to cover.

"Peter," he asked, "how do I go about withdrawing the money? I'll need it in cash."

"Call me on my private line and I'll arrange it. Don't speak to anyone else," David replied, writing his telephone number on a piece of paper. He did not give Garth a business card.

When Garth got home, he phoned Berndt Fischer and triggered the transfer of the funds to their new offshore account.

"Can you do two hundred Van Riebeecks?" he asked, using the code word they'd agreed to. A Van Riebeeck was the code for one thousand Rand, and he wanted to move the full two hundred thousand that he'd deposited with Peter Collins.

"I'll call you when it's done," Berndt replied abruptly and put down the telephone.

Berndt called back two days later. "Garth?" he enquired when Garth answered the phone.

"Yes," Garth confirmed.

"Your parcel has been delivered."

"Thank you. I'll call back once I've received confirmation." The phone clicked and the line went dead.

Garth turned to Caitlin. "The money has been transferred. Could you type a fax to David Brown in Barbados and confirm that the funds are in our account?"

The next morning a fax from Barbados confirmed that the funds were there. Now they had to make the payment.

Garth phoned Berndt Fischer, and a meeting place and time was arranged. He put down the phone and dialled Collins's private number. The bank manager answered on the second ring, and Garth made an appointment to draw all the funds in the account – in cash and in two hundred Rand notes, the largest denomination he could get.

Preparing to leave, Garth strapped his holster and revolver to his calf. Caitlin checked her Glock and put it in her handbag, and they drove to the bank. When they asked for the bank manager the receptionist placed an internal call.

She spoke into the phone, nodded, replaced the receiver and stood up. "This way please," she said, and showed them to a booth. Then she disappeared.

Peter Collins was nowhere in sight.

Caitlin whispered to Garth, "I hope she isn't going to bring the money out here in front of everyone."

"I doubt it," Garth said, thinking of something else. It was odd that Peter Collins hadn't come to meet them, as he had the first day. He swallowed and felt claustrophobic. "What if it's a set up, a police trap?"

Caitlin looked around and scanned the people in the bank. There was an old lady at the counter in front of one of the tellers – the second teller's position was closed, and a woman with a child in a pram stood in line behind the old lady. A man was leaving. Two muscular young men with short, cropped hair and wearing dark suits sat at desks behind the counter. They didn't look like bankers. She stared suspiciously at the young men. "Should we leave?"

"It's too late now. But if this goes wrong I'll say that you don't know anything. Just play dumb, go home, take Shanon and Scott and leave the country. My dad will bail me out. Then I'll get him to fly me across the border in his Bonanza, and I'll meet you in Zim." He had thought it all out.

The receptionist walked up, high heals clicking. They both turned, pulses racing.

"This way," she said. Garth and Caitlin pushed back their chairs and followed her down a passageway.

"Well, this is it," Garth said, under his breath. He wiped a hand across his forehead.

"I hope there isn't a swat team waiting for us back there," Caitlin replied softly, trying to make a light-hearted joke. But it didn't work for either of them.

The receptionist stopped and unlocked a door by punching in a code, and showed them in. They hesitated in the doorway and gave each other a final look of encouragement, and then they walked into the room to whatever faced them there. With a wave of relief they realized that the room was empty. There was no swat team. On the conference table in the centre stood four neatly stacked bundles.

"Sir, would you mind counting the money?" the receptionist enquired. Garth indicated that Caitlin should do the counting, and she sat down in front of the bundles. "You've requested two hundred thousand Rand," the woman confirmed.

Garth nodded and Caitlin drew the pile of money towards her. She separated the bundles into the packs that had been strapped together in bank-style paper strips. All of the notes appeared to be the colour of the denomination they had requested. She counted the packs. One hundred packs. If each pack had ten two hundred Rand notes the total was correct.

Caitlin looked up. "Do I have to count the individual packs?"

"It's up to you. The currency counter counted and strapped the notes, and the bundles have been weighed as a precautionary check."

"Good," Caitlin said with a look of relief. She hadn't been looking forward to counting one thousand notes individually.

The woman slid a receipt across the table. "Sir, could you sign the withdrawal slip, please?"

Garth leant forward. He was the signatory on the account, so he picked up a pen and signed the paper.

"Thank you," the woman said, separating the receipt from the carbon copy and giving Garth the duplicate. "There's a small balance on the account, the interest for the period. Would you like to draw the balance and close the account?"

"Not right now, thank you," Garth replied.

"Will that be all, then?" she asked.

"Yes, thank you," Garth replied. He opened his briefcase and stacked the bundles neatly inside in rows, locked it, and they all stood up.

The woman escorted them to the bank's exit. At the door she paused, blocking the way. The two short-haired men they had seen earlier approached from behind. It struck Garth that this was the time they could be caught with all the evidence of the transaction on them. He looked at the men closing in. Was this going to go down now? he asked himself.

He stooped and put down the briefcase, readying himself for the lies he would have to tell to explain why he had withdrawn so much cash. He felt hot and cold at the same time. Caitlin turned to Garth and he returned her look. He took a deep breath. Fear thrummed in the back of his skull. His brain screamed – Hurry! Run! Get out! He looked past the woman, watched as an afternoon wind blew pockets of dust across the parking lot.

"Excuse me," one of the men said. Garth turned stiffly and the man and his colleague stepped around him and the woman, and walked away. To Garth's surprise they didn't appear to be interested in them.

The receptionist moved aside, and Caitlin walked out with a look of relief on her face.

"Have a nice day," the woman said.

Garth blinked at her, pulled himself together and managed a feeble smile. He mumbled thank you, picked up his briefcase and walked slowly out of the bank towards his car. He wanted to run, to get away as fast as he could, but his legs felt like rubber. He paused and surveyed the vehicles in the parking lot. There was no one who looked suspicious or interested in them.

He clicked the remote and the BMW's doors unlocked. It was a new car, replaced aftr the robbery. Caitlin climbed in, and he opened the boot and placed the briefcase inside. He was shaking slightly when he started the car; he still expected a tap on the window at any moment, and a cop to show his badge.

"So far so good," he said, breathing out a gust of air. He reversed out of his parking spot.

"My nerves!" Caitlin exclaimed.

"Mine too," Garth admitted. He looked left and right searching for the men in the bank, for anyone out of place. There was no one. "I'm still not happy. I'm not sure if we've done anything illegal yet, but those two guys from the bank, or someone else, might be waiting to follow us and catch us red handed with Berndt's people."

He drove out of the parking lot and, glancing at his rear view mirror, pulled up and waited to see if anyone followed. Caitlin looked left and right, turned in her seat and checked behind.

"No one's following," she confirmed.

Garth waited three minutes and then entered the traffic flow. He headed onto the R59 highway towards Johannesburg, and an hour later took the off-ramp, and drove across town towards Rosebank. Under his arms his shirt was sweat-soaked, in spite of the air-conditioning, and he angled the air vents towards himself. The traffic flow increased and Garth had another thought.

"What if we're hi-jacked?" he asked uneasily. They'd been so immersed in the intricacies of the transaction that they hadn't anticipated the danger of being car-jacked, but it was certainly something to consider. "We've got all this cash in the car." He pulled out his revolver and placed it on the seat between his legs.

"Don't even think about it, I can't take any more stress."

In spite of what she said, Caitlin opened her purse and made sure that her Glock was readily accessible. They drove on in silence anxiously watching the other vehicles and keeping an eye on the traffic. When a pick-up truck pulled up close behind their tension mounted. Garth's eyes flicked to his rear view mirror.

There were two black men in the front, three in the back.

"Fuck," Garth said and put his hand on his revolver, "here goes." Caitlin picked up her Glock and looked for a way out.

Garth checked his rear view mirror again. "He's indicating, turning off." He exhaled, and Caitlin put her Glock back in her purse – but left it open.

"Whew," Garth said, as he pulled up at a red traffic light. He took a moment to compose himself. So far so good, they were still safe and nearly at their destination. He noticed movement to his left. A black man was running towards them, something in his hand – possibly an assault weapon. Garth tensed again. It was the stuff nightmares were made from. Traffic was flowing across the intersection, and cars were bumper to bumper behind. They were trapped.

Caitlin pulled out her Glock. Garth raised his revolver, and they both pointed their guns. The man skidded to a stop, his eyes widened, and he lifted a squeegee.

Garth lowered his gun. "I... don't... want... my... bloody... windows... cleaned," he mouthed through the window. "Now fuck off!" he yelled at the top of his lungs.

"Calm down, Garth, it's not his fault." Caitlin opened her window and tossed a couple of coins into the man's hands. "Sorry," she said, slipping her Glock back into her purse.

The traffic light turned green and Garth accelerated away – still angry after the fright the man had given him. He drove in silence through the suburbs and onto Oxford Road, peering into the rear view mirror every sixty seconds – just as he'd been doing since leaving the bank.

"Turn here," Caitlin said, breaking the silence, and Garth turned out of Rosebank into Melrose.

"Next road right into Jameson Avenue," she said, consulting her map. "Go five blocks and the house will be on your right," she said once he had executed the turn.

She called out the address and Garth cruised slowly along the tree-lined street. It was a wealthy area with large houses, tall walls, fancy gates and plush gardens. Garth slowed as they approached the address they were looking for, turned into the driveway, and before he pressed the intercom the gate opened. It looked as if someone was watching.

"Stay in the car and lock the doors," he said abruptly as he drove up the short driveway. Ahead of them a double-garage door opened and a man directed him inside. Garth drove in and the door slid closed. "Shit," he hissed under his breath.

Florescent strip-lights cast a hard white light over everything. Two men were waiting in the garage next to a black Mercedes sedan with tinted windows.

Garth got out. "Good afternoon," he said.

One of the men nodded. He had a beard of the type that could be gone tomorrow, and his hair appeared to be a darker black than it should've been. The other had a recent buzz cut and his scalp was pale underneath. He wore sunglasses inside. The man with the buzz cut indicated with a spin of his hand that Garth should hurry up. Garth walked to the boot of his car, popped it and took out his briefcase, then went around and placed it on the bonnet. He took out the money and Buzz Cut took it and placed it in his own briefcase.

"Two hundred thousand Rands? I don't have to check it do I?" he asked in a threatening voice.

"No, it's all there," Garth said.

"Good, let's go," he said to his sidekick.

He snapped the briefcase closed and both men climbed into the black Mercedes. The double-garage door slid open and they reversed out.

Garth got into the BMW and reversed out too, the doors closed and the Mercedes drove rapidly away.

Garth drove out onto the street, the gate closed behind him and he carried on a short way before he stopped the car. He held up his hands. "I'm shaking like a leaf."

Caitlin nodded, glancing at her own shaking hands. "Me too. I wouldn't like to tangle with those two."

Caitlin looked at Garth, then she giggled, a touch of hysteria edging her laughter. "That was like something out of a movie."

Garth laughed too. "It was."

He drew away and navigated down the street to Oxford Road. "We should celebrate. Our first transfer has gone through without a hitch."

"Let's go out for dinner. We could go to River Lodge. It's quite nice, and it's close to the farm."

"Sounds good. We'll take Shanon and Scott, they'll enjoy it."

Three quarters of an hour later they drove into the farm and Jackson looked up from his work. A line of keloids, tough, irregularly shaped lesions, followed the scar around his neck like a hangman's rope. And his injured eye, although healed since his accident, watered from the dust. Four labourers worked alongside him with bush cutters and machetes clearing bush and grass from the perimeter of the fence.

Garth pulled up and rolled down the window.

"*Middag, Baas, Middag, Missus,*" Jackson greeted them both.

"*Middag,* Jackson. How are Nelly, and the children?" Caitlin asked.

"They are well, *Missus,* thank you."

Jackson turned and surveyed the firebreak they had created. "Is that wide enough, *Baas?*" he asked.

Garth climbed out of the car and looked at their work. He nodded, "That's good, thanks Jackson."

Jackson looked skeptical. "If there's a strong wind, the fire will still jump onto the roof." He flicked his fingers upwards, indicating the rapid spread of flames and they both looked at the thatch roof on the farmhouse.

"I know," Garth replied. "But there's not much more we can do. The firebreak will give us more time to put out the fire before it gets that close. If there's a strong wind, we won't stand a chance, however wide we make it."

"*Ja, Baas,*" Jackson glanced at his watch. "It's five o'clock, time to *chaile Baas* – time to go home."

"That's fine, Jackson. Have a nice evening," Garth said.

"*Nag, Baas, nag, Missus,*" Jackson wished them a good night, and then he shouted to his men in their own language that they were finished for the day.

Garth climbed back into the car and, as he drove through the gate, Gotcha loped alongside. Elias and Maria were leaving, they waved, "*Nag, Baas, nag, Missus.*"

The riverfront restaurant where they went for dinner that evening was in the original farmhouse on a farm that had been converted into a timeshare resort. Caitlin had curled her hair, applied more make-up than usual and was wearing stretch jeans and a black sheen top. Shanon looked striking in a short dress with a broad belt cinched at the waist. Scott and Garth were both in their best jeans, and Garth smelt of aftershave. Garth and Caitlin were in high spirits after their success that day, and the four of them enjoyed their dinner accompanied by a full-bodied red wine, but were home before midnight.

Back home Caitlin went into the kitchen to feed Gotcha and the rest of the family went off to prepare for bed. Minutes later Shanon came back, a bemused expression on her face.

"Mom," she said. "I think there's a leak in our bathroom cupboard, its spraying water. But it's also making a noise!"

"What kind of noise?" Caitlin asked, scooping dog food into a bowl.

"Like snoring," Shanon shrugged and reproduced the sound, "ggah." It came out in a guttural gargle.

Caitlin glanced up from her task. If there was a leak there would be no sound, perhaps a gentle hiss.

"Did you open the cupboard?"

"No," Shanon made a face, "it was too weird."

Caitlin turned apprehensively and followed Shanon into the bathroom. It was strange and she didn't like the sound of it. She cracked the cupboard door open and a goose-like hiss warned her back. She went into high alert. Approaching more carefully, she opened the door marginally wider, and peered in. A long shadow sped towards her, dark and as fat as an arm. She realized in time that it was a snake and managed to close the door just as the reptile slammed into it, its anger evident. Caitlin recoiled as the door bounced on its hinges.

"It's a snake. Fetch Dad!" she told Shanon.

Shanon raced off. "Dad! Dad!" she yelled as she ran to him.

Garth could hear the fear in her voice and responded immediately. "What is it?" He met her partway with Scott who'd also heard the commotion.

"Come quickly, there's a snake in our bathroom."

Caitlin didn't look away from the cupboard as they entered. "There's a very, very big snake in there," she said, making a circle with her apposing index fingers and thumbs touching.

At the sound of voices the snake struck the door and hissed angrily. Garth didn't bother to confirm what Caitlin said, he knew it was true. He paced the length of the passageway, a worried expression on his face. He headed back. The most common snakes they encountered were the Rinkhals, mostly black with a dark belly and one or two light-coloured cross bands on the throat, a meter to a meter-and-a-half, or three to five feet long. Also, the Mozambique Spitting Cobra which was slightly bigger, slate to olive grey, a salmon pink to purple yellowish underneath, with black bars across the neck. Both could spit accurately up to two-and-a-half meters (eight feet), and they usually spat in their victim's eyes, which could cause impaired vision or blindness, if left untreated.

Their bite could cause severe tissue destruction, and neurotoxic symptoms causing respiratory failure and, eventually, death.

"Scott," Garth said in a distracted voice. He was thinking that this was a big snake in a confined area, and confronting it would be very dangerous. He'd killed a lot of snakes on the farm, but this was an unusual circumstance that required careful planning. He didn't want anyone bitten or for them to get venom in their eyes. "Fetch the swimming goggles."

"Goggles?" Scott queried. It was a strange request at a time like this.

"It's probably a Spitting Cobra, we must protect our eyes," Garth explained. "Shanon," he continued with his strategy, "fetch my bull whip from the umbrella stand at the front door."

He kept the whip handy because a moving target like a snake was easier to hit with a pliable whip than a stick, which has a small striking surface. Shanon had seen her father kill a snake by bringing a whip down hard in a vertical swath across its back, and didn't ask questions. She hurried to do as her father asked, and Scott ran off to do the same.

"How're we going to do this? You can't go in there," Caitlin pointed out. The snake had been momentarily silent, but now that it heard her speak it struck the sides of the cupboard fiercely. Caitlin stepped back involuntarily and then she took a moment to study the bathroom and assess the danger. "If you open the cabinet, its door is going to block the bathroom doorway. You won't be able to get out."

It was a small room with a single basin in a cabinet with one louvered door that faced the toilet. There was a bath on the far side under the window, and the cabinet opened towards the bathroom door. Caitlin had a point. When they opened the cabinet door it would block the exit.

"There's only one way to go about this," she continued. "I'll climb onto the basin, push the snake out of the cabinet with a stick or something, and then you can kill it."

Garth bit down on his lip in thought. He didn't want Caitlin so close to danger, but there was no other way. He couldn't do both the extracting of the snake and the killing. He nodded with grim determination.

"I'll need something to hook the snake out of the cupboard," Caitlin observed, continuing her train of thought, "maybe a broom or something with a long handle." She went into the kitchen and returned with a broom at the same time that Shanon arrived with the whip.

Garth took the whip.

Scott came back and gave Garth one set of goggles, and another pair to Caitlin, who put them on.

Caitlin looked at Garth. "Are you ready?"

"Yes," he replied, his voice serious.

Caitlin steeled herself. "Hold this for me while I climb up," she handed the broom to Scott then looked at the vanity. The door was closed, the slats on the door were narrow, and the snake couldn't strike her with the door closed, but it could still spray venom through the gaps. She decided to approach from the side avoiding exposure to the door, and then she could climb onto the vanity where the snake couldn't reach her.

As she started out the snake heard the movement and hit the door, hissing louder. Caitlin took a deep breath and closed her mind to the snake. She climbed up, slid onto the basin and scooted into place. Her back against the wall, her feet well up on the cabinet. She took a moment to catch her breath, sickeningly aware of the snake below her. It had gone into a frenzy. Caitlin's pulse was racing. Her hands shook as she reached out for the broom.

Scott looked at her. "Are you okay, Mom?"

Caitlin nodded. She was frightened, but she knew Garth would kill the snake before it could get close. She trusted him. She made an encouraging movement with her fingers and Scott handed her the broom.

"Ready?" Garth asked.

"Yep," Caitlin said, adjusting her goggles.

Garth stood poised, his eyes focused on the door of the cabinet. "Okay, open the door."

The children stepped out of the way.

It was now or never. Caitlin leant forward and nudged the door with the tip of the broom. It swung open and there was a terrible pause. Caitlin could imagine the snake recoiling, ready to strike. Then it hissed loudly, warning. She inserted the broomstick into the cupboard, fished around, felt the broom strike against something rubbery, pulled the stick up and aimed it further back into the cupboard, behind where she imagined the snake to be. Once she had it in place, she moved the broom forward until she felt the rubber resistance of the snake again. She put her weight behind it and the snake went into a frenzy hitting the side of the cupboard again and again, hissing furiously. Caitlin yanked and pushed back and forth, hoping to weaken the snake. She leant back tired. She could feel a trickle of sweat run from her scalp down the length of her jaw. The heat in the bathroom seemed to intensify. She leant forward again and yanked back ferociously. She dipped her head and lifted her shoulder to dab at the itchy run of sweat. With both hands wrapped around the broomstick she threw her weight once more against the stick. A mist of venom blew through the door below accompanied by the gooselike hiss. She tugged on the stick, but there was no leverage. She didn't have the strength anymore, her muscles were singing from the strain.

"It's no good, it won't budge," she said.

"Maybe you've hooked the pipe. Try again."

"I haven't, I can feel the snake moving against the broom. It's incredibly strong." She repeated the manoeuvre twisting and shoving and yanking. She adjusted her position, seesawed back and forth. The snake hissed and smashed against the side of the cabinet. Caitlin shook her head and leant back against the wall. "It's not working."

Garth considered their predicament. They could continue fighting to get the snake out of the cabinet or he could shoot it where it was – either way, it meant the same thing. The snake had to die. He made a decision, there was only one thing left to do.

"Scott, bring my Astra revolver and the box of birdshot." Birdshot is a cartridge loaded with multiple lead shot designed to be fired at close range. The spread was especially useful for animals that moved quickly and unpredictably changed direction. "Caitlin, get down. If we can't get the snake out, I'm going to shoot it where it is."

Caitlin retreated off the vanity and the snake quietened once it couldn't hear activity. They stood in silence and waited until Scott came back with the Astra and a box of ammunition. Garth took the gun, ejected the bullets in the chamber, and inserted the new cartridges.

"Caity, open the cupboard and stand back," he instructed.

Using the broom Caitlin flung the door open, and stepped away.

Garth moved into the space she'd vacated, aimed and shot off three shots directly into the open cabinet. A burst of blood mixed with glass, face cream, and pills splattered against the walls and bathtub. It was strangely quiet after the boom of the gun.

"Pass me that broom!" Garth handed the whip to Caitlin and took the broom. "Keep the whip ready, I might need it again."

Garth pushed the broom into the cupboard and heaved on the injured snake. He shook his head. "It's coiled around the pipes, no wonder you couldn't get it out. Scott go and fetch the long *braai* tongs, I'll get this bastard out."

By the time Scott came back with the barbeque tongs, the snake was no longer moving, and there was silence from the cupboard. Garth gripped the snake with the tongs and shook it like a Jack Russell shaking a rat, and the snake came free. It appeared to be dead as it slid out of the cabinet. Garth dragged it to the door, down the passage, and along the kitchen floor leaving a long smear of blood. It looked like a Cape Cobra, one of the most dangerous species of cobra in all of Africa. Dark brown with black stippling and blotches. As long as a tall man, and as thick as his arm.

He dropped it on the paving outside, and it moved showing life.

"Bring the whip," Garth yelled. Scott ran back inside and returned with the whip. Garth took it and hit the snake. A wet mark spread on the paving. He hit it again – and again, and again. The snake moving with every strike. Long after its lingering reflexes stopped, its skin broken, bloody and torn, Garth continued the beating. His mouth had pulled into a grimace of hate and rage, his breath came in sharp gusts, his shirt was wet with sweat.

"Dad. Dad! I think it's dead," Scott pointed out the obvious.

Garth didn't stop, he was beyond hearing. He drew back and hit the snake again, his body moving in rhythm with the whip, back and forth over and over again.

"Garth, stop!" Caitlin yelled. Garth finally looked up.

"It's dead, Garth," Caitlin said in a quiet voice.

Garth's shoulders heaved from exertion. The whip, dark with blood, hung slack at his side. They were staring at him. Garth looked down at the snake.

"It's dead, Dad," Scott looked apprehensive. "It's been dead for quite a while."

Garth lifted his head and noticed their expressions. He saw the question in their eyes and realized that he'd overreacted. "I don't know what came over me," he said, apologising. "I saw this snake as everything that's evil in this country. I saw Spider, I saw the car-jackers, and I imagined Holomisa and Peter Mokaba taking my farm from me. I was just overwhelmed with anger." He frowned. "Why should I leave my country because of these black bastards? This is where I was born." He lifted his arms slightly and dropped them to his sides. His shoulders slumped – he was suddenly tired. "My father was born here, and so was my grandfather. Now I'm treated like a pariah, an outcast, and the money I've worked for isn't even my own."

He stopped and looked up at them. "I just... I just saw the snake and I lost it. I'm... I'm sorry," he said.

TWENTY-SIX

IN THE THICK OF IT

B ack in Bloemfontein it was Kazi's third day looking for his brothers. At four o'clock in the afternoon, Isaak rapped on the door. Kazi and Thandi were seated at the kitchen table where they had spent hours talking about their future. Kazi had told Thandi of his plans to spend the year looking for his brothers, to work and earn extra money, and then of his vision to move to Cape Town to be with her, and go to university.

And now they had to say goodbye.

"When will I see you again?" Thandi asked. A single tear ran unheeded down her cheek.

"I don't know," Kazi replied dismally. He took her in his arms and kissed the tear. "Goodbye, my darling," he whispered tenderly.

"Be careful," she said, her tears running freely now.

He stepped back, his hands on hers, his eyes on hers. "You are my life. My reason for living."

"And you are mine," she replied, crying freely as he let go and walked backwards to the door keeping his eyes on hers. He was struggling to maintain his composure.

"I love you," she called desperately and he ran back.

He enveloped her in his arms and crushed her in his embrace. He kissed her longingly.

"I love you," he said, looking at her as if he wanted to burn the impression of her face into his brain. Then he turned, walked out, and closed the door behind him. He stopped for a moment and felt Thandi's presence on the other side. He wanted to go back in and never leave her side, but he knew what he had to do and he walked with determination down the steps.

"Hello," he said abruptly when he reached Isaak.

"*Molo,* Kazi," Isaak replied. "Can you leave the Nomad here? It'll be stolen if we leave it parked at the station. We'll take a taxi and you can fetch it when we return."

Kazi nodded, feeling too raw to speak as they walked in silence. Although Thandi was leaving that day, he was sure the Nomad could stay where it was. Her aunt wouldn't be back for a while.

After a few minutes Isaak saw a taxi, lifted his finger and the mini-bus stopped.

"Train station?" Isaak asked.

"*Yebo,*" the taxi driver confirmed. "But first I go to taxi rank to fetch passengers. Okay?"

"It's okay," Isaak nodded, and climbed in with Kazi following. A small sign on the dashboard told them their driver's name was Sepho.

Sepho had a fat round face and a deep warm voice. "Where you from?" he asked.

Kazi left Isaak to reply, and the two men started a conversation that continued until they reached the taxi rank. Sepho parked, climbed out and walked away to greet a fellow taxi driver.

Hundreds of passengers and drivers milled around. There were also bony boys, obviously homeless from the look of their scruffy clothing, offering chewing gum and cigarettes for sale. Scraggy old women sold cooked mealies and shrivelled fruit, and drunks and glue addicts begged for money.

It was hot in the mini-bus and Isaak suggested they get out, so Kazi opened the sliding door, and they both climbed out and stood on the sidewalk. A small group of prospective passengers congregated next to the taxi, but Sepho carried on with his conversation.

Kazi looked around with interest. "Isaak?" he asked. "I've noticed that some of the taxis have pictures of a *takkie*, or a running shoe, on the back window. Why is that?"

"Each gang has a sign identifying them, and their own designated area to work in. It's a way of controlling their turf, they ..."

Before Isaak could finish, a white mini-bus, similar to their own taxi, pulled up on the other side of the road and a black man holding a gun leant out the window. Kazi looked at him in amazement, and then he heard the spit of bullets. He dove behind their taxi as glass erupted from its windows. A fat woman attempted to crawl beneath a nearby vehicle, and people on the sidewalk screamed. Sepho lay in the gutter clutching at a wound in his chest while a bloody froth bubbled from the corner of his mouth. The mini-bus sped away and Isaak rushed to Sepho. Kazi was frozen where he stood behind the taxi, stunned with disbelief. The fat woman crawled out sobbing, her legs red with blood. Sepho gripped his chest in pain and then his eyes widened suddenly and he gasped. His body jerked once, then he lay motionless in a steady stream of blood that pooled on the road.

Isaak straightened shaking his head. "He's dead," he announced in a flat monotone.

Kazi's stomach heaved, and he turned and vomited into the gutter. Then he leant against the taxi, shaking.

"W-why, w-what happened?" he stammered, trying to make sense of what he'd witnessed.

"The taxi groups are like Mafia," Isaak said. "They have territories, and if they infringe on each other's area, there's war."

"But they killed our driver!"

"I know, Kazi, this happens all the time in the cities. It's possible that Sepho shouldn't have picked us up. Maybe we weren't in his jurisdiction."

"But we could all have been killed." Isaak shrugged. Kazi's gaze returned to Sepho's body, then at the people milling around and returning to business. "It's unbelievable. Look at those people carrying on as if nothing happened."

Isaak shrugged again. "What else can they do?"

"But how do they cope with seeing someone killed right in front of their eyes! They could have died too."

"This is their life! Crimes like this happen every day, and they've grown used to it." Isaak took Kazi's arm. "Come," he said, "we'll miss our train if we're here when the police arrive. They never find the culprits, or do anything other than delay us by taking down statements. They don't care if another black man dies."

Kazi followed Isaak and climbed reluctantly into another taxi. His stomach still felt queasy and, as their taxi drove away, he turned and looked over his shoulder at Sepho's body lying in the road. Sirens blasted past, speeding in the direction of the slaughter, and Sepho's body became smaller and smaller with distance.

At the station, which was a dirty squat building with an architecture that dated well back in history, taxis honked ceaselessly for business, people shouted greetings, and hidden loudspeakers announced arrivals and departures. They climbed out of the taxi, paid their fare, and hurried towards the building. Isaak studied the arrivals and departures board and led Kazi towards a ticket booth.

In the booth, a sour-faced white woman scowled at them from behind a small grill window.

"Excuse me, ma'am. How do we get to Ulundi?" Isaak asked.

"There are no trains that go direct to Ulundi," the woman snapped. "You have to take the train from platform three and get off at Ladysmith. From there you can take a train to Ulundi. Hurry up now, do you want tickets or not?"

Isaak nodded, "Yes. Please," he added politely, ignoring the woman's attitude.

She slapped two tickets on the counter and Isaak paid.

"Which way, ma'am?" he asked.

The woman pointed irritably as if it wasn't her job to show passengers where to go, and Kazi and Isaak walked towards platform three. Grime caked the walls and there was an overpowering stench of urine. On the platform the benches were packed with weary passengers, so they leant against the dirty wall.

"Damn," Isaak exclaimed. "I forgot to bring something to eat."

Kazi couldn't think about food, he was still overwrought. He patted his pocket. "Thandi gave me a couple of sandwiches. You can have them, but they're probably squashed after the shooting at the taxi. I don't want to eat. I can't get Sepho out of my mind."

"You'll feel better later on and then you'll be hungry," Isaak assured him. He leant forward and peered down the tracks as twin pinpricks of light indicated the distant approach of their train. "Get to the front," he instructed.

Kazi followed Isaak through the crush of bodies as the train drew to a stop and, when the doors slid open, they pushed through the disembarking passengers. Isaak managed to find two seats and they slid into them. Kazi had to fold his knees to one side to avoid touching the man facing him, and his hip was against Isaak's. He looked around. The vinyl seats were cracked and torn, the windows caked with dirt, and the interior walls between the graffiti and smudges were a dirty beige. Moments later metal protested loudly, the train moved forward and headed down the tracks. After a while the steady motion made Kazi sleepy. He was tired and hadn't slept much in the last couple of days, but each time he nodded off, his head fell forward, jolting him awake. Isaak was snoring softly and he envied the ease at which the older man slept through the discomfort and noise.

To pass the time he gazed out at the passing fields, and in the faint moonlight he could see fields of tall, shadowy sunflowers. Without stopping the train passed through small towns with names like Sannaspos, Tweespruit, and Westminster. Then it took on a different sound as they climbed through Van Reenan's Pass, and began the descent from the high Drakensburg Mountains. In the early hours of the morning they chugged into Ladysmith, and Kazi and Isaak disembarked to take the train to Ulundi. A sign showed that the ticket counter would be closed until 5am, so they settled themselves on an uncomfortable bench and shared Kazi's crushed sandwiches. As Isaak had said, Kazi was hungry.

Once they had eaten, they drank water and did their ablutions in the public washrooms, and after that they just sat and waited. The station clock ticked its way towards five o'clock and on the hour, the shutters on the ticket window opened with a clack. They moved forward and asked the ticket master for tickets to Ulundi.

The man guffawed loudly. "Ha, ha," he laughed. He was obviously in a good mood, which was surprising for such an early hour. "The milk train to Ulundi, ha-ha-ha," he laughed jovially, "hope you're not in a hurry." Kazi and Isaak looked at each other. "You don't get it. The train stops at every station," the man laughed again hitting the keys on his till, "that's why we call it the milk train." He placed two tickets on the counter and pointed to a bench on the other side of the small platform. "Over there, half an hour," he said, still chuckling.

On the train the man's joke was explained when the train stopped at each and every small town. Kazi lost track after jolting to a stop in Pepsworth, then Elandslaagte, Wasbank and Glencoe. He turned his attention to the changing scenery and noticed that the landscape was greener and lusher as they approached the KwaZulu Natal coast. They passed through fields of cattle, and green crops stretching into the distance, until at last the conductor called out, "Vryheid, next stop Vryheid."

Isaak prodded Kazi. "Get your things together. Ulundi is the next stop after Vryheid."

Kazi nodded, stretched a hand under the bench and pulled out the few items he had brought with him. He had travelled lightly.

"Ulundi," the conductor yelled and the train stopped at a small platform and they climbed off. A few passengers climbed aboard and the train pulled away again to disappear rapidly out of sight down the track.

Isaak had directions and, after a greasy meal at a small café in Ulundi, they began the long trek on foot.

Keeping at a constant pace they reached the outskirts of the small town and soon left all signs of civilization behind. Dotted sporadically on the slopes were the occasional huts, goats, and cattle. After an hour an old man stopped and gave them a ride on his donkey cart for a couple of miles until he turned at an intersection, and left them to continue on their own. At that point they decided to rest for a few hours before continuing when the heat of the day passed, and they sat down under a tree alongside the road. Other than the road there was nothing to see but aloes, thorn bushes, red soil between course savannah grass, and widely spaced, scattered trees.

Sweat beaded Kazi's forehead and drenched his back. It was a different kind of heat to what he was accustomed to, humid and muggy, and he fidgeted with a blade of grass, chewing on it as he watched a troupe of monkeys chattering in a nearby tree.

"Kazi," Isaak said, "sleep if you can, tonight will be our only chance to go to the Inkatha camp. You don't want to be tired."

"Okay," Kazi said and lay back in the shade with his hands cupped under his head. Suddenly the fatigue from the sleepless train trip caught up with him, and he fell sound asleep in spite of the heat. He woke hours later to the constant buzz of mosquitoes. Thick air seemed to have descended to trap him in a humid bath and, even though the sun was setting, the evening offered no relief from the day's heat.

Isaak stirred and walked into the bush to relieve himself. He was gone for a long time, and when he returned, he was carrying a dead rabbit by its back legs.

"How did you manage to catch that?" Kazi asked, dumbfounded.

"I set up a trap earlier." Isaak lay the rabbit down and chopped off the feet, tail and head, and then he made a horizontal incision, removed the entrails and pulled off the skin. "Go and collect some wood for a fire so that we can cook," he said, without looking up from his task.

"Okay." Kazi strolled off into the veld. He passed an outcrop of prickly pear plants and wished the fruit was ripe.

Looking for wood he spotted an Acacia tree, but avoided it because of the thorns. Then he found a Red Beech tree with dead branches scattered underneath its canopy. He returned to their camp site with an armload, built the fire, and lit it while Isaak finished skinning the rabbit. When the coals burned down Isaak skewered the rabbit on two long green sticks, and suspended the animal above the fire.

The fat sizzled in the heat and the smell of roasting meat rose. Kazi realized that he was hungry. The sandwiches were long gone, and his stomach had already forgotten the meal they'd eaten in Ulundi that morning.

"Let's get some water while we're waiting," Isaak suggested. He nudged a couple of embers into place under the rabbit and left it to cook while they searched a nearby ravine for water. They found a slow trickle of a stream and drank thirstily, then washed off their faces and necks, cooling and refreshing themselves. When they returned, the meat was brown and crisped, and they devoured it hungrily wishing for something more to add to their meal. After they had eaten, they covered up the remains of their fire with sand and set out again.

By then it was quite dark with only a segment of moon for light. They kept to the road until they turned to follow a track, and twenty minutes or more passed before Isaak stopped suddenly. Kazi bumped into him.

"What is it?" he asked.

"I've lost the path."

Kazi scanned the ground ahead and behind. He decided to go back and pick up the trail and start again. He walked back, couldn't find it and moved to the left, searching in a grid pattern. He walked ten meters, turned back and, as he started out in the other direction, something shifted in the grass under his foot. The earth exploded. Landmine! he thought as he leapt back, a scream dying in his throat. He fell hard, dust flying, small stones pelting down stinging his face. He felt for his legs and feet, wondering why he couldn't feel pain. Something brushed against his face and he shrank back as a small owl flew away, screeching furiously.

Isaak towered over him. "It's only an owl," he laughed, leaning forward to offer Kazi a hand up.

Kazi ignored Isaak's hand and got to his feet by himself.

"Sorry, Kazi," Isaak chuckled. "I shouldn't have laughed, but it was so funny I couldn't help it." He turned away and said, "Come on, let's find that path."

They searched in silence, Kazi still upset and Isaak chuckling under his breath, until they found the trail and set off again. The path steepened until they crested a hill, then it eased towards the Mfolozi River where they noticed activity.

"Shush," Isaak whispered. "Down," he said, indicating with his hand. "We'll wait here for a few minutes and see if there's a guard," Isaak whispered.

They waited in silence, watching. It looked like a typical Zulu village with clusters of round huts. The distinguishing factor was that there were no women or children. No chickens scratching in the dirt and no animals. The most important fact was that the men had assault weapons slung over their shoulders or lying on the ground where they sat.

Kazi looked at the camp with interest. It was obvious that there was no European or Russian influence here. He had heard that the South African government was secretly funding the Zulu Inkatha Freedom Movement to help them become an opposition party to the ANC. When he had first heard about it, he had been astounded that the white run government would rather see the collapse of the country through tribal war before handing over to a black government run by Nelson Mandela. But, Kazi thought, if the Inkatha didn't receive backing from someone, then they would be crushed by the powerful ANC who had international funding. And then he remembered the reason for his being there, and his sympathy for the Inkatha dissipated.

"There's no guard," Isaak's whisper interrupted Kazi's thoughts. "I'm sure we can slip into the camp without being noticed."

"Are you crazy?" Kazi whispered back. "Someone is sure to speak to us, what then?"

"Just keep your head down and grunt. Look, it's the only way if we want to see if your brothers are there."

Without waiting, Isaak slunk through the bush until he was close enough and then, without hesitation, walked through the opening in the wall. Kazi followed with his heart beating so loudly he thought everyone would hear it. As Isaak had suspected, the men in the camp continued what they were doing. A young man, about Dumani's age, was leaning over a bucket of water washing, dragging the wet cloth over the back of his neck and head. Droplets of water gleamed in the glow of firelight. His profile was Goodwill's and his stance was achingly familiar. Kazi rushed forward, his mouth already mouthing his brother's name when Isaak put a cautionary hand on his arm. Kazi nodded, realizing his mistake, and moved carefully around the camp until the boy's face was more visible. With a stab of disappointment he realized the boy was a stranger.

He continued unobserved on the outskirts of the firelight and around groups of older men until he found a group of youngsters. One boy in particular was talking loudly, bragging of his day's conquests. Kazi was watching the young men when suddenly he felt a knife pushed against his back just hard enough for him to feel it through the cloth of his shirt.

"Move," a voice prompted in Zulu, pricking him a little harder. Kazi couldn't see Isaak and fear coursed through him as he realized that he had been caught.

His captor marched him up to a man who was obviously the leader of the camp. His face was ugly and threatening.

"Who are you?" he demanded.

Kazi stood frozen, unable to answer.

"What are you doing here?" Kazi didn't reply. All he knew was that he wouldn't give Isaak up. The man's fist lashed out hitting him hard. "I asked you a question. Answer me!" he yelled.

Again and again the fist smashed into his face, and Kazi fell back. He felt his lip break open, his eye swell closed, as blood filled his mouth. A boot connected hard with his chest and he slumped over winded, the pain excruciating. The two men continued kicking him and hitting him until thankfully, a dark silence took over, taking with it all feeling of pain.

"We'll find out who he is tomorrow. Musa, take him to the hut," the man commanded.

The next morning pain filtered through the haze of Kazi's brain. His tongue stuck to the roof of his mouth, he desperately needed water. As his mind cleared, and his memory returned, the horror of his situation dawned on him. He felt his stomach clench in fear and he brought up the remnants of the rabbit. He wiped his mouth and tried to sit up, but pain shot through his chest and back. He groaned and held his ribs, rolled onto his side and managed to get himself upright.

A shadow blocked the door and the same large Zulu bent as he came through the low entrance into the hut. It was Musa, he must have heard his groans.

"So you're awake," he growled.

Kazi wanted to run but there was no way to escape, and he didn't think he could run. He remembered that Isaak must have got away and hopefully would help him.

"Who are you?" Musa asked. Kazi remained silent. "You're a Xhosa ANC mongrel, that's who you are," Musa spat with naked aggression. His mouth slid down at the corners. His nose flared.

"I'm not ANC," Kazi managed to say through split and swollen lips.

"You're lying!" Musa exploded angrily.

"No, no you must listen …"

"You're an ANC spy."

"No, I told you …"

"You are. You're the dog they sent to spy on us."

"I'm on my own! I'm not ANC," Kazi repeated.

The Zulu's fist swung back, Kazi got ready to block the punch but the man froze at the sound of gunfire and ran outside. Kazi realized this would be his only opportunity to escape and dragged himself to the doorway. There was chaos outside; men shouted, others barked commands, and soldiers shot at unseen attackers. He saw the young man who'd been bragging at the fireside crawling towards the opening in the wall. He was leading three others out into the bush, probably in an attempt to take the intruders from the rear. Kazi looked around. The rest of the Zulus had forgotten him in the gunfight, and he ran crouched over towards the wall. Adrenaline ran through his veins and his heart thudded like a fist in his chest. He reached the wall and threw himself over it, his muscles and ribs screaming in protest. He landed painfully on the ground and lay without moving. He wanted to cry out, but forced the impulse down and stayed still while listening for one of the Zulus to shout a warning to the others of his escape. He took a few shallow breaths and every breath was a new torture.

Before he could decide on what action to take, a hushed voice called out, "Kazi, this way." He lifted his head a fraction and looked in that direction.

"Here." Kazi recognised Isaak's voice and scrambled towards it.

"Get up, get up, hurry," Isaak urged, leaning over him.

Kazi squinted in the direction of Isaak's voice. "Okay," he croaked, pulling himself to his knees.

"Hurry," Isaak repeated.

Kazi got to his feet and Isaak slipped under his arm. "Lean on me," he said and together they staggered forward.

Three other men joined them. Isaak gave a signal and they spread out, running through the tall grass. Kazi leant heavily on Isaak's shoulder and they pushed on until they reached a hidden cart.

"Here," Isaak said. "Get on."

Kazi did as he was told. One of the men covered Kazi with sacks.

"Go now," Isaak's voice was gruff. "Take him to the safe house."

Kazi lay back, his mind blank as the cart bounced over the uneven track. Every bump hurt, and every breath filled his lungs with dust from the sacks. After what seemed an unbearable time the cart stopped. Above him Kazi could hear muffled voices and his heart pounded as a hand grasped the sacks and pulled them away. He shrank, his eyes adjusting to the light. Then he recognised the stranger from the cart and felt a rush of relief.

"We're here. You can get up," he said.

Kazi slid forward until he reached the tailgate, threw his legs over and stood up gingerly. A man walked towards them. "Go into the hut," he said.

Without question, Kazi hobbled forward. He had no other option but to trust these people. The hut was a round rondavel with a thatch roof sewn to poles with grass rope. The walls had been constructed of stone, and the floor had been finished with a dung mixture to make it hard and smooth.

"I'll send the old woman to tend to you," the man said.

Kazi wondered who the old woman was, but he lowered himself onto a flimsy bed and waited in the gloomy hut. The wild beating of his heart stilled and his breathing quietened. He began to feel better.

An elderly woman entered the room. She had the dark colouring of a Zulu, but spoke Xhosa. "Take off your shirt," she said, opening a jar of reeking ointment.

He did as he was told and she began to apply it to his bruises, Kazi flinching at her touch.

"You have a cracked rib, but there's nothing broken. Don't worry, you're young and will heal quickly." The woman moved rapidly, smoothing ointment over the bruises on his chest, eye and cheek. She took long strips of cloth and wrapped his chest firmly. "Come with me," she said, replacing the lid on the jar. He went out with her, and she indicated a three-legged stool near the fire. He sat and she gave him a plate of food. "Eat. Isaak will be here to fetch you soon." She placed a mug next to him. "Be sure to drink that."

He wasn't hungry but he took a long thirsty swallow from the mug and gagged – the liquid was as bitter and foul as the ointment. The woman nodded at his grimace. "Drink it," she smiled sympathetically and she reminded Kazi of his mother. "There are herbs in there that will give you strength for the rest of your journey."

Kazi had barely finished when Isaak came crashing through the bush behind the hut, his shirt stained and torn. He looked over his shoulder. "Kazi, we have to go, hurry." He scooped a cup of water from a pail by the door and drank thirstily, then took a fistful of food from Kazi's plate and shoved it into his mouth.

Kazi had a million questions rushing through his mind, but he knew better than to ask them now. There would be time for that later. He stood immediately, thanked the woman and followed quickly, feeling stronger from the brew she had given him and the bandages that braced his ribs. He felt ready to move on.

They jogged as far as they could, then moved away from the road and found a place to rest. Their ragged breathing quieted. They sat, neither knowing what to say. A Stinkwood tree cast a deep shade over them. Birds were feeding on the yellow-brown berries. A snake slithered away.

Isaak began to speak. "It went wrong. I'm sorry, you shouldn't have been there," he said. "I shouldn't have brought you."

Kazi nodded silently, his mind seething with questions. He decided to let Isaak talk. He suspected now that Isaak was somehow involved between the rival factions of the ANC and the Zulu Inkatha.

Isaak continued, "We heard rumours about a Zulu encampment, and we needed to confirm that it was a military training camp for the Inkatha. I had to find out how many men there were and what weapons they had. Kazi, I really did want to help you find your brothers. I thought I could combine your search with my mission. I thought we could just have a look and that it would be easy. I'm sorry."

"Who are you really?" Kazi demanded.

"Umkhonto we Sizwe," Isaak admitted.

"So you're with the ANC army."

"Yes, Kazi, I am."

"Oh." Kazi felt betrayed. Isaak had helped him, but he had also deceived him.

"Kazi…"

"Isaak, I don't want to talk. I need to think."

"As you wish, we'll rest until tonight, and then we'll get back to Ulundi for the train."

When Kazi woke from a restless sleep, fraught with nightmares and the pain in his ribs, he noticed that night had fallen. The sky was clear and the stars so close that he felt he could reach up and touch them. It was beautiful, perhaps more so than ever before, because now he appreciated his life and freedom.

In Ulundi, Isaak and Kazi parted ways. Kazi caught the next train and the trip back to Bloemfontein was difficult to bear, but it gave Kazi time to think, to realize that his quest to find his brothers was useless. He had no idea where to look next or what to do.

He fetched the Nomad and drove home feeling defeated. Outside the gates to the farmhouse he stopped. His bruised eye ached, and the skin on his face felt stretched and dry from the sun and wind on the return trip in the open Nomad. It had seemed longer and more exhausting than the trip there when he was full of optimism. He sat for a moment to gather his thoughts, then he pushed the buzzer on the intercom. He heard a voice ask him to identify himself, he did, and the gate swung open.

Scott opened the door before he could knock. "So you're back," he said, smacking Kazi cheerfully on his shoulder.

Kazi winced. "Yes," he replied. After all that he had been through, he found it hard to come to terms with Scott's boyishness. He felt old now, a man already. He tried to smile.

"You should hear what happened," Scott said exuberantly, "There was a snake in our bathroom cabinet. A massive Cape Cobra ..." He stopped and looked properly at Kazi for the first time. "What the hell happened to you?"

Kazi lowered his head. "Scott, it was far worse than I ever expected, and I haven't found my brothers. I suppose I was stupid to think that I would."

"What happened?" Scott asked. "Do you want to come in?"

"Not now, my parents will be waiting."

"You've got a black eye," Scott leant towards him checking out the bruises on his face. He lifted Kazi's T-shirt. "You're covered in bruises."

Kazi pulled away. "It was bad Scott, people were killed."

"Killed?" Scott said, horror in his voice.

Kazi nodded. "I'll tell you about it later, I have to go now. Thanks for lending me the Nomad. I hope I didn't keep it too long."

"No, it was fine, I didn't need it."

"Well, thanks for your help. I'll catch up with you tomorrow and tell you what happened."

"Before you go at least tell me about Thandi," Scott said. "Did you see her?"

Kazi's face softened, the hard angles disappeared and he smiled briefly. "I love her, Scott, and I've given everything a lot of thought during the trip home. I'm going to stop this idiotic search for my brothers. I'm going to move to Cape Town and study journalism at UCT."

"Journalism?" Scott queried.

Kazi nodded. "After what I've been through I want to expose what's really happening in South Africa. And," he paused and smiled, "I'm going to marry Thandi."

Scott nodded and his smile mirrored Kazi's. "I'm pleased that you can move on now, it's time. And Thandi's a great girl, you'll be happy together."

"I know," Kazi said, and with a wave he was off, striding towards the labourers' houses.

Kazi told his parents as much as he felt he could about his search for his brothers. He left out Sepho's murder, the Inkatha massacre, and he skimmed over the facts of his capture and beating.

He looked at Martha, "I'm sorry I didn't find them, *Umama*."

He turned to his father, "I've come to accept that I must just hope that they come back on their own one day."

Goodwill put his hand gently on Kazi's shoulder. "Kazi, you've obviously been through an ordeal that you don't want to talk about. I should be angry with you for putting yourself in danger like that, but now I am just thankful that you've returned safely. You have tried to find them, and now it is in God's hands."

"Yes," Kazi agreed sadly, he wondered if his faith would ever be as strong again. "In God's hands," he repeated.

TWENTY-SEVEN

MADNESS

1991· 1992 · **1993** · 1994 · 1995 · 1996 · 1997 · 1998 · 1999

On the 10th day of April 1993 Chris Hani, the Secretary General of the South African Communist Party and former Chief of Staff of the Umkhonto we Sizwe armed resistance movement, one of the most popular figures in the ANC, was shot at point blank range in front of his home in Boksburg. The situation in the country was precarious, and there were concerns that his death could set off a racial war. Nelson Mandela spoke to the nation on television and radio, trying to calm the people. The Finleys were listening – it was Easter break and Scott and Shanon were home for the holidays. Kazi was there too.

"Tonight," Nelson Mandela said, "I am reaching out to every single South African, black and white, from the very depths of my being," he spoke slowly with emphasis. "A white man, full of prejudice and hate, came to our country and committed a deed so foul that our whole nation now teeters on the brink of disaster." His face was serious as he looked into the camera. "Now is the time for all South Africans to stand together against those who, from any quarter, wish to destroy what Chris Hani gave his life for – the freedom of all of us."

A picture of the arrested assassin, a Polish immigrant and member of the right wing Afrikaner Resistance Movement, flashed onto the television screen. With the photograph was a police artist sketch of the driver, who was still at large.

Scott and Kazi sat forward simultaneously.

"That looks like Jacobus!" Scott exclaimed.

"*Ja*," Kazi agreed, "could be."

"Who, the driver or the assassin?" Caitlin asked.

"The driver, Mom, I think he's the man they're looking for," Scott replied. "He is a member of the Afrikaner Resistance Movement, and he's fanatical enough to get involved with something as drastic as this."

Garth looked at the artist's sketch; he'd seen Jacobus in the village and knew what he looked like. "You're right, there is a remarkable similarity. He's got the same jaw and nose. Same colour hair."

"What should we do?" Scott asked.

The news finished and Garth switched off the television. "You should notify the police."

"But I'm not totally sure it's him," Scott said.

"How sure are you?" Caitlin queried, looking from Scott to Garth to Kazi.

Scott pulled the corners of his mouth down and shrugged, "Pretty sure, Mom."

Kazi nodded too. "Could be him, Mrs. Finley."

"I also think it could be him," Garth agreed. "Go on, Scott, call it in."

Kazi nodded again. He hated Jacobus and would love to see him on the wrong side of the law.

"But, Dad, I told you I'm not sure," Scott said.

"My boy, it's up to the police to follow up on leads. If it's not him, then its not."

"Okay." Scott got up reluctantly. He came back a few minutes later with an unhappy expression on his face. "I have to go to the police station to make a statement. You coming, Kazi?" he asked.

"Sure," Kazi said with a vengeful grin, he was still thinking about Jacobus and how he'd dismissed him like a piece of garbage.

The two boys drove away in the Nomad and Garth turned to Caitlin.

"I've deposited the money from the property we sold in Schoemansville. We're ready to do another transfer, but there's been a slight change." Caitlin waited for him to carry on. "You remember the bank manager in Vereeniging?"

"Peter Collins?"

Garth nodded. "He's moved to another branch."

"Which one?"

"Joubert Street in Jo'burg. We'll have to go there to fetch the money."

Caitlin pulled a face. "That means we have to drive into the centre of town."

"Let's make an outing of it. We'll drop the kids off at Sandton City on our way in, go to the bank, draw the cash, do the transaction with Berndt's people, and then we'll pick the kids up and go to a movie."

"Sounds good to me. It'll be nice to do something with Scott and Shanon before they go back to 'varsity."

Scott walked in with Kazi.

"I heard my name, what's up?"

"Dad and I have business to do in town next week, we thought we'd go and see a movie afterwards," Caitlin replied.

"Great! Can Kazi come?"

Caitlin turned and smiled at Kazi, "Of course, any time."

"Thank you, Mrs. Finley," Kazi said enthusiastically. He never went to the movies or out to dinner unless it was with them.

"We'll go on Monday afternoon." Garth stood up and went into the office to trigger the next transfer. It was the fifth and they were used to the process. It was becoming routine and wasn't as frightening as it had been at first.

On Monday Garth and Caitlin were running late and there wasn't time to drop Shanon, Scott and Kazi at the mall. Garth decided to go straight to the bank. He would have preferred to leave the youngsters at Sandton City, but he had his appointment at the bank and couldn't be late. He wasn't overly concerned about having them with him. They could wait in the car while he and Caitlin went inside. The only danger he could foresee would be a car-jacker when they left the bank, but car-jackers didn't generally target carloads of people; there was too much risk. He would take them to the mall after they had picked up the money, but before they did the transfer with Berndt's people. There wasn't any real danger there either, but he didn't think it would be right to expose them to Berndt's shady hoodlums, and he certainly didn't want to attract Kazi's curiosity.

He drove straight to Johannesburg and parked in the secure parking below the bank. It was cool in the parking garage and Shanon, Scott and Kazi waited in the car and listened to music while Garth and Caitlin went inside. Within half an hour Garth and Caitlin were back and Garth drove out, turned right towards Jeppe Street, and could go no further.

The road ahead was a mass of thousands of militant, angry black people. They writhed and churned like a dark river filling the street as far ahead and as far back as they could see. Black men punched the sky with clenched fists, faces passed by, contorted with rage and naked aggression.

Suddenly a group broke away and came towards them. They pounded on the car, eyes wild and vengeful, and spit flew from open shouting mouths. An angry youth leant towards the window, bashed it with his fist and stared in at the white people with dark, hard eyes. And then he pulled his hand across his neck in a throat slitting motion and grimaced.

"What's white for you today will be black for us tomorrow," he snarled.

"I'll shoot the bastard," Garth growled menacingly and reached for the revolver strapped to his ankle.

"Garth, don't let them see the gun, it'll just infuriate them and they'll kill us all," Caitlin urged. "We don't have enough firepower to take on a mob like this. Let's get out of here."

"How the hell do you suggest I do that?" Garth shouted angrily above the increasing noise. He looked over his shoulder. A mini-bus filled with shouting demonstrators blocked their retreat and the mob of people blocked the street ahead. Further to their left was a street with a no-entry sign.

A police siren blurped and a policeman, on a motorbike on the street with the no-entry sign, yelled over his loud hailer.

"You," his voice boomed over the commotion. "You in the silver BMW, this way, get a move on, this way." He waved permission for them to go the wrong way up the one-way street.

Garth spun the wheel and manoeuvred through a small gap in the crowd.

"Stop!" Kazi shouted suddenly. "There's Dumani!"

Garth slammed on the brakes and, without waiting for the car to come to a complete stop, Kazi pushed open his door and jumped out.

"Go, go, go!" he shouted, waving them away and he was quickly absorbed into the crowd.

Garth drove on through the crowd of rioters. It was slow going. People continued to block his way and to beat on the roof and sides of the car and shout obscenities. When they refused to move, Garth pushed them out of the way with his front bumper. He reached the one-way street, spun the steering wheel, and turned into it. Oncoming traffic had been stopped by the traffic officer and Garth drove up the road as fast and as far as he could. At the first opportunity he turned, punched the accelerator and sped away from the scene of the riot.

"This, Caitlin," Garth said angrily, "is the straw that breaks the camel's back. We've got to get out of this bloody country. It's obvious these bastards hate us. We've got to decide where we're moving to and make our application soon. The country has changed and we had better move before it changes us."

"What do you mean 'move' Dad?" Shanon asked in a quiet voice.

"Dad and I have been considering ..."

"Leaving South Africa," Garth finished.

"But what about us?" Shanon glanced at Scott, "What about university?"

"We'll move somewhere where there's a university," Garth stated.

"Where will we go?" Scott asked.

"We don't know. Canada, New Zealand, Australia..." Caitlin shrugged. "We would have to apply and see where we can get in."

"When were you going to tell us?" Shanon asked.

"We haven't made a final decision yet, but we've been building up a nest egg offshore in case we decided to move," Caitlin replied. "We were going to talk to you when the time came."

"Well, I have decided, today, in fact right now," Garth snapped. "After seeing those *kaffirs* going berserk like that, and the car-jacking and the way the country's going, I've made up my mind. We are leaving."

"But what about Chad and I?" Shanon asked, thinking about her boyfriend.

"We'll go as a family, or not at all," Garth replied sharply. "We have to stick together through this," he said.

There was silence in the car while everyone absorbed Garth's statement.

"This makes me all the more sure of what we should be doing. We have to get out of here, that's obvious from what we just saw," Garth continued, his voice hard and tense. "The writing's on the wall. There's no future for whites in South Africa and we've got to get out while we still can."

No one said anything. Then Caitlin remembered the money in the boot. She drew in a sharp breath.

"I forgot about the money in the back." She looked over her shoulder. "We've got two hundred and fifty thousand Rand in the boot," she said, dismay in her voice.

Shanon straightened. "What are you talking about? Is there really that much money in the boot?"

"Yes," Caitlin admitted quietly.

"In cash, in the car?" Scott exclaimed. The riot had been bad enough but to have that amount money in the car was lunacy.

"This is part of the money we're moving overseas, so that we can start up again if we have to."

Shanon frowned. "I don't understand what that has to do with cash in the car."

"It's complicated, but in short, we're buying US dollars."

"But I've heard you say time and again that you can't take money out of South Africa."

"Dad found a way around it."

"How?" Scott asked intrigued.

"On the black market; I ask for a transfer, the money is deposited in an offshore account in any currency I want, and then I pay for the transfer in cash," Garth replied.

"How do the funds get transferred?" Scott asked; he wanted to know more.

"It may have something to do with weapons exchanged for diamonds," Garth replied. "It's a case of no questions asked or given."

Shanon was quiet while her thoughts tumbled into place. "Diamonds… there's only one country that would deal in illegal diamonds and that would be Angola. Blood diamonds, sold to fund their war, or exchanged for arms and ammunition. And since sanctions and the arms embargo against South Africa, Armscor develops weapons locally."

Scott put it together. "So they take your money and buy weapons from Armscor, swap them for diamonds, smuggle them out of the country, and sell them overseas. And there's your money."

"Maybe," Garth said, "we don't really know. I never meet the people that do the actual transfer; I deal with a middle man."

"Shanon, Scott," Caitlin turned towards them, her tone serious, "you realize that this is illegal. You can't tell a soul that we're doing this, or even that we're thinking of moving. There are jealous people who can't move. If they hear what we're doing, they might tip off the government and a spotlight will be turned on all our transactions. We'll have to leave the rest of our assets behind, and that includes the farm. We could even go to jail."

Scott and Shanon nodded.

"Not even Chad must know about this," Garth replied, his voice firm. "And not Kazi either," he said, glancing at Scott. "Not a word to anyone, okay?"

"Got it, Dad," Shanon retorted.

Garth looked at his watch. "Damn," he said. "Now we're late for our meeting with Berndt's men. We'll have to go straight to the drop off. The windows are tinted, I'm sure they won't notice Scott and Shanon in the back. It'll only take five minutes, I'll just hand over the money like I usually do and we'll be out of there in no time."

They drove into the same driveway as before, and the people were obviously waiting for them because the gate opened the minute they pulled up and so did the garage doors. Garth pulled in and the door closed behind him.

"Stay in the car, keep a low profile," he said and climbed out.

He went around to the boot and took out his briefcase.

Buzz Cut came forward to meet him; his hair was no longer short. He walked up and noticed Scott and Shanon immediately.

"What the hell are those kids doing here?" he pointed to the car. "What the fuck!" he yelled.

"Let's just get down to business," Garth said. "They've got nothing to do with you."

The dark-haired man came forward. "Give me the money." His mouth twisted, "Bloody kids shouldn't have seen us."

Garth handed over the briefcase and Buzz Cut took it without opening it. He stalked away with the briefcase and its contents.

"Now go," Buzz Cut said. "We'll talk to Berndt; this is a serious breach of policy."

"Idiot," the dark-haired man cursed and climbed into the Mercedes.

The two men raced away in their car and Garth climbed into the BMW and followed. The garage door, and then the gate closed silently after them.

"Do you guys still want to go to the movies?" Garth said in a sombre tone. "We can still go if you want." Garth was still shattered by the day's events. All he wanted to do was go home, pour himself a couple of stiff drinks and think, or even better to forget about the day.

"Not really," Shanon said.

She had to choose between Chad and her family. She felt crushed. She looked out the window at the passing traffic and wicked away a tear. She didn't speak again and brooded about her situation. She had only just met Chad, but they got on well and had a lot in common. She thought she might even love him. How could she leave? But she couldn't stay either. It was a terrible choice to face, and she was in an agony of indecision. She didn't want to be responsible for the whole family's decision.

"I don't," Scott replied. "I'm worried about Kazi and want to get home in case he comes back. I should go and tell Goodwill what happened."

"I don't either," Caitlin said. She was still shaken by the mob that had surrounded them, the hatred in their eyes.

When they got home Shanon ran into her bedroom. Gotcha padded in behind her, sensing her distress, and she slammed the door. She sat down on the floor, put her arms around the dog and sobbed into his fur. After a while, she stopped crying and straightened.

"And what about you, Gotcha? What's going to happen to you?" She broke into fresh sobs. She stroked the dog and he licked the salt off her face.

"I guess I've no choice. I have to go, don't I?" she asked the dog.

He looked up at her and wagged his short tail.

"I can't make a decision for the family based on something that might not work out. It's too soon to know, but I think I love Chad." Her mouth turned down and she wanted to cry again. She looked at the dog and he gazed back. "Come on, let's go for a walk in the garden," she said, standing up.

She walked out of the room and Caitlin looked up.

"Are you okay?" she asked, noting Shanon's red-rimmed eyes.

"Yes," Shanon snapped. She wanted to hit out at everyone around her, even though she knew it wasn't their fault. She couldn't hold the family back, she had to go. She knew she had to bite the bullet and agree, but that didn't change the fact that she was angry and bitter, and she hated them all.

Caitlin was feeling drained. She had been functioning on adrenaline and the effect was wearing off. She didn't know what she could say to Shanon that would ease her pain. She was at a loss, and her own heart was breaking because she had to leave her beloved grandparents. She had always been a mainstay in their lives. Her grandfather was ninety-one and her Gran, although much younger, had a pacemaker and suffered from a variety of ailments. If something happened to Gran, who would help Granddad if she, Caitlin, was no longer there?

Caitlin had warned him that they may leave South Africa, and Granddad had encouraged her. He believed the 'time of trouble and turmoil' in the scriptures was imminent. He was a religious man, a retired minister and missionary in Zambia, which had been called Northern Rhodesia during his time there.

Caitlin had her own losses, her own heartbreak to contend with, and she realized for the first time in her life that she wasn't capable of helping her daughter. Her own life was in turmoil and was sliding in a direction where she was no longer in control.

After the Finleys left Kazi on Jeppe Street in the middle of the riot, Kazi raced after his brother.

"Dumani, Dumani," he shouted to his brother's receding back. Dumani didn't hear and continued moving further and further away.

Kazi realized that the young man chanting and punching the air next to Dumani was Mandiso. He shouted their names again, pushing hard, fighting his way through the crowd. A mob of people were breaking windows with bricks, and others were looting as they went. What had begun as a peaceful demonstration after Secretary General Chris Hani's murder was turning into an uncontrolled riot. People were venting rage that had been suppressed for decades, and their eyes held a madness bred from a need for revenge. Kazi pushed on desperately through the press of bodies. A chanting shout passed from mouth to mouth.

"*Amandla!*" Power!

"*Amandla!*" Power!

"*Amandla!*" Power!

Clenched fists rose in unison with each call.

Suddenly Kazi broke through the crowd and he was there, face to face, with them, his brothers, after so long. After all the searching they were there, free. He held out his hand in greeting. He would have recognised Dumani anywhere. He was lean, the same height as Goodwill, the same dark intelligent eyes, oval face and high cheekbones. Mandiso had Martha's dark colouring, but no longer looked like her. He was now taller than Dumani, also thin, but muscular. His nose had been broken and was flat and misshapen, his eyes were dark and angry. Dumani took Kazi's hand, but Mandiso turned coldly away, ignoring Kazi's outstretched hand.

Bewildered Kazi turned to Dumani but, before he could speak, a policeman in riot gear launched tear gas into the mob, and people ran pushing and shoving to escape. Kazi held his breath for as long as he could. A young woman fell, her head trampled into the pavement by the charging mob. People were screaming. Policemen moved forward in V formation, dark helmets covering their faces, shields held out and batons smashing into the crowd. Kazi glanced around looking for escape. Dumani gripped his arm and pulled him along. Mandiso was gone. A policeman, grim-faced behind his protective helmet, swung his baton down across Kazi's head and he fell hard. Dumani fell next to him. The batons rose and fell and people collapsed around them.

Dumani and Kazi were handcuffed and thrown into a police van. As far as Kazi could tell, Mandiso had managed to escape. His elation at finding his brothers was curbed by this unexpected change of events. He sat bent over on the hard metal bench in the back of the police van, trying to make sense of what had happened. His eyes and throat burned from the tear gas, his nose ran and he coughed uncontrollably.

The police van drove away. After a while it stopped, and the doors opened. Kazi stepped out and a policeman gave him an unsympathetic shove towards the police station. Inside they were herded down a passageway and into a large cell, the handcuffs were removed, and he heard the clunk of the door closing and the rattle of keys as they were locked in. A florescent bulb protected by a heavy wire mesh hung in the centre of the room. Its light showed rows of metal benches along the walls and a filthy toilet in the corner. The cell smelt of urine and faeces, and the close confinement of dirty people. Young men sat on the benches and on the floor. There was no one under the age of fourteen or over forty. Some were bleeding, others had dark bruises. Kazi was angry. He had done nothing wrong, and didn't deserve to be there. They obviously did. He found a space against the wall and slid down to sit on the cold concrete next to Dumani.

Kazi turned on Dumani. "Why didn't you come home?"

Dumani turned towards Kazi, his eyes were dull, devoid of emotion. "At first we didn't know where we were, we didn't know where to go and we were frightened. No one came to fetch us. We waited and waited and when we realized that no one was coming for us the people we were with became our family, our brothers."

"But Dumani, I did search for you. They forced our father to hold political meetings against his will because they had you. We did everything to get you back."

"Well, it wasn't enough, was it?" Dumani accused, looking away from him.

Devastated by Dumani's reaction, Kazi stared down at the floor. His eyes followed a cockroach scuttling across the ground. He didn't know what to say.

Keys rattled and the prison door clanged open. Kazi lifted his head, expecting another prisoner to be shoved into the already full cell. Perhaps Mandiso. A prison guard stood in the doorway.

"You're not being charged," he told them. "You can leave." He sounded disappointed.

Kazi and Dumani got to their feet, followed the others through the prison, and walked out into the fading sunshine. One of the prisoners lifted his fist in the freedom salute and punched the air as he sauntered away. Dumani turned and, with a brief wave to Kazi, walked away with the rest.

"Goodbye, Kazi," he called out, "perhaps I'll see you again sometime."

Kazi stood, hands slack at his sides, watching as his brother left with the comrade brothers he had chosen over his own. He set out towards the farm, walking, or hitching a ride when he could. His mind wandered, and he allowed it to in order to escape the day's ordeals.

Late that night, when he arrived back, he went first to the farmhouse knowing that Scott and the Finleys would be worried. He reassured them but avoided their questions, his emotions still too raw to speak. Now he had to tell his parents that his brothers were alive and free in body, but their souls were lost.

He turned away and walked slowly home, head down, wondering how to break the news. He saw his parents waiting. Scott must have told Goodwill and Martha that Kazi had seen Dumani and Mandiso, and they were watching the road for his return. At his approach his father came to meet him, and his mother stood up and waited near the fire passing her hands dryly over each other, over and over again. His expression must have revealed that the news was not good because his father took his arm and led him gently to the fire, and his mother silently pulled a chair close to its warmth for him. He sank gratefully onto it while they pulled up chairs on either side of him and waited for him to speak.

When he began to tell the story his voice was flat. Clearly it was painful for him to say what he had to tell them.

"I saw them," he said, "but they're not coming home. There's too much hostility and anger in them."

His father's head drooped towards his chest, his mother's hands stopped their incessant movement, and the fire flickered softly.

Goodwill lifted his head. "Don't worry, Martha, they are of our blood and we must believe in that bond. We will pray that they will come home one day."

The pain within Kazi grew like a black shroud threatening to envelop him. He stood up, needing to be on his own. He needed time to think, time to sort out his feelings of anger and frustration. He left his parents at the fireside and walked away into the shadows, yearning for solitude. Unerringly he found the old Coral tree in the dark and leant gratefully against its trunk, feeling the strength flowing from it. He closed his eyes and stood silently reflecting on the events of his life, the tragedies, the loss of his brothers to the family, and the sorrow his parents had suffered. His breath caught in his chest and he wrapped his arms around himself hugging his torment. Angrily he pushed away from the tree and staggered blindly back towards the house.

A form stepped out from the shadows.

"And what do we have here?" it sneered, "The little white boy's friend!"

Kazi recognised Spyder and his chest contracted. He thought back to the night when his sister had been raped, and a burning anger began to build low in his stomach. He could feel a pulse beating rapidly in his neck and his heart race with adrenaline. He felt the blackness expand in his head and he leant into a punch, taking Spyder by surprise on the side of his jaw. Before he could react, Kazi followed with three rapid blows. Blood spurted from Spyder's nose and he staggered back. Kazi followed ruthlessly, punching Spyder again and again. Spyder hunched forward and Kazi pushed him down.

"You bastard," he said. "I hope I never see you again."

A muscle in his jaw bunched and he turned away, his anger still seething and his breath coming in short, panting movements. He hadn't realized that his body was now lean and strong, and more powerful than Spyder's.

TWENTY-EIGHT

CHANGING PLACES

1991 · 1992 · **1993** · 1994 · 1995 · 1996 · 1997 · 1998 · 1999

At the farmhouse on the morning after the riot, Caitlin walked into the office as the sun caught the burglar bars and threw dark bands across Garth's face. He put down the phone. Now that they were considering leaving South Africa he wanted to assess their options and was booking their overseas flights. They had met with an immigration specialist, but wanted to go to the countries they had been told would accept them. They wanted to judge for themselves where they would fit in.

"Our tickets to Auckland, Sydney, and Vancouver are booked," he told her. He hadn't wasted time.

"Did the travel agent apply for our visas?"

"She's getting them," Garth confirmed. "Here's the itinerary."

Caitlin glanced at the sheet of paper Garth had handed to her. "I'll call Jackie tonight," she said, mentally working out the time in Sydney, Australia, where her sister lived. "I'm sure we can stay with them." She paused and ran through the things she had to organise in her mind. "Shanon and Scott will be at university, so they'll be fine. Our passports are up to date, Maria will feed Gotcha, Elias will look after the horses."

"And Goodwill and Jackson will take care of the farm, they can get hold of Dries if there's an emergency," Garth added.

Three weeks later, on May the 2nd, Garth and Caitlin left South Africa with a mixture of excitement and trepidation. They flew to Australia first.

As the doors to arrivals slid open Caitlin's sister waved. "Caity, Caity, over here!"

Caitlin waved back. "Jackeee," she yelled. It had been fourteen years since she had seen her sister and she was excited. She wove her way through clusters of people greeting family and friends, and, on reaching her, hugged her close. She stepped back to look at her sister. Jackie's long hair had been cropped into a short bob. She wore little make-up, and fine lines at the corners of her eyes were the only evidence of the years that had passed. She had Caitlin's same blond hair, streaked by the sun, and the same colour eyes – brown flecked with green. "You're looking good, Sis."

Jackie grinned, "Yeah, you too."

Caitlin turned to the little girl clinging to Jackie's hand, hiding behind her skirt. "You must be Ashley," she said, dropping to the same level. Ashley was wearing a dungaree style denim dress, white pumps, a pink shirt, and her hair was tied back into a ponytail. Caitlin reached into her bag and placed a Cabbage Patch doll in her eight-year-old niece's arms and the little girl's eyes lit up.

"Thanks," she said timidly, still shy of the aunt she'd never met.

Caitlin turned to the boy standing expectantly behind his sister. He was dressed in shorts, T-shirt and runners. He had light brown hair like his sister's and the same grey-green eyes. "You must be Tyler," she said holding out a box, dying to hug him, but knew to bide her time.

"Dinkum!" he exclaimed, opening it.

Jackie's husband, Kevin, embraced Caitlin, and shook Garth's hand. He picked up Caitlin's suitcase. "Didja have a good trip?" he asked with a mixture of accents – Australian and South African. He was tall, rugged, had a day's growth, light brown hair, deep-set, grey-green eyes. It was obvious that the children took after him.

"It was long! Fourteen hours in that bloody tin can." Garth hefted his own luggage.

"Yeah, we've done it a couple of times. One of my home brews will sort you out pretty quick. Let's get going."

Garth and Caitlin followed Kevin, Jackie and the children outside to Jackie's Honda Accord station wagon and Kevin's bright red V8 Holden SS, parked side by side. The men loaded the luggage into the station wagon, and the children climbed in. Kevin turned to Garth.

"You ready to go for a hoon?" he asked, indicating his sports car. "The girls can ride together."

Garth looked puzzled, and Kevin explained that a 'hoon' was a ride. "Sure," he said, climbing into the Holden and clipping his seatbelt.

Kevin cranked over the engine and catapulted away from the curb. Jackie took off after him, but he lead-footed it into a roundabout and popped out onto a side road with a last minute flick of his indicator. He drove like a rally driver, and Jackie soon fell back.

When she and Caitlin pulled up in front of the house both men were already out of the Holden looking under the bonnet. They glanced up, Kevin closed the bonnet, and they walked across to the station wagon. The children leapt out and disappeared into the garden to play with their new toys, and Caitlin looked around with interest. Proteas lined the driveway, obviously a reminder of South Africa, and she noticed a table and chairs set out invitingly beneath a large ash tree. From outside, the house appeared to be a rancher. It was painted white, had a tile roof, a carport, and a single, closed-in garage.

Kevin opened the back of the station wagon, and Caitlin turned away from her observations to help with the luggage while Jackie unlocked the front door.

Inside, a large open-plan living area led onto a deck, and Jackie threw open the doors allowing a light breeze to blow in, bringing with it the sound of the children's laughter mingled with the calls of loud birds. On the deck a patio table and chairs stood under a vine-draped pergola. A well-used barbeque hung with forks and cooking utensils. In the garden below the lawn had been neatly mown, the beds were trimmed, and a swimming pool sparkled invitingly. Next door to the left, a ginger-haired teenager laboured behind a lawnmower. To the right, a woman lounged in a hammock; she looked up and waved. Jackie acknowledged the woman and turned to go inside.

"Come on, I'll show you your digs," Jackie said, drawing out the "i" into a long "ee". She led them downstairs to a lower level that Garth and Caitlin hadn't expected from outside. The stairs opened out into a family room with a television and a fireplace. A passage led to the bedrooms.

Jackie stopped in a doorway. "I've moved Ashley in with Tyler, so you'll be in here. Biffy's over there," she turned and pointed up the passage. "Would'ya like to freshen up before dinner?"

Caitlin put down her bags chuckling inwardly at Jackie's Aussie vocab. She'd pronounced dinner as deenah, and her words flowed together just as Kevin's had. "That would be great, thanks." She was dying to sit down and talk, but knew that once they started it would be impossible to stop. Her mind was full of memoires waiting to be remembered, waiting to be spoken about, but she would have to wait.

Kevin placed Caitlin's suitcase next to the wall. "Come on up for a pint as soon as you're done."

"Thanks," Garth said, putting his case next to Caitlin's.

Caitlin hurried through a shower, left unpacking for later, and she and Garth went upstairs to the deck where Jackie and Kevin were waiting. By then a finger of moon showed on the horizon and clusters of stars packed the sky. A wombat's eyes shone from the pergola where it was stealing the last of the grapes from the vine. The smell of eucalyptus from a nearby tree filled the evening air. Although winter was approaching, it was mild and pleasant outside.

Over drinks Jackie asked about Shanon and Scott. During the conversation she got up from time to time to check on dinner, and the aroma of food cooking drifted through the open door. At seven they went inside and Jackie served up a feast of roast chicken, potatoes, golden crisp on the outside, buttered vegetables, and sweetened, cinnamon-spiced pumpkin.

After dinner, the remnants of their meal forgotten in the kitchen, Caitlin and Jackie began to talk. They bristled at remembered transgressions, cried over memories, shared feelings, and laughed about their childhood cook who ate mopane worms. Between them they recalled their first nanny's name, talked about their parents, their grandparents. Asked after friends. The men, bored by their conversation, moved downstairs to watch sport on television. The children, refusing to go to bed, fell asleep huddled under blankets on the couch.

Caitlin and Jackie spoke until the early hours of the morning – old jealousies were put aside, a new bond formed. The conversation ebbed and flowed. A river of catching up until they went to bed not wanting to sleep, but knowing they should.

At dawn, although exhausted, Garth and Caitlin woke to the maniacal cackle of a kookaburra. There was no chance they could go back to sleep, so they got up, made tea, and took their mugs outside to the table and chairs under the ash tree. A bird feeder hung from a branch and the noisy birds they'd heard the evening before, colourful lorikeets, white-crested cockatiels, and blue, red, and green king parrots squabbled over the seeds.

Jackie wandered out, her hair still tousled with sleep. "You're awake already!" She placed a plate of South African rusks on the table and the birds flocked to the biscuits as tame as house birds.

"Time change," Caitlin said ruefully. "Our bodies haven't worked out whether it's day or night yet. I hope we didn't wake you."

"No worries, I'm usually up early," Jackie said, chasing the birds away.

Caitlin took a rusk and dunked the hard biscuit into her tea to soften it. "Jacks, I'm nervous about leaving South Africa and all that I'm used to. Tell me what it's like. Was it difficult?"

Jackie turned to Caitlin considering whether to be honest or not. She decided on the former. "To be frank, it's bloody hard. When you first arrive there's no one to pop in, to drop by for coffee or a casual meal. You hav'ta make new friends, and create family outta those friends. Until then you celebrate Christmas on your own, and birthdays aren't special. It takes a long time. A lot of new immigrants don't survive and go back. We wanted to, but we couldn't. We didn't have the money."

Jackie continued, her accent and terminology distinctly Australian. "When we moved we were young and naive and came across with Kevin's job offer, a couple sticks of furniture, and nothin' else. We thought it was going to be a breeze, but we were wrong." She looked unhappy as she sipped her tea. "I was depressed, homesick." She looked away to hide tears, blew out a sigh at the memory.

Caitlin put her hand on Jackie's. "I had no idea, Jacks. You never said anything."

"I know. I didn't want to admit that we'd made a mistake." She sighed again. "Houses were more expensive than South Africa and all we could afford was a mouldy, drafty old place. It was bloody dreadful."

Kevin came out, overheard what she said, took a rusk and sat down. "It was worse than dreadful, the bloody place shoulda been torn down."

"The other thing we hadn't anticipated," Jackie continued, "was that the Aussies didn't accept my qualifications. It took a lot of hard yakka to crawl back to where I am now." She swatted an insistent bird off the table.

"You've done well since then," Catlin indicated the house and garden.

"Things came right. I just wanted you to know that it's not easy. To let you know what you're letting yourselves into before you decide to leave South Africa."

Garth listened to what she had to say, imagined their hardships, and made a conscious decision not to move unless they had enough money out of South Africa to start a new life without the same struggles Jackie was describing.

"Did you make friends easily?" he asked thinking of things they should know before they chose a country to move to. He wanted to ask about taxes, health care, cost of living, education – he had a whole list of questions.

"In the beginning we were busy making ends meet, we didn't have time for friends. And then I was stuck at home with a squalling baby, and a second one within twelve months."

"It was easier for me," Kevin said. "I had the chaps at work, and I joined a rugby club." He stood up. "I've got to head out. Come on, Mate," he said, speaking to Garth. "I wanna show you my biltong drier before I leave. You'll have to learn howta make the stuff if you're gonna leave South Africa."

"You make it yourself!" Garth got to his feet, and the two men headed towards the house discussing recipes and the best method to dry meat.

Caitlin turned back to Jackie. "You're okay now, aren't you? You look happy."

"Oh yeah, I'm alright. It was just hard in the beginning."

Jackie looked at her watch, stood up, and tossed the crumbs off the plate onto the ground. The birds squabbled after them. "I've gotta get the keeds to school. Kevin has to work, but I'll take you around."

Caitlin tipped her head to one side. "I can't get used to your Australian accent," she smiled.

"That's funny," Jackie chuckled. "The Aussies think I've still got a South African accent! You'll see, you'll never lose the connection. It doesn't matter where you go, you'll always be a South African."

After the first day the rest flew by. Jackie showed them around and imparted as much knowledge as she could. Kevin took them to the fish market and made paella for dinner one night. Garth and Caitlin collected real estate magazines, immigration information, university application forms, newspaper articles, and business listings. They caught the Jet Catamaran ferry with Jackie, had lunch in Darling Harbour, strolled around the vibrant shops and kiosks at The Rocks, stopped to listen to an aborigine play the didgeridoo, admired the magnificent Opera House, patted a koala at the zoo, and swam in a moon-shaped bay in spite of the chill autumn water. Caitlin and Jackie had become strangers over the fourteen years with only a couple of letters and photographs to sustain their link, but they made up for it during the seven days together. They spoke about every subject under the sun, often not finishing the previous subject before starting the next. They shed tears, laughed, renewed their bond, and Caitlin got to know her niece and nephew.

In bed on the last night Caitlin spoke softly so that she didn't disturb the rest of the family. "Do you think you'd be able to move to Sydney?" she asked Garth.

"I don't know," he whispered back. "Living in town would be an enormous adjustment. I can't stand the thought of people looking over my shoulder all the time. Perhaps we could find a small holding, or live out in the country."

"I don't think we could afford it, not near Sydney anyway."

After a while they fell asleep wondering if they could leave what they had in South Africa behind. They'd been farmers all their adult lives, and now they would have to learn to be something, or somebody else.

At dawn the kookaburra woke them as it had every morning.

"Bloody kookaburra," Garth grumbled.

New Zealand was next. They stayed in a bald little room, on the second floor of a reasonably priced two-story hotel, in a suburb close to the business district and the city of Auckland.

On the first day they met with Immigration and went to the university. The immigration people were non-committal – the country was in the middle of economic reform at the time, and immigrants were not encouraged. At the university they learnt that South African university credentials were treated skeptically and, due to the high unemployment rate, a large percentage of skilled workers lived overseas and many new graduates found employment in Australia or Britain. The next day they researched businesses and housing and were beginning to feel discouraged.

On their third evening, after another day of research, they bought a bottle of wine, take-away food, and went back to their hotel. Garth pulled up in front of the split-pole fence separating the hotel parking lot from the apartment block next door, and they climbed out of the car feeling depressed and de-motivated. Out of sight, on the far side of the fence, a woman spoke, apparently to herself. She sounded drunk, so Garth and Caitlin ignored her and went upstairs. Caitlin looked forward to a long soak in the bathtub, and Garth to watching a South African rugby team play Auckland.

As Caitlin unlocked the door to their room the revving of an engine and squeal of tires made them both turn. A pick-up truck spun into the parking lot behind the fence, skidded to a halt, and from their vantage point Garth and Caitlin noticed a man climb out and speak harshly to the woman. She didn't appear to respond, so he pulled her to her feet and shoved her towards one of the apartments. She stumbled and he grabbed her arm, yanked her inside and slammed the door.

The lights were on in the apartment and Garth and Caitlin had a clear view. The man pushed the woman and she fell. She tried to sit up, but he cuffed her with a flat hand, and she fell back. He picked up a stick, or what could have been a bat, and struck her again. Her screams punctuated the blows, and with every blow Caitlin flinched in sympathy.

A small pigtailed girl in a nightie came out of an upstairs room and the movement made Garth and Caitlin look up. She stopped on the top step sucking her thumb. A boy, slightly older than the little girl, ran past and down the stairs. He threw himself at the man.

Garth and Caitlin heard him scream. "Don't hit my mommy, don't hit my mommy!"

The man twisted, grabbed the boy, and tossed him like a toy across the room. The boy hit the wall and slid to the floor. He lay without moving. The woman shrieked a long shuddering wail, and the man hit her again, a solid clout across the head. She lay completely still.

Motivated, Caitlin ran inside, her face mirroring her emotions, and dialled the emergency number listed on the phone.

Minutes later a police car drew up, two policemen went into the apartment, came out with the man and escorted him into the back of the police cruiser. A couple came out of the neighbouring unit, picked up the boy, took the little girl by the hand, and led them to their own apartment. An ambulance arrived and the woman was lifted onto a stretcher. The police car and the ambulance drove away as the manager from the hotel walked idly up the stairs towards Garth and Caitlin.

"Did you call the cops?" he asked.

"Yes," Caitlin replied, "I did." She thought the man had come to thank her for calling the police.

"Well, in future," he said brusquely, "mind your own business." He turned on his heel and left.

Caitlin sucked in a breath, stared after his retreating back, gazed at the window in the apartment across the way. The lights were still blazing and in her mind she could still see the man standing over his wife, the boy on the floor against the wall in the corner, and the little girl crying on the stairs. She went back inside, and sat down.

Garth followed her into the room, sat down next to her, stared at the wall, his hands on his thighs. He was silent, thinking. After a while he stood up, walked to the counter where he had left the bottle of wine, poured two glasses, gave one to Caitlin. "We are not going to move here." Caitlin nodded and Garth sat down in front of the television. "I'm going to watch the game."

Caitlin hadn't moved. "What are we going to do now?"

"Find somewhere to relax for a few days until our flight to Canada."

Caitlin nodded again, "Good idea." She picked up their travel guide, carried the guide and her glass of wine to the bathroom, poured the entire bottle of cheap hotel bubble bath into the tub, and closed the door.

The Bay of Islands, near the tip of North Island, was listed as a popular holiday destination, and Garth and Caitlin travelled up to it the next morning in their rented Toyota Corolla.

On their way they witnessed more evidence of the recession, and the efforts to reduce the trade deficit, in the restored vehicles – Morris Minors, Ford Prefects, Austin A40's, and old Massey-Harris and Farmall tractors – on the roads and in the farm lands.

They found a hotel fronting onto the water, booked a room with a balcony overlooking a sparkling bay and a golden beach, fetched dinner from a food stand and ate outside on the sundeck. It was glorious, and a welcome reprieve from the stress, the need to find a place where they could fit in.

By the end of their holiday they had another perspective of New Zealand; rolling pasture land, narrow twisting roads, scenic beaches, quaint inns, delicious roast lamb, and friendly people. But none of it erased the memory of the events at the hotel and, although they wouldn't make their decision based on that one isolated incident, they could not ignore the facts – the country was in a deep recession, there was high unemployment, as immigrants they would be resented, and uppermost on their minds was the probability that Scott and Shanon would leave home once they got their degrees. None of those things fit their criteria. They were moving because they wanted quality of life. New Zealand was in a difficult period of transition, and it would not be an easy road for new immigrants to travel.

Three time changes in the same number of weeks and Caitlin collapsed onto the bed of their hotel room when they arrived in Vancouver, Canada, and was asleep in seconds.

The following day they woke early, hired a car, and went on a brief tour of the downtown core to familiarize themselves with the city.

"Vancouver reminds me of Cape Town," Caitlin observed after a few hours.

"Mm," Garth replied, concentrating on driving on the opposite side of the road.

He parked at Canada Place, an eye-catching building with a roof that looked like a series of white sails. The day was crisp, cool, but clear. Three cruise ships were in berth and the couple took a leisurely stroll along the wharf. When they went inside Caitlin stopped at a giant debt clock, Garth craned his neck. The clock was enormous, twelve feet long by eight-and-a-half feet high, and it displayed the per-second increase in debt along with the share for each Canadian family, and the deficit.

Caitlin's heart sank. "This doesn't look encouraging." She cocked her head. "What's the difference between debt and deficit?"

"No idea." Garth shrugged. "From what I can see the debt's something over five hundred *billion*, if I've read that correctly."

They were both silent while they absorbed the figure.

"Do you think the whole world is in financial crisis?" Caitlin's brow creased at the thought. She'd heard enough about debts and deficits, and now she was worried they would never find a safe, politically and financially stable country, and a country open to immigrants. "I wonder what South Africa's debt is?"

"We're mushrooms in South Africa."

"What do you mean?"

"Kept in the dark and fed shit," Garth laughed.

Caitlin laughed too. "Jokes aside, I think we should find out more before we do anything else."

Garth pointed to a sign listing all the offices in the building. "I'm sure someone at the Chamber of Commerce will answer our questions."

"Good idea." Caitlin followed him towards the elevator.

Inside it was explained that the debt was the total amount of money the country owes and deficit the amount the country loses each year. They were told that Canada had an economic plan going forward, and was not in a crisis. They left feeling more confident with a heap of information to read at home – the Canadian federal budget, taxation in Canada, the economy in Canada, government budget deficit, and public debt. They also had brochures and pamphlets on business opportunities.

After the Chamber of Commerce, they drove to two universities – the University of British Columbia and Simon Fraser University, where they were well received.

The next day they had an appointment with the Department of Immigration and were encouraged. They were given more booklets and information on moving to Canada, and an immigration officer suggested they would adapt better to the dryer climate in the Okanagan or Vancouver Island. Neither Garth nor Caitlin thought to ask why the official had mentioned the weather. They weren't aware that Vancouver endured, on average, 161 rainy days a year! Instead they raised the question of universities. Once it was established that there was a university in Victoria on Vancouver Island, and none in the Okanagan, they decided to go to Victoria in a final effort to complete their research.

Caitlin had a hollow feeling in her stomach. They were running out of options and time. If they didn't like Victoria, there was nothing left. She doubted they would adapt to city life in either Vancouver or Sydney. And Auckland had been stuck off their list.

On their third day in Canada, they caught a ferry from Tsawwassen on the mainland to Swartz Bay on Vancouver Island. The Spirit of British Columbia carried two thousand passengers, and approximately four hundred cars and trucks. Once on board Garth and Caitlin walked around taking everything in. They noticed doors to the outer deck, and went outside where the wind whipped up the water and chilled their faces. Small boats and yachts skimmed by. Seagulls scooped down to fly alongside. The ferry turned into Active Pass, the waterway leading through the Gulf Islands to Victoria. The deck trembled under their feet. Another ferry sounded its horn as it sailed in the opposite direction. They passed islands with green forests of Douglas-fir, Western Red Cedar, and Hemlock. Two deer foraged in one of the log-strewn bays. And a red and white light house flashed its beacon at the tip of an island. Garth and Caitlin's shoulders relaxed, their tension eased, and the stress of their trip and previous months fell away.

When the ferry docked, they turned off the highway instead of following the flow of traffic to Victoria, and took a scenic route. Driveways sloped away to hidden houses, and thick brush and towering trees grew to the edge of the road. They noticed a chip trail, parked and followed it to a small cove where they sat on the rocks at the water's edge until a cold wind whipped up off the water. Becoming chilled they decided to drive on, and crossed the same highway they'd seen when they came off the ferry earlier. They passed crops, cows and barns. Flat lands leaping up towards mountains. An airport with small planes landing and taking off. The sky shone a peerless blue, untouched by cloud, and gardens were crammed with flowers. Wooden stands were stocked with eggs, fruit and farm produce. No one in attendance, just an honesty box, and the thought struck Garth and Caitlin that in South Africa the produce, the stand, and the money would have been stolen. Children played on the sidewalks. Dogs in a park chased Frisbees and balls. There were no burglar bars on the houses they passed.

As dusk fell they drove into a small hotel overlooking a strait and a distant snow capped mountain. At the entrance, daffodils, tulips, rhododendrons, and cherry trees bloomed invitingly. Garth went inside and came back smiling.

"Come on, Caity, we've got a room with a view and an appointment with a realtor," he said, holding out a slip of paper.

She looked confused. "But we haven't decided to move here yet."

"That's exactly what I told the manager, but he was so enthusiastic I couldn't stop him. He phoned the realtor while I was in his office, and she insisted on showing us around tomorrow."

It sounded optimistic. "Well, I guess there's nothing to lose," Caitlin shrugged.

The realtor arrived after breakfast. It was another warm spring day and she had the top down on her Jaguar convertible. She climbed out.

"Pat," she introduced herself with a warm handshake. Garth and Caitlin introduced themselves, and Pat looked at her watch. "If you're ready we should go." She spoke with a lovely lilt, each word a separate entity. A soft mix between British and American English, with a hint of something else, Scottish perhaps. "I've got a couple of open houses to show you," she said, sliding the seat forward. Caitlin squeezed into the back.

"I can put the top up if you like," Pat offered.

"No, this is great," Caitlin replied, pulling a hair-band out of her handbag and twisting her hair into a ponytail.

"I'm also fine with the top down." Garth zipped up his jacket as he climbed into the passenger seat.

"Good, we've got to take advantage of the weather while it lasts." She expanded her arms to encompass the sky.

As she accelerated away, a fine mist rose off the sea, and the air smelt of salt and seaweed. The road twisted through a forest of conifers and into a suburb of average-sized houses. They saw a doe and her fawn browsing on someone's tulips, and a woman ran out yelling. Undaunted the deer barely lifted its head.

They left the suburb behind and drove through a cluster of small holdings, and Garth and Caitlin perked up and asked about prices. Pat offered to drop off a portfolio of listings at their hotel, and then she drove them around the university, took them through open houses, and fed them lunch in a cosy bistro. By the end of the day they were friends, and Garth and Caitlin could see themselves settling in Victoria.

The next day they continued their research on their own, and that evening they went for a walk on the beach. A lone woman and her dog walked in the distance and Garth and Caitlin followed at their own pace on the log strewn stretch of sand. It was different from what they were used to, but it had its own rustic beauty.

At sunset they turned back towards their hotel. The mountains behind had turned a bluish-black, the water to mercury, the sky a coral pink. A bird called and Caitlin turned her head.

"That's a Piet-my-vrou," she said. She didn't realize that she was wrong. It was a Quail, but it gave her comfort to hear a familiar bird call so far from home.

As the sun eased down beyond the water and the mountains a shooting star drew a bright light across the sky and vanished.

"Did you wish?" Garth asked.

Caitlin looked thoughtful. She would have liked to wish that things in South Africa would come right, but that was impossible. You couldn't wish for something that was unattainable.

"I guess I'd wish we could move here, to Victoria."

Garth felt a deep feeling of relief. "What about Australia?"

Caitlin's expression turned serious. "In my heart I'd have liked to live near Jackie, but in my mind I know there are other things to consider."

She took Garth's hand as they walked towards their hotel and they were both silent, their thoughts tumbling into place.

Both felt as if a weight had been lifted. A move to Victoria would be like ripping off their skin and trying to grow a new one, but this might be the easiest place to do it.

When they returned to South Africa, their Canadian residency permits were approved and Caitlin went to tell her grandfather. It broke her heart to see how old he looked. His white hair was receding, bags underlined his eyes, and loose skin sagged under his chin bringing her attention to how much weight he had lost.

He drew her closer and she knelt in front of his chair. He put his dry old hands on either side of her face and looked into her eyes; his were delft blue and crystal clear.

"Caity, there's no hope here," he assured her. "You must forge forth and start a new life. If I were a younger man, I would come with you and help you start again, but the Lord will not spare me for much longer."

Caitlin tried to object, but he stilled her. "I am not scared of the life hereafter, and you mustn't worry." Caitlin held back tears as he continued. "My dear," he looked at her with an intensity that shook her. "*I will not drink henceforth of the fruit of the vine,*" he quoted Matthew 26, "*until the day when we meet again in my Father's Kingdom.*"

And Caitlin realized that he had accepted the fact that he would die without her at his bedside, when she was gone, gone when he needed her most, and she felt her heart shatter into a million pieces.

part three

freedom

TWENTY-NINE

TURNING THE PAGE

1991 · 1992 · 1993 · **1994** · 1995 · 1996 · 1997 · 1998 · 1999

Seven months later, January 1994, a year after graduating from school, Kazi was leaving for university. Goodwill looked on with pride, and Martha smiled broadly. Neighbours and friends congregated in front of the house to wish him well. The farm women dressed colourfully and the men in their Sunday best; pants shiny with use and jackets ill-matching, but still it was their best. Bare-butt children chased squawking chickens, and no one bothered to reprimand them. The reason for the festive atmosphere was that Kazi was the first of the labourers' children to go to university. It was a great day for them all.

Before he left, Kazi looked up at the mountain that had always listened in stoical silence to his problems and given him strength during hard times. For one last time, his eyes followed a fish eagle floating on the thermals. He heard a baboon bark on the mountain, laughed, and called back, "Goodbye, baboon!"

Then it was time to go. He hugged his sister; he could feel her ribs through her thin dress and wondered what was wrong. Something niggled at the back of his mind, but he couldn't put his finger on it. He had forgotten his thoughts a year earlier when he had wanted her to see a doctor. Lately she dragged herself through her chores as if she had no energy and coughed from a continual cold. She often complained that her bed was soaked with sweat when she woke in the morning. He closed his mind to the fact that she could have AIDS from when she was raped by Spyder. It just wasn't right that she was sick all the time, but maybe he was just being overly protective. Kazi consoled himself with the fact that she had seemed happier since she'd met Almon. He appeared to be a nice guy and treated her well.

"*Sala kakuhle* – stay well, Ntokoso," he said. "I'll see you in December."

She smiled. "*Yebo, Hamba kakuhle*. Go well, my brother."

Then he looked down into his cherished father's face. His back was more stooped and the lines of his face had deepened over recent years, but there was a new energy in his eyes that made it easier to leave.

"*Sala kakuhle,* my father."

"*Hamba kakuhle,* my son."

Then he held his mother in a bear-hug for a long time until she stepped back and waved him away. He climbed into the Nomad with Scott and suddenly everyone was shouting goodbye and calling out last minute advice. Children ran behind the car in the trailing dust, shouting and waving until, one by one, they turned back laughing and chattering.

Kazi was grinning as they sped down the road. "Thanks for taking me to the station." Scott nodded. "When do you leave for Stellenbosch?" Kazi asked. He didn't know that the

Finleys were immigrating. Hard as it had been, Scott had kept his promise to his parents and had not told Kazi anything.

"Tomorrow. My folks are driving us down. Dad's going to take the trailer 'cos we've got so much stuff."

Kazi thought about university and felt a flush of eagerness. He was on his way at last.

"I don't know what strings your dad must've pulled to get me into UCT; it was the only university I really wanted to go to."

"I wonder why! It wouldn't have something to do with a certain pretty girl that lives in Cape Town, would it?" Kazi smiled. Scott could tease all he liked, his dreams were being fulfilled. Scott continued. "My dad's a master at getting people to do things they don't want to do. I heard him talking to the admissions department. He used charm and, when that didn't work, he used the racism card. And when he said he was going to hire an affirmative action lawyer, the deal was sealed."

Kazi shook his head, "I guess I should avoid admissions for a while."

"That would be wise."

Kazi sat back and enjoyed the feeling of spinning along in the Jeep with the sun blazing down, and a breeze cooling his skin. He took a deep appreciative breath and beamed. "I'm so happy. I don't have to hang around Skeerpoort for another year. I've found my brothers, even though it didn't work out, and I'm going to be with Thandi. Life is good."

They drove on for a while, each thinking his own separate thoughts about the impending year, Kazi a fresh start and Scott looking only as far ahead as the next semester at Stellenbosch. He didn't know when they were going to leave South Africa and didn't think it would be any time soon. Their immigration applications had been accepted, but it would take time to sell the farm. The thought of leaving brought him mixed emotions, excitement for a new adventure, but sorrow too when he thought of all he would lose.

Kazi was too tangled up in his own thoughts to notice Scott's sudden emotional shift. He carried on with his own thoughts. "I wonder if UCT has an initiation week like Stellenbosch. *Jool* sounded like so much fun."

Scott shrugged off his feelings; it would be months or maybe even years before they left.

He nodded, "I think it's called Week-0 or something like that. We'll get together and compare notes. Stellenbosch is only about an hour from Cape Town."

He changed lanes and took the ramp onto the N1 highway.

"Where are you going?" Kazi asked.

"Jan Smuts airport."

"But we're supposed to be going to the railway station." Kazi looked at his watch. "You'd better take the next off-ramp and step on it. We're going to be late!"

Scott chuckled. "Here," he tossed a white envelope onto Kazi's lap.

"What's this?" Kazi asked. He tore open the envelope and drew out the contents. "An aeroplane ticket!" he exclaimed.

Scott grinned, "It's a gift from my parents."

"Scott, this is incredible, I've never flown before. Wow!" he said, looking at the ticket in his hand again. "Wow!" He continued to stare incredulously at the ticket. "I don't know how I'll ever repay your parents."

"It's a gift, Kazi."

"No, you don't understand. It's not just the tickets. They helped set up the school during the boycotts, and I would never have finished matric without that. Then your mom organised my university grant, and your dad got me accepted at UCT. I'm indebted to them."

"Kazi, they don't expect anything. To see you succeed will be enough."

"I will succeed," Kazi promised. "Oh shucks," he straightened. "I forgot about Thandi. She's fetching me at the station. How am I going to let her know?"

"She knows already," Scott grinned, following the signs to the airport.

"She knows! And she kept it secret from me!" Kazi shook his head in amazement. "Thanks, Scott. Thanks for everything."

Scott glanced away from the road, at Kazi. "You're welcome, my friend."

At the airport Scott toured the parking lot searching for a space, found one, and they went inside and booked Kazi's luggage through. At the gate they shook hands for one last time promising to get together in Cape Town, and Kazi joined the other outbound passengers on a bus that took them across the apron to their aeroplane. He climbed out of the bus and looked up at the aircraft. He had never been this close. He looked around to share his excitement with someone, but the other passengers seemed to be in a hurry to get to their destinations. He climbed the rolling stairs and admired the jet from up close. It had the familiar South African Airways flying springbok logo on the tail, and he wondered what type of plane it was. Perhaps he could ask someone on board.

He stepped inside and felt a pressure building in his chest. He breathed out and tried to calm himself. He looked around wondering where to go.

A flight attendant held out her hand. "Boarding pass please," she said, and with a glance at it, pointed in the direction of his seat. "Enjoy your flight, Sir."

"Thank you," he grinned cheerfully. He'd been called sir for the very first time, and was about to experience his first flight.

He walked down the isle checking the seat numbers, feeling nervous and excited at the same time. He found his row and checked his boarding pass against the diagram overhead. His seat was in the middle. An elderly man was already seated next to the window, and a woman was in the seat on the isle.

He noticed that there was a luggage compartment, so he stored his carry-on bag. The woman stood up for him to get by, and he quickly moved in and sat down. He looked at the man on his right and the woman on his left, and observed that they had put on their safety belts. He found his and fiddled with it until he found out how it worked, and adjusted it to fit. He looked around to see where the toilets were. After that he spotted magazines and brochures in a pouch in front of him, pulled them out, flipped through them, and saw that one of them was an information sheet with a diagram of their aeroplane on it. He returned the magazines to the pouch and studied the sheet. It had all the information he wanted. He read the statistics, studied the interior, and searched for the life jacket that the diagram showed was under his seat. He set the direction of the air flow, and looked for the oxygen mask.

The elderly man turned to him. "Your first flight?" he asked. He'd noticed Kazi's excitement and the fact that he had tightened his seatbelt very securely, and checked for the life jacket and oxygen mask.

"It is," Kazi replied, nodding enthusiastically.

"Name's Bill," the man held out his hand.

Kazi shook it. "Mine's Kazi." He looked at the woman on his left, ready to introduce himself to her too, but she shifted away and carried on reading her book.

"We're lucky, it's going to be a nice flight," Bill said, looking out at the weather.

Kazi turned and looked past Bill out the window. The service trucks were pulling away, the stairs were being removed, and the engines were already running. The flight attendant closed the door. He became aware of the plane moving as it was pushed away from the apron and felt a stirring in his chest. He took a deep breath; this was the most exciting thing that had ever happened in his entire life.

The plane came to a stop and the engines spooled, first the left and then the right. They screeched softly and the plane shuddered forward and taxied slowly towards the runway. From where he sat, Kazi could see other planes lining up and taking off. At the front of the plane the flight attendant went through the safety announcements. Then she took her seat facing them and strapped herself in.

The pilot announced, "Cabin crew, we are cleared for takeoff."

The engines thundered and a nervous sensation fluttered through Kazi's stomach. The plane sped up and accelerated down the runway, and Kazi's heart raced. He looked out of the window and saw the buildings speeding past. There was a roar and the jet's nose tilted up. An invisible force pushed him into his seat and he felt a sinking sensation and a slight feeling of nausea. There was a thump and he gripped the hand rests.

Bill touched his arm, "It's just the landing gear retracting."

Kazi managed a weak smile, grateful for the reassurance, but was worried he was going to throw up. The plane levelled out and the queasiness in his stomach disappeared. He sighed with relief and his earlier excitement returned. He looked out the window and noticed that the houses had dwindled to the size of match boxes. They flew over the hazy slum of a township, and out into the country. The jet passed through a series of white clouds. Kazi felt an exhilarating freedom. He was as high as the clouds!

It wasn't long before the flight attendant brought a trolley of food and drinks. He accepted a Coke, but no food because he couldn't trust his stomach. While he drank his cool drink he and Bill exchanged information about their lives, and then the flight attendant returned to pick up the empty cups and food trays. The seatbelt sign came on again, and a voice came over the intercom asking the passengers to return to their seats and fasten their seatbelts. The plane began to descend and pressure built up in Kazi's ears.

Bill pointed out the window and Kazi looked down. Below them were long stretches of beach and the pilot announced that they were beginning their descent into Cape Town. As the plane began to drop it banked and flew alongside Table Mountain. A cool wind had swept in from the Antarctic condensing into a light blanket of mist that hugged the mountaintop, it furled gently over the rim and dissolved in feathery wisps as it rolled down the steep face. The plane banked again and Robben Island lay below, isolated in the middle of the ocean. There were jagged rocks on the shoreline and the sea looked dark, deep, and rough. The shadows of sharks could be seen circling. The island itself was stark and barren; a few buildings from its days as a prison camp were evident, as was the lime quarry where Nelson Mandela had worked when he was imprisoned on the island.

The plane slanted down and there was a whine.

"Flaps," Bill explained, and he pointed out the window at the wing changing shape. The plane banked again, descended rapidly and there was a loud thump. "Landing gear," Bill said.

The aeroplane touched down and taxied down the runway. Kazi felt a forward force as the reverse thrusters slowed the plane, and then the pilot brought the plane around to stop in front of the terminal.

A few minutes later they were allowed to disembark.

"It was great meeting you, Bill." Kazi's grin was as wide as it could get.

"Likewise, Kazi," Bill shook his hand. "Good luck with your studies."

The passengers moved forward and Kazi followed them down the aluminium steps that had been rolled up to the plane. From the apron he could see Thandi waving wildly behind glass windows in the terminal, her lips forming words that he could only imagine. He turned to point her out to Bill, but he had lost sight of him, so he turned back. He hurried through the remaining passengers and went through the doors and into the airport.

"Kazi!" Thandi screamed and flew into his arms.

He picked her up and spun her in a circle. "Thandi," he laughed, putting her down and kissing her thoroughly.

Surrounding passengers clapped, and they broke apart, grinning self-consciously. Kazi picked up his hand luggage, grabbed Thandi's hand, and together they went to fetch his bags. Then matching his pace to hers, they walked across the parking lot to her battered old Datsun.

A hot dry berg wind was blowing from inland and her skirt flicked gaily around her legs.

It felt good to be there with exciting opportunities and a new life opening before him.

Kazi settled into the routine of university, and he and Thandi embarked on their new lives together with enthusiasm, marred only by a letter from Scott.

30th March 1994

Dear Kazi,

I'm writing to say goodbye. You're probably wondering why I'm saying this and I have no easy way of telling you. You see, my parents have decided to sell the farm and immigrate to Canada, and Shanon and I are going too. I thought we'd get together in Cape Town or that we'd see each other on the farm during our holidays so that I could tell you in person, but we're leaving sooner than I expected.

I'll be sad to leave the farm and everything that I'm used to. We've lived all of our lives in South Africa, and so have my grandparents and their parents. Our roots are here, and our hearts, but ever since the car-jacking and being caught in the riots after Chris Hani's murder, my parents have been thinking seriously about leaving. It's been a difficult decision, but my dad hasn't been able to forget the aggression and hatred in those people's eyes during the riot. And, as you know, my mom was very traumatized by the car-jacking.

I tried to persuade them to move to the Cape, but dad feels that it would be a temporary move until the violence begins there too. Mom and Dad are worried that South Africa is going to follow the way that Zimbabwe, Congo, Kenya and other African countries have gone. They feel that it would be foolish to ignore history and the violence against white people that has happened in the rest of the continent. Dad says it'll take a powerful leader to bring everyone together peacefully under one roof. Maybe Nelson Mandela will be that person. Who knows? I certainly hope so.

I'm sorry that I can't say goodbye in person, but I'll write often.

Hope things go well, say hi to Thandi.

Scott

Kazi was crushed. He could already feel the void Scott and the Finleys would leave in his life. They'd always been the one constant he could rely on. He shoved Scott's letter in his pocket and went for a walk. The day had turned bleak, a charmless grey. A light drizzle began to fall. He kept his head down and strode past the engineering building, the science labs, the library, and out to the sports fields. After a while his pace slowed, and water dripped off his nose, down the back of his neck. He began to shiver and turned back to his dorm. In his room he pulled his shirt over his head and dropped it on the floor. He threw a towel over his shoulders and picked up a pen. He wanted to tell Scott not to leave. He wanted to ask why they were leaving just when the government was changing. He wanted to tell him that the country needed people like them. He wanted to voice his sorrow and his concern for his parents who had lived and worked for so many years on the farm. He poured out his feelings on paper. He wrote every feeling he had, and then he scrunched up the letter and threw it in the bin. The letter he finally wrote was brief. He left out his feelings, tried to be understanding, and he didn't mention his parents. He could only hope that the new owner would offer them employment. Even so, the changes would be difficult for them.

Dear Scott,

I'm very sad to hear that you and your family are leaving South Africa. But I understand your fears. Considering the decades of political denial, there will be those people who will seek revenge, and they won't differentiate between a good white man and a bad one. I agree that there's continuing violence across the country, and we're living through difficult times.

We will have our share of teething problems when the new government comes in, but naturally I see things from a different perspective to you – as a black man, I see a future filled with promise. Nelson Mandela is going to win the election, I'm sure of that, and I have great faith in him. I also believe he'll be a strong leader.

I hope you'll return one day but, in the meantime, my greatest wish will be that you come back for my wedding.

Thandi joins me in sending regards to your parents and to Shanon.

Stay well,

Kazi

THIRTY

VOTING DAY

1991 · 1992 · 1993 · **1994** · 1995 · 1996 · 1997 · 1998 · 1999

April 27th 1994, the first day of elections, dawned crisp and clear. The heat of summer was over, but it was not quite winter yet. The sky was a soft blue with wispy windblown clouds, and the day promised to be warm and comfortable. Young people of voting age, old people, black and white stood side by side under the April sun in long snaking lines on dirt roads, on sidewalks, on the grass outside town halls and schools, waiting patiently to vote.

An old black woman, her face a wrinkled map, grinned happily showing three yellowing teeth in an almost toothless smile. She spoke to the white woman standing next to her, lisping slightly through the gaps in her teeth. "*Mevrou*, I feel like a human being for the first time in my life. I am free to vote!"

The white woman took her hand and replied. "Yes, *Mama Khulu* – Great Grandmother. We can be proud that we live in a free country at last."

Kazi and Thandi stood arm in arm waiting their turn. They had arrived late, the line was long, and they had to wait in the sun for most of the day to vote, but they didn't mind. Today they would be voting for their past generations who'd been denied the privilege. They chatted happily to the people around them and kept a place for the young couple in front of them when they wanted to fetch something to eat, and for a middle-aged businessman behind them when he needed to relieve himself.

After the votes were counted, Nelson Mandela was sworn in as the first black president for the New South Africa, a country of many races, the Rainbow Nation.

In his speech he said, "Never, never again shall it be that this beautiful land again experience the oppression of one by another." He smiled victoriously, "The sun shall never set on so glorious a human achievement. Let freedom reign. God bless Africa!"

And the country basked in the afterglow of the elections. Violence ceased and differences were set aside. Everyone hoped that it would be a true government of national unity. The Nationalist party had won in the Cape, Inkatha won in Kwa-Zulu Natal. And the ANC won just less than two thirds of the country's vote. After more than three centuries, the country had been turned over to black rule, but no one group held all the power.

THIRTY-ONE

THE HONEYMOON IS OVER

1991 · 1992 · 1993 · 1994 · 1995 · 1996 · 1997 · 1998 · **1999**

In 1999, five years after the general elections, Thabo Mbeki was hand picked by Nelson Mandela as deputy president and was slated to take over when Mandela retired. The second general elections were scheduled to be held in five months time, in June – but, in the meantime, the honeymoon seemed to be over. ANC officials were being accused, amongst other things, of corruption and coercing members from other parties out of fear for their lives to join its ranks.

At least forty percent of the adult population were unable to find permanent employment, AIDS was an epidemic sweeping the country, and tension was rampant in KwaZulu Natal following the assassination of Dan Nkosi, the ANC branch secretary. In Johannesburg, people were being shot or mugged by black youths, armed since the resistance, and lacking in work skills after years of school boycotts. In Cape

Town there had been bombings, the most recent at Victoria and Albert Waterfront, and Planet Hollywood.

There were reports all over the country of drug running, pipe bombs, murders, muggings, rape, and it was obvious that the government was struggling to maintain law and order.

In January, Scott kept his promise and returned to South Africa for Kazi and Thandi's wedding. He and Shanon travelled together, and they stepped from the Boeing 747 into a humid summer day and stripped off their jackets. Scott paused as he entered D. F. Malan Airport, renamed Cape Town International Airport, and the local accents took his thoughts back to another day at another airport in South Africa.

He recalled the day they left as if it were yesterday. He could remember his grandfather's hug, the tears in his aunt's eyes, and the choking lump in his own throat as he said goodbye. And then the journey to Victoria in British Columbia, Canada, had seemed never-ending. Twenty-eight hours after leaving South Africa they'd landed in Vancouver exhausted, their emotions in tatters. They'd staggered through customs and immigration, found a hotel and tried, in the strangeness of that first night, to find sleep. And the following day they'd caught the ferry to Victoria.

At Shanon's touch Scott came back to the present. The luggage carousel had started up and their suitcases were plummeting down the chute towards them. He pulled them off, and they made their way through customs where a black official stamped their Canadian passports and, recognising their accents, said, "Welcome back to South Africa."

The doors to the airport slid open. Summer heat descended on them once again and both Shanon and Scott were relieved they'd changed into summer clothing while waiting for their luggage. Although it rarely snowed in Victoria the ground had been white with frost when they left, and they'd been dressed for winter.

Minutes later Scott swung out of the parking lot onto the highway in their hired Ford Escort, flooring the accelerator to catch up with the traffic that was travelling well above the speed limit.

"I wish I was in a BMW," he said, leaning back in his seat and straightening his arms like a racing driver. "This is awesome."

Shanon laughed. "You realize you've just joined the statistics," she said pointing to a billboard that read, 'Drivers not speeding last week …16%', "but I should point out that you're one of the 74% percent who *are* speeding," she added, glancing at the speedometer.

"C'mon Sis, the speed limit's just a suggestion here. This isn't Canada." Scott laughed and slowed for a herd of goats on the side of the highway. A scruffy boy, obviously from the squatter camp nearby, noticed Scott reduce speed and darted across the road. Scott braked for the child.

"Watch out for the kids," Shanon quipped, "and I don't mean baby goats."

"Ha-ha, very funny," Scott said speeding up again. They drove on in silence enjoying the sensation of being home – the smells, the familiar architecture, trees and shrubs, and Table Mountain in the distance.

"Which off-ramp must we take?"

Shanon took out a folded email with directions to deliver a parcel for a friend. "Buitenkant Street," she read.

"Why is it that there's always someone who wants you to take something when you mention you're travelling abroad? You could be going to Timbuktu and somebody would know someone there."

"I know," Shanon agreed. "There's the off-ramp ahead." As Scott took the off-ramp she read out the rest of the instructions. "Follow the street past the Castle of Good Hope. The building's on the right."

A group of protesters had gathered on Buitenkant Street and Shanon turned in her seat to look. Many of the people were dressed in typical Muslim clothing, the women's faces and heads were covered with veils, the men's with kufiyas. Some carried banners saying 'One bullet, One Blair' and 'Blairy Killer Go Home – Eff Off.' Others were shouting 'Death to Tony Blair.'

"What's going on?" Shanon asked.

Scott shrugged. "I've no idea. I guess we've been away too long to understand the local politics. What's the address? Let's get rid of this parcel and get out of here."

Shanon repeated the number while scanning buildings as they passed.

"There it is," she touched Scott's arm and pointed.

Scott pulled into an open parking spot.

"That was lucky. I'll be as quick as I can. Stay in the car and lock the doors," he told her.

Shanon rolled up the windows and locked the doors. She looked around at the people, ordinary people going about their business. No one seemed to be interested in her. It was hot in the car and her legs stuck damply to the seat. She opened the window a crack and put her head back. It had been a long trip and she was looking forward to a shower. Leaves on a nearby shrub fluttered on a mild breeze, and she wished she could get out. Everyone looked so normal and she began to feel foolish sweltering in the hot car. She reached for the handle and opened the door slightly. A plump black woman walked by and smiled, Shanon smiled back. A group of coloured youths looked in at her and she felt uneasy again. A business man strode past. It was still hot in the car, and she looked towards the doorway where Scott had disappeared and hoped he wouldn't be long.

She heard the pop of gunfire and slammed the door locking it, her heart hammering in her chest. It came from the direction of the protestors and she peered over the back of the seat. Policemen at the Castle of Good Hope were aiming rifles and hand guns into the crowd. There was chaos amongst the demonstrators. A man dove across the road, his legs spread-eagled in a desperate leap for safety, his hand flung out across his head for what little protection it could give. A white-haired man had a young Muslim boy in his arms and raced for shelter, and a woman lay on the ground, her legs bleeding. Tear gas poured from canisters and people fell, screaming.

Shanon hunkered down on the seat, not sure what to do. Where was Scott? Her worst nightmare was happening and Scott was nowhere to be seen. If the shooting moved up the street, she wouldn't be able to do anything. She couldn't drive away, Scott had the car keys. She looked again for Scott. Where was he? What was taking so long? Couldn't he hear the gunshots? Maybe she should get out and run up the street away from the demonstration. She looked back at the door hoping to see Scott. Surely he'd heard the noise. She looked at the demonstrators and saw the police converge on the mob. She looked back at the building just as a door opened. It was Scott. He dashed across the street in a long-legged run and Shanon unlocked the driver's door. She pushed it open and Scott jumped in, pulling the door closed.

"What the hell!" he gasped locking the door behind him. His hand shook as he inserted the key into the ignition. He started the car and accelerated out of the parking place, barely missing the car in front.

"What the hell's going on?" he asked.

"I don't know. Thank goodness you came; I didn't know what to do."

Scott glanced at his sister. "You okay?"

She nodded, her heart was still beating hard, and it took some time before she calmed down.

When they reached their Bed and Breakfast, Scott phoned Kazi.

"Scott, I can't wait to see you. How was your flight?"

"Good, just tiring. How are you? Can we see you tonight?"

"Of course, Thandi's standing by. How's Shanon?"

"She's okay, just a bit shaken up after this afternoon." He told Kazi what had happened.

"Were you there?" Kazi sounded astounded. "I heard about it from one of our reporters. The protestors were a group of Muslims who call themselves PAGAD, the name stands for People Against Gangsterism and Drugs. They initially formed a gang to fight crime and drugs, but their new leader is an extremist and now they often feature quite negatively in the news with regard to bombings, shootings, and gang wars."

"What does that have to do with Tony Blair?"

"He's presenting medals to a group of British defence experts who helped the South African National Defence Force during the integration process. PAGAD are protesting against Britain and America's bombing of the Iraqi people a few weeks ago."

"I guess we'll have to check Tony Blair's schedule next time we visit South Africa. We'll make sure not to coincide our visit with his."

Kazi chuckled. "What time should we pick you up?"

"We're going to unpack and have a quick shower. Let's say an hour."

"Good, see you then."

Kazi arrived within the hour and Shanon and Scott piled into his car, Scott in front with Kazi and the girls in the back.

"It's great to see you," Scott said, shaking Kazi's hand vigorously, assessing him. Kazi was now a full fledged journalist and had a maturity that he had lacked before. He was dressed in jeans, an open neck shirt, and a casual jacket. His handshake was firm. Thandi's hair had grown but she still kept it braided, and hadn't changed at all. She kissed them both, once on each cheek.

"You've got an accent, it's cool," she exclaimed.

"Why, did I say '*eh*'?" Scott emphasised the word, broadening his accent and adding a common Canadianism. The joke was weak but they were still laughing when Kazi pulled up outside Minnesota Spur.

Over dinner of BBQ spare ribs and thick potato fries Shanon asked about the farm. Kazi hadn't been back and couldn't tell them much, and then Scott asked about Dumani and Mandiso.

"Have you heard from your brothers?"

"No," Kazi shook his head sadly, "not a word. They're alive, they're free." He shrugged. What more could he say.

"How's your dad?" Scott changed the subject.

"He's getting old, but he's fine."

"When do they get here for the wedding? I assume your dad's performing the ceremony."

"He is. They arrive tomorrow. And your parents, how are they? How's their construction business going?"

Scott swayed his hand. "Up and down, but they're doing okay."

They chatted through dinner and over coffee Shanon brought out a photograph album, which they paged through until the ten hour time difference caught up, and then Kazi dropped them off at their Bed and Breakfast for some much needed sleep.

That night Scott lay in bed listening to the barking of dogs, gun shots in the distance. He wondered how people could put these sounds out of their minds and sleep soundly. Perhaps they had to, he thought, because they couldn't cope with what they meant. He fell asleep worried that he didn't have a gun next to his bed.

The next day they drove up Chapman's Peak, stopped to buy African carvings on the side of the road, and ate ice creams on a beach in Camp's Bay. There was so much to talk about, so much to catch up on. They spoke all day and didn't manage to finish any one topic. It was magical, relaxing, and glorious to be back.

That night they went to a restaurant at Spier Wine Estate and sat under a Bedouin tent, amongst ancient oaks. A young woman washed their hands in an ebony bowl of rose water and painted their faces in tribal designs. There was a tempting array of South African dishes, and between them they ordered a couple of bottles of Spier Shiraz and enjoyed their meal while native men and women in tribal dress entertained them with music and dancing.

During the evening, Thandi watched Kazi and Scott laughing together. She envied their friendship, the incredible bond they shared, perhaps because Scott never had a brother and Kazi had lost his. She marvelled at the fact that they had built up such a close friendship, in spite of apartheid.

"Would you come back to South Africa?" Thandi asked, knowing that it would be Kazi's deepest wish.

Scott shook his head. "Much as I love South Africa, I couldn't come back now."

"But doesn't the weather get you down?"

"Sometimes, but the summers make up for it."

"*Vloeibare sonskyn* – liquid sunshine," Kazi jibed.

"Wise-ass," Scott laughed.

When they stopped laughing, Thandi asked about earthquakes. She was hoping to find something that would persuade them to come back.

"Thandi, there's a whip for your back wherever you go," Shanon replied gently, reminding Thandi of their own problems in South Africa, and Thandi had to relinquish her argument. She realized that they would only come back if she and Kazi could prove that their fears were groundless. She changed the subject and they moved on to lighter topics.

On the third day, Kazi asked what their plans were for the following day, as he had to get back to work.

Scott pulled a long face. "The girls want to go shopping at Tyger Valley."

Shanon punched him playfully. "Come on, we'll have fun. And you want to buy a present for Thandi and Kazi, so don't moan."

Scott did enjoy the morning. They had coffee at Mug and Bean, went to all their favourite shops, had lunch at Fishmongers, and finally to Woolworths for the wedding present.

In Woolworths a siren went off as they waited in line at the till.

Scott looked around. "Everyone appears to be ignoring it, so I guess it's nothing."

Thandi shrugged and they moved forward in line.

A security guard hurried past.

"I hope he switches the darn thing off," Scott remarked. "It's giving me a headache."

The man continued towards the entrance, but when he got there he didn't turn off the siren. Instead he turned to face them and shouted, "There's a bomb! Please evacuate the building!"

Scott went cold. Shanon dropped what she was holding. The shoppers, who'd ignored the alarm until then, reacted immediately. Mothers pulled their children closer, people in change rooms rushed out adjusting clothing, and others shouted names.

Over it all the guard yelled, "Please leave unpaid merchandise in the shop."

Thandi was unperturbed. "It's probably just a scare. Happens all the time."

"Please evacuate the building!" the guard repeated.

It struck Scott that the man kept saying please, that he remained polite under the circumstances. His own heart was hammering. Shanon was ashen.

Scott wasn't sure whether to believe the guard, or Thandi. He decided on caution and reached for the girls' hands. "Let's go," he said, dragging the girls into the stream of shoppers making their way out.

The mob flowed out into a swelling crowd in the mall.

"Where's the closest exit, Thandi?" Scott asked.

"Over there," she pointed. Scott nodded and they moved in that direction.

Near the exit they were forced to slow down. Women with prams and shopping carts clogged the door, and people behind pushed against them to get outside. An old woman stumbled and Shanon helped her up. A young woman held a screaming toddler. Four teenagers formed into a single file holding hands. A man had been separated from his wife and was yelling her name. The alarm clanged and Scott forced his way through the melee, dragging the girls along. They reached the exit and outside the crowd fanned out in different directions. The mood changed as anxiety was replaced with relief. People spoke in normal tones and laughed again. Two girls carrying large take-away sodas giggled about not paying because of the bomb scare, and a plump woman took the time to check on her baby. Shanon stopped and took a photograph.

Thandi put a hand on her arm. "Shanon, it's probably a scare, but I think we should keep moving. We won't be safe until we're out of the parking lot – the last bomb was in a parked car."

Shanon picked up her pace and they joined a group of people standing on the sidewalk. The wail of sirens converged and emergency vehicles, police cars, fire engines, ambulances, and paramedics, sped in and parked at the mall's entrance. A bomb disposal unit pulled up, and men in grey protective suits and helmets hurried into the building.

It was hot in the sun, yet nothing appeared to be happening.

After a while a man said, "Looks like they think the bomb's inside, not out here. I'm going." He walked into the parking lot, and one or two people glanced around and followed.

Time passed. The sun moved over to the west and their shadows stretched.

More people left.

"Should we go?" Scott asked.

"May as well," Thandi replied stepping off the sidewalk and walking towards their car.

Scott followed, looking left and right. He paused when he noticed keys hanging from the trunk of a car. It struck him as odd. It didn't make sense, not in South Africa where crime was a factor, and a shiver of fear ran through him for the second time that day. Perhaps the bomb had been placed in this car!

"Thandi," he pointed. Thandi turned at the urgency in his voice and looked at what he was pointing at. She seized his hand.

"Move!" she instructed.

They took off running in a short cut between the cars, reached their own, got in as fast as they could, and Scott pulled away flooring the accelerator. Thandi was silent.

"Probably just a scare," Scott said.

"Probably," Thandi replied.

Silence fell while they all thought about what had just happened.

Scott turned on the radio. "Maybe it'll be on the news."

"We should phone Kazi," Shanon suggested.

"Good idea." Thandi replied. "Our nose-to-the-ground reporter will know what's happening. And furthermore, he knows we're at Tyger Valley. He'll be worried if he's heard about the bomb." She opened her cell phone and listened for a dial tone. "Crap," she said and put the phone away. "I forgot that it wouldn't work. The police shut down cell phone channels if there's a bomb threat."

"Why?" Shanon asked.

"In case the bomb is detonated by a cell phone," Thandi explained.

On the radio a newscaster interrupted the program with a newsflash, he confirmed that a bomb had been found in a department store at Tyger Valley mall, and it was suspected that Muslim extremists belonging to PAGAD had been involved. He went on to say, "The latest move follows fears that People Against Gangsterism and Drugs, a violent vigilante group allied with Muslim organisations, are mounting a new wave of attacks after the death of twenty-two-year-old Yusuf Jacobs during a protest in Cape Town."

Thandi's face fell. "I'm sorry this happened while you're here," she said dismally.

"Don't worry about it, we'll dine off this story for months," Scott said, making light of the situation.

Shanon and Scott dropped Thandi off.

"I'm looking forward to getting home," Shanon said quietly, once they were on their own.

"Me too," Scott said, realizing that for the first time they had spoken of Canada as home.

Kazi looked up as Thandi entered the chapel. Her dress clung to her figure in silken folds, and an elegant hood covered her head and gently framed her oval face. She walked towards Kazi, he smiled, and they turned towards Goodwill. He held out his hands, and as they bowed their heads, sun streamed through the stained-glass windows and enveloped them in a warm glow, as if they were being blessed.

After the ceremony the reception was held under a cool canopy of trees that grew on the banks of a slow moving river. Young men played football, girlfriends and wives lounged on blankets, older people sat in chairs in the shade, and a fragrant smoke drifted from meat that turned slowly on a rotisserie over a fire.

Scott walked over to where Goodwill was standing. The man looked aged beyond the five years they had been in Canada. He had lost weight and his jacket hung loosely from his shoulders.

"Goodwill, how are you?"

"I'm good, *Klein Baasie*," he said, using the labourers' term of affection for Scott – Little Boss.

"How're things on the farm?"

"Not the same as when your parents were there, *Baasie*."

"That's a pity. And how's Jackson?"

Goodwill shook his head. "He took the workshop tools your father gave him and set up a shop in Brits. But he lost everything."

"How did he manage that?"

"Through drink. He's been worse since your parents left."

"Is Nelly still with him?"

"She is. I don't know why, but she is."

"How does the farm look?"

"*Baas* Jan is a good farmer, but he doesn't live on the farm. He doesn't really care about anything but the crop. He's not good to us like your father."

"I'm sorry to hear that." Scott withdrew an envelope from his pocket and gave it to Goodwill. "My dad said to give you this."

Goodwill slit the seal and withdrew a bundle of notes.

"I'm grateful, please thank your father." He placed the envelope in his inner pocket and smiled across at Martha who was watching from where she sat. "Are you and *Missus* Shanon coming to the farm?" he asked.

"I don't think so," Scott shook his head. "All our friends have moved away. But, to be honest, we don't want to see someone else living in our old house. It would make us sad."

Goodwill nodded sagely. "And what about *Missus* Shanon's boyfriend, Chad? She will see him?" he asked.

Scott shook his head, "No that's over. They're still friends, but she has another boyfriend now."

"A Canadian?" Scott nodded. "Huh," Goodwill said, insinuating that he didn't approve.

Kazi came up and interrupted their conversation. "Scott, Thandi and I have to leave now," he said. "I've come to say goodbye." He took Scott's hand and shook it in the traditional manner, three times. Hand over hand. "*Hamba kakuhle,* go well," he added his face sombre. "Thank you for coming."

"*Sala Kakuhle,* stay well my friend," Scott shook Kazi's hand a second time. He wondered when he would see him again. He turned towards Thandi who was standing behind her new husband and hugged her. "Goodbye, Thandi, look after my friend."

"I will," she smiled sympathetically, recognising the permanence of their loss.

THIRTY-TWO

REVENGE OF THE ANGELS

1995 · 1996 · 1997 · 1998 · 1999 · 2000 · 2001 · 2002 · **2003**

Thandi became pregnant two years after they got married, and when their son Bongani, which means to give thanks, was a year old, they went back to the farm for the christening. Kazi could remember the day his son was born all wet and wrinkled, and how he had held Bongani to his chest, wanting to wrap him in his arms and keep him safe. His world had been transformed and he knew his parents would feel the same way about their first grandchild.

They climbed down from the mini-bus and Kazi lifted Bongani onto his shoulders. He took Thandi's hand and together they walked through the farm entrance and followed the dirt road to his father's house. He sighed with pleasure at the thought of being home and drew in deep breaths of the familiar air. As far as the eye could see were the valley, mountains, and river, the land where he had spent his childhood. Turning to Thandi he said, "I am home." He felt invigorated and excited. It had been nine years since he'd been on the farm, and nothing appeared to have changed during his absence.

As they walked towards the house Kazi saw his mother bent over the cooking fire. Her movements were stiff and arthritic and it caught him by surprise. He hadn't expected to see her so aged in the short time since he had seen her at their wedding. "*Molo*! Hello!" he shouted.

Martha straightened with difficulty. "You're here at last!" she cried, coming to meet them.

She called over her shoulder to children playing nearby. "Fetch Goodwill! Hurry, his son is here!"

Kazi lifted Bongani from his shoulders and, when Martha reached them, placed his child into her outstretched arms.

She stroked the baby's plump cheek. "You look just like your daddy," she said to the baby.

Kazi winked at Thandi and then he noticed Ntokoso coming towards them. She was heavily pregnant and Kazi took her into a gentle hug. "My little sister," he pulled away and looked at her. She had been sixteen when he left for Cape Town, and in his head she'd remained a teenager. He'd forgotten that she would be in her mid-twenties. "When is the baby due?"

"Any day now," she replied, happy that he was there.

Thandi came forward and hugged her too. "I hope it's while we're here."

"It's possible," Ntokoso smiled.

"Where's Almon?" Kazi asked, looking around for Ntokoso's common-law husband.

Ntokoso's face fell. "He left me. I…"

Kazi frowned, he remembered thirteen years ago when Spyder raped her. It was a long time in most people's lives, but rape was not something you could easily overcome. He wondered if it had affected her relationships. She did appear to find it difficult to trust men. Perhaps that was why Almon had left.

A shout drowned out Ntokoso's next words.

"Hello, hello!" Goodwill yelled as he hurried towards them. His hair was grey now, his cheekbones stood out, but he had energy in his stride.

Moments later Jackson and Nelly appeared, they had come specially to see them. They too had aged. Jackson's face showed the ravages of alcohol and a careless lifestyle, and Nelly, a middle aged woman, was no longer pretty. Piet, Frans and Elliphas arrived with some people Kazi had never met before, and everyone began to speak at once.

It was nice to see them, but when they left, Kazi was pleased to be alone with his family.

Night fell and Goodwill put more wood on the fire in the *lapa*. An owl hooted in the barn where it hunted for mice. Kazi stared into the flames and the smells, the sounds, brought memories flooding back.

Thandi placed her hand on his leg. "Tomorrow you must show me all the places you've told me about."

Kazi came back to the present and looked fondly at her. "I'm looking forward to it. We'll go up the mountain, and to the river, I'll introduce you to Ahmed at the shop, and I'll show you where I went to school."

The next day Kazi and Thandi walked together hand in hand. Bongani rode on his father's shoulders supported by Kazi's firm hand on his leg. They walked past the irrigation dam where a canoe Garth had made for him and Scott lay forgotten and rusted. It reminded him of the fun they'd had, and he pointed it out to Thandi. "I think we spent more time in the water than in the canoe," he laughed.

The path curved up the mountain, steepened and Kazi moved Bongani onto his back. The slopes were dotted with kippersol trees, thorn bush, and aloe, each shaggy plant carrying a candelabra of fiery, poker-like blossoms. He began to anticipate the place that had been his and Scott's favourite refuge and in his excitement he stretched out his stride. Rounding a rocky outcrop he disturbed a family of Meerkat, and Bongani laughed as the group of mongoose lifted onto their hind legs. At the sound, the little animals scampered away. They reached the log where Kazi and Scott used to sit, and Kazi lifted Bongani from his back and sat down. Thandi sat next to him, and together they looked out at the valley and mountains.

Kazi remained silent and Thandi left him with his thoughts, allowing him time. When he began to speak, his memories were heartfelt and touching. He spoke of Scott, Johannes, Juby, and Spyder. With the mention of Spyder's name his voice turned hard. "Did Ntokoso tell you?" he asked.

"No, what is it, Kazi?"

"She went to the clinic. Apparently a blood test is routine before the birth."

"And?"

"She…" He stopped, unable to speak. "She has AIDS."

"No!" Thandi stared at him. "Surely it's HIV?"

He shook his head. "No, it's full blown AIDS."

"Was it Spyder?"

"She thinks so."

It was late when they left the mountain. In the distance they could see Jackson walking towards them, his pace fast, taking the same path as theirs. He drew closer, and by the look on his face, their meeting was no coincidence.

When they were close enough to be heard Jackson called out, "Kazi hurry. Ntokoso is in labour. Your father says you must come quickly."

Kazi handed Bongani to Thandi and sprinted away, a cold fear rushing over him. Ntokoso's baby had grown within her while the disease had begun its dreaded course, and she was weak. When Kazi reached the house his father was waiting outside, obviously in prayer. Through the thin door he could hear Ntokoso's groans and Martha's soothing voice. Kazi stood there feeling useless. Why had she ignored the disease? he thought.

And then he heard the thin wail of a baby, and Martha called Goodwill into the room. After a while Goodwill opened the door and beckoned to Kazi. The room was darkened and he entered moving quickly to his sister's bedside. She spoke softly and he lowered his ear towards her mouth.

"Please, Kazi, take my baby and look after him as your own."

He knelt and lifted her hand to his chest holding on to her as if it would pass his strength to her, his heart beating against her hand.

"I promise, Ntokoso, I promise."

Then she died. Her eyes were open and she looked directly into his eyes as if she still wanted to say something. He tried to think of what Ntokoso might have felt before she died, her life cut short. She might have married. She would have lived to love her child, to see him grow. He stood there for what seemed to be a long time. Then he turned slowly away.

He felt a great weight of sadness wash over him. He didn't want to face anyone yet. He went to his room and closed the door. He lowered himself onto the bed and began to cry. He cried for Ntokoso, Johannes and Phineas, for the men who had died in the Zulu camp, for Sepho the taxi driver, for all the people who had died so senselessly. He had suppressed his feelings for a long time.

He roused himself and the muscles of his jaw bunched as he strengthened his resolve. Night had fallen and the darkness was the colour of violence. He was angry and his loathing bloomed fresh. He never thought that hate could be like this, so singular. He went outside and pushed his way through the darkness searching for Spyder. He reached the house where he lived and banged his knuckles on the door. The man who opened it had beer on his breath and his eyes were dark.

"Spyder, where is he?" Kazi snarled.

The man looked at him and smirked, he knew who Kazi was. Then recognition dawned on Kazi, he remembered the face from Spyder's gang of extremist followers. It was Matla. From the deep shadows of the house another man stepped forward; Kgasi, he remembered. Kazi wanted revenge. He could taste it, and he felt the rush of adrenaline as he hit Kgasi, leading with his right fist. Then he followed rapidly with a left uppercut. Kgasi fell to his haunches. Matla slammed Kazi driving his head back. Kazi stepped away and Matla came towards him with hatred in his eyes.

Kazi aimed a punch at his flat wedge-shaped nose, but Matla stepped out of reach. Kgali pulled himself to his feet moving in on the fight, two against one. Kazi kicked out, catching Kgali off balance, downing him again. He flew into Matla with clean hard punches into his nose, and mouth. Matla fell back, blood splattered across his shirt. Kgasi stayed where he was clutching his leg, groaning.

Kazi pushed his way past them into the house, his neck cabled with tendons. He was looking for Spyder. He heard a sound in the back room and followed it, his anger lending him strength to finish the fight. The room stank of illness. A dim light shone on a mattress, and a thin grey blanket lay lumpy and tangled on it. Kazi ran his eyes around the room. He knew Spyder was here. The blankets moved slightly and Kazi stepped forward throwing them aside. Spyder lay there, his face skeletal, eyes deep dark holes. His clothes were stained with filth, the sheets wet with fever. Kazi looked down at him without sympathy. He was dying a slow and agonising death, the one that he deserved. Kazi turned. His mind empty now. He held no feeling. He walked away feeling drained and hollow. He had gone for vindication, for vengeance. He didn't know if Ntokoso's death was vindicated by Spyder's same death so close, yet the suffering drawn out. Perhaps it didn't matter because for the first time in years he felt release, release from hatred.

The next night, as shades of blue and grey tinged the darkening sky, the fire died down to glowing coals. A nightjar called from somewhere in the dark, a peaceful bubbling sound without menace. Bongani had settled on his grandfather's lap, and Ntokoso's baby lay contented in Thandi's arms.

As Kazi stood up to add more wood to the fire he noticed two long shadows moving towards them. He slit his eyes and tried to see who it was as the shadows broke through from the darkness into the firelight. He realized that it was Dumani and Mandiso. They had come home.

Martha screamed. She looked at her two boys and her legs gave out beneath her. She sat down on the ground and raised her arms towards the sky.

"God, God, thank you, God!" she cried. Dumani came to her and picked her up.

She didn't know whether to laugh or cry. She touched Dumani's face, searching for the son she remembered in the tall man that stood before her. "You were so small when they took you!" she sobbed.

Then she turned and looked up at Mandiso, trying to recognise something in this stranger. He was lean and angular, a stubble of growth on his chin. He stared back, his eyes dark, daring her to reject what he had become. His hands were fists, and he balanced on the balls of his feet ready to escape.

Martha held out her arms. "It's okay, my boy, you're home now," she said, her voice gentle.

Mandiso lost the wariness in his eyes, and Martha saw in them a shadow of the boy he used to be. She smiled encouragingly, and he stepped into her embrace.

"*Umama*," his voice cracked. "*Umama*," he repeated.

Goodwill put Bongani down and hurried across the *lapa*. He threw his arms around Dumani. Martha's sobbing subsided and Mandiso let go of her, hugged his father and held on. Martha sank down onto one of the cracked old stools. Tears ran down her cheeks.

Kazi reached out and Mandiso placed his wrist against Kazi's wrist. "Blood brothers," he said, his pulse matching Kazi's.

Kazi grinned, "Blood brothers," he agreed, reaching for Dumani, shaking his hand in the traditional way, hand over hand. Then he threw his arms around both his brothers' shoulders and pulled them together until their heads touched.

When he let them go Mandiso turned around, "Where's Ntokoso?" he asked.

"She was sick," Martha replied. Her newfound happiness melted away.

"Well then, let's go to her. Is she inside?" Mandiso asked expectantly.

"I'm sorry," Goodwill replied miserably. "She is not with us anymore."

"What do you mean, not with us?" Dumani demanded.

"She ..." Goodwill's voice cracked, "she died yesterday. I'm sorry," he repeated.

"She died?" Mandiso said. "Yesterday?" he asked, looking from one to the other, confused.

"Yes, yesterday."

Martha pointed to Ntokoso's baby in Thandi's arms. "This is her baby."

Dumani looked at the baby. "This is hers?"

"He was born the day she died," Martha said, tears on her face. "I wish she could have seen you. She would have been so happy to see you, to know that you were back."

"We are too late." Dumani looked defeated.

A shadow flitted across Goodwill's face as he thought about Ntokoso and the life that she had lost, but he put his sadness aside. "No, my son, you're not too late," Goodwill said. "You are here, and it is a blessing that you've come back to ease our loss."

Kazi went inside and came back carrying the little carving of the horse. It was worn and shone from all the times that he had rubbed it over the years, and he handed it to Dumani. "Your horse," he said gruffly.

"You kept it!" Dumani took the horse and looked at it. "You kept it all this time?" he said, running his hand over the horse's back. He looked up at Kazi, "I'll keep this horse forever, and it will remind me that there's always hope no matter how bad things may seem at the time."

Martha made food and once they had eaten Kazi built up the fire, and they sat talking into the early hours of the morning. The two young men told of their lives from the day that they were taken away.

"My memories are like dreams," Mandiso said. "I remember when we escaped. There were men with guns and all the people were running. There was so much confusion that we just ran into the bush. Someone said that we should walk south, so we just started walking."

Dumani took over. "There were lots of us. Our feet burned and most of the time we had no food or water. We survived eating lizards, frogs, and berries. When we were desperate we ate leaves, but some of the berries must have been poisonous because we had terrible stomach cramps and were often sick."

Dumani continued, "After many days of walking, we came to a wide river. We realized that it was probably the same river we had crossed when the men first brought us to the camp in Zimbabwe. We knew we had to cross it, but we could see crocodiles. After a while we all just jumped in. Some drowned and some were attacked by the crocodiles. We pulled one of the boys to the edge, but he'd been badly mauled."

"He died and we couldn't bury him," Mandiso added. He looked up at them, his eyes intense with the memory. "We piled stones on top of him. It was all we could do."

"Those of us who reached the other side just walked on. We saw people but we were scared we'd be sent back, so we hid."

"Those who made it back just stayed together," Mandiso said, "and we joined the armed struggle." He looked at his mother. "I'm sorry we didn't come home. I suppose too much time had gone past. Too much had happened to us."

Their story finally told, Kazi recounted his search for them. This time he included his beating at the Umkhonto we Sizwe camp, Sepho's murder, the Inkatha massacre and his capture. After all was done, Goodwill's eyes were wet with unshed tears. He bowed his head and thanked the Lord for the safe return of his sons to the family. Then he prayed that the bloodletting was over, and he prayed for peace for his family and for South Africa.

GLOSSARY

AFRIKAANS	ENGLISH
Ag	Term of frustration
Baas	Boss
Babalas	Hangover
Baie	Very
Burgerlike Beskerming	Civil defence
Biltong	Air cured, spiced beef
Bliksem	Scoundrel
Boere	Farmers
Boet	Brother
Dankie	Thank you
Dom	Stupid
Droog	Dry
Duim vas hou ou maat	Hold thumbs old friend
Ek is die pa	I am the father
Ekskuus	Excuse me
Engelsman	English man
Geen Wetenskap	No knowledge
Gooi oor	A group of people pool their money and use it on a rotation basis
Ja	Yes
Ja broer	A person who is always in agreement
Jong	Young boy or slang for man
Kaffer	Kaffir - Black African (a derogative term)
Kafferboetie	African lover (a derogative term)
Keel	Throat
Klap	Clout
Klein Baas	Young boss
Kraal	Corral
Lapa	Outside cooking area

Loop dop	A drink for the road
Mealie	Corn
Mealie-pap	Corn meal
Meid	Maid servant
Meneer	Mister
Moedertjie	Little Mother
Moer-toe	Destroyed
Môre	Morning or as a greeting = Good morning
Nagmaal wyn	Communion wine
Nee Dankie	No thank you
Nommer asseblief	Number please
Oom	Uncle – sometimes used as a term of respect
Oppas	Be careful
Pannekoek	Pancake
Polisie stasie	Police station
Shebeen	Illegal pub
Skadonk	Old car - beater
Skrik	Fright
Sonskyn	Sunshine
Sout Piel	A South African with British heritage called Sout Piel because he has one foot in South Africa and one foot in Britain with his penis dangling in the salt water (it is a derogative term.)
Spook en diesel	Ghost and diesel (A slang term for brandy and Coke)
Stille Nag	Silent night (A Christmas carol)
Swaer	Brother-in-law or term of affection
Takkie	Canvas shoe or Running shoe
Tjoep stil	Totally quiet
Twak	Tobacco or slang for nonsense
Veld	Grass lands
Vensters	Windows
Vetkoek	Bread dough cooked in oil
Vloeibare	Liquid

Volkstad	Home land
Vroutjie	Little woman
Wag 'n bietjie	Wait a while
Wonderlik	Wonderful
Wragies	Truly
Jislaaik	To express astonishment

ENGLISH	**ENGLISH**
Kaffir	Black African (a derogative term)
Tsotsi	Young criminal

ZULU/XHOSA	**ENGLISH**
Amadoda	Male
Amandla	Power
Baba	Friend
Bwana	Boss
Chaile	Time to go home
Hamba kakuhle	Good bye - when person is leaving = go well
Hau	An exclamation of surprise
iAfrika	Africa
Maruti	Preacher, religious leader
Mayibuye	Let it come back
Mdala	Old man/Grandfather
Molo	Hello
Morogo	An edible weed similar to spinach
Ngawethu	Is ours
Nnyane	Honestly
Nyoka	Snake
Sala Kakuhle	Good bye – when a person remains = stay well
Sangoma	Witchdoctor
Umama	Mother
Utata	Father
Yebo	Yes

ACKNOWLEDGEMENTS

I am grateful to everyone who has assisted me on this journey. My husband, Neil, for his love, understanding, and inspiration. My debt to you is immeasurable, as is my love.

My daughter Verna, my son Greg, and my sister Lynn,
thank you for reading the first draft
and encouraging me to keep going.

Lynn le Roux, for your perceptive reading of this
manuscript, and your honest, valuable suggestions.
Amanda Breedt, for pointing out medical discrepancies.
Any errors after the fact are mine.

My editor, Ann Westlake, your suggestions strengthened the
story and smoothed out the rough edges.
My illustrator, Neil Powell, your illustrations
match the story perfectly.
Kobus Van Wyk for creating the basis for my website and
introducing me to the mechanics of a marketing platform.
Johanna Socha for proof reading, web design and layout.

ABOUT THE AUTHOR

Caren Powell lived in South Africa for 38 years during the apartheid era and the changeover to democracy, and now lives on Vancouver Island on the west coast of Canada with her husband Neil and two Jack Russells.

Caren is currently working on her next book.

www.carenpowell.com